Please return/renew this item by the last date shown. Books may also be renewed by phone or internet.

🖥 www.rbwm.gov.uk/home/leisure-and-culture/libraries

☎ 01628 796969 (library hours)

☎ 0303 123 0035 (24 hours)

'Beautifully writte... ill capture your

D1421834

95800000218568

Heidi Stephens has spent her career working in advertising and marketing; some of her early writing work includes instruction manuals for vacuum cleaners, saucepans and sex toys. Since 2008 she has also freelanced as a journalist and, on autumnal weekend evenings, can be found liveblogging *Strictly Come Dancing* for *The Guardian*. Her debut novel, *Two Metres From You*, won the 2022 Katie Fforde Debut Romantic Novel Award. She lives in Wiltshire with her partner and her Labrador, Mabel.

By Heidi Stephens

Two Metres From You
Never Gonna Happen
The Only Way Is Up

HEIDI STEPHENS

THE ONLY WAY IS UP

ACCENT

First published in 2022 by Headline Accent
An imprint of HEADLINE PUBLISHING GROUP

1

Cataloguing in Publication Data is available from the British Library

ISBN 978 1 4722 9355 8

Typeset in 11.6/15pt Bembo Std by Jouve (UK), Milton Keynes

Printed and bound in Great Britain by Clays Ltd, Elcograf S.p.A.

Headline's policy is to use papers that are natural, renewable and recyclable
products and made from wood grown in well-managed forests and other
controlled sources. The logging and manufacturing processes are expected
to conform to the environmental regulations of the country of origin.

HEADLINE PUBLISHING GROUP
An Hachette UK Company
Carmelite House
50 Victoria Embankment
London EC4Y 0DZ

www.headline.co.uk
www.hachette.co.uk

To Mum, with love and thanks for everything

PART ONE.

CHAPTER ONE

Daisy Crawford perched on the stool in her bedroom, trying to relax as Edith artfully dabbed and blended foundation into her forehead. A glass of champagne fizzed away on the dressing table, hidden among the mountain of pots and jars and tubes that had been decanted from Edith's multitiered cosmetics case, but Daisy hadn't touched it. There would be rivers of booze at the various after-parties later, and twenty years of the National Television Awards had taught her not to go too hard, or too early.

She thought about the evening ahead, mentally preparing herself for the red carpet she'd walked countless times before. *Spotlight* would pick up a talent show award or two – as it always did – and Daisy would miss out on the TV Presenter of the Year Award – as she always did. For the past eleven years, Joe McDonald had won and now it was considered an TV inevitability, like the *Strictly* Curse or a Christmas family meltdown on *EastEnders*. Daisy would smile and clap for the cameras, pretending she didn't mind, yet all she really wanted was to win; to feel like twenty-five years of hard work had been recognised. Finally.

The format for the evening felt familiar and comforting, but the big difference this year was that Daisy would be walking the red carpet with Christian, the first time she'd taken a date in the best part of a decade. It was also their first public outing since their engagement, but of course nobody knew about that yet. They hadn't even bought a ring, and she needed to tell Ruby first. That was a conversation she really wasn't looking forward to – Ruby was nearly sixteen and guaranteed to be less than enthused about having Christian as a stepfather.

Daisy watched him out of the corner of her eye, lounging on her enormous bed and tapping frantically on his phone, his brow furrowed and his body taut with tension. Not that Christian's body was ever NOT taut – a long career as a professional tennis player had given him a lean, athletic physique. He hadn't even had a shower yet, but then these events were easy for men. A quick wash half an hour before the limo arrived, throw on a dinner jacket, splash of after-shave, done. Daisy had been getting ready since yesterday, when she'd had a spray tan, a manicure and pedicure. Today it had taken three hours to do her hair and makeup so far, notwithstanding the half day she'd spent last week trying on dresses and shoes. The stylist was due any minute – a young Spaniard called Victor who had been recommended by her manager as 'up and coming'. She had a regular stylist, Paul, for her *Spotlight* outfits, but he always spent the autumn in LA, pretending he wasn't originally from Huddersfield. So the NTAs were a good opportunity to try someone new, mix things up a bit.

There was a soft knock on the door, and Karim's head appeared. He was primarily Daisy's driver, but also the only person she trusted to deal with deliveries or arrivals while she was glued to a chair. And most importantly, Karim would guarantee she left on time.

'Victor's here,' he said quietly, before being swept aside by

4

a tall man in a cream suit that showcased his narrow hips. He was carrying a huge dress bag over one arm and wheeling a holdall of shoes and accessories.

'Daisy,' breathed Victor. 'You look like heaven.'

'Hi,' said Daisy, catching Christian's extravagant eyeroll before he slipped his phone into his pocket and left the room.

'Do NOT come any closer,' said Edith, glaring at him. 'I'm still working.'

'Fine,' hissed Victor, vaguely kissing the air two metres from Daisy's head before retreating to the other side of the room to wait in reverent silence.

'How's the dress?' asked Daisy, trying not to move her face.

'Fabulous,' said Victor. 'I have made all the adjustments and now it will fit you like a glove. But no panties.'

Daisy laughed nervously. 'Not even a thong?'

'You cannot wear a thong with this dress,' said Victor firmly. 'Commando only.'

Daisy said nothing, listening to the wind buffeting the sash window and wondering whether she'd make it to the end of the red carpet without getting goosebumps on her muff. She closed her eyes so Edith could do her smoky eyeshadow, listening to Christian singing John Legend's *Ordinary People* in the shower next door. Considering the circus currently playing out in her bedroom, the irony was not lost on Daisy. She did some mindful breathing exercises and reassured herself that it was all going to be fine.

'You're done,' said Edith fifteen minutes later. 'I've left a few bits for your handbag in case you need to touch up.'

'Thanks,' said Daisy, knowing that she'd only need a slick of lipstick. Her makeup was trowelled on like a death mask and set with a mist of superglue – she'd probably need an orbital sander to shift it later. She walked around the room while Edith packed away all her pots and brushes, happy to be out of the chair and able to stretch.

'Victor says I can't wear knickers with this dress,' said Daisy as Christian came back into the bedroom, now looking unfeasibly handsome in a white dress shirt and black trousers. He handed her a pair of gold cufflinks and held out his right sleeve.

'No panties,' said Victor, his face implacable as he gently extracted several acres of fabric from the bag. 'Everything is a perfect fit.'

'I'm always OK with you not wearing any knickers,' whispered Christian, leaning forward so his lips brushed her ear. 'I promise to keep you warm.'

Daisy blushed under her makeup, looking at his beautiful hands and imagining them disappearing up her skirt in the back of the limo. He'd *definitely* have to wait until the drive home. Ignoring the anxiety and desire fluttering in her chest, she finished Christian's cufflinks and took off her bathrobe in front of the full-length mirror, trying not to be embarrassed at her naked reflection. Victor politely looked away, but Christian unashamedly looked on with a lascivious smile. He had persuaded her to have a full Hollywood wax the previous week, and she was still getting used to being as smooth as a snooker ball down below.

Daisy leaned on Victor's shoulder for support as she carefully stepped into the dress and slid it over her naked body. She turned to inspect the rear view; the dress was insanely tight. Sheer and sparkling, it was made from a black stretchy fabric that fitted her body like a pair of opaque spangly tights to the top of her thighs, before gently flaring into a long, heavy skirt. The top half had some built-in boob scaffolding and was surprisingly comfortable, hugging every one of her gym-honed curves and smoothing her out in all the right places. She was relieved to see that at nearly forty, her bum was still holding up. She silently gave thanks to her personal trainer for the thousands of squats she'd done over the years.

Her one stipulation had been that the dress didn't flash any cleavage, and Victor hadn't let her down. Instead his chosen outfit gave the impression of two completely different dresses depending on which side of Daisy you were looking at. From the left it had a shoulder strap and a skirt that pooled on the floor with a touch of old-school Hollywood glamour. But from the right her shoulder was bare, and the skirt had a dangerously daring thigh split on the side seam. Daisy liked the subtle hint of provocation but felt much more comfortable on the covered-up side. Uncertainty flickered for a second, and she wondered if she should have a drink after all.

'See?' said Victor triumphantly, helping her into vertiginous silver heels and handing her a matching clutch bag. 'Better with no panties.'

Daisy examined every inch of her reflection and grudgingly agreed that the outfit looked and felt better without underwear. The stretch fabric still gave her plenty of room to walk, and she'd just have to remember to keep her legs firmly closed as she got out of the limo.

As she watched, Victor deftly tied Christian's bow tie and helped him into his jacket, before stepping back so that Daisy and Christian could stand side by side in front of the mirror.

7

Daisy's hair was pinned around the back of her neck and hung in loose curls over her bare shoulder, the glow of her tanned skin reflected in the huge diamond drop earrings Victor had borrowed for the evening. Christian looked tall and lean and effortlessly sexy in his classic dinner jacket, his dark eyes drinking in every inch of Daisy's body. Together they looked like the new 007 and his Bond Girl; the press were going to go mad for them.

As soon as she exited the limo – without mishap – Daisy was warmed by the familiar rush of adrenaline from the cameras, questions thrown at her and the cheering from the waiting crowd at the O2. Christian handled the press with his usual boyish charm, his hand resting gently on the small of Daisy's back as he smiled and twinkled and answered questions from the waiting press. Yes, Daisy could play tennis, but no they hadn't played together yet; yes, he was enjoying the switch to black tie after a career in sportswear, but no he didn't have a couple of spare balls in his pocket. Everyone laughed and simpered as they moved on to the next entertainment reporter and repeated the whole circus again.

Inside the O2, Daisy and Christian hovered around the celebrity seating, which was laid out in cinema-style sections in front of the stage. The arena crowd rose in tiers around them, all flashing cameras and thunderous noise. Daisy doled out air kisses and posed for selfies with celebrity friends and colleagues, including a few of the new wave of reality TV stars that she didn't know at all, but who approached her like they were best friends. She tried to be generous with her time, promising to catch up with everyone for drinks later and making arrangements for brunches and dinners that would almost certainly never happen.

Daisy had been a familiar face on TV since she was fifteen, when she'd presented a mid-nineties teen pop show on Saturday mornings. She'd missed the pinnacle of the Ladette movement by a few years, instead providing a more wholesome girl-next-door alternative as she progressed from weekend mayhem TV to shows about budget home makeovers for twenty-somethings cashing in on the early noughties boom. Later she'd married heartthrob breakfast TV presenter Simon Burton, then had Ruby. Winning the job of presenting *Spotlight*, the biggest talent show on TV, had been the icing on the cake of a long and impressive career.

The simple fact was that people liked Daisy. She was kind to production staff, worked hard and never took her success for granted. She was never late and remembered people's birthdays. Her most outrageous diva demand was to ask if someone could find her a peppermint teabag during a live broadcast from a lighthouse in Aberystwyth. There were plenty of other TV stars who did a great job of being edgy, unpredictable or outrageous, but Daisy had no problem with being famously *nice*.

Being easy to work with had paid off and, after nearly twenty-five years, Daisy's star was still burning bright. *Spotlight* continued to top the ratings as the biggest family entertainment show on TV, and she had advertising deals with fashion, beauty and skincare brands, as well as two bestselling cookbooks. She had a cabinet full of awards, just not the trophy she really wanted. Yet, despite the inevitable outcome of tonight's proceedings, there was something comforting about being in the company of so many people who wished Daisy nothing but success.

Christian, meanwhile, did not look comforted in the least. She could tell that he'd rather be anywhere else but here. Yes, he was politely shaking hands with endless strangers, but he was forcing himself to hover in the reflected glow of Daisy's fame. Every now and then his hand brushed over her backside in a way that felt both proprietary and provocative, and it was clear to Daisy that his only interest in her dress was how quickly he could get her out of it.

They took their seats in time for the live broadcast to begin, presented by TV legend Des Parker, who was Daisy's longstanding friend and mentor, as well as Ruby's godfather. He'd been a huge support when her four-year marriage to Simon had broken down – even though Daisy had given her full and public support to Simon's announcement that he was gay, she'd been devastated. But there was nothing to be gained from airing her grief in public, and she cared about Simon too much to punish him for finally having the courage to be himself.

Everyone clapped and cheered politely as the awards were handed out – *Factual Entertainment*, *New Drama*, *Daytime*, *Comedy*, *Quiz Show*, *Drama Performance* . . . The nominations, speeches and thank yous all started to blur into one another. Christian was getting bored; drumming his fingers on the arm of the chair and making little effort to hide his yawns. Daisy tried not to be annoyed with him; this was probably pretty tedious for someone who didn't work in the industry or watch a lot of TV, but he could at least try to LOOK like he was having fun, especially with so many people watching.

Christian briefly rallied when *Spotlight* won the award for Best Talent Show, and the cameras swung to him clapping and smiling as Daisy went up onto the stage with the rest of the team. She said a few words of thanks alongside the executive producer and accepted the award for the sixth time. It was always an honour, but it still wasn't the big one.

The atmosphere changed as Des introduced soap legend Susie Docherty, who was presenting the award for Best TV Presenter. After eleven years, the possibility that Joe McDonald might be knocked off his podium was tantalising, but the result would make the front page of the tabloids tomorrow either way. Susie read out the nominations and clips were played from each of their shows.

As Daisy smiled for the cameras and gave a humble wave, Christian leaned in and whispered in her ear, 'Don't be too gutted, babe.'

It felt like a punch in the gut. She was still fighting back tears when Susie opened the envelope and the arena fell quiet.

'And the winner is—' Everyone held their breath. '—*DAISY CRAWFORD!*'

The crowd went bananas.

Daisy stumbled to her feet, her hands over her face as she struggled to breathe. Between her fingers, she could just see Joe giving her a standing ovation, and soon the rest of the celebrity audience joined him, a sea of faces clapping and cheering.

Christian gave her a lingering kiss as the cameras flashed frantically. Daisy tried not to cry, reminding herself that her face was going to be all over the papers tomorrow, and was live on TV right now.

11

Look happy. Don't blub. For God's sake . . . hold it together.

Daisy could barely feel her legs as she walked towards the stage. It felt like miles. She'd never done this walk alone before; the *Spotlight* team had always been with her. She could feel the anxiety rising. She hadn't prepared a speech; she'd never expected to win. Who should she thank? It felt like one of those fever dreams where you had to sit an exam you hadn't revised for. She tried not to panic as she teetered up the steps. As long as she acknowledged the *Spotlight* team and the public for their years of support, everything else would be fine. Nobody wanted a speech that rambled on. She wasn't Gwyneth Paltrow at the Oscars.

She lifted her skirt delicately in both hands as she walked across the stage, her eyes fixed on the smiling faces of Susie and her darling friend, Des, and the silver award in his hands. Then everything seemed to slow as she stumbled, the heel of her left shoe catching on something. It snapped and crumpled beneath her. She toppled sideways, dropping the skirt to save herself, arms windmilling as she tried to right herself, her other foot going down to find purchase. But the heavy, voluminous fabric caught under her right heel, the thigh split giving way along the seam as Daisy's legs slid in opposite directions. Susie shrieked and Des's face turned from joy and pride to utter horror. They both reached out to catch her, but it was all too late.

The next thing Daisy knew she was flat on her back, winded and disoriented, the bright stage lights blinding her and an agonising throb in the back of her head. After a moment she struggled to sit upright, ignoring the untenable pain as she untangled herself slowly from what felt like acres of skirt fabric bunched around her head. Her left leg was bent backwards at an unnatural angle and there was a sharp pain coming from her knee, and her other foot was splayed outwards, the heel of her shoe wedged firmly under a cable leading to a light fixture at the edge of the stage.

Within seconds Des was squatting in front of her, his face full of horror and concern as he touched her shoulder and said some words. But her ears were full of a strange ringing and the pain in her head was blinding. A camera flashed nearby, then another. Des leapt up and pushed someone away, then struggled out of his jacket and laid it across her lap, which felt cold, for some reason. He squatted back down and held her hand as shadows appeared, people gently moving her legs and touching her arms. Beyond Des, Daisy could see hundreds of tiny lights, flashing, exploding, like a sky full of fireflies. *How beautiful*, she thought, and then she passed out.

CHAPTER TWO

'So, Daisy. How are you feeling?'

The assembled team all looked at her with sympathetic head-tilts and caring smiles. She'd shed a bucket of tears in the past few days and was not in the mood for being handled with kid gloves, like she wasn't entirely stable and might go into meltdown at any second. She gave Clara, the executive producer of *Spotlight*, a look that she hoped was respectful, but also clearly communicated that she was not to be messed with.

'I'm fine,' Daisy murmured. 'Remind me why we're here?'

Clara cleared her throat and tossed her glossy curtain of jet-black hair. They all knew why. The meeting was ostensibly to talk about what was now being referred to as *The Incident*, but Daisy wasn't going to apologise or beg. It wasn't her fault.

They were assembled in the offices of Cloud Productions, the company which made *Spotlight*, on the first floor of an ugly concrete block in Covent Garden that overlooked the back of a theatre and a row of huge wheelie bins. Daisy idly wondered if they were planning to toss her straight out of the window and save time.

Daisy sat on one side of the glossy meeting table, flanked by her manager, Katie, and her agent, Roger, who had copies of Daisy's contract in his briefcase and was prepared to waft them around, if required. Clara sat on the other side, alongside three members of the *Spotlight* public relations team who looked like twenty-something hostages who hadn't been fed in weeks and seemed to be there for no other purpose than to ensure Clara had more people in the room than Daisy.

'We need to make a plan,' said Clara. 'It's been four days since . . . well, The Incident, and we haven't yet put out a statement, as you know. The press is demanding to know what our position is.'

'And what *is* your position?' Daisy stared Clara down, as one of the Hostages gave an involuntary shudder.

Clara smiled and sat back in her chair, her voice softening. 'Daisy, darling, we're not the enemy here. We've all worked together a long time, and I hope you think of us as your friends.' She turned the palms of her hands upwards. 'Of course, I'm here to represent *Spotlight*, but I'm also here to help. I thought that between us we could come up with a plan to deal with all the noise, then get back to what we're all best at.'

Daisy slumped in her chair, momentarily defeated. 'I'm sorry. I don't mean to be a bitch. The whole thing is so awful, and I've got no idea who's on my side any more.'

Clara leaned across the table, covering Daisy's hand with her own. Her nails were a glossy red, filed to a perfect oval, in contrast to the remnants of Daisy's red-carpet manicure, which had been chewed and picked to a raggedy mess.

'We're definitely on your side, and it's our intention to give you our full support. We plan for *Spotlight* to kick off next July with you at the helm, as usual.'

Daisy breathed out for what felt like the first time in days. 'And was that a unanimous decision?'

'Of course not!' laughed Clara. 'Several people here AND at the Beeb demanded your head on a spike. Family show, terrible press, blah-blah-blah. I reminded them how many

15

dubious characters have been given top jobs on British television over the years and asked if they were really intending to fire you over an unfortunate wardrobe malfunction. I also reminded them that it would NEVER happen to a man, because men aren't expected to wear that kind of nonsense on the red carpet.'

'It's not just the NTAs though, is it?' Daisy could feel a headache building.

'Well, no.' Clara's tone was brisk, all business. 'So that's what we're here to talk about.' She nodded at Hostage One, whose pale, spindly hands reached into his man bag to extract a brown cardboard folder of press cuttings and website printouts. 'To work out where all this other noise is coming from, and the best way to put a stop to it.'

Hostage One placed the folder in front of Daisy like it might explode at any minute, while Clara opened her laptop. The screen projected onto the huge TV on the wall, showing a headline from the *Daily Mail* that read '*Whoops-A-Daisy! TV Treasure Takes a Tumble*'. Underneath was a picture of her and Christian smiling on the red carpet, alongside a press photo taken from the edge of the stage, showing her bare legs spread at right angles and her dignity covered by a blushing face emoji.

'Jesus,' gasped Daisy, putting her head in her hands as Katie patted her arm. It wasn't the first time she'd seen the picture, but the feeling of sickness and humiliation was still raw. Clara kept scrolling through the other tabloid front pages – '*From Red Carpet to Red Face – TV Darling Daisy Accidentally Bares All*' in the *Daily Mirror*, and '*Wax The Way To Do It!*' in *The Sun*. Thankfully, the fifteen-second delay on the live broadcast meant ITV had been able to cut to a different shot of the arena after The Incident, so her naked lower half hadn't been broadcast into the nation's living rooms. But it seemed like half the audience in the O2 had taken a highly pixelated picture of her nether regions on their phones, so it was everywhere on social media anyway.

While the immediate coverage was horrific, it was at least vaguely factual. The following two days had unleashed two of Daisy's least favourite things – speculation and opinion. The speculation, all attributed to conveniently unnamed 'sources', was that Daisy was drunk, or possibly on some kind of medication. While nobody actually used the word 'drugs', the source still managed to make it sound like Daisy habitually injected heroin into her eyeballs.

Meanwhile the opinion pieces offered various points of view on Daisy's main misdemeanours – wearing ridiculous heels, not wearing any knickers, and waxing off all her pubes. All three had opened up a feminist debate that involved a great deal of outrage, a small but vocal seam of support – and not very much middle ground. After a columnist in the *Telegraph* wrote a piece comparing and contrasting Daisy's waxing choices with Julia Roberts' armpit hair at the *Notting Hill* premiere in 1999, she sat on the toilet and wept for twenty minutes, before asking her team to wade through the festering swamp of press and social media coverage on her behalf. That meant that some of the latest stories that Clara was scrolling through on the screen were news to Daisy. It was like a horror film, and did nothing to ease her headache.

Another 'source' said Daisy had been seen drunk in a nightclub a couple of weeks ago, implying there was some kind of behaviour pattern that suggested her 'fall' was possibly a 'collapse'. Then there was a petition. A *petition*! That called for

17

Daisy to be sacked, stating she was symptomatic of Britain's 'moral breakdown'. Yet another source claimed that Daisy was known to have a temper and had once 'thrown a shoe at her dog', with the headline *Dangerous Daisy throws a Jimmy Choo-huahua*. Daisy rarely lost her temper, but more to the point had never even owned a dog. In fact she'd never thrown so much as a sock at any animal, although right now she'd happily unleash every stiletto she owned on the flock of press – the Vultures, she called them – trailing her around London.

She and the team worked through the possible sources of the stories, analysing the details for clues, but came up with nothing. Chances were the tabloids had just made them up. It wouldn't be the first time.

The one thing Daisy was grateful for was that Ruby was safely away at boarding school, and it seemed like the piss-taking about her mother's wardrobe malfunction from her fellow students had mostly stopped. Daisy had never been more grateful for the capriciousness of teenagers. Ruby was due home for half-term in a couple of weeks so they could talk properly – aside from smoothing over Ruby's mortification about The Incident, Daisy needed to get to the bottom of why her daughter wasn't keen on her fiancé. Another headache to deal with another day.

As Clara used phrases like 'deflection strategy' and 'revolving celebrity news cycle', Daisy's thoughts drifted to the aftermath of her fall. She couldn't remember seeing Christian after The Incident, although apparently he'd been escorted backstage straight away and hovered around the paramedics until she regained consciousness, at which point she'd yelled at him to go away. He'd messaged a few times since to ask if she was OK, along with hundreds of other friends and colleagues and hangers-on, some of whom were probably revelling in her downfall from Darling Daisy to Sentient Vagina. From most loved, to most laughed at.

'—so in essence what I'm saying is that our response strategy should be two-pronged . . .' Clara continued.

Katie, Roger and Daisy's phones buzzed simultaneously. Daisy ignored hers: it never stopped buzzing these days. Katie quietly slid her iPhone off the table and glanced at the message, her brow furrowing as her clicks and swipes became more frantic.

'First, we need to—'

'Sorry, can I stop you there?' Katie looked worriedly at Daisy, who raised her eyebrows in question. 'Er, Christian has just announced your engagement. On Twitter.'

'He's done WHAT?' Daisy's mouth fell open, her eyes bulging as she snatched Katie's phone from her hand and stared at the tweet.

> Guys its supposed to be a secret but I cant keep it in. Two weeks ago I asked Daisy to be Mrs Walker and she said YES. Best feeling ever. Better than winning on centre court! SO stoked!
>
> 💬 567 🔁 1,983 ♡ 12.8k

'Oh God!' Any remaining colour drained from Daisy's face. *Jesus Fucking Christ.* I need to call Ruby.'

Daisy took deep yogic breaths as she waited for Irene, the Milton Park School secretary, to track down Ruby – apparently she had a study period so could be in any number of places right now. Daisy calmly explained that it was urgent that Ruby call her back, ringing off after gaining assurance from Irene that she would find her daughter straight away. Daisy trusted Irene to do what she'd asked without any fuss; Milton Park had no shortage of famous parents, and Daisy's downfall was by no means the biggest celebrity scandal it had weathered.

She was sitting in a tiny meeting room where Hostage Two had ushered her so she could call Ruby in private. There was a montage of black-and-white photos of *Spotlight* winners on the walls; Daisy was in most of them, handing over the giant glass trophy and beaming with happiness. She studied all the versions of her smiling face, knowing that in those moments she'd been feeling both joy for the winner, but also relief that another series was over and she could take a break. It wasn't the kind of thing you ever talked about: nobody wanted to hear from a wealthy, successful celebrity how tiring and stressful their job was. You just kept smiling, which was why everyone wanted to be Daisy Crawford – the glitter, the clothes, the face, the boyfriend, the lifestyle. Until the NTAs, anyway.

She checked her phone again, then leaned forward, pressing the heels of her hands into her eyeballs and trying to unscramble her thoughts.

Benny, Christian's manager, had to be behind the engagement announcement; he was a Machiavellian puppet-master who knew exactly how to pull Christian's strings. At thirty-three, Christian had just retired from the international tour and was coming to the end of his first tennis-free summer since he was six. Daisy knew that his new mission was to be a 'TV personality', and that had been moderately successful, largely thanks to Benny. Christian's appearances on telethons and quiz shows had revealed a dry wit and a bucket of charisma that he'd clearly been hiding away in his racquet bag. It also didn't hurt that he was tall, dark and extremely handsome.

So Benny would have told him to make the announcement, no doubt to make him look like the hero of the hour. A Disney Prince standing by his Fallen Woman. Benny would also know that Daisy couldn't kick off publicly without looking mean-spirited in the face of Christian's charming outpouring of emotion. She frowned as she put the pieces together. Maybe Damien, Christian's agent, was involved too. She knew he was in negotiations for Christian to join the BBC Wimbledon commentating team, but the contract hadn't been confirmed yet – and only a handful of people knew about it, including Daisy. Christian had never won a Grand Slam tournament, but the public loved him – and his relationship with Daisy marked him as a star in the ascendant. Christian was hot property right now, and they needed to get the Wimbledon deal signed as soon as possible.

Daisy picked up her iPhone, scrolled to Christian's number and stabbed at the screen, only to throw it onto the table seconds later as it went straight to voicemail.

Again.

Daisy's ears were ringing from Ruby's tears and recriminations when she got back to the meeting room. She felt lightheaded and unsteady on her feet, like her world had been tilted on its axis for the second time in four days. What had Christian been thinking? How could he have done something so thoughtless? Poor Ruby. She felt so guilty, and just wanted to give her daughter a hug.

21

Daisy collapsed into a seat at the table and picked up the glass of water, trying to stop her hands from shaking as she took a sip. She looked at Clara, doing her best to look like she was holding it together. 'Right. Shall we talk about your two-pronged strategy?'

Clara gave a barking laugh and tapped her nails on the desk. '*Dar–ling*, it's just sprouted several new prongs.'

An hour later, they had the makings of a plan. Daisy's biggest problem was the Vultures, who were determined to keep the story alive. They clearly weren't going away any time soon, particularly in view of Christian's announcement.

'What about getting out of London for a while?' suggested Hostage Three. 'Like, somewhere secluded where the press can't get to you. Behind gates, or security, or whatever.' The other two looked up from their phones, waiting to see Daisy's reaction before they arranged their sunken faces into expressions of awe or disdain.

'What about a health retreat?' said Clara. 'You could go abroad.'

'No,' said Katie firmly. 'The press could spin that as some kind of rehab.'

'Hmm,' said Clara, nodding thoughtfully. 'OK, bad idea.' She glared at Hostage Three, who tried to disappear into her chair, tucking away her limbs like a folding bicycle.

'No, it's not,' said Katie. 'But Daisy needs to stay in the UK. Somewhere with peace and privacy, but where she can be seen out in public. That way we can manage the story and squash any rumours the minute they surface.'

Daisy sat forward in her chair, suddenly inspired. 'Willow Cottage.'

'Where's Willow Cottage?' asked Hostage Two.

'It's in the Cotswolds. Simon and I bought it years ago. He kept it in the divorce and now goes there with his husband.'

Hostage Two's eyes narrowed as her brain processed this unconventional family tree, then she nodded approvingly. 'Cool.'

Daisy hadn't been to Willow Cottage in thirteen or fourteen years, and even before that she'd only visited a dozen or so times, mostly early on in her relationship with Simon when things had been great between them. She recalled how secluded it was, part of a private school estate with a gated driveway and too many footpaths in and out for the Vultures to cover. It was in a village in the arse end of nowhere but only ten miles or so from Ruby's school, so she could come home at weekends if she wanted to. It would give Daisy a chance to do some repair work on their mother–daughter relationship and beg for forgiveness about the engagement. And she could deal with Christian from a distance, without any sharp objects to hand. Daisy could come back to London in a few weeks after Ruby's half-term, by which time somebody else's genitalia would be keeping the nation entertained and The Incident and the engagement would all be ancient news.

Simon sounded relieved when Daisy called him, but he knew her well enough not to ask too many questions. He confirmed that the cottage was free for as long as Daisy needed it, and in return she promised to call him later for a proper chat. Already she was itching to get out of town and start putting all this mess behind her.

Daisy was taken home by Karim, who had also driven her back from the O2 after she'd been given the all-clear by paramedics and crawled into his car so she could die of shame at home. She liked that he was discreet and reliable, and in over a decade he had never asked her for insider gossip or free tickets to *Spotlight*, although she offered the latter to him every year. He drove her himself whenever he could, or sent one of his brothers if he wasn't available; it was an arrangement that worked for everyone, and in Daisy's tight-knit circle of trust, Karim was a valued member of her team.

Today Karim's job was to act as bodyguard as well as driver. He helped Daisy out of the car, navigating her through the pack of Vultures waiting outside her Highgate Village townhouse, a protective arm around her as they bombarded her with questions. *Was Christian's proposal a publicity stunt, Daisy? Have you been sacked from* Spotlight, *Daisy? What does your mum think of what happened at the NTAs, Daisy?*

She thanked Karim and firmly closed the door, then made a cup of tea and tried Christian again. This time he answered.

'Hey,' he said quietly. Daisy could hear the trepidation in his voice and felt a wave of exhaustion wash over her. She was all out of fight for one day.

'What were you thinking?' she asked, trying to keep her voice calm and measured when inside she was screaming. 'Why would you announce something like that without talking to me first?'

'I was being spontaneous,' said Christian. 'I wanted to be supportive. You know, after . . .'

'But Ruby *didn't know*,' hissed Daisy through gritted teeth. 'She found out from people at school that her mum's getting married. She's incredibly upset.'

'Oh,' said Christian. 'Is she upset that you didn't tell her, or that we're getting married?'

Both, thought Daisy, but she wasn't getting into that now.

'What does it matter?' she said. 'You had no right to go public without talking to me first.' She raked her hand through her hair in frustration. 'In my world, there's a way of . . .' She stopped short, feeling stupid. There WAS a way of doing these kind of things – a ring, proper photos, a statement, an Instagram announcement, maybe a deal with *OK!* if you were that way inclined. But it was patronising to suggest that Christian wasn't part of her world.

'I didn't think about that, I'm sorry,' said Christian, but she could already hear the boredom in his voice. 'I was just excited, and it felt like the right moment.'

'I'm getting out of town for a while,' said Daisy. 'The press are everywhere, so I'm going to stay in a friend's place in the Cotswolds.' She didn't mention that it had once been a romantic bolthole for her and her ex-husband.

'Right, I totally get that,' said Christian. 'But I need to stay in London right now. The Wimbledon contract and . . . stuff, you know.' Daisy could hear him stifling a yawn and pressed her lips together in fury. *I wasn't inviting you anyway.*

'Fine. I'll call you in a few days,' said Daisy.

'OK,' mumbled Christian. 'I gotta go, my personal trainer is here. We'll talk soon.'

Daisy ended the call, feeling like she had plenty more to say, but all of it could wait until she felt less frazzled. She threw her phone on the sofa and sipped her tea. Was she overreacting? Could Christian's show of support actually be quite helpful? Weren't women always asking men to be more open, to show their emotions? Judging by the Twitter response, the public seemed to think it was adorable. So why was she so unsettled?

CHAPTER THREE

Daisy manoeuvred the BMW along increasingly narrow and winding lanes, wishing the relentless rain would stop. One of her windscreen wipers squeaked and had been grating on her nerves since Oxford, but she couldn't bring herself to stop at a garage and get it fixed. That would involve interacting with members of the public, which ordinarily she didn't mind, but right now it was all knowing smiles, elbow nudges and whispering. Anyone would think they'd never seen a fanny before.

Hopefully, once she arrived in Shipton Combe, she wouldn't need to use the car again for a while – she had a boot full of groceries and could get Ocado to deliver whenever she needed to. Everything else she needed was stuffed into a couple of weekend bags, with a nod to practicality rather than glamour. She definitely wasn't planning any cocktail parties.

Ordinarily October was Daisy's favourite month of the year; because it marked the beginning of her annual autumn break. *Spotlight*'s gruelling run of live shows finished in mid-September, and Daisy's manager and agent were under strict instructions to keep her TV schedule free until the end of the year. She was happy to do the odd interview, brand endorsement or charity thing, but mostly this was her time to relax and unwind. After the NTAs, Daisy usually had no major plans until she and Ruby went skiing the week before Christmas. That was their family time, and something thankfully Christian had shown no interest in – snow sports had been deemed too dangerous while he was on the tennis circuit, which was pretty much his entire life. So he'd never learnt to ski, and Daisy suspected his objection was mostly about embarking on a sport at which he might not immediately shine.

As Daisy waited at some temporary traffic lights on a hedge-lined lane, she thought back to when she and Christian had first met. Christian had taken part in a one-off *Spotlight* charity special, performing an uncannily good rendition of 'I Feel It Coming' by The Weeknd. Since Christian had been largely assumed to be an all-round personality vacuum, the fact that he could hold a tune and occupy a public stage without needing to towel his face every sixty seconds came as a surprise. It was a performance literally nobody asked for, but everybody subsequently talked about.

After the show he approached Daisy in the BBC bar and handed her his phone, casually rolling out the line 'I think there's something wrong with my phone – it doesn't seem to have your number in it.' Daisy had been at first amused by his confidence, then charmed by his persistence, and finally bowled over by his desire. The news that Christian and Daisy were dating had sent the tabloids wild – he was square-jawed and brooding, while she was a wholesome English Rose with a colourful family history and a messy divorce that the tabloids never tired of raking over.

On Daisy's insistence they had played the relationship down and kept things classy, mainly for Ruby's sake, but also because despite her job, Daisy was a private person. Her

TV persona was public property, but her personal life was not for sale. She knew Katie was now being bombarded with six-figure offers for her and Christian's engagement interview and photos; no doubt Benny was getting the same, if not actively encouraging a bidding war. And while Christian would want to make hay while the sun shone, Daisy just wasn't interested. She'd been reminded in the past week that for every person who was kind and supportive, there were plenty of others who were cruel and judgemental. Lifting the lid on her off-screen world just invited the keyboard warriors in, and she no longer had the stomach for it.

Daisy swung the car towards the gates of Shipton House School, her hair getting soaked in the autumnal downpour as she leaned out of the window to enter a four-digit code on an electronic keypad. The metal gates clanked open and she drove slowly down the impressive drive, taking in the looming grey manor house with Jacobean gables and spooky-looking towers. A dozen or so cottages lay scattered across the fifty or so acres of school grounds, most lived in by staff. She turned off the drive towards Willow Cottage, one of a pair of identical houses built from honey-coloured Cotswold stone. Even from the car she could see that Beech Cottage next door looked cosy and lived-in, with a pair of muddy wellies flumped sideways by the front door and a bicycle with a wicker basket leaning against the wall. She spotted a shadowy flicker of movement in the dim light behind the curtains and wondered who lived there. In contrast Willow Cottage looked dark, cold and abandoned.

Sixteen years ago, this place had seemed hopelessly romantic to Daisy, but that was another life. She remembered being shown around the cottage by an estate agent – Daisy blooming and blissful in pregnancy, Simon full of enthusiasm for the house's potential as a family hideaway. Now she felt an unexpected wave of mixed emotions as she looked at the tiny wooden porch, the leaded windows and the crooked tiled roof.

For a year or two after Ruby was born, this had been a happy place for Simon and Daisy – a chance for them all to spend time together away from London and the Vultures. But later it was the scene of some of the worst times, including the eventual showdown when Simon had confessed that he had been spending quality time with Archie, his now husband. Daisy hadn't set foot in this village since, but now wasn't the time to relive past traumas – God knows, she had enough to deal with in her present.

She dug Simon's key out of her handbag and climbed out of the car, hurrying through the rain to the cottage. The heavy front door opened into a tiny, dark lounge that reeked of furniture polish and a sickly lavender room spray. Presumably Simon's cleaner had done a quick whip round in the hope of making it feel lived in; instead it smelled like a pensioner's sock drawer. On the upside, it was clean enough and the heating was on, with an inviting fire laid in the wood burner, so Daisy would soon have it feeling snug.

By 4 p.m. Daisy was unpacked, hooked up to the WiFi and restored to something vaguely resembling normality by a cup of tea and a cheese sandwich. The rain was easing off, so she decided to go for a walk around the village before it got dark. She put on a pair of wellies and a waxed coat of Archie's, who was the same height as Daisy and had equally slim hips. Up close, she supposed she could be recognisable, but from afar she might be mistaken for Archie.

And anyway, who would be expecting Daisy Crawford to be in Shipton Combe? But it was a small village and realistically she wouldn't be anonymous for long. So, might as well make the most of it.

She closed the front door and headed across the field towards the school; since it was Saturday, there was nobody around apart from birds and squirrels. She did a lap of the main building, wondering what it must be like to obtain a very expensive education in what was clearly a haunted prison. The place felt familiar but only in the vaguest sense – she and Simon had never socialised or made friends here as a couple. Willow Cottage had always been somewhere they used for running away and hiding. No change there, then.

She made her way along a footpath which followed a row of old beech trees already showing tinges of autumn colour, meandering past a small lake with a weedy and overgrown island in the middle. By the time Daisy made it to the gate that opened onto the main road at the far end of the village, it had started to rain again, so she turned up the collar of Archie's raincoat and picked up her pace.

Shipton Combe was little more than a road about a quarter of a mile long, with a village hall, children's play area and tennis court at one end, backing onto a cricket pitch with a smart white pavilion. Pretty houses lined both sides of the road, all seemingly of a similar era to Willow Cottage, which suggested most of the village had been built to accommodate workers at the original Shipton House. Some had names echoing their former role – The Old Laundry, The Old Dairy, The Old Schoolhouse – but now they were all family homes with chimneys belching woodsmoke and windows firmly closed against the increasing deluge.

At the other end of the village a rather lovely Norman church was flanked by a large, ramshackle rectory, opposite the main school gates that Daisy had driven through hours earlier. Next to the rectory was a cosy-looking pub called the Shipton Arms, which looked like it had undergone some gentrification since Daisy had last visited. She remembered it as a shabby, spit-and-sawdust local pub, but now there were signs for organic ales and a venison delivery van parked outside. The door was open, but she resisted the temptation to get out of the rain and order something warming. She could just imagine the headlines if she were spotted knocking back a brandy in the middle of the afternoon.

The rain was coming down in sheets as Daisy hurried towards the school gates, so she didn't notice the car approaching until it was right behind her, tyres hissing on the wet road. She'd barely glanced at the dark four-wheel drive before it drove at speed through a huge puddle, soaking her from head to toe in a sheet of cold, muddy water.

'Oh my God! What the fuck?!' Furious, Daisy turned to watch as the car slammed to a halt; then started to reverse. The driver lowered the window. It was a man with dark hair and a green jumper, looking at her in horror, but Daisy couldn't tell much more than that because her fringe was now dripping into her eyes.

'I can't believe you just did that.' Daisy waited for an apology so they could at least move past the awkwardness and laugh it off, but the man said nothing, continuing to stare at Daisy, his mouth opening and closing like a goldfish. She was used to this kind of reaction from people who recognised her, but it wasn't what she'd expected from somebody who'd just drowned her with a Toyota Land Cruiser. The

31

man finally looked away, then looked back, then looked away again, then silently closed the window. He drove off without a word.

She watched somewhat incredulously as his car swished along the flooded road towards the far end of the village, his tail lights casting red shadows in the standing water.

'Jesus! What an arsehole!'

She wiped the sleeve of Archie's coat across her dripping face, but the waxed cotton made the gesture entirely pointless, so shivering, she hurried through the school gates, feeling the cold, clammy squelch of wet socks inside her wellies.

As she half-jogged down the tree-lined driveway in what was now a torrential downpour, she forced her thoughts away from the Toyota Wanker to the slightly more alluring prospect of Christian. She was still furious with him, but this was the longest she'd gone without having sex in six months, and she had to admit she was missing it. Christian was insatiable, and if he was here right now they'd be rushing back to get their wet clothes off, before warming each other up on the rug in front of the fire with a great deal of human friction.

Given the choice, Daisy preferred making love by candlelight in a pillowy nest of bliss, and on these occasions Christian was happy to play the romantic seducer. But he also liked to have spontaneous, dirty sex, wherever and whenever there was a window of opportunity – in her shower, on the kitchen table, even once in the master bathroom at Richard and Judy's house while everyone partied downstairs. She'd drawn the line at a disabled toilet in BBC Broadcasting House, but he usually managed to talk her round. The way Daisy looked at him made him hard, and the way he looked at Daisy made him hard to resist.

Daisy shivered, this time from more than the cold and wet. Yes, she was still livid with him – he'd made an awful week infinitely worse AND landed her in this miserable village. But maybe she'd call him later and get a few things off her chest, and then they could both take matters into their own hands.

CHAPTER FOUR

As Daisy walked around the old stables towards the warmth and shelter of Willow Cottage, a bicycle whisked past at high speed. She recognised the wicker basket from the house next door and caught a glimpse of a man in a blue anorak and a canvas hat with a large brim. He was emptying provisions from the basket as she walked around the corner – a box of eggs, some muddy vegetables and a very dead chicken with a dangling head and all its feathers. He barely gave Daisy a glance before disappearing inside the house and slamming the door behind him.

The knock came five minutes later, after Daisy had struggled out of her wet coat and boots and was busy draping everything over a couple of chairs by the fireplace to dry. She opened the door a crack to see the same man standing in the rain, holding two bunches of wonky carrots by their green stalks.

'You got any coffee?' The accent was more East End than Gloucestershire. Clearly Daisy wasn't the only outsider in this village.

The question disarmed her; it wasn't what she was expecting from a man holding carrots. But she nodded, rationalising that she could spare a few instant granules before her next Ocado order. 'Sure. Hang on, I'll get you some.'

'No. Sorry. Can you make me a coffee? I'm not allowed to make it myself.'

Daisy was baffled and wondered if the man was drunk. He appeared to be in his fifties with a scruffy thatch of silvery hair, a straggly beard and an oversized Fair Isle jumper that was mostly holes. He also looked familiar, but Daisy couldn't place him. She raised her eyebrows questioningly, and he huffed.

'God, this is fucking ridiculous. Can I come in? I'll explain, but I'm getting soaked out here.' He noticed her discomfort and held out his veg-filled hands in a gesture of openness. 'I'm a gay chef, not an axe murderer. *I promise.*'

Daisy eyed him carefully, then the pieces fell into place and she finally worked out who he was. Justin Drummond, former TV chef and restauranteur. He'd disappeared from public view a few years ago after a scandal involving . . . what was it? Tax? Creative accounting? Something like that. Definitely nothing involving beating women to death with root vegetables. She opened the door wider and he bustled past into the warm room, immediately shaking himself like a wet dog.

'I'm Justin. Have a welcome gift.' He thrust the carrots at her, which were dripping on the carpet, so she took them.

'Daisy,' she muttered, disappearing into the kitchen to dump them in the sink.

'Oh yeah, course. Sorry, didn't recognise you.' Daisy waited for the inevitable 'with your knickers on' but it didn't materialise. 'I've been out of circulation for a while, house don't have a TV or internet or anything. Are you still doing that talent show thing, what's it called?'

Daisy was momentarily stunned, unsure if he was joking. '*Spotlight.*'

'That's the fella. That still going strong?'

'Yes. Doesn't start until next July though, so I've got a bit of a break.'

'Good for you. I'll be long gone by then.'

Daisy put the kettle on and put a spoonful of coffee into a mug as Justin loomed over her shoulder. He smelled quite organic, like he hadn't troubled a bar of soap or a box of Persil in a while.

'Pop another spoonful in there, will you? Nice and strong, lots of milk.'

Daisy obliged, reaching further along the counter to retrieve a box of chocolate fingers. Justin pulled the plastic tray from the box with a moan, visibly salivating.

'Oh God, do you promise you won't tell?'

He started stuffing biscuits into his mouth until they were poking out like fangs and he could no longer speak. Daisy folded her arms and waited for him to swallow, then watched, mesmerised, as he washed everything down with half the mug of coffee.

'Why would anyone care about you eating biscuits?'

Justin gave a barking laugh, his mouth still glued together with chocolate fingers. 'I'm writing a book.' He drained the mug and held it out, so Daisy spooned in more coffee for a refill.

'A book?'

'It was a stupid fucking idea but I can't afford to sack it off now. I'm living off grid for a year, got four months to go, then I can get out of this festering shithole.'

Daisy was intrigued. 'How off grid, exactly?'

'Very,' Justin mumbled through another mouthful of biscuits. 'No phone, no electricity, no internet, no food that I don't grow or rear myself. I've got a smallholding over by the school with veg and chickens and pigs and a goat. Got a polytunnel and some beehives, I can forage fruit and stuff locally. The kids help out and I do some lessons in exchange for firewood.'

'And why here, exactly? Why not somewhere nearer London?'

'It was my publisher's idea,' huffed Justin. 'One of the senior editors owns the cottage next door; she used to live here and thought it would make a great location. I should have asked why she left before I agreed to move in.'

Daisy raised her eyebrows. 'Is it actually that bad though? It's not like you're living in a tent and eating grubs.' She was impressed when Justin managed to stuff more biscuits in, even if it wasn't at all pretty.

After some sticky chewing, Justin shrugged. 'It was brilliant in the summer. Loads of fruit and salad. Spending all day outside, plenty to do. Now it's all root veg and pickled stuff, and I have to actually write the fucking book. I don't have a computer. The house is freezing, I have to make my own soap and some days I would flog my right arm for a coffee.' He looked at the empty box of biscuits. 'And a chocolate finger. Don't tell anyone. I'd probably have to pay back my advance. Fuck, I really miss flour and proper sugar.'

'Do you want another coffee?'

'No, thanks, I'm buzzing off my tits already.'

Justin leaned back against the kitchen counter, his arms folded over a healthy belly that suggested he definitely wasn't going hungry, however much he was missing bread and pasta. He eyed Daisy appraisingly. 'So, what are you doing in Shipton Combe? It's not exactly a celeb hotspot.'

'It's a long story. I'm only here for a few weeks, my ex-husband owns this cottage.'

Justin raised his eyebrows and gave her a salacious smile. 'Ah yeah, I remember. Simon wotsit. Left you for a hunky man. Big old scandal back in the day.'

Daisy shrugged. 'It was a long time ago. We're still close friends and we have a lovely daughter.' God, how many times had she said those same words over the last decade? She sounded like a robot.

'It's fine,' Justin grinned. 'We're keepers of each other's secrets now. You can call him a *cheating twat* if you like.' Daisy laughed and decided Justin might not be the worst neighbour ever. Even though some of that homemade soap definitely wouldn't go amiss.

After Justin left to pluck his chicken, throwing out a vague invite to Daisy to come over for dinner later in the week, Daisy closed the curtains and turned on the lamps around the cottage. It was warm and cosy, and she momentarily felt sorry for Justin who was managing with oil lamps and candles and no heating other than the wood burner in the lounge and a wood-fired AGA in the kitchen. The bedrooms would be damp in this weather. No wonder he wasn't in a hurry to get naked for a shower. Did he even have hot water?

Dinner was cheese on toast washed down with a small glass of wine. Daisy had decided she was going to limit herself to one glass a day, having found herself reaching for the bottle as soon as the clock struck five since The Incident.

Daisy's mother was an Olympic-standard drinker, so she always tried to be careful with her booze intake.

So instead of giving into the urge to get stuck into the bottle and drown her many sorrows, Daisy made a peppermint tea and decided to call Christian, hoping he might be up for improving her mood. None of their previous calls had gone much beyond checking in – Christian always seemed to be busy, although she suspected he was avoiding heavy conversations. This time didn't bode any better, certainly not for phone sex, anyway: she could tell he was in a sulk from the moment he answered the phone.

'I'm getting loads of grief on Twitter from mad feminists,' he mumbled. 'Apparently some people think me announcing our engagement is a sign of me being an emotionally abusive control freak.'

Daisy shrugged. 'It was your decision to put it out there. You had to expect some kind of backlash.'

'And here's me thinking you might defend me,' snarked Christian.

Daisy sighed. 'Can you really not see any issue? I know we haven't got into the details, but would it help if I explained exactly what I'm upset about?'

'Sure,' mumbled Christian. 'If it makes *you* feel any better.'

'Actually, it does,' said Daisy, with a headmistress-like tone that Christian would probably find quite sexy, knowing him. 'First, you blurted out our personal business on Twitter without speaking to me beforehand – but we've already talked about that one. Second, you said I'd agreed to be "Mrs Walker", which I categorically have not. I didn't change my name for Simon; I'm certainly not doing it for you.'

Christian was silent for a moment. 'Why wouldn't you want my name? That's totally something we need to discuss.'

'I agree, but you jumped the gun, remember?' Daisy's tone was firm. 'My answer would have been the same. I've been Daisy Crawford for nearly forty years, and I'm not changing it for you or anyone else.'

She could pretty much hear Christian pouting at the other end of the phone, trying to work out his next move. When he said nothing, she ploughed on. 'THIRD, you used the announcement of our engagement to remind everyone that you once won a match on Centre Court, which is absolutely pathetic—'

'It wasn't a MATCH, it was a TOURNAMENT,' spat Christian.

'Oh for God's sake,' Daisy's tone was withering. 'You were fourteen. *It doesn't count.*'

'It fucking does!' whined Christian. 'It was the Boys' Singles in 1999, and that win over Marcus Elliot set me on course for British Number Two.'

Daisy rolled her eyes, again wondering why men were such needy children.

'Look, I've said I'm sorry.' Christian was clearly tired of this conversation. 'I don't know what more you want.'

One hundred miles away in Shipton Combe, Daisy suddenly realised that she didn't know either. Why did relationships have to be so complicated?

CHAPTER FIVE

A week later, Tom Clark sat in the headmaster's office at Shipton House School, reading through the grade predictions for this year's batch of Year 13s and wondering for the thousandth time why he'd ever become a teacher. Shipton House couldn't afford to be selective; they had barely three hundred students across the seven secondary school years as it was. So they usually ended up with the kids who didn't make the grade for other local private schools, and this year's lot was even more underwhelming than usual. The exception was Will Forbes-Glover, who was on track to be their first Oxbridge candidate in several years.

He put down the sheet of paper and stared out of his office window, across the field to the stables and the just-visible chimney of Willow Cottage, which he knew from the staff WhatsApp group had now been rented to Daisy Crawford. That rumour had originated with Lesley, the landlady at the Shipton Arms, who'd heard it from Avril, the local cleaner, who'd heard from the owner of Willow Cottage, who was Daisy's ex-husband, Simon Burton. Ms Crawford being in Shipton Combe was of no interest to Tom unless she could add twenty extra pupils to his register by next year, although he felt a twinge of guilt over soaking her with his car last week. Seeing her in the village like that, actual Daisy Crawford outside the school gates; it had stopped him in his tracks.

In the heat of the moment, he'd lost his mind and driven away – not exactly his finest hour, true, but it was too late now.

Tom stood up and looked at his reflection in the framed mirror above the fireplace. At forty-two, after twenty years of hard work and thousands of mostly tolerable children and universally ghastly parents, he'd achieved his ultimate career goal. He still had his own teeth and hair, and if the come-to-bed looks from some of the mothers (and a few of the fathers) were anything to go by, he was still what Tessa had called 'a dish'. So why did he feel like he was wearing lead boots?

He stuffed a folder of old A level papers into his bag and put his coat on, rousing Henry the chocolate Labrador from his slumber by the radiator under the bay window. He'd drop them off at Will Forbes-Glover's house, then give Henry a walk while he ran a couple of errands in the village. His old dog stretched and yawned grudgingly, then trudged after him down the stairs.

'Thanks for bringing those over.' Will caught Tom's eye for the briefest of seconds. He was a smart kid, and good-looking enough that the girls in the school pursued him relentlessly, but he was also cripplingly shy and awkward. It was one of the many reasons Tom liked him – Will reminded him of himself twenty-five years ago. Tessa had been good friends with Will's mother, Melanie, which had given Tom the opportunity to get to know him a little over the years. In school, Will treated him with the same eye rolling disdain as every other student. But in private, Tom liked to think Will saw him as some sort of family friend.

'No problem.' Tom sat on a stool at the kitchen island while Will fished a carton of milk out of the fridge and swilled a teabag in a mug. 'Is your heating broken?' It was only early October and it was already damp and freezing in here. Tom could practically see his own breath.

Will shrugged and disappeared back into the fridge. 'It's always like this. Dad likes the cold.'

Tight-fisted, or broke? You couldn't tell with Gerald Forbes-Glover; he sometimes came across as the kind of man who'd leave the rest of his family to freeze while he checked himself into a five-star hotel. Tessa had never liked him, but Tom was more inclined to see the best in people. He glanced over at the open textbooks further along the counter. 'How are you getting on with *The Handmaid's Tale*?'

'OK,' Will shrugged. 'It's actually pretty good. I thought it would be a girls' book, but it's not really.'

'What's the essay?'

Will mooched over and picked up his homework diary, a tangle of teenage limbs in a baggy grey hoody and black joggers with a crotch that hung halfway to his knees. '*In Gilead, love no longer exists,*' he read tonelessly. '*Examine this view of Atwood's presentation of relationships in* The Handmaid's Tale.'

'Christ!' Tom laughed. 'What do men like us know about love and relationships?'

Will half-smiled, then looked away, blushing furiously. 'Tell me about it,' he mumbled, cramming a chocolate digestive into his mouth and holding out the packet to Tom.

He took one. 'How's your dad?'

Will shrugged again and slid a mug of tea towards Tom. 'OK. He and Mum are currently obsessed with that telly woman who's moved into the village.'

'Daisy Crawford.' Tom rolled his eyes. 'It's no great surprise that people are talking, I guess. Nothing much else happens around here.'

'My dad had printed out her Wikipedia page.' Will pulled a face. 'I went into his office earlier and saw it on his desk. Age, career, everything. He's even highlighted bits of it in yellow.'

Tom nodded, not really surprised. Before his fall from grace, Gerald Forbes-Glover had been Conservative Member of Parliament for North Gloucestershire. Seven years earlier, he'd been caught having a fumble with a House of Commons intern and had been invited to resign. From what Tom had been able to gather from the usual village gossips, Gerald's mother had died not long before the scandal broke and had left him Shipton Rectory, so he'd scuttled out of Westminster and hunkered down here with his second wife, Melanie, and their son, Will, who was now seventeen. It wouldn't shock anyone if Gerald pointed his legendary sword in the direction of a woman like Daisy Crawford.

'What about your mum?' asked Tom, taking a swig of tea. He knew that Will's home life was fractious, and he made these visits every now and then to check up on him, timing it for when he knew Gerald and Melanie would both be in church. The line between headteacher and trusted adult was a fine one, and Tom had to be careful not to overstep.

Will shrugged. 'She's, like, a massive *Spotlight* fan, but it's not like they've got anything in common. And anyway, Mum wouldn't want to give Dad a chance to . . .' His voice trailed off as he brushed his floppy fringe out of his eyes, a sign of anxiety that Tom had seen in the young man too many times before.

Tom cleared his throat and picked up the exam papers again, sifting through them. 'Give me a shout when you've had a look at these. You've got a few months to think about university, but I'm really happy to chat about your options.'

'Dad's still saying I should do PPE at Cambridge, like he did.'

'And that isn't what you want?' Tom sipped his tea and looked at Will intently. It wasn't always easy to get him to talk, but if Will was in the mood to, he was definitely listening.

'I dunno,' he shrugged. 'I want to go travelling first, then maybe. But Dad says he won't pay for me to hang out with wasters in some crack den in Thailand.'

Tom clamped his lips together in restraint. 'Maybe if you get a deferred place, he'll think differently.'

Will shrugged again. 'Can't see it. I'll find a way to pay for it myself.' He picked up his copy of *The Handmaid's Tale* and started flicking through it, and Tom knew that his time was up.

'I need to return some Tupperware to the vicar.' He stood, draining his mug. 'Thanks for the tea.'

Will nodded and turned back to his books, so Tom let himself out.

'Do you think her being here might boost the congregation?' asked the Reverend Miriam Mayhew, handing Tom yet another mug of tea. It had '*Need an ark? I Noah guy*' printed on the side. Definitely in the God tier of Christian puns. The reverend put a flowery plate of custard creams on the kitchen table, then helped herself to two.

Tom took a biscuit. 'No idea. She doesn't seem like much of a churchgoer.'

45

'Troubled, though,' mused Miriam through a mouthful of biscuit. 'Maybe I can tempt her into the fold.'

Tom looked away, recalling the many times the local vicar had tried to lure him into the Church of St Mary the Virgin. Tessa had been a regular and, after she'd gone, Miriam had decided he was ripe for saving. So far he'd managed to fob her off. Perhaps the arrival of Daisy Crawford would keep her off his back for a while longer.

'Maybe,' Tom hedged, then added, 'It would definitely help the fundraising for the vestry.'

Miriam visibly perked up at the mention of her favourite subject. The vestry project had been ongoing for nearly five years and they were still only halfway to their target. The roof was falling in, the toilet was half-open to the elements and every winter it got worse and more funds were needed. Tom couldn't help but admire her resilience and commitment to what seemed to be a futile fundraising effort.

'Perhaps the Lord has sent me a saviour.' Miriam pressed her hands together in prayer, looking upwards at the cobwebby light fittings.

'Well, let's not get carried away,' chuckled Tom. 'She might not be here for long. But you should probably pay her a visit.'

Miriam nodded, clearly already plotting her next move. Tom remembered what Will said about Gerald and wondered who else in the village would be setting their sights on Daisy Crawford.

'Gerald and Melanie in church this morning?' he asked casually.

'Mmm,' Miriam muttered through another mouthful of biscuit. 'Enough space between them on that pew to park a donkey. And I couldn't help but notice that Melanie had a ladder in her tights.'

Tom raised his eyebrows, not wishing to get into idle speculation on the state of Melanie Forbes-Glover's hosiery.

'And she never sings during the hymns,' added Miriam in a stage whisper. 'Gerald sings, but Melanie *mimes*.' She gave Tom a significant look, like mouthing the words to 'Lead Us Heavenly Father Lead Us' was a recognised cry for help.

Tom drained his mug and gathered his coat and Henry's lead. Once Miriam got the bit between her teeth about something, she could keep you in Church House until Evensong.

Tom spotted Melanie Forbes-Glover as he closed Miriam's front door behind him. She was standing on one leg on the opposite pavement as she removed a shoe and pulled a pair of holey tights over an exposed toe. He turned away and pretended to rummage in his bag, not wanting her to know he'd seen her. Somehow seeing the bare toes of a woman like Melanie felt oddly intimate.

'Hello, Tom.' Melanie sounded breathless, like she was speaking for the first time that day. 'I was just on my way to see Miriam.' She reached down to pat Henry, who licked her hand.

'I'm just leaving,' said Tom with a warm smile, taking in Melanie's limp hair and shapeless clothes. She couldn't be a day over forty, but she dressed like a woman thirty years older and twice her size. Tom wondered, not for the first time, what on earth had happened to her. If she'd ever confided in Tessa, she'd never shared the details.

'Have you met our new celebrity neighbour yet?' he asked, hoping to hold her in conversation a little longer.

'No. Have you?'

'Not yet,' he said, conveniently ignoring the whole puddle incident. 'I'm not sure Shipton Combe has much to offer someone like her.' Melanie's eyes widened, and he realised he probably sounded a bit snarky. 'Not much celebrity night-life, you know,' he added lamely.

'Well, maybe that's part of the appeal. I was thinking of taking over a rhubarb crumble. Should I knock, do you think? Or just leave it on the doorstep?'

Tom considered the question for a moment. 'I'd knock. But take a note in case she doesn't answer. Leave your address or number, so she can say thank you. She probably won't, but at least she has the option.'

Melanie nodded. 'That's a good idea. Poor woman, being all over the papers. Must have been so humiliating.'

'Hmm.' Tom wondered if Melanie was actually talking about herself. 'Well, I'd better get on.'

'Enjoy your Sunday,' said Melanie with a weak smile. Tom returned it, feeling a wave of sympathy for Will's mum and wishing he could say something that might make her day better. But he'd already committed to helping her son, and Gerald was a whole other mess. It wasn't his job to res-cue the whole family; some days he could barely help himself.

Tom crossed the road with Henry and slipped through the school gates. He'd pop in on Justin, then head home to microwave a roast dinner and watch the rugby.

As he knocked on Justin's door, Tom couldn't resist a glimpse at Willow Cottage, but the curtains were drawn and the house was silent. Perhaps Daisy Crawford had already left the village. Marcus appeared in the doorway, which was

48

no surprise – he often popped over on a Sunday after Justin's tennis lesson.

'Is that Tom?' yelled Justin from the kitchen. 'We were just talking about my new neighbour.'

Tom left Henry to settle down on the ancient rug in front of the wood burner and wandered into the kitchen, where Justin was chopping onions for yet another chicken soup. 'Smells good.'

'It needs salt,' said Justin glumly. 'Doesn't matter how many fucking herbs I throw in, everything needs salt. Should have done this stupid stunt near the coast. Could have made my own.'

'How long have you got left?' asked Tom.

'Less than four months. First of February is my freedom day. I'm going to spend it stuffing my face with Dairy Milk and Pringles, as far away from this dump as possible. Just need to get the book finished first.'

He looked so depressed that Tom hurried back to the lounge before Justin launched into another monologue on the bleak state of his unfinished book. 'How are you?' he asked Marcus, who was sitting on the sofa with his arm stretched along its back.

'Fine,' he replied, raking his hand through his dirty-blond hair. 'I've just been telling Justin about my connection to Daisy Crawford.'

'Oh, you'll love this,' shouted Justin from the kitchen. 'It's proper juicy.'

Tom sat down on the other sofa, hoping he wasn't about to hear about one of Marcus's many sexual conquests. He was considerably younger than Tom and used his ridiculous good looks and talents as a tennis coach to get into the

49

knickers of every bored housewife in the county. Tom had never particularly warmed to him, but male company was quite hard to come by in Shipton Combe. Most of the time, Marcus made a refreshing change from a bunch of stuffy teachers, and it meant he got to hang out with Justin, who he considered a friend.

'I know her boyfriend,' Marcus drawled. 'Well, fiancé now. Christian Walker. He beat me in the Wimbledon Boys' Final in 1999.'

'Wow,' said Tom, grudgingly impressed.

'Anyway a few days later I was replaying the final set in my head when I got knocked off my bike by a car,' continued Marcus. 'Broke my leg and pelvis and never played at that level again.'

'Shit,' said Tom, his eyebrows raised. 'Why do I get the impression that's still an open wound?'

'Stealing his fiancée would be worthy revenge, don't you think?

'For beating you in a tennis match nineteen years ago?' said Tom incredulously. 'Or was he driving the car too?'

'It's not just that he beat me,' explained Marcus. 'He was a proper smug wanker about it.'

Tom laughed. 'You were, what, fourteen? All boys that age are smug wankers.'

'Still,' Marcus grinned. 'Might be fun to try. Liven things up a bit around here.'

'Maybe she won't fall for your charms, mate,' shouted Justin from the kitchen. 'I've met her, and she's in a whole other league.'

'Yeah, but she's still a woman.' Marcus's confidence was something Tom could only aspire to. 'A bored, middle-aged woman, probably with a shitty backhand. They're my speciality. Justin, tell Tom what she was like.'

Justin wandered in from the kitchen, carrying three mugs of herb tea that smelled like the school compost heap. He handed one each to Tom and Marcus, both of whom immediately abandoned it on the coffee table.

'I liked her.' Justin sat down on the sofa next to Tom. 'Beautiful, obviously, but not in a super-glam way. She didn't have a scrap of make up on when I met her last week and looked amazing. Quite an achievement considering what she's been through.'

'Did you even know what she'd been through?' Tom was aware that Justin had no TV or radio, and definitely no internet.

'Didn't have a clue,' Justin said amiably. 'I had to go to the pub to get the lowdown. I feel like the only man in the country who hasn't seen Daisy Crawford's minge.'

'I can show you if you like,' Marcus announced cheerfully, pulling his phone out of his pocket.

'I'll pass,' said Justin, holding up his hand. 'Lady bits are very much not my bag.'

'Well, I'll bag it on your behalf,' Marcus grinned. 'Bet you both twenty quid. But don't say anything about how I know Christian. Might put her off.'

Tom shook his head, torn between amusement at Marcus's confidence and outrage on Daisy's behalf. He pushed that aside, confident that she was a woman he could never, ever be friends with.

'I'm not getting involved in your sordid little games.' He stood up, quickly pulling his coat on before Justin could make him drink the evil tea. 'Must get Henry home.'

51

'The game is ON, my friend,' Marcus said, happily ignoring Tom.

'She's way out of your league,' Justin replied. Tom could still hear them bickering as he led Henry out, closing the front door firmly behind him. He glanced at Willow Cottage again and saw that the lounge curtains had been opened. So, she was definitely in, then. The woman who'd hovered at the edge of his and Tessa's marriage, even though she'd never known a thing about it. He tried not to let the old resentments bubble to the surface, but everything felt so overwhelming. He'd stopped trying to make sense of it years ago.

CHAPTER SIX

Justin drained his mug of coffee and held it out to Daisy for a refill. She smiled and passed him a plastic box filled with homemade coconut macaroons.

'Dear God, you're an angel,' Justin crooned. 'How have your first couple of weeks been?' He stuffed a macaroon into his mouth and made a sound like he was having a tiny orgasm.

'Unexpectedly busy,' replied Daisy. 'You've inspired me to write another cookbook. My agent has been nagging me to do it for years.'

'Blimey, I'm honoured.' Justin took another macaroon. 'What's this one about?'

'Cooking for teenagers,' Daisy said. 'I wrote a baby cookbook when Ruby was little, then another when she was eight with lots of recipes to make with your kids. This one completes the set; I'm hoping Ruby might help me write it.'

'Is that likely?' Justin pulled a sceptical face.

'Probably not, but she'll happily take her share of the royalties.'

'Must be nice to know it will be an instant bestseller,' Justin grumbled.

Daisy didn't deny it. There was no point. Even with everything that was going on, *Spotlight* brought her an instant audience. 'If it's any consolation, it will piss off my mother no end.'

'How come?'

'She's Stella Crawford. She presented TV cooking shows in the eighties.'

'Shit, I'd forgotten that!' Justin waved his biscuit about. 'I'm pretty sure I remember learning to make a scotch egg from one of her books. Didn't they base school Home Economics lessons on her stuff?'

'They did,' Daisy nodded. 'At least until schools stopped teaching kids to cook.'

That was a long-standing source of bitterness for Stella, along with the fact that Daisy hadn't used her fame and influence to engineer a Mary Berry-style comeback for her own mother. Stella had been notably silent after the engagement announcement and The Incident, which meant she was either furiously blanking her daughter, or more likely had done a deal to talk to a newspaper instead. Daisy had dropped her a message out of courtesy to let her know her new address but hadn't received a reply. The silence was blissful, but ominous.

'So, what else has been going on?' Justin was eyeing up the last macaroon like it might melt before his eyes. Daisy slid over the box before he started drooling. 'Met any of the locals yet?'

'Lots. People keep popping round with food. The path to this cottage is paved with jars of marmalade and fruit crumbles.'

'You need beefy security, like one of those Kardashians,' mumbled Justin through macaroon crumbs. 'Sorry I haven't been around to fight them off, I've been teaching bloody awful kids about bees and pigs . . . Who have you met so far?'

Daisy ticked them off on her fingers. 'Couple of teachers, a nice woman who runs the pub. The vicar, who seemed rather disappointed to learn that I'm a heathen. Also Archie's cleaner, who came to ask if the cottage needed deep cleaning. I've only been here a couple of weeks – what does she think I'm doing? Oh, and another woman. Posh, sensible shoes. Melanie? Melody?—'

'Ah, Melanie Forbes-Glover,' Justin finished. 'She's married to Gerald Forbes-Glover. He lost his job as an MP after getting an illicit blowjob in the Palace of Westminster.'

'Oh shit!' Daisy's eyes popped. 'I remember! That poor woman. Why would you stick by a man like that?'

'They have a son at the school,' said Justin. 'Will. He's a great kid, super smart. Presumably Melanie has nowhere else to go. We call her Lemony. Because she's so bitter.'

'Who's we?' said Daisy, raising her eyebrows.

'Me and Marcus. He's our local tennis coach.'

'Ah,' smiled Daisy. 'He put a card through my letter box, welcoming me to the village and offering me a free tennis lesson.'

Justin shrugged. 'He's a good coach, but he fancies himself as a ladies' man. Also his mum is your cleaner and the biggest gossip in the village, so he'll find out all your filthy habits.'

Daisy laughed. 'I've yet to meet a cleaner who isn't a massive gossip, or a tennis player who doesn't fancy himself as a ladies' man.'

'Right.' Justin raised his eyebrows. 'Talking of which, where *is* the handsome fiancé?'

That was actually a very good question.

'He's busy in London, but hopefully visiting soon,' she replied, trying to sound convincing. She knew he was meeting his manager Benny for dinner in London tonight, some place in Soho that Christian couldn't remember the name of. Daisy made a point of calling him every day but it always seemed to go to voicemail. He called her back eventually, but his mood was unpredictable and Daisy found it emotionally draining. There was no progress on the Wimbledon contract and the whole thing was stressing him out. She wondered if getting started with wedding plans might give them something else to talk about.

Justin looked sceptical. 'Sure he is. Tell you what, I'm just about to put a chicken in the oven, so come round in a couple of hours and help me eat it. You might want to bring your own salt. You can meet Mr Clark.'

'Who's Mr Clark?' asked Daisy.

'The school headmaster,' Justin muttered, wiping the crumbs from his mouth and scattering them down his jumper. 'Tom. He's a nice guy. You'll like him.'

Daisy headed to Justin's clutching a bunch of cream roses, bought in a panic dash to Waitrose in Evesham when she realised any dinner offerings of food or wine would be inappropriate for her host's dietary limitations, even though he probably wouldn't complain. The spotty youth on the checkout had given her a knowing look and been rewarded for his impure thoughts with a beaming smile from Daisy. She wasn't going to apologise for The Incident or let total strangers shame her. Her manager Katie had told her never to flinch because that gave power to shitty opinions. This kind of Katie wisdom was one of the many reasons why Daisy loved her.

Justin accepted the flowers with a hug and bustled off to the kitchen to find a milk bottle to put them in, leaving Daisy to warm her cold hands by the crackling wood burner in the lounge. The layout of Beech Cottage was identical to Willow Cottage, other than this place needed a really good scrub. Chemical cleaners were a no-no in Justin's current world, which left him experimenting with herb-scented water, fresh beeswax and general neglect.

She jumped at the knock at the door, which immediately opened with a booming 'Hello!', presumably from the mysterious headmaster. Daisy instantly felt nervous, like she was about to get a dressing-down for some minor infraction of school rules. She may have spent her childhood at stage school, but she still knew what a bollocking from an angry teacher felt like.

As Tom Clark strode into the room trailing a dripping brown dog, Daisy had two simultaneous thoughts: first that a telling-off from this headmaster might be well worth misbehaving for, and second that this was definitely the man who had given her a drenching with his car on her first day in Shipton Combe. Now she could see him properly, his dark hair and blue eyes reminded her of James McAvoy, which was never a bad thing. In fact, he was really quite dishy, which made it all the more disappointing that he was evidently a Toyota-driving arsehole. To make things worse, he looked at her first with shock, and then with pure loathing, so the feeling was clearly mutual.

Daisy held out her hand and smiled. 'Hello, you must be Tom. I'm Daisy.'

Tom nodded and took her hand for the briefest possible second, immediately looking away. 'I didn't know Justin had another guest. Is he in the kitchen?'

He hurried off without waiting for her answer, leaving Daisy with the dog and a slightly sick feeling in her stomach. Was he one of those stuffed-shirt morality campaigners who had cancelled Daisy entirely, or had he been hoping for an evening with Justin alone? For the first time it occurred to her that they might be a couple, and she felt bad about cramping their style. Presumably Justin's restricted diet didn't prevent him going down on the locals.

Justin returned from the kitchen, carrying three grubby glasses and a ceramic flagon stuffed with an old champagne cork. 'Come on, you two. It's time to try my homemade mead.'

By the time Justin served baked apples with honey and goat's milk ice cream, Daisy was comprehensively pissed, and also one hundred per cent sure that, despite Justin's assurances, Tom Clark was not a nice guy and she didn't like him one bit. He might be ridiculously handsome, but it was obvious he hated her guts, for no reason she could fathom other than he was clearly an uptight, judgemental bastard who thought her somehow unworthy of his attention.

'Tell Daisy about that time my goat escaped and trampled through sports day,' said Justin, valiantly trying to keep the conversation going.

'I can't imagine Daisy would find that very interesting,' said Tom. 'I'm sure we all seem quite sleepy and boring compared to . . .' he trailed off and took another swig of mead, suddenly fascinated by the books on Justin's shelf.

'Compared to what?' said Daisy, infuriated that he wouldn't

look at her. He'd barely glanced at her all evening; she felt like a ghost. 'All my exciting celebrity friends?'

Tom shrugged and stacked up the pudding bowls, then took them into the kitchen.

'I'm sorry,' whispered Justin, looking mortified. 'I've never known him like this before, otherwise I wouldn't have put you in the same room. I've got no idea what's up.'

Daisy smiled like it couldn't matter less, even though it stung like hell. But Justin had more than made up for Tom, and she'd somehow managed to have a fun evening despite the malevolent prick sending bad vibes over the table. She hoped he was nicer to his dog than he was to women.

She looked up, to see Tom staring at her from the doorway to the kitchen. The expression on his face was unfathomable – it could be hatred or pain or lust – but she could feel the depth and intensity of it, like he suddenly knew all her secrets. She shivered and felt heat flood to her cheeks, and this time she was the one who looked away first.

'I'm off,' she said, giving Tom a nod and Justin a heartfelt hug before she wobbled back to her cottage, warmed by mead and the pleasure of laughing herself silly with a new friend. After a hot shower, Daisy dragged her flushed and tingling body into bed, trying to push away the creeping mead-induced headache and thoughts of horrible head-masters by getting her vibrator out of her underwear drawer with a view to achieving a sleep-inducing orgasm. She closed her eyes and imagined Christian's beautiful hands and deft tongue flickering across her body, but in the end it was Tom Clark's brooding, stricken face buried between her legs that sent her tumbling over the edge as the rain started to hammer against her window.

CHAPTER SEVEN

Daisy and Ruby chatted about nothing much as they waited for their table to be ready in the Shipton Arms, both of them pretending that the entire pub wasn't breaking their necks to get a look at them.

'Do you think they got this because of you?' asked Ruby, picking up a monthly women's magazine from the table of reading matter by the front door. It had Daisy's face on the cover, issued a couple of weeks before The Incident.

'I have no idea,' said Daisy, smiling at the landlady as she led them to a quiet table in a nook by the huge fireplace, away from all the other diners. Daisy chose the chair that positioned her with her back to the room, so she could enjoy her lunch without feeling like a zoo exhibit.

'It's a nice picture, it's just a shame it doesn't look anything like you,' Ruby smirked, holding up the magazine. Daisy's beaming face smiled back, alongside the headline '*Beauty Secrets from the Queen of the Spotlight*'.

Daisy couldn't deny that the glossy-haired blonde on the cover of *Womanhood* magazine bore little resemblance to the real thing. In the right light with the support of an army of stylists and makeup professionals, Daisy could look about seventy-five per cent as fabulous as this. But the magazine had worked some extra digital magic, blurring out every tiny blemish and wrinkle, whitening her teeth and adding extra lift and gloss to her artfully curled hair. She also vaguely remembered a wind machine, but that might have been a different photoshoot. Any signposts towards middle-aged turkey neck were covered by a heavy turtleneck sweater up to her chin. She looked pink-cheeked and sparkling, like she'd just come in from a brisk autumn walk and was ready for an afternoon making jam and listening to Radio 4.

Ruby soon tired of the magazine; the interviews were all the same and her mother's face on the cover was old news. Daisy realised how little time they'd spent just the two of them this year – they were always in the company of Simon or Christian or a group of friends. In a couple of months Ruby would be sixteen, and it felt like the clock was ticking on their quality time together. Talking of which, there was a conversation she needed to have with her daughter, and right now seemed like as good a time as any.

'Rubes,' said Daisy carefully, 'we need to talk about Christian.'

Ruby rolled her eyes. 'And we were having such a nice day. Why did you have to spoil it?' She gave her mother a bucket of side-eye, then pretended to read the menu.

'Please don't be a bitch.' Daisy pursed her lips. 'It doesn't suit you. I've said sorry a hundred times.' Ruby looked contrite, so Daisy ploughed on. 'Look, when all this noise has died down, he and I are going to start making wedding plans. I'd really like you to help. It might be fun.'

Ruby looked unimpressed and gave a theatrical yawn. 'It *might* be fun, I guess. If you weren't marrying Christian.'

Daisy sat back in her chair, trying not to get defensive. 'What is it, Rubes? Is Christian really the problem, or is it just that I'm getting married again? Your dad is fine with it.'

Ruby's head snapped upright, her face thunderous and so very like her father's. 'It's got NOTHING to do with you getting married again, and actually Dad isn't fine with it at all. He hates Christian too.'

This was news to Daisy. Clearly, she and Simon needed to have a chat. She took a deep breath. '*Hate* is quite a strong word, Rubes. What specifically are your objections?'

Ruby put her water glass on the table and folded her arms. 'Fine. He's a selfish manbaby, and I think he's using you to boost his TV career.'

Daisy flinched. 'Selfish manbaby' was definitely a phrase that had come from Simon's mouth. 'Anything else?'

'Yes. He looks at other women when you're together,' continued Ruby, 'like he wants to have sex with them. I've seen him do it, and it's creepy. Why don't you mind about that?'

Daisy stared at Ruby, not knowing what to say. It shocked her to hear her little girl talking about Christian's wandering eye. Of course she'd noticed, but she'd put it down to his ridiculous sex drive. The man was horny all the time; he thought about nothing else. She'd brushed it aside as just window shopping.

'Somebody at school sent me this thing they found online.' Ruby picked up her phone and scrolled through her WhatsApps.

'What thing?'

'A gossip newsletter. I don't know, maybe it's not about Christian. But it felt weird. Here.'

Daisy took the phone from Ruby and scrolled through the text. A funny story about a pop star, a rumour about a member of the royal family. Then a paragraph that made her heart stop.

Which hunky sporting star is known to be knocking up with his female personal trainer? He's not only been doing extra-curricular workouts behind his famous fiancée's back, but he's also been spotted honing his backhand at exclusive Soho sex parties. New balls, please . . .

Daisy's hand flew to her mouth as a thousand disconnected thoughts and fragments of recent phone conversations tumbled forth like jigsaw pieces from a box, then her brain deftly fitted them together. In that moment, she knew with absolute certainty that she was being taken for a fool.

She took a deep breath and forced a smile as she handed back Ruby's phone. Whatever game Christian was playing, she was determined it wouldn't ruin the first weekend she'd spent alone with her daughter in months. 'Shall we do some online shopping later? Find something for your dad's birthday?'

Ruby reached over and took her mum's hand, forcing Daisy to suppress a sob. 'That would be nice,' she said brightly, adding an extra squeeze for good measure.

'What are you staring at?' Daisy asked an hour later, as the landlady cleared their plates and Ruby's attention drifted to a table near the bar.

'No, don't turn round!' whispered Ruby. 'It's a boy doing his homework. Don't look.'

'OK,' Daisy smiled. 'What's so interesting about him?'

'He's super-cute, and he's reading *The Handmaid's Tale*,' replied Ruby.

'Ah, one of your favourites. For school, do you think, or is he just a fan of dystopian feminist classics?'

'It's an A level text, so he must be a year or two older than me. He looks like Timothée Chalamet.'

63

Daisy raised her eyebrows in amusement. 'Goodness, that's quite the recommendation.'

'He just accidentally smiled at me, then blushed bright red,' Ruby muttered.

Daisy smiled at her daughter, her eyes glittering. 'OK, here's a little challenge for you. I'm going to the bar to order some tea. By the time I get back you need to have found out his name, how old he is and where he lives.'

Ruby smiled and stretched her neck from side to side like an athlete warming up, interlacing her fingers and pushing them inside out. 'You're on.'

Daisy leaned on the bar and watched Ruby approach the boy out of the corner of her eye. He was tall and thin with a floppy mess of dark curls that fell over his face, like the pictures she'd seen of Simon as a New Romantic in the early eighties.

'Hi,' said Ruby. 'How's the book?' *A good start*, thought Daisy. Always ask an open question.

The boy opened and closed his mouth for a few seconds, then found his voice. 'It's good. Better than I thought it would be, I suppose.'

Ruby smiled at him, looking like an angel with her hair hanging in loose curls around her shoulders; the poor boy didn't stand a chance. He stared at her in awe for a moment then looked down at the book again, hiding his face behind the curtain of fringe.

'Why are you doing your homework in the pub?' asked Ruby as Daisy placed her order for two cups of tea. *Subtle, Rubes.*

The boy looked up again, his face now scarlet. 'Oh. It's warmer in here. My dad won't put the heating on, so the house is freezing.'

Ruby's brow furrowed. 'Wow, that's harsh. Where do you live?'

The boy nodded to his right. 'In the rectory next door. It's freezing. Full of ghosts, probably.' He blushed again, and Daisy felt momentarily glad she wasn't single, then remembered the gossip about Christian and felt a wave of sickness in the pit of her stomach.

Ruby gave a tinkly laugh. 'I'm Ruby.'

The boy pushed his hair out of his face and attempted a smile. 'Oh. Um, I'm Will.' Daisy glanced at him with renewed interest, realising he was Melanie's son, the boy Justin had mentioned.

'Is this for A level?' asked Ruby. 'How old are you?' *God, Ruby*, thought Daisy. *Let the poor boy breathe.*

'I'm seventeen, so just started second year,' said Will. 'English Lit.'

'I'm sixteen in a couple of months,' Ruby ploughed on. 'GCSEs next year, I've got my mocks after Christmas. I'm at Milton Park.'

Will nodded as Daisy headed over with two cups and saucers. His eyes widened, no doubt putting two and two together and recalling a specific photo he'd probably seen on social media. Daisy took a deep breath and smiled.

'Mum, this is Will.' Ruby waved at the blushing young man. 'He's seventeen and lives in the rectory next door.'

Daisy gave Ruby a triumphant grin, then looked at Will. 'Hi, Will, nice to meet you.' She twisted her head to look at his book. 'You should ask Ruby about *The Handmaid's Tale*, she's read it loads of times.'

Will looked at Ruby, his mouth half open. 'Really?'

Ruby nodded. 'If you need any essay help, I'm your gal.

I'm going to my dad's on Monday though.' She took his pen and deftly wrote her phone number on the corner of his notepad, then returned to their table.

'How was that?' whispered Ruby as they sipped their tea.

'A masterclass,' said Daisy with a smile.

Ruby's phone buzzed as she and Daisy were halfway down the school drive, enjoying the squelch of wet leaves beneath their boots and the misty tendrils of afternoon sunshine casting long shadows through the beech trees. She opened the text and showed it to Daisy.

If you're serious about helping with my essay then yes please. Here for a few more hours, or tomorrow? Will.

Daisy was impressed. 'Man, you work fast.'

Ruby looked smug. 'I learnt from an expert.'

'I'm going to assume you're talking about your dad,' Daisy laughed. 'What do you want to do?'

Ruby thought for a second. 'I'd quite like to go back, I guess. But does that look desperate?'

'Who cares? You're going to your dad's on Monday and I'll be back in London soon, so you'll probably never see him again. Fill your boots.'

'Oh God, that's really depressing,' said Ruby with a sad pout. 'He was cute. Best I head back then.'

Daisy tucked her scarf around Ruby's neck and kissed her on the forehead. 'Don't go anywhere other than the pub and be back before it gets dark. If for any reason he can't walk you home, call me and I'll come and meet you by the school gates.'

Ruby smiled and nodded, then turned and headed back up the driveway. Daisy watched her go, feeling a mix of love and grief bubble up in her chest. Ruby had her head screwed on, and Daisy hadn't forgotten how it felt to be fifteen. In her case every minute of her day had been monitored and managed by adults, including Stella. She didn't want that for Ruby, she wanted her daughter to be free to make her own decisions and navigate those choppy teenage waters alone.

And talking of choppy waters, it was time to decide what to do about Christian.

CHAPTER EIGHT

In the end it was two weeks before Daisy could deal with anything, because by Sunday Ruby was begging to stay in Shipton Combe for the whole of half-term so she could spend more time with Will. Daisy didn't mind and Simon was OK about it, since Ruby was spending Christmas with him and Archie. So, Will and Ruby spent part of each day doing their homework and playing board games together in the Shipton Arms, and Daisy made the most of the opportunity to spend quality time with her daughter. They cooked, watched movies and carved Halloween pumpkins together, and Daisy managed to push Christian from her mind for a decent chunk of each day.

This was made much easier when he announced he was going to China for a few weeks to commentate on a tennis tournament for Sky Sports. The time difference made it easy to avoid speaking or seeing him – WhatsApp messages were less tense, and by the time he got back she'd have decided what to do. She'd been keeping an eye online for any other gossip about him, but there was nothing new, so maybe it was just idle speculation. But Daisy's gut told her it was more than that, and now she couldn't help but think of all the times she caught him looking at other women and dismissed it as nothing. Christian had an insanely high sex drive, but Daisy hadn't seen him for weeks. Was it out of the question that he'd go elsewhere, even though they were engaged? She could only put off finding out for so long.

Daisy arranged the call with Katie for Ruby's final Sunday morning while she was saying her goodbyes to Will, taking advantage of the fact that his parents were in church. Through some gentle questioning Daisy had established that there'd been some kissing, a first for both of them. But Will wasn't pushy or anything, and mostly they just hung out and chatted. So Daisy pushed the million mum-anxieties aside and took her phone over to the sofa by the fire, taking a minute to catch up on a few messages from friends and colleagues, all saying how much they missed her and asking if she was going to be at this dinner or that industry event. Replying with 'I'm away for a while' felt like such a relief, like she was finally having the chance to decompress after twenty-five years of the same parties and the same faces.

She and Katie chatted for a while about the press situation. There had been a few mentions on social media that Daisy had been spotted in the Cotswolds without Christian, and a blurry photo of her buying flowers in Waitrose, but nothing that Katie was worried about. And they caught up on Daisy's progress with the recipe book, which was now the official reason as to why Daisy was holed up in the Cotswolds.

'So why have you actually called me?' Katie asked astutely; she never missed a trick. 'This is all Monday morning stuff. You never ask to chat on Sunday unless it's urgent.'

'I'm sorry,' Daisy said miserably. 'I've just sent you a screengrab from one of those celeb gossip newsletters. It's from a few weeks ago, but there's something in it that I think you should read.'

'Hang on.' Daisy could hear the tapping of Katie's fingers, then a short silence as she read the text. '*FUCK.*'

'Quite,' Daisy nodded. 'It might be nothing, but obviously I need to know one way or the other.'

'Yeah. But you don't think it's nothing, do you?' asked Katie carefully.

'No. I don't think it's *nothing*. But before I do anything, I need to know how big a *something* it is.'

'Right. When's he back from China?'

'In a week or so.'

'Hmm. OK. Leave it with me. I know some people who can find out. Super-discreet people.'

'Are you sure?'

'Of course. Don't worry about it.'

'Thanks.' Daisy gave a huge sigh of relief. 'I don't know what I would do without you.'

Katie gave a hollow laugh. 'Who knows? Maybe you'd be free from all this celebrity bullshit and meet less worthless men.'

'Ouch.'

Daisy felt a little lighter after her call with Katie, like she'd briefly offloaded the problem onto someone else's shoulders. She still felt bad about burdening her with her domestic dramas, but she was helpless to deal with Christian without proof. Either way the deed was now done, so she decided to clear her head with a walk into the village. She could meet Ruby and they could spend some time together before the drive back to Milton Park.

Daisy expected Ruby to be a little despondent after saying goodbye to Will, but to Daisy's surprise her daughter seemed fine. Perhaps not every relationship was a roller-coaster of high drama. She'd brought some bread so they could stop and feed the ducks at the lake, something they'd done a few times over the course of half-term, even though it was off the public footpath and she had no idea if they were allowed.

'Mum, there's a man coming. Are we in trouble?' Daisy noted that Ruby had stuffed the bag of bread in her coat pocket.

Daisy spun round to look; her heart sank. 'Oh, bollocks!'

The Horrible Headmaster was striding towards them with his dog, no doubt getting ready to tell her to stop poisoning his swans or something.

'Who is he?' whispered Ruby, leaning into her mother.

'School headmaster,' muttered Daisy. 'Absolute knob.'

Ruby snorted with laughter. 'Quite fit though, for an old guy.'

Daisy ignored the slight. 'Yeah. Still a knob.' She stopped talking as he came closer and glared, determined not to put up with any more of his rudeness. Not in front of Ruby.

When Tom was a few metres away, Henry bounded over to Daisy to say hello. She'd never owned a dog, but this one seemed harmless and in need of attention, so she crouched down and gave him a fuss. When she stood up, Daisy was startled to see Tom was smiling. It transformed his face from hostile and forbidding to drop-dead gorgeous, showing off his killer cheekbones, his blue eyes sparkling in the autumn sunshine. He was disarmingly attractive; if you liked total shits.

Daisy resumed glaring, reminding herself of his appalling behaviour at dinner. 'Is there a problem? Are we trespassing?'

Tom immediately stopped smiling and cleared his throat awkwardly. 'No, not at all,' he stuttered. 'I saw you from my office window and . . .' There was an awkward silence.

'Well, we're heading home now. Come on, Rubes.' Daisy gave a tight smile and trudged off, leaving Ruby still kneeling in the leaves holding Henry's left paw, which he'd kindly offered her.

'Honestly, he was SUCH a bastard at dinner,' mumbled Daisy as she stumbled through a ditch full of muddy leaves. She could hear Ruby now puffing to keep up. 'Barely spoke to me, just ignored me all night.'

'I'm really sorry.' Not Ruby.

Daisy spun round so fast she lost her footing, sliding sideways onto the grass and flailing about madly until a strong hand grabbed her arm and hauled her upright. She frantically brushed the mud from her hair. Ruby was still twenty metres away, throwing leaves into the air for Henry to chase.

'Oh God,' she gasped, spitting out mud. 'I thought you were Ruby.'

'Evidently,' said Tom with a weak smile. 'Look, I *was* a total shit at dinner, and I'd like to have the opportunity to apologise and explain. I'm not a bastard, I was just having a really bad day. Please let me say sorry.'

Daisy scowled at him, bridling at the mention of a 'bad day'. HE'D had a bad day? She'd had her fanny plastered all over the papers and been forced to move to this boggy village to avoid the Vultures. Then there was Watergate, when he'd soaked her and driven off. And then his behaviour the other night! All she'd tried to do was make friends and he'd treated her with the same shitty judgement as everyone else. *Bad day?* She'd give him bad day. How about bad fucking year?!

72

'I'm not interested in your apology.' She brushed the wet leaves from her coat. 'Apart from anything else, it's two weeks old.'

'I'm sorry. Really sorry,' Tom pleaded. 'I've been away since the morning after we met. I only got back yesterday. I was planning to pop round later but I saw you from my office window.'

Daisy put her hands on her hips and pressed her lips together. He was gorgeous, but so was Christian. Men like them always thought that a square jaw and puppy dog eyes would get them off the hook.

'You soaked me with your car and were unforgivably rude to me and disrespectful to Justin,' she snapped. 'Let *him* have your apology. I don't want it.'

Tom recoiled, his face desolate. Slowly, he turned and headed back towards Henry, whispering a few words to Ruby as they passed each other. She laughed awkwardly, then jogged back to her mother.

'What did he just say to you?' asked Daisy, her eyes narrowed.

'He said he messed that right up,' Ruby's expression was soft. 'But that it was no less than he deserved.'

CHAPTER NINE

On Monday morning Daisy gathered all the frozen recipe samples she'd made and stacked them up on the counter. She and Ruby had eaten a decent chunk of her output, but the rest had been painstakingly portioned into foil containers and carefully labelled with dietary information and reheating instructions. Daisy found a green canvas shopping trolley in the cupboard under the stairs and packed all the containers inside. She'd been putting it off for a month, but it was time to return all the visits from people in the neighbourhood and offload some food.

Her first stop was Church House, official residence of the Reverend Miriam Mayhew. It was a tiny cottage sandwiched in the middle of a row of three, identifiable by a black metal fish hanging over the door, engraved with faded gold lettering. Two hundred years ago Reverend Mayhew would have lived in the splendour of the rectory, but of course two hundred years ago the Anglican church would have needed smelling salts to countenance the idea of a female priest.

Daisy handed over a few containers of food for Miriam's freezer, and the vicar blushed and gibbered away, thanking Daisy effusively and clutching the containers like she'd just unwrapped a bottle of frankincense at the nativity.

'It's so kind of you,' she gushed. 'We're so excited to have you here. Although of course it's tricky for some, I think. At the school, you know.'

Daisy smiled thinly. Presumably her arrival had created some negative press for the school; perhaps they didn't like her being in such close proximity to impressionable teenagers in case she accidentally flashed at them. She wondered if Tom was behind whatever was making it 'tricky' and took a moment to hate him even more.

'Well, I won't be here much longer,' said Daisy, taking a sip from a mug of tea that was as weak and flavourless as the conversation. She made a swift exit once Miriam started dropping clanging hints about fundraising for the vestry and the village winter fete at the end of January. She wasn't wholly against a bit of community involvement, but she had every intention of being long gone by then.

Daisy's next stop was the rectory, which had an ancient Ford Mondeo parked outside and some overgrown borders that needed cutting back before winter. She crunched across the gravel and pushed the doorbell, hearing it jangle somewhere deep inside the house. Less than a minute later, Melanie Forbes-Glover opened the heavy door. The pleated skirt, beige blouse and shapeless cardigan were neat and clean but far too old for Melanie, who couldn't be more than a year or two older than Daisy. She had a pale but striking face and a tall, willowy frame under all that sludge-coloured polyester. Perhaps Gerald had married her for her shorthand; it certainly wasn't for her killer wardrobe.

Melanie invited Daisy into an equally drab kitchen, staring at her in a way that made her wonder if she had food on her face. Daisy wondered if this was Melanie's general demeanour or a response to being in the company of a 'celebrity'; some people behaved really weirdly. The house was dark, freezing and clearly run down – the wallpaper in the hallway faded and peeling, and part of one of the kitchen floorboards was missing, the hole currently occupied by an angry-looking ginger cat with a squashed face. No wonder Will did his homework in the pub; this place felt like a haunted shack in a Scooby Doo cartoon.

'Sorry to drop in like this,' Daisy said easily. 'I was passing and thought I'd say hello.'

Melanie smiled nervously and fussed with the kettle. 'It's kind of you to visit,' she said, her voice wispy and insubstantial.

Daisy started unloading some trays. 'I've been cooking. Testing, you know, for a recipe book. I've been sharing the spoils around the village since I can't fit any more in my freezer. Feel free to say no, but I brought some over for you and the family. Lasagne, stroganoff, a couple of bean chillis and a—' she squinted at the lid, '—chocolate fondant pudding.'

'That's so kind, thank you. Will never stops eating, he'll get through these in no time.' Melanie looked like she might cry as she organised the containers into a neat pile on the kitchen counter.

'Ha, I'm amazed he's eating at all,' Daisy laughed. 'Doesn't young love take away your appetite?'

Melanie looked confused, and in a flash Daisy realised that Will hadn't told her about Ruby. She blushed and fidgeted, but it was too late to go back now. 'Oh, listen to me,' she continued airily, 'I'm such a blabbermouth. Your son met my daughter, Ruby, over half-term, and I think they might be rather taken with each other. But you know teenagers.'

Daisy felt terrible at how stricken Melanie looked – she

was so used to Ruby telling her everything, it never occurred to her that Will might have cut his mother out of his life. She tried to find the right words, but Melanie rallied. 'Well, good for Will,' she replied with forced cheerfulness. 'It's always nice to make new friends. I'm sorry my husband isn't here to say hello; he's upstairs in his office but he doesn't like to be disturbed. And Will's at school, of course.'

They waded through ten more minutes of inconsequential small talk about the weather and the history of the church before Daisy gathered her belongings and left, planning to make a couple of further food drops to some other villagers who'd been kind enough to leave gifts on her doorstep. She walked across the driveway thinking about Melanie, a clearly lonely woman rattling around in a huge house with a philandering husband and a son who didn't talk to her.

Daisy was almost at the gate when she heard the crunch of gravel behind her. She turned to see a man in a pinstriped suit grinning and holding out his hand. She immediately recognised him as Melanie's husband, the disgraced MP she'd seen in the papers years before. He was handsome in that raffish, full-lipped way of fifty-something, upper-class Englishmen. Like Hugh Grant, or maybe Alan Rickman.

'I'm sorry we haven't met sooner.' He clasped Daisy's hand in both of his like he was greeting the mayor at the Town Hall. 'I'm Gerald Forbes-Glover.' He smelled of woody aftershave and pure lust, and Daisy's skin immediately began to crawl. She tried to extract her hand.

'Nice to meet you, Gerald,' Daisy murmured, backing away to the gate. 'I'm afraid I need to be getting on, but it would be lovely to catch up another time.' *Not.*

'I'll make sure of it.' Gerald smiled at Daisy like a hungry wolf. She waved, then hurried off down the road as fast as she could without actually running.

It was lunchtime by the time Daisy had offloaded the rest of her food, and groups of students were hanging around in the school grounds getting some mandatory fresh air before returning to their afternoon lessons. She kept her head down as she walked down the drive in the hope that nobody recognised her, only glancing up as she passed the huge cedar tree at the side of the school. Will Forbes-Glover was walking in circles beneath it, his hands buried in his pockets, his shoulders hunched over.

Daisy watched him for a moment, wondering what stage of lovesick teenage angst he was currently enduring. He looked up and caught her eye, so she gave him a wave and waited for him to amble over and talk to her.

'Hi, Will,' she said softly, hoping that her smile communicated her understanding of his feelings right now.

'Hey.' Will scuffed his feet on the gravel path, his face a picture of pure misery.

'I'm sorry Ruby won't be back for any more weekends before Christmas. It's hockey season.'

'I know.' Will turned away but Daisy could see his blush.

'She gets some free time after lunch on a Saturday, if that's helpful? Milton Park isn't that far away.'

Will looked up at her with renewed interest. 'Really?' His eyes flickered in all directions as the cogs in his brain whirred. 'Could I cycle it, do you think?'

Daisy shrugged. 'It's ten miles and pretty hilly. Depends how much you like cycling.' *And Ruby.*

'I don't mind cycling.' Will pulled himself up a little taller. 'Where have you been?'

'To see your mum, among other things. You should talk to her; she might have some ideas.'

Will blushed and looked a little ashamed. 'Yeah. I will.' He looked around, realising some of the other students were frozen in awe at the sight of him chatting to Daisy Crawford. 'It's such a headfuck you being here,' he said. 'Must be a nightmare for our headmaster.'

'So I hear,' said Daisy, deciding she quite liked the idea of Tom getting grief from the governors and parents about having yet another disgraced celebrity living in the school grounds, so soon after Justin and his tax evasion. Serves him right for being a prick.

Daisy gave Will a reassuring smile and walked away, joining the path that cut across the field between the back of the school and the lake. A movement above made her look up. It startled her to see Tom Clark watching her from a first-floor window, his face curiously blank. He held his hand up in acknowledgement, and Daisy instinctively twitched her hand to wave back, before thinking better of it and burying it in her pocket instead.

She dragged the now empty trolley across the field and around the side of the stables, when she noticed someone, a woman, sitting on Justin's front step, holding a tankard of what looked like mead. Justin was unloading logs from a wheelbarrow, his shoulders shaking with laughter as he regaled the person with a story. Daisy caught the words 'pigshit' and 'teacher' as her brain finally computed what she was seeing.

As if on cue, the heavens opened and a murder of crows took flight from a nearby tree with a discordant rattle of caws and flapping wings. A suitable entrance, Daisy thought sourly, for her mother.

CHAPTER TEN

'—Most daughters would be delighted that their mother had come to support them during a challenging time,' Stella muttered. Daisy was sitting on her mother's bed in the small room above the bar in the Shipton Arms, trying not to feel too oppressed by the overly busy wisteria wallpaper. Stella was hanging clothes in the wardrobe with a level of aggression that made Daisy fear for the collection of floral chiffon blouses.

Daisy took a deep breath, then exhaled slowly, thinking mindful thoughts. 'Yes, but it's been weeks since the NTAs. So what are you doing here?'

'After everything I've done for you. I paved the way for your success, smoothed the path. You have no idea of the sacrifices I've made. And what do I get in return? Obscurity, borderline poverty, total lack of appreciation—'

Here we go. Daisy had heard variations on this speech thousands of times. 'Please don't talk to me about lack of appreciation. I paid off your mortgage from the proceeds of that skin cream deal.' She began ticking off a list on her fingers. 'The villa in Portugal which you can use whenever you like. Clothes, gifts, tickets to shows, red carpet events. The fact that I'm here, even willing to LOOK YOU IN THE EYE . . . after you sold me out to the tabloids—'

'That was a misunderstanding.' Stella jiggled a cardigan

81

onto a hanger, tossing her head to flick her salt-and-pepper hair out of her eyes. 'What do they call it? Entrapment.'

'What? Both times?' Daisy said sarcastically.

'All I'm asking for is your help, to get me back on TV. Prue Leith can't do *Bake Off* forever—'

'No.'

'You're selfish, just like your father,' Stella announced bitterly. 'He was gone before I even knew I was pregnant, and I had to spend the first part of my career pretending to be a tragic widow. Whatever the producers of *Waste Not, Want Not* said at the time, being a single mother finished my career.'

'Are you blaming me now for being born?' Eyes wide, Daisy held out her hands in disbelief.

'No, of course not,' snapped Stella. 'But I put my needs aside despite everyone's petty judgement and raised you to be a superstar. And what thanks do I get, either from you, or the people who made millions off you? *None.*' She rammed the cardigan into the wardrobe, causing several other hangers to clatter to the floor.

'Which takes me back to my original question,' Daisy said, forcing herself to stay calm. '*Why are you here?*'

'Because now you know what petty judgement feels like,' said Stella quietly, her eyes filling with tears, although Daisy was hard pushed to see if they were real or manufactured.

Daisy jogged to the village tennis court in a state of high anxiety, hoping it would start raining again so she could hide in the cottage with the door locked. The call with Katie yesterday had helped her feel more in control of the situation, and the visits round the village had convinced her that this break could be relaxing, potentially productive, maybe even fun. But thanks to Stella, everything had gone to shit again.

It wasn't that Daisy didn't love her mother or appreciate the efforts Stella had put in to give her the best start in her career. Scraping together the funds for stage school, introducing her to her TV network, giving her a gentle push in the right direction. Daisy didn't underestimate the value of Stella's leg-up, but how long was she supposed to repay that debt? Everything that followed was down to Daisy's hard graft and talent; there was no question that she had succeeded on her own merit. But, twenty-five years on, Stella fully expected Daisy to return the favour and revive her TV career.

Daisy refused to do it – and there was a very long list of reasons why, among them that Stella absolutely couldn't be trusted. It was a hard thing to say about your own mother, but it was true; she'd aired her grievances in the tabloids too many times. Her mother liked a drink – not in a Mary Berry 'ooh, I love a cheeky tipple' kind of way, but in a 'wine is a major food group' way that had made her sloppy and obnoxious. Any attempts to talk to Stella about her drinking were batted away as nonsense; and even Ruby had intervened on occasion. Daisy worried about her mother's physical health, her mental well-being and what she was capable of when she'd had a few. Stella's arrival in Shipton Combe was nothing but bad news.

Daisy trudged slowly back through the school grounds in the gathering dark, past the lake and Tom's dark office window, her racquet bag slung over her shoulder and her head full of chaotic thoughts. The free lesson from Marcus had been a write-off, and mentally drawing Christian's face on a barrage of tennis balls hadn't really helped at all. As for Marcus doing his best to charm her – there absolutely wasn't room for another man like that in Daisy's life. And talking of other men – she squinted – what was Tom Clark doing loitering outside Willow Cottage? Daisy started to beat a hasty retreat, but it was obvious he'd seen her.

'I'm sorry to doorstep you.' Tom's voice wavered as he took a step forward. 'I just need five minutes of your time. Please.'

Daisy noticed the dark circles under his eyes, like he hadn't slept. He was still unfeasibly handsome, but he looked bleak and a little broken. She really didn't have the energy to make him feel any worse so she nodded and unlocked the door, leaving it open as she started to head to the kitchen to put the kettle on. She glanced at the clock – it was more or less five, so she grabbed a bottle of wine and two glasses instead.

Gesturing Tom to one of the squashy sofas near the wood burner, Daisy poured them both glasses, then sat in awkward silence as they sipped their wine. Henry the lab was stretched out on the rug, toasting his belly, seemingly oblivious to the tension in the room. Finally, Tom cleared his throat, turning his empty glass round in his hands. 'Look, I said I wanted to explain about dinner at Justin's. I feel terrible about it. My behaviour was aw—'

Daisy's phone rang loudly, the vibration rattling it across the coffee table. 'Christian' lit up the gloom. They both stared at it as it continued to jump around.

Tom stood up. 'Sorry . . . Now clearly isn't a good time.'

'It's fine, I'll call him back,' Daisy said quickly, but Tom was already pulling on his coat.

The phone rang again a few more times then stopped.

'I need to get going anyway,' Tom insisted. 'We'll do this another time when you're less busy. Thanks for the wine.' He nudged a disgruntled Henry to the door.

Daisy shrugged. 'It's fine,' she said. 'I'm sure I'll see you around.'

'Maybe,' said Tom, colour rushing to his cheeks. He hurried out into the cold, giving Daisy a vague wave before disappearing around the side of the stables. She closed the front door shaking her head in confusion. What was all that about? Reluctantly, she picked up her phone. She'd already ignored two calls from Christian today. With a sigh, she pressed the button to return his call, willing it to go to voicemail.

'Hey, babe,' Christian answered. She could hear the rumble of traffic noise in the background. 'Just in a cab back from a night out with the crew. Thought I'd try and catch you.'

Alone? Didn't score a woman, then, she thought uncharitably. 'Sorry I haven't answered your calls,' she croaked. 'Been a bit under the weather. I've spent most of today in bed with a hot water bottle.'

'Ah babe, I'm sorry.' Christian dropped his voice to a whisper. 'I could be your hot water bottle. I'd make it all better.'

Daisy shivered as a wave of heat coursed through her body. She was furious that Christian still could have this effect on her. She swallowed. 'That's tempting, but I feel like death.'

'I could definitely get you in the mood,' Christian persisted. Daisy could hear the provocation in his voice and knew he was getting turned on right now. Christian had a thing about cars; just being in one made him aroused. Sometimes while he was driving, he'd silently take her hand and put it on his rock hard crotch, wanting her to know that even at temporary traffic lights on the outskirts of East Barnet, he was thinking about having sex with her. Now she was irritated that he wasn't taking her illness more seriously, even if it was fake.

'It will have to wait for a while,' croaked Daisy.

'Hopefully not too long. I miss you. China's fun, but not as fun as you.'

'I miss you too,' lied Daisy. 'I'll call you in a couple of days.'

'OK. See you soon.' Christian blew her a kiss and hung up.

Daisy put her phone on the sofa and lay back on the cushions, torn between relief that she'd got that out of the way and annoyance that he could still push her buttons in spite of everything. But there was something else nagging at her brain, something about their conversations. All their conversations. After nearly eight months of being together, hundreds of hours of incredible sex and a proposal of marriage, Christian had never once said he loved her.

PART TWO

PART TWO

CHAPTER ELEVEN

Tom grabbed a bucket from the shed in the corner of Justin's vegetable allotment and rattled it on the fence of the goat field. Actually 'field' was probably pushing it a bit, it was more of a grassy enclosure with a shelter for Nancy to sleep in at night during the cold weather. The goat stuck her head out at the noise and trotted over, bleating a good morning symphony.

'Do you want me to milk her?' he called to Justin, who was forking steaming manure from the back of a trailer into a wheelbarrow next to the polytunnel.

'No, I'll do it.' He glanced at Tom's battered leather shoes as he wandered over, still breathing heavily. 'Those boots aren't made for milking. Anyway, I'll probably miss her when I'm gone.'

'You won't give any of us a moment's thought,' laughed Tom.

Justin grinned. 'I can already smell the sweet food and spicy men.'

Tom laughed. 'How's the book coming on?'

This question usually sent Justin into a state of high dudgeon, but today he smiled happily. 'Better now Stella Crawford's here. She's written loads of cookbooks, so she's helping me turn my nonsense into something coherent. She's given me renewed hope.'

'What's she like?' asked Tom. Daisy had lingered at the edge of his thoughts ever since their non-conversation over wine two weeks ago. News of the arrival of her mother in Shipton Combe had been an unexpected twist; Daisy hadn't mentioned it, but to be fair he had only lasted all of about four minutes before he'd lost his bottle and run away. *What. A. Dick.*

'Stella's great,' Justin smiled. 'Funny and outrageous. And she's got plenty of time on her hands to help me out, which I'm definitely not complaining about.'

'You'd think she'd be spending her time with Daisy.'

'Yeah, there's some family beef there,' said Justin, pulling a dramatic face. 'I'm not getting into it. My life is currently beef-free.'

'Probably best,' Tom agreed.

'I hope Daisy hangs around, though. Because then Stella might stay too.'

I *hope Daisy hangs around* too, thought Tom, the realisation taking him by surprise. He hadn't consciously been avoiding her for the past two weeks, in fact he found himself looking for her around every corner, wandering the grounds with Henry in the freezing cold hoping he might bump into her. But after his disastrous visit to Willow Cottage, he wasn't sure if he should bother her again. No doubt she already thought he was a hopeless twat, and she had enough on her plate right now without the local headmaster loitering around her yard like a teenager with a crush.

Justin squatted down in the grass and started to milk Nancy with practised hands, so Tom strolled over to the enclosure where the two remaining pigs were snuffling about in the mud. The rest had all gone to piggy heaven in earlier months, and next week, one of these would be heading the same way.

Tom would get some homemade bacon sandwiches and Year 10 would learn how to make sausages.

'What's the plan for Nancy?' Tom asked, watching Justin deftly milk the goat. 'After you leave in a few months?'

Justin shrugged. 'She'll make a lovely goat curry.'

Tom looked horrified. 'Oh God, really?'

Justin smirked. 'I don't know. Maybe. It's up to you, I guess. Is the school going to keep this project up, or should we just have a farewell party of curried Nancy before I burn everything to the ground?'

Tom's brow furrowed. 'Shit, I suppose I'd better give it some thought. I'd like to keep it up, really; the kids love it and it looks good on the website. But I really don't have time to milk a goat every day.' He cleared his throat and looked wistfully towards the chimney of Willow Cottage.

'Have you seen her yet?' asked Justin knowingly. 'Since you were a massive bellend over dinner?'

Tom gave a hollow laugh. 'Yeah. A couple of weeks ago.' Justin raised his eyebrows; he hadn't told Justin about his cowardly visit yet. 'I went over to explain about the whole Tessa thing, but then the tennis player rang so I bottled it and ran.'

'Is there anything you can't fuck up?' Justin said affectionately.

'Apparently not.'

'I've barely seen her at all, but I s'pose the weather's been bloody awful. And I think she's avoiding Stella,' Justin mused. 'She goes out for a walk really early then spends all day cooking. She's pretty much got her own Ocado van.'

'Right,' Tom grinned, mildly heartened that he wasn't the only one she was avoiding.

'Fuck me,' said Justin with a grin. 'You're properly *smitten*.'

'Am not,' Tom denied hotly. 'Not like that, anyway. I'm just annoyed at myself for being such an arsehole.'

'Hmm, can't argue with that. Are you ready to meet The Mother?'

'I don't know. Am I?'

'I'm not sure you have a choice,' chuckled Justin. 'She's on her way over.'

He gestured behind Tom, who turned to see a woman bumbling across the field, looking charmingly eccentric in several layers of rainbow knitwear and a pair of Hunter wellies. She was darker and stouter than her daughter, and he idly wondered what Daisy's father had looked like. A Scandinavian love god, maybe.

Stella beamed at Tom and held out her hand. When he took it, she engulfed it with both of her own. 'You must be the elusive headmaster,' she said breathlessly. 'I've heard a lot about you.'

Tom smiled nervously. 'From Daisy? Oh dear.'

'No, from Justin.' Stella raised an eyebrow. 'Daisy hasn't mentioned you.' Tom blushed and turned away, Justin smirking silently as he funnelled the bucket of goats' milk into a large thermos flask.

'What are we doing today?' Stella asked. 'Fixing fences? Digging vegetables?'

Justin grinned. 'I've got a special job for you.' Stella clapped her hands excitedly as Justin screwed the lid on the flask. 'See those two pigs over there? *You* get to choose which one lives and which one dies.'

Tom laughed at Stella's horror.

'Oh my—' she gasped.

'Hello, hello,' a voice behind them called. It was the Reverend Miriam Mayhew, huffing towards them in a plum-coloured coat, a green kilt and sensible shoes, her face wrapped in a yellow scarf. She looked purposefully at Tom, ignoring Stella and Justin.

'Sorry to bother,' Miriam said, looking anything but. 'How are the pigs?'

'One of them is fine,' said Tom, 'but the other is about to get some very bad news. How can I help, Reverend Mayhew?'

'You really must call me Miriam, we're all friends,' she beamed. 'Well, since you ask, I'm here about the church winter fete. I've started planning, but I just wanted to check that we could use the school halls and gazebos again. Same as last year. End of January.'

'Yes, of course. Just drop my secretary a note and confirm the date. Let us know what you need.'

'Will do, will do,' sang Miriam. 'I'm hoping to secure our local celebrity as a special guest, that's bound to boost the numbers. All very exciting.'

Tom glanced awkwardly at Stella, who looked amused. 'Reverend Mayhew, can I introduce you to another guest in the village? This is Stella Crawford, mother of our . . . of Daisy Crawford.'

Miriam's hands flew to her face in horror. 'Oh goodness, I'm so sorry,' she cried. 'I'd heard you were visiting, but I didn't recognise you. I thought you were a member of staff.'

'It's fine,' said Stella with a polite smile.

'I was SUCH a big fan of yours,' continued Miriam excitedly. 'Well, of course I still am. My copy of *Waste Not, Want*

Not is the most-used cookbook in my kitchen. When you cook for one on a stipend, you need to be frugal.'

Stella beamed, clearly thrilled at this five-star review of her work. 'That's so lovely to hear. Thank you.'

Miriam continued, evidently keen not to lose Stella's attention. 'Are you staying in the village for a while? I'd love your input on the fete.'

Stella looked momentarily wrong-footed. 'Goodness. Well, I'm not sure how long for, but obviously I'm happy to help in any way I can while I'm here.'

'Oh, how wonderful!' Miriam clapped her hands. 'Can we meet later? I've got lots of ideas and would love to bounce them off someone. Have a little brainstorm, you know.'

Stella nodded and smiled gamely. 'Well, I don't see why not. I haven't had a chance to look round the church yet. Perhaps you'd give me a tour this afternoon, then we can chat over a sherry?'

Tom glanced at Justin and raised his eyebrows. Miriam had just delivered a masterclass in how to recruit another helper to her lost cause. But looking at Stella, he wondered if she might have just met her match.

CHAPTER TWELVE

Daisy was on her third attempt at a butternut squash risotto when her phone rang. She was tweaking the recipe, and while it might be a bit of a faff to make for teenagers, it was cheap, filling and a good, healthy vegan option. She glanced at the screen and saw Katie's name, almost dropping the phone in the pan in her haste to answer it.

'Hi,' said Daisy, taking a deep breath.

'Hey,' replied Katie, her voice as calm and in control as always. 'How are you?'

'I'm fine, I think,' replied Daisy, although she was stressed and on edge. 'Ask me again at the end of this call. Do you have any news?'

'I do.' Katie paused. 'You're not going to like it.'

Daisy held her breath, squeezing her eyes shut. 'Just give me the headlines – is he cheating on me?'

'Yes,' Katie murmured. 'I'm sorry. I've had a private investigator on the case. She's a friend, and she's the best.'

Daisy took a deep, juddering breath. 'Right. So, what did she find out?'

Katie sighed. 'OK, brace yourself. Christian entertained a woman at his house in Cheshunt on Friday evening. My friend traced her car: she's a personal trainer.'

'How do you know they weren't doing a training session?'

'He had his tongue down her throat on the doorstep as

95

she left,' Katie said briskly. 'They might have got hot and sweaty, but it definitely wasn't that kind of exercise.'

'Right.' Daisy swallowed, tears prickling the corners of her eyes. She took a deep breath. 'What else? There has to be something.' She could tell from Katie's voice.

'He met two women in Soho on Saturday and they went to a sex club. One of those high-end places, all coked-up socialites and leather dungeons. And then . . . last night, he went to a house party.'

Daisy closed her eyes as her hand flew to her pounding chest. 'What kind of house party?' she asked faintly, already wishing she hadn't.

'A sex party,' Katie said. 'A swinger's soiree, a suburban shagfest . . . call it what you like. Lots of people drinking Pornstar Martinis and fingering each other in the hot tub.'

Daisy suppressed something between a sob and a scream. 'Where? Where was the party?'

'In Romford.'

'Romford?' squealed Daisy. 'Wait. Are you telling me that Christian went to an orgy in Essex on a Sunday night?'

'I'm really sorry, Daisy.'

Daisy gripped the edge of the kitchen counter and took deep breaths. 'Don't ever apologise for my terrible taste in men, Katie. Just . . . thank you, and let me know how much I owe your friend.'

'I will. And now I'll ask you again – how are you?'

Daisy's head was spinning. She needed to get off the phone so she could scream and kick herself for being such an idiot. 'I'll be OK, Katie, don't worry about me.'

Katie was quiet for a moment. 'Daisy, we've been friends for a long time – I always do.'

CHAPTER THIRTEEN

Tom hovered outside Willow Cottage holding Henry's lead in one hand and a box of freshly laid eggs in the other. Justin could have dropped them off, but after two weeks Tom was ready to give apologising to Daisy another go, so he'd pilfered them from the shed. He cuddled the eggs to his chest, ignoring the fact that his friend was watching him beadily from his window next door. He hesitated for a moment, then pushed aside any nagging doubts and knocked decisively on Daisy's door.

After a few seconds it cracked open and a red and puffy face peeked out, barely recognisable as Daisy. She had clearly been crying, and seeing Tom set her off on another round of racking sobs. He instinctively stepped forward and gathered her into his arms, manoeuvring her back into the room as he kicked the door closed behind him.

'Hey, it's OK. It's OK.' She smelled of apple shampoo and flowery perfume, clutching at his jumper with her clenched fists like he was a lifeboat.

After a minute the tears subsided and Daisy pulled away, crossing the room to pull a tissue from a box. 'I'm so sorry,' she said, blowing her nose with a honking sound.

'What's happened? Are you OK?'

Daisy smiled weakly and hiccupped. 'Nobody's died, I promise. Just trouble in paradise.'

Tom sniffed, then looked towards the kitchen. Something was burning. 'What's that smell?'

'Oh fuck, it's my *risotto*!' Daisy wailed.

'Stay there,' said Tom. 'Sit down and pat Henry. I'll be back.'

He headed into the kitchen and found smoke emanating from some kind of sticky, orange lava welded to a pan on the AGA. He opened the back door, then grabbed the pan with an oven glove and tossed the whole thing onto the lawn, hearing it hiss as it hit the wet grass. He left the door open to allow the smoke to clear and fished a bottle of white wine from the fridge and a couple of glasses from one of the cupboards.

By the time he returned to the lounge, Daisy had mostly stopped crying and was curled up on the sofa with Henry, gently stroking between his ears. Tom handed Daisy a glass of wine and sat on the other sofa, nursing his.

'Now,' he said. 'What's happened?'

Daisy swigged half the wine and looked at him, through swollen eyes, her hand clamped over her mouth. 'Christian . . . he . . . I . . . oh fuck. It's awful, but I really can't talk about it. I'm sorry.'

Tom nodded, wondering if she couldn't talk because it was too painful, or because she didn't trust him not to blab her private business to the press. Probably the latter. 'Is there anything at all I can do?'

Daisy shook her head, breaking into a new round of racking sobs. Tom scuttled across the rug on his knees and gathered her into his arms again. 'Hey, it's OK,' he whispered, gently stroking her hair as she wailed like a wounded animal.

After a minute she pulled away, taking deep breaths. 'Oh God. I'm so sorry.'

'You don't have to apologise.' Daisy turned away to blow her nose again, and Tom took the opportunity to retreat back to the sofa.

They sat in silence for a moment. 'Is there anything else you want to talk about? Can I get you anything? Call your mu—?'

'God no,' said Daisy quickly. 'Stella and I are . . . well, let's not talk about that either. I'll be fine. It's not an emergency, honestly. Just a bit of a shock. You caught me at a bad moment.'

Another short silence. 'Would you like me to go?'

Daisy took a deep breath and nodded. 'I think that would be best,' she said. 'I'm really sorry I cried all over you.'

Tom smiled and stood up. 'I don't mind. You know where I am,' he said quietly.

Daisy smiled weakly. 'I do. Thank you, Tom.'

Tom opened the door and half-jogged away from Willow Cottage, across the school grounds, his cheeks burning with humiliation and helplessness and a whole confusion of other emotions. He could still feel the warmth of Daisy's body in his arms, and it occurred to him that it was the first time he'd held a woman in over three years. In the heat of the moment, it had felt like the most natural thing in the world. What did that say about him?

He looked down at Henry, who was panting by his side, and got a glare in return. Tom couldn't tell if he was being judged for his lack of finesse with women, or for making an old dog run.

CHAPTER FOURTEEN

Daisy poured another glass of wine and took a few deep breaths. She couldn't handle Tom Clark, not right now. She was too messed up, too vulnerable, too willing to offload her secrets – or, even worse, fall into the arms of the first handsome man who offered. God, how embarrassing. She'd been an incoherent mess. What must he think of her?

She hadn't consciously been avoiding Tom for the past two weeks, but she hadn't sought him out either. Well, not actively, anyway – it was hard not to glance up at his office window as she walked across the school grounds, or keep an eye out for his people-soaking car in the village. But she hadn't been out much, to be fair – the weather had been awful, and she'd tasked herself with nailing a new recipe a day. There had been some days where the furthest she'd travelled was the school gates to collect another Ocado order. Most people round here grew their own food or went to the farm shop, but she was very much a city girl.

Daisy went to the bathroom and splashed water on her face, taking in the shadows around her eyes and the dry ends of her hair. Right now all she wanted was to talk to Ruby, who was both sane and oblivious to the mess Daisy was in. She answered after a few rings, but she was getting ready for movie night, the latest *Fantastic Beasts* film, which Ruby informed her was set in the Harry Potter universe but didn't actually feature Harry Potter.

'How's Will?' Daisy asked.

'He's fine.' Daisy could hear the smile in her daughter's voice. At least she was happy.

'Have you seen him since half-term?'

'Yeah, he's cycled over a couple of times on Saturdays. We meet down by the woods and go for a walk. And he messages me after school every day, so it's all cool.' There was a finality to Ruby's tone, like this was all the detail Daisy was getting.

'Any thoughts on your birthday present?'

Ruby was quiet for a second. 'I've had an idea, but I'm still thinking it through. Can I call you next week and confirm?'

'That doesn't give me much time, Rubes,' said Daisy. 'It's only a few weeks off, and I've got Christmas to think about too.'

'It's not a big thing, I promise. I just need to decide if it's really what I want.'

'OK, fine,' Daisy pouted.

'Film's starting,' Ruby muttered. 'I need to go, Mum.'

'Have fun,' said Daisy with a smile. 'Love you.'

'Love you, too.'

Daisy ended the call and sipped her wine, feeling calmer and more focused. Her marriage to Simon had been a disaster, but Ruby had made it all worth it. Their daughter was happy, secure and grounded, and it was up to Daisy to keep her that way. And how could she do that if she didn't deal with Christian? It was time to put her Big Girl Pants on and write an email.

Christian

I'm emailing because to be honest I don't want to talk to you in person.

I know about your personal trainer, the Soho sex club and the party in Romford. I don't know how long you've been cheating on me, but you're not the man I thought you were.

Our engagement is off, obviously. Please ask Benny to liaise with Katie on a public statement. I have no interest in being vindictive, so in exchange for me not airing your grubby laundry perhaps you could do me the courtesy of never contacting me again.

Daisy

'The email's good,' Katie said an hour later. 'Thanks for copying me in.'

'I'm sorry; I should have run it past you first.'

'You don't need to consult with me on how to dump your fiancé, Daisy,' Katie muttered. 'To be honest, I'm surprised you were so restrained. I'd have sent someone round to chop his balls off with a rusty bread knife.'

Daisy snorted. 'I have a lot of questions for him, mostly about how he thinks it's OK to bang his personal trainer on Friday, then go to a sex club with two other women on Saturday, then go to an orgy in Romford on Sunday.'

'This is the worst Craig David song ever.'

Daisy giggled, then started to cry. 'I just feel so stupid and humiliated,' she wailed. 'How could I not know?'

'Why do you think I only date women?' Katie asked. 'Men are awful. Well, I'll take things from here – I'll give Benny a couple of days to respond, then start hassling him. Does anyone else know?'

Daisy hesitated. 'No. The school headmaster, a guy called

Tom – he turned up just after I got your call and found me having a meltdown. But I didn't tell him why. Well, not really.'

'Can you trust him? I can give him a call if you like.'

Daisy thought about it for a second. Did she trust Tom? Was he likely to be on the phone to the tabloids right now, telling them what he'd seen? Her gut said no, he wasn't the type. But then her gut had also told her Christian was husband material – look how that had turned out. 'No, it's fine. I do trust him, actually.'

'Because if—'

'I know, Katie. He caught me in a vulnerable moment, but I'm not worried. I can speak to him myself if it makes you feel better.'

'OK.'

'I'll call you tomorrow.'

'Sleep well.'

Daisy knocked on Tom's door, her coat wrapped tightly around her. It was only nine, so surely he would still be up? The lights were on, and his office window had been in darkness. She breathed out as footsteps sounded on the other side of the door, before it was pulled open.

'Hi,' Daisy greeted Tom with a weak smile.

'Hi.' Tom was wearing the same clothes as earlier – dark cords, a blue check shirt, a navy wool V-neck with a hole in the cuff. Probably moths.

'Sorry to bother you,' Daisy murmured. She had yet to look him in the eye.

'It's fine,' said Tom softly. 'Come in.'

'No,' Daisy said quickly. 'I won't, if that's OK. I just wanted to say sorry for earlier and thank you for being so nice. You caught me having a bit of a moment.'

'You don't have to apologise,' Tom leaned against the doorframe, his smile soft. Daisy smiled back as Henry appeared by his side, sniffing the air for treats. 'I'm just glad you're OK.'

'It's just—' Daisy looked away. She felt awful about this conversation, but Katie was right and it needed to be said. Henry nuzzled her hand, the gesture comforting. 'There are lots of people who would make quite a big deal out of that situation if they knew, and . . .'

Tom held up his hand. 'It's fine. I understand. I haven't told anyone, and I promise not to. I would never do that.'

Daisy smiled gratefully and let out a slow breath. 'Thank you. Please don't be offended, but I've been let down before.'

'I know,' said Tom. 'It's OK.'

She nodded. 'Well, I'd better get back.'

'I came round earlier to explain my behaviour,' Tom said quickly before she could go. 'Which I should have done two weeks ago – I chickened out. I'd still like to have that chance. When you're up to it.'

Daisy hesitated. Tom had been kind earlier, and she could still feel the warmth of his broad chest as she leaned into him. She probably owed him this and yet . . .

'I should get back and sort myself out,' she said. 'I look like shit.'

'I wasn't going to say anything,' shrugged Tom. 'But you really do. Pure shit.'

For a moment they were both still, then Daisy properly laughed for what felt like the first time in weeks.

'Look, come in.' Tom opened the door a little wider. 'I'll make us some tea.'

Daisy hesitated for a second, then nodded.

'I used to be married.' Tom squeaked out the words, like air being released from a balloon. 'Until a few years ago. The end was incredibly difficult. I can't really talk about it.' He glanced up at Daisy, his face pale and desolate.

'OK,' Daisy said gently, wondering where he was going with this.

'The thing is . . . you look like her. Tessa. A LOT like her. Same eyes, same face, same . . .' He blushed and vaguely waved his hand in the direction of Daisy's body, 'er, shape.'

Daisy stared at him, her mouth hanging open. She wasn't sure what she'd been expecting, but it wasn't this.

'Your hair is more blonde,' he continued, lost in memories, 'but otherwise you could have been twins. You're nothing like her personality-wise, obviously, but when we were together, people used to mistake her for you all the time. It was a running joke.'

He looked up at Daisy and smiled sadly. 'Once she even signed an autograph for somebody. They looked so happy to meet you and she didn't want to burst their bubble. God, it's so strange to be telling you this.' He rubbed his hand across his stubbly jaw, then raked it through his hair.

'Wow,' Daisy was nonplussed. 'I, um . . . wow.' She thought about the vicar's comments about her presence being *tricky for some at the school*, and then Will saying *it's such a headfuck you being here, must be a nightmare for our headmaster*. People here weren't being weird because she was famous – or infamous, after The Incident – it was because she was the spitting image of Tom's ex. *Awkward.*

'So, when I saw you in the village that day, and then at Justin's house,' Tom put his glass down, pressing his thumbs into his eye sockets, before looking bleakly at Daisy again, 'well, everything that happened came flooding back. It was like Tessa was there, but wasn't, and it messed with my head. Obviously, that wasn't your fault. It was a shitty thing to do. I'm so sorry.' He looked up at Daisy so sadly, she had a sudden urge to crawl into his lap and snog his face off. Probably not a great time, all things considered.

'It's OK,' Daisy shrugged. 'You've explained now. It's a little weird knowing I have a doppelganger, but let's forget it. How's Justin? I haven't seen him about recently.'

'I apologised to him too,' Tom admitted. 'He never met Tessa, so he had no idea why I was being such a dick. He was considerably less nice about it than you.'

'I think he's got a lot on his plate,' Daisy remarked wryly. 'None of it adequately seasoned.' Tom laughed and it felt like a shock to see him properly relax. He was dazzlingly good-looking. She felt her insides start to liquefy.

'I also need to apologise about driving through that puddle.' Tom looked shamefaced. 'I'm really sorry I made you so wet.'

Daisy snorted with laughter, prompting Tom to slop his tea down his jumper. 'Oh God,' he laughed. 'I'm so bad at this.'

'I'll tell you what,' Daisy said softly. 'Let's pretend the soaking and the dinner never happened. Shall we start again?' She stood up and held out her hand across the table. 'Hi, I'm Daisy Crawford. I'm a disgraced TV presenter.'

Tom smiled gratefully and stood up to join her, his hand feeling warm and strong around hers. 'Hi, I'm Tom Clark. I'm headmaster of a third-rate independent school.'

Daisy beamed as Tom started to laugh again. Maybe the world wasn't so bleak, after all.

CHAPTER FIFTEEN

On Saturday morning, Daisy lit the wood burner and settled on the sofa with her laptop, ready for a call that Katie had requested. Katie didn't bother with pleasantries, which suggested she had important stuff on her mind.

'Two things. First, I haven't heard back from Benny, so either he's cooking up some dastardly plan, or more likely Christian is licking his wounds and hasn't told him yet. I'll give him until Monday, then I'll give him a kicking.'

'Benny or Christian?'

'Benny, but I'm happy to put a Doc Marten up Christian's arse too.'

'Thanks,' laughed Daisy. 'What's the other thing?'

'Check your emails, I've just sent you a link.'

'Hang on, I'll open it now.' Daisy clicked onto her emails and saw the new arrival from Katie. The link took her to a tabloid website. '"*Game, Set but No Match?*"' Daisy read aloud. '"*Christian parties in London while Daisy hangs out with handsome Head in heavenly hideaway.*" I mean, you have to admire the alliteration.'

'Read the rest later,' Katie instructed. 'It's just gossip and speculation. They've heard a few rumours about Christian but can't corroborate. I'm actually more interested in the story about you and the headmaster. Somebody down there is talking to the press. Any ideas who?'

'Could be any number of people,' Daisy sighed, tucking her legs up on the sofa. 'But there's nothing to tell. I had dinner with Tom at another house in the village when I first moved down here, then he came over on Monday when he found me having a meltdown. I popped over to his house later that evening to ask him not to blab to the papers, but we just had a cup of tea and a chat for half an hour. Anyone could have seen us if they were passing by.' Her mind turned first to Justin, who was the most obvious candidate since he lived next door; then to Stella, who certainly had ample form. Or of course it could be Tom himself. The thought made her itch, so she pushed it to one side.

'I believe you, although I also wouldn't blame you,' laughed Katie. 'There's a picture of him later in the article, they call him "Tragic Tom". He's pretty hot, even by my standards.'

'I can neither confirm nor deny,' replied Daisy with a smile. 'Why Tragic Tom? What's tragic about him?'

'Didn't he tell you?' asked Katie. 'The whole thing with his wife, a few years ago?'

'Yeah,' said Daisy. 'She left him.'

Katie was silent for a moment. 'No, that's not it. She was in a road accident. She didn't leave him, Daisy. She's dead.'

After the call Daisy sat in silence on the sofa for a while, trying to process what Katie had told her. Tom had never specifically said that Tessa had left him, but he definitely hadn't mentioned that she was dead.

With nervous hands, Daisy searched 'Tessa Clark Shipton Combe' online and found the report of the inquest. Tessa had been shopping alone in Cheltenham on a September

Saturday three years ago when she was run over by a van at a junction. The inquest recorded a verdict of accident; by all accounts Tessa had stepped out into the road on a red light. The van had come round the corner and hadn't seen Tessa because the view of the junction was blocked by a road maintenance truck. The van had hit her head on, causing devastating head injuries. No blame was attributed to the driver, who was unhurt, although he'd received extensive treatment for PTSD by the time of the inquest. Tessa was thirty-four and fourteen weeks pregnant at the time.

I used to be married. The end was incredibly hard and I can't really talk about it. That's what Tom had said on Monday. No wonder he'd lost his mind at the sight of Daisy in Shipton Combe; it must have brought back the worst time of his life in vivid technicolour.

Daisy thought about the press rumours about Christian and Tom this morning, and what would happen if that story blew up. It would only take a little digging by a curious journalist to discover how much Tessa had looked like Daisy, which would be too good a detail to resist. Christian's suburban sexploits would elevate the story from gossip newsletter speculation to the front pages of the tabloids, no doubt implying that Tom was somehow a third party in this whole sordid business. He was too handsome and his back-story was pure tabloid fodder. Daisy picked up her phone and called Katie straight back.

'I need your help,' said Daisy. 'We need to protect Christian.'

'Okaaay,' said Katie. 'NOT what I expected you to say. Why?'

'Because right now it's a small story,' replied Daisy, 'but if

Christian's cheating gets out it will be huge. And if it gets huge, the life of a really nice man is going to be turned upside down for the second time.'

The only reason Daisy had agreed to have a regular lunch with her mother in Willow Cottage was to manage the time they spent together, thus avoiding Stella rocking up at the house whenever she liked. Right now most of her mother's free time seemed to be spent on the allotment with Justin, or planning a village fete with the vicar that seemed to get more ambitious by the day. Both were fine by Daisy – if Stella was busy, she wasn't causing trouble.

'I saw the news story about you and the headmaster,' said Stella, spooning carrot and coriander soup into her mouth. 'What's the situation with you and Christian?' Her purple cardigan smelled of a Floris perfume that took Daisy back to being a teenager, being ferried from audition to audition, Stella never far away.

'Just ask away, Mum,' said Daisy snarkily. 'Don't hold back.'

Stella raised her eyebrows and smiled sweetly. 'I'm your mother, I'm not obliged to beat around the bush.'

Daisy sighed and put down her spoon. 'We're going through a sticky patch.' Daisy's mood darkened, thinking about the number of sticky patches Christian had probably slept in recently. 'I really don't want to talk about it.'

'So, nothing in the rumours about you and Tom Clark, then?'

'No.' Daisy gritted her teeth, but once her mother was on to something she was like a dog with a bone. 'We've chatted two or three times, both times to talk about the recipe book.'

Daisy cast around wildly for a reason she might have done that, before having a moment of divine inspiration. 'I'd like to test the recipes out on some of his students.' This had been the first thing that came to mind, but now she'd said it out loud it actually sounded like a really good idea.

'Oh,' said Stella, sounding impressed but also disappointed. 'Well, I'm sure that would be very useful.'

Daisy made a mental note to tell Katie her latest plan and talk to Tom about it, ideally before Stella did. She had a tennis lesson with Marcus now, but she'd swing by the school and see him on her way back.

As Daisy finished her lesson and said goodbye to Marcus, who had once again spent an hour trying to charm his way up her tennis skirt, to no avail, she was surprised to see Gerald and Melanie heading across the village hall car park towards the court. Gerald was wearing a waxed jacket and corduroy trousers in a putrid shade of salmon, while Melanie was wearing something vaguely resembling sportswear big enough for a pantomime horse. She was also clutching a tennis racquet. Daisy gave her a warm smile as they approached.

'I didn't know you played.'

'Oh,' said Melanie, blushing furiously. 'Well, I—'

'It's a fortieth birthday gift from Will and myself,' announced Gerald, like he'd just gifted her a super yacht. 'Melanie used to be a keen player, so we've booked her a course of six lessons. A new racquet, too.'

Daisy raised her eyebrows at Melanie, who smiled in return. 'It's a lovely present,' the woman said quietly. 'I'm very rusty, though. I hope that's OK, Marcus.'

'Rusty is fine. We'll ease you in gently.'

'Enjoy your lesson, I'll see you later.' Gerald gave his wife a half-hearted kiss on the cheek before turning to Daisy. 'Shall I walk you back?'

Daisy couldn't come up with a convenient excuse, so she allowed Gerald to fall into step beside her as they walked back up the road. His pungent aftershave made her eyes water, and it occurred to her that maybe the timing of Melanie's tennis lesson wasn't a coincidence. Surely Gerald hadn't offloaded his wife for an hour in order to spend time alone with Daisy? She was so paranoid these days. She must be over-thinking it.

'And how are you settling into Shipton Combe?' asked Gerald, with the kind of pompous tone a waiter might use to ask if the lobster thermidor was to her liking.

'Fine, thank you,' said Daisy. 'I'm keeping busy.'

'I'm sorry we haven't had time to catch up properly,' continued Gerald. 'It seems we both have many demands on our time.'

'Well, I'll be here for at least a couple more weeks.'

'Is that so?' exclaimed Gerald. 'How lovely. Why don't I walk you back to your lovely cottage, and you can tell me all about your plans?'

Daisy shuddered, now certain that this whole situation had been engineered as part of Gerald's master seduction plan. Grim.

'I'm afraid I have another meeting.' Daisy quickly glanced at her watch. 'And I'm actually a little late. I'll have to run. But thank you for the offer – perhaps you and Melanie could come over for a drink another time?' She gave him the briefest of smiles, then jogged across the road to the gate that led to the school grounds.

Daisy hurried through the woods, periodically checking

113

behind her to ensure he wasn't following and making a mental note never to be alone in a room with Gerald Forbes-Glover. She'd definitely invite Melanie over for a drink, but if Gerald insisted on coming, she'd have to get Justin round to act as a human shield.

She hadn't lied about having a meeting. Katie had been hugely enthusiastic about her recipe-testing idea as a means to explain her meetings with Tom, so she'd got his number from Marcus and messaged him to ask if she could pop over for a quick chat. He'd suggested his office, which seemed rather formal for a Saturday; perhaps after reading the press coverage he wanted to keep a desk between them.

Tom met Daisy by the main door to the school, wearing old jeans, lace-up leather boots and a cream cable-knit sweater that made him look like a sexy fisherman. His office was warm and cosy and joyfully chaotic, with a desk piled with papers, books and folders and empty coffee mugs. Henry huffed over to say hello, then returned to his favourite spot by the clanking radiator.

'Have a seat,' said Tom stiffly. 'Would you like a cup of tea?'

Daisy laughed. 'I feel like I'm being interviewed for a job.'

Tom blushed and fiddled with a stapler on his desk. 'I'm sorry. This is all a bit awkward, isn't it?'

'It's me who should apologise.' Daisy sat down in the visitor's chair. It was hard and uncomfortable and clearly designed to ensure visitors didn't stay for very long. 'I've got you caught up in my nonsense. I wanted to let you know because there's a possibility other tabloids might pick up on it. Probably just websites, not the Sunday papers or anything. My manager is dealing with it.'

'How does that work?' asked Tom. 'How do you deal with something like that?'

'Well,' Daisy frowned, 'usually we provide an alternative story. Something boring and not remotely salacious. For example, we could say that the reason you and I have met a couple of times is to discuss me testing out my new cookbook on some of your students.'

Tom's eyes widened. 'Oh wow, that's a great idea. But . . . if the press print that, doesn't it mean you'll actually have to do it?'

'Ideally, yes,' Daisy nodded, 'but to be honest I'd absolutely love it, as long as it's not a huge inconvenience for the school. Some input from your students would be incredibly useful.'

'Well,' Tom settled back into his chair thoughtfully. 'I'm sure we can make that work. The parents will be thrilled.'

Daisy beamed. 'Maybe after Christmas? You don't have to decide now, but if you could give it some thought that would be amazing.'

'Of course, no problem.' He looked considerably more cheerful, which was a huge relief. They sat in awkward silence for a moment, Tom fidgeting in his chair as Daisy looked out across the wet and windblown school grounds.

Tom spoke first. 'Is everything OK? After whatever happened on Monday?'

Daisy shook her head. 'No, but I'll be fine. Why didn't you tell me about what happened to your wife?'

Tom took a deep breath, like he'd known the question was coming but it was still a punch in the chest. 'I guess I find it really hard to talk about. It's been over three years but sometimes it still hurts like it was yesterday.' He looked down at his feet, his shoulders slumped in defeat. 'We were so excited about the baby.' Tom reached out and touched a photo frame on his desk.

Daisy leaned forward. 'May I?'

He picked up the frame and handed it to her, then walked to the window and stared at the view across the school fields, his hands buried deep in the pockets of his jeans. Daisy looked at the picture and suppressed a gasp of shock – it was true that Tessa had looked remarkably like her, although her hair was a warmer blonde than Daisy's. But everything else – the eyes, the shape of her face, the full lips, the dimples – it was like looking in a mirror. The photo was a holiday selfie, Tessa and Tom laughing into the camera, looking tanned and happy. Daisy couldn't imagine how deep that loss must feel; her heart ached for him.

Carefully, she put the photo down, then walked to the window and stood beside Tom, her arms folded. 'Do you want to talk about it?'

Tom gave a sad laugh. 'Funnily enough, you're the one person it's particularly hard to talk to about it. You've always been part of what happened, somehow.'

'What do you mean? Because we looked alike?'

'Partly that, yes. But also . . .' his voice trailed off.

'Also, what?'

He met her gaze and smiled. 'I don't want this to come out the wrong way, like I've ever blamed you in any way. But it was a Saturday in September, and she was in a hurry, rushing around, because . . .'

The pieces slotted together in Daisy's brain and she thought she might be sick. 'She wanted to get back for the *Spotlight* final.'

Tom nodded. 'It had just started on TV when the police

knocked on my door. I knew something was wrong because she'd never have missed it.'

Daisy was horrified. 'God, I'm so sorry.'

Tom rubbed his face with both hands. 'Tessa was such a huge fan of yours, I think she felt like you had some kind of connection, somehow. You living in the village would have blown her mind – she'd have been doing everything possible to make you her new best friend.'

'I'm sure I'd have liked her.'

Tom smiled. 'I'm sure you would too. I'm afraid I've never been able to watch your show since.'

'No. It certainly explains why you were so upset the first time we met.' She reached out to touch him, then withdrew her hand. 'I'm so sorry, Tom. It must be really hard.' *Especially seeing me here, like a ghost.*

Tom's face was grim, his eyes vacant and unseeing, then he shook his head. 'I'm told it will get easier. And it has a bit, I suppose. I've accepted it was just an accident and stopped blaming everyone else. I've met the van driver a couple of times, a guy called Martin. He's torn himself apart over it, poor bastard.' He turned from the window and looked at Daisy. 'Some days I almost feel ready to move on, other days not so much. Apparently one day the fog will lift. I'm really looking forward to it, actually.'

Daisy instinctively put her hand on his arm, but the crackle of static from her sports top made her jump, so she refolded her arms and walked back to the chair. She should probably leave, even though she felt the pull of something indefinable which made her want to stay.

She put on her coat. 'I've taken up enough of your time. I'm going skiing for the week before Christmas, so why don't I drop you an email next week about the cooking classes? Let you know what I'd need so you can have a think about it.'

Tom nodded and walked back to his desk. 'We still have an old domestic science classroom, although we haven't taught that in years. I could ask the maintenance team to give it a spruce up while you're away, make sure it's up to code.'

'That would be amazing,' Daisy murmured, her eyes searching his. 'I'll cover all the costs.' Tom smiled softly, and Daisy felt that thing in the pit of her stomach again. She shook it off and headed for the door before she made a fool of herself.

Just before ten, Daisy's phone rang. It was Ruby. She never usually called this late.

'Hey, Rubes,' said Daisy with concern. 'Are you OK?'

'I'm fine,' Ruby assured her. 'Better than fine. I'm amazing actually, and I know exactly what I want for my birthday.'

'Hooray, about time,' Daisy said happily. 'What is it?'

'I want Will to come skiing with us.'

CHAPTER SIXTEEN

The following Sunday morning Daisy power-walked up the school drive towards the rectory, her breath creating clouds of vapour in the still air. She'd spent over a week procrastinating about going to see Will's parents, hoping that Ruby might change her mind. Of course she could have refused point blank, but Ruby rarely asked for anything and she could see how much she liked Will. Considering her upbringing, she'd been a surprisingly undemanding child. So, Daisy really had to give this her best shot. Even if it might mean breathing the same air as Will's father.

As she crossed the road to the gates of the rectory, Daisy was surprised and relieved to see Melanie walking across the gravel drive. She was dressed in the same hideously ill-fitting sportswear as last time, and carrying her tennis racquet.

'Hello. Heading for another lesson?'

Melanie nodded. 'It's nice to play again, so I thought I'd get one in while it's dry. Gerald's playing golf.' She looked happy, so Daisy gave Gerald a temporary pass – he might be a dreadful letch, but at least he bought his wife nice presents.

'Can I walk with you?' asked Daisy. 'I'm heading your way.' She fell into step with Melanie, wondering how best to engage her in conversation before she threw in 'by the way, can I take your son on holiday?' as idle chit-chat.

'I saw the story,' said Melanie nervously. 'In the news.'

119

'Hmm,' said Daisy with a hollow laugh. 'I get that kind of thing a lot.'

'I know how it feels,' said Melanie, looking at her feet. 'When it's just speculation, but no actual facts.'

'Of course you do,' said Daisy, feeling a brief moment of connection with Melanie. They were quiet for a moment, neither of them in any hurry. 'It's hard for Ruby too. She's been through a lot over the past few months. Meeting Will has made it a lot easier, actually.'

'I'm glad,' said Melanie with a soft smile. 'Will struggled too, when everything about Gerald was in the papers. He was only ten and didn't really understand why we suddenly had to move here.'

'It must have been a nightmare,' said Daisy, thinking that she, Melanie and Tom could write a book about emotional roller-coasters. 'Out of interest, did you know Tessa? Tom's wife?'

'Yes,' said Melanie. 'We were good friends. We used to do the flowers together at the church.' Her eyes widened as she looked at Daisy. 'She was lovely. I'm sorry, it's just so uncanny . . .'

'I know,' said Daisy. 'Tom told me. Let's talk about that another day.'

'OK,' said Melanie. They were both quiet for a moment, walking side by side through the sleepy village. 'So what was the news story all about?' she asked tentatively. 'Are things between you and your fiancé OK?'

'We'll be fine,' said Daisy with a shrug, not wanting to lie any more than she had to. 'And what about you? How are things between you and Gerald?'

Melanie looked at her warily. 'Oh, well. Fine.'

Daisy touched her arm 'Look, Melanie. I don't mean to pry. But I don't know many people in this village, and I'd really like us to be friends. I think we have things in common, our children apart.' She took a deep breath. 'We've both had our personal lives slapped all over the tabloids.'

Melanie was quiet for a moment, clearly battling with how much to say. 'I suppose you know all the details about what happened with Gerald.'

Daisy gave her a reassuring smile. 'I'm not going to pretend. That would be embarrassing for both of us. I do know.'

Melanie smiled weakly, a pink glow on her cheeks. 'I'm sure you've gathered what he's like. Things . . . haven't been easy for a while.'

Daisy nodded encouragingly. She got the impression Melanie didn't speak to many people and, Ruby and Will aside, she genuinely hoped they could be friends. Both of them knew what it was like to be with someone famous with a roaming eye. 'I guessed that much.'

Melanie took a deep breath. 'He can be difficult. Moody. Cold, sometimes. I've learnt it's easier just to stay as invisible as possible.' She glanced down at herself miserably. 'I didn't used to be like this. But Will . . . well, he gets me through the day.'

Melanie stopped walking and turned to face Daisy. 'And I do still love him. I know people think I stayed for his money or for Will, but it's more than that. We used to have something really special.'

Daisy nodded. 'I get that.' She thought about Simon, and how much she still cared about him despite everything. That thing they'd had at the very beginning couldn't be erased, no matter what followed. She wouldn't want to because without it there'd be no Ruby. She imagined Melanie felt the same about Will, even if they seemed a little distanced from each other.

121

'So now it's my turn,' said Melanie with a mischievous smile. 'Is any of the stuff in the papers true?'

Daisy gave a hollow laugh. 'Which bit?'

'About your fiancé – and you having a fling with Tom.'

'Well, things with Christian have been difficult, but I'm afraid there's nothing to report on the headmaster front. He's just helping me out with my latest project.'

Daisy relaxed a little when she realised Melanie wasn't judging her, just seemed genuinely interested. She was surprised at how easy she was to talk to, and it was nice to chat to another woman. Other than Katie and her mother, things had been a bit dry in that department.

Melanie nodded happily. 'I knew it was just gossip. Still, he deserves to be happy.'

They were almost at the village tennis court, so Daisy realised she needed to get to the point. 'So look, Melanie, you know by now that Ruby and Will are an item?'

Melanie smiled. 'Yes, Will told me. I have to say, he seems rather smitten.'

'I think they're both rather smitten,' laughed Daisy, 'which by the way I have absolutely no objection to. Will seems like a lovely young man.'

Melanie beamed. 'He really is. I'm very proud of him.'

Daisy took another deep breath. 'The thing is, we're going skiing for the first week of the school holidays, to celebrate Ruby's sixteenth birthday. And she's told me that what she really wants for a present is for Will to come with us.'

Melanie stopped dead in the car park. 'Skiing? With you?'

'Yes,' said Daisy helplessly. 'A week on Friday.'

'Where?'

'Austria,' Daisy said, wondering, not for the first time, why Ruby couldn't have asked for a bloody pony.

Melanie wrung her hands and shuffled her feet, her face full of anxiety. 'Well, I don't—Gerald wouldn't . . . We can't . . . Oh, goodness! I don't know what to say.'

Daisy put her hand on Melanie's arm. 'It won't cost you and Gerald a penny,' she reassured. 'The chalet belongs to a friend and it has loads of spare rooms.' *This was true.* 'A couple of friends have dropped out at the last minute, so Will can have their ski hire and lessons and things.' *This was absolutely not true, but it was for a good cause.* 'And I can transfer one of their flights to Will's name.' *Also a lie, she'd have to buy him a seat.*

Melanie looked panic-stricken. 'But . . . but he's never been skiing, he doesn't have the right clothes or anything.'

'There's a big cupboard full of ski wear, we can kit him out when we arrive—' That was actually true: the chalet was home to twenty years' worth of outgrown and unused ski clothing.

'—Honestly, everything is covered,' continued Daisy, 'and I will look after him like he's my own son. I'm picking Ruby up from school on the Thursday, then flying first thing on Friday and we'll be back on the twenty-first, so you'll have Will back in time for Christmas. All you need to do is give me his passport.' Daisy smiled hopefully. 'I know it's a lot to ask, but you'd make my daughter very happy. Your son too. And Ruby's had such a tough time recently.' *Emotional blackmail – why the hell not? In for a penny.*

'Goodness,' said Melanie, obviously flustered. 'It's just so much to take in.' She looked around awkwardly. 'Look, I don't mean to sound ungrateful, but can I think about it? I'll come and see you first thing.'

123

It wasn't an outright no, and probably the best Daisy could hope for right now, so she smiled at Melanie.

'Of course. Absolutely no problem.' *Quite a big problem, actually, but what's another lie?*

Daisy was mooching around the cottage, making notes for a new recipe, when there was a loud knock at the door. She found Melanie on the porch looking stricken but determined; she was still dressed in her tennis gear.

'I thought you were coming round tomorrow?' Daisy said, ushering the woman into the kitchen.

'I was, but I already know what my answer is, so I thought I'd come now.' Melanie leaned against the AGA, pulling her sweatshirt tightly about her.

'Do you want tea? You look freezing.' Daisy filled the kettle with water and rummaged in the cupboard for biscuits.

'Will can't come with you,' said Melanie, her expression pained. 'I can't tell you how much I appreciate the offer, but he can't. I'm so sorry.'

Daisy had been half-expecting this, but it was still a blow. Ruby would be gutted, but at least Daisy could say she'd done her best. She put the biscuits down and turned to face Melanie. 'Can I ask why? You can tell me it's none of my business, if you like.'

Melanie hesitated, clearly torn about whether to offload, then she visibly deflated. 'It's Gerald,' she said finally. 'He's a proud man, and he won't like it. Personally, I want whatever makes Will happy. But if Will goes, Gerald will make life very difficult for me.'

Daisy's eyes widened in horror and Melanie held up her hands, laughing shakily. 'No, don't get me wrong. Gerald is

124

many things, but he isn't violent or anything. He's just . . . so cold.' She looked away. 'I can tolerate it for the small day-to-day things; Will makes everything easier. But I can't handle a week alone with him. I'm not strong enough. I really wish I was. For Will.'

Daisy didn't say anything for a minute, instead turning back to the kitchen counter and busying herself with making the tea. 'Why do you stay with him, Melanie?'

Melanie sighed and hung her head. 'I do still love him. I can't explain it, really. And he's Will's father. And, yes, on a practical level, I can't afford to leave. I don't have any money of my own, and no family now I can turn to.' She stared at her feet, her face red with shame. Daisy was sure there was a story there.

'Everything we have is Gerald's family money,' she continued. 'Not that there's much of it left, but it's enough to pay Will's school fees and keep a roof over our heads. He only has one year left, then he'll be off to university and not financially dependent on Gerald.'

'What if I spoke to Gerald?' asked Daisy. 'Explained the situation and asked him myself? Do you still think he'd say no?' Daisy handed over a mug of tea, which Melanie hugged gratefully. Her knuckles were white with tension.

Melanie shook her head bleakly. 'He'd say yes. Will would never forgive him if he said no, and he does care what Will thinks, even if he doesn't show it. But he'd still make life miserable for me while you were away. It would be unbearable. I'm so sorry. I know that's selfish.'

Daisy thought for a few seconds, then put her mug down and faced Melanie squarely, hands on her hips. 'Fine,' she said decisively. 'There's nothing else for it, I'm afraid.' She smiled at the woman broadly. 'You're just going to have to come with us.'

CHAPTER SEVENTEEN

'Remind me why we're doing this, again?'

Daisy's left arm was wedged against the door to the van, her right pressed into Stella's shoulder. Her mother smelled of hairspray and patchouli; the ancient van reeked of manure. The combination reminded her of a boutique music festival she and Simon had once gone to on a farm in Wales, bopping along to Toploader in a slurry-splattered barn. Sometimes it felt like the blisters from that weekend of dancing in rubber wellies had lasted longer than her marriage.

'I told Justin I'd go with him to the pig place—' Stella murmured, looking out of the window at the passing greenery.

'The pig place,' Daisy raised her eyebrows.

'She means the slaughterhouse,' said Justin with a grin. 'It's time for Pig Three to meet her maker.'

'I thought it would be a nice opportunity for us to spend some time together. A little adventure,' Stella continued, ignoring both of them.

'Whose van is this?' asked Daisy. She knew she sounded tetchy, but she was tired and far from looking forward to dealing with Gerald later. Not for the first time she wished she was back at the cottage, lounging on the sofa, rather than trapped in a fusty old van with her mother, Justin and a doomed pig. But by agreeing to 'go on a little road trip' with her mother now, she could maybe avoid having a one-on-one lunch with her later. She'd cross her fingers if she could move her arms.

'It's mine,' said Justin. 'I sold my midlife crisis motorbike when I started this fucking nightmare and bought this instead. It's much more useful for lugging firewood and livestock.'

'Poor Prue,' said Stella sadly.

'Who's Prue?' asked Daisy.

'That's the name the students gave Pig Three,' said Justin with a grin. 'They named them all after famous TV chefs. I prefer not to give them human names: it makes them harder to kill. Easy for the kids, they're not the ones who have to make this journey and pick up a butchered carcass at the other end.'

'So, where are Pigs One and Two?' asked Daisy, although she suspected she knew the answer.

'Ah, Gordon and Delia,' said Justin wistfully. 'They both met Mark the Slaughterman just in time for Halloween.'

'How very . . . *appropriate*,' mused Daisy.

'So why are there two pigs in the back,' asked Stella, 'if only Prue is being put to sleep?'

Daisy smiled wryly at Stella's sugar-coating of today's outing, then twisted in her seat to look through the tiny window into the back of the van. There were two happy-looking pigs snuffling around in a bed of straw.

'Because pigs don't like living alone,' Justin explained. 'They're social creatures. If we're turning Pig Three into loin chops, we need to find Pig Four a new home.'

'Nigella,' Stella pronounced. 'Pig Four,' she added when Daisy looked at her blankly.

'If you like,' shrugged Justin. 'On the way back from

127

dropping off Prue, we're taking *Nigella* to her new home. She's joining a smallholding that belongs to one of the school parents. They plan to use her for breeding.'

'Lucky Nigella,' said Daisy.

'She never needs to know how close she came to being pumped into the school sausage machine,' added Justin wickedly.

'So what's going to happen today?' asked Stella, wringing her hands in the passenger seat.

'Today, nothing,' said Justin calmly. 'We'll drop her off, and Mark will keep her in a pen overnight so she's all calm and settled. She'll be slaughtered tomorrow and hung in Mark's fridge. We'll pick her up on Thursday morning and do some butchering. Some cuts for me, some for Tom and the school freezer, the rest for the Pig in a Blanket.'

'What's the Pig in a Blanket?' asked Daisy.

'The winter barbecue I'm having for a few friends on Thursday night, at Tom's place. You're invited.'

Daisy nodded, feeling the now familiar frisson of butterflies in the pit of her stomach at the prospect of seeing Tom again. They'd exchanged a few emails about the recipe testing since that meeting in his office, but she'd kept her distance. In her current fragile emotional state, everything about Tom Clark felt like trouble. And as far as everyone else was concerned, she and Christian were still a couple.

'I've never been to a slaughterhouse before,' mumbled Stella.

'I don't suppose you have,' said Justin agreeably. 'Mark's the best. He only deals with local farmers and smallholdings, not big meat factories. He's all about the animal welfare, so it will help us write that bit of the book.' He looked at Stella hopefully, but it was clear to Daisy that her mother wasn't convinced. 'Tom's meeting us there,' he added.

'Tom's coming today?' Daisy looked at Justin in alarm.

'Yeah.' Justin shot her a knowing smile. 'He's bringing his Year 11 RE class, part of the ethics module. Mark's giving them a tour.'

Daisy tried to look calm, but her stomach was doing somersaults that had nothing to do with the narrow, windy roads. If she'd known Tom was coming, she'd have at least brushed her hair. She thought about their conversation in his kitchen and how he made her feel when he smiled. She realised she was looking forward to seeing him, even if the location wasn't exactly her first choice for a hot date. *Date?* Where had that come from?

'—Do you have to come back tomorrow?' asked Stella.

'For the killing?' Justin shrugged. 'I wasn't planning to. I know what Mark does and I respect it, but I'd rather not fucking watch—'

'No.' Stella patted Daisy's arm like she used to when Daisy was small and *she* was actually feeling anxious, not her daughter. 'Poor Prue,' she muttered again.

'There's still time to change your mind,' Justin grinned evilly. 'You can sacrifice Nigella to save Prue.'

Stella shuddered and glared at Justin. 'Absolutely not. But you're a terrible man for making me choose.'

Justin burst out laughing and Daisy joined in, suddenly aware that spending time with the two of them was actually kind of fun. She took Stella's hand in her own and squeezed it, ignoring her mother's start of surprise, and happy for the first time in years just to be in her company.

★

Tom was waiting next to the school minibus, eight or nine students milling around him. A grey-haired man in blue overalls and an impressive wizard-like beard, who Daisy assumed was Mark, stood nearby. The students goggled at Daisy and chuntered excitedly as she climbed out of the van, and a few pulled out their phones in the hope of grabbing a photo. Justin and Mark quickly herded them off, with Stella jogging along behind, leaving Daisy and Tom alone.

'Not going in?' asked Daisy, wandering over to the back of the minibus, which created a buffer against the wind and hid them from the turned heads of the retreating students and any stray cameras.

'No.' Tom shook his head emphatically. 'I've seen it all before. I'm really only here to drive the minibus. Sandra Pearson is their RE teacher, but she won't come. Vegan,' he added at Daisy's enquiring look.

'You're kidding.'

'Nope,' shrugged Tom with a grin. 'It's important the students are free to make up their own minds, but Sandra worries *she*'ll go rogue and start setting all the animals free.'

Daisy laughed, hugging her coat around her tightly, wishing she didn't look quite so much like she'd just rolled out of bed.

'How are you?' asked Tom quietly. He moved a little closer to her, his breath making clouds in the icy air. Considering the inauspicious location, the moment felt oddly intimate.

'I'm fine,' she replied with a soft smile. She met his gaze, feeling the intensity of his stare and wondering, not for the first time, what it would be like to kiss him.

'I'm glad,' he replied. 'I've got a flask of coffee in the front – do you want some?'

Daisy nodded happily, marvelling at how quickly her life had reached a point where drinking instant coffee out of a thermos in an abattoir car park gave her more joy than the coolest cafés in London.

Daisy pressed the doorbell of the rectory with sweaty palms, wondering why this encounter with Gerald felt so high stakes. Of course, Ruby would be disappointed if Will couldn't come skiing, but it was hardly parenting fail of the year. She'd acknowledge that Daisy had done her best and they'd have a lovely holiday anyway, just as they always did. She checked her watch – Melanie did the church flowers at 12.30 on a Tuesday, and they'd agreed that Daisy would turn up ten minutes later, then message when it was safe for Melanie to return home. Daisy didn't feel great about rail-roading Gerald, but you couldn't appeal to the better nature of somebody who didn't have one, could you?

Gerald answered the door with a predatory grin, like he'd known it was only a matter of time before Daisy would be lured to the rectory by his animal magnetism. Daisy repressed a shudder and gave him her best primetime TV smile.

'Hello, Gerald. So sorry to bother you.'

'My dear Daisy, what a lovely surprise. I'm afraid Melanie has gone out.'

Daisy cranked the smile up a notch. 'Well, I actually came to see you. Do you have a minute?'

'Yes, of course.' Gerald stepped to one side with a flourish, like Hugh Hefner opening the door to the Playboy Mansion. '*Do* come in.'

'Do you mind if we take a walk around the churchyard instead?' Daisy replied cheerfully, already stepping away. 'It's so nice to get some fresh air. I've just got back from a slaughterhouse.' Today's heavy skies were now accompanied by a biting wind, but nothing was going to tempt Daisy over that threshold.

'Oh. Yes. Why not?' said Gerald gamely, grabbing a Barbour jacket and a pair of leather strangler's gloves from the coat rack by the door. Daisy led him through the wooden gate at the side of the house into the oldest section of the churchyard, where gravestones crusted with moss and lichen listed sideways like drunk old men. The ground was hard with frost and the church looked bleak and forbidding. Snow was forecast before the weekend, although it wasn't expected to amount to much.

Gerald closed the gate and fell into step beside her, close enough that his shoulder brushed hers. He steered her towards the back of the churchyard, which was hidden from the rectory and the road by the looming stone hulk of the church.

'So, Daisy, what can I do you for you?'

'I wanted to ask you something. A favour, actually.'

'I can't imagine ever saying no to a woman like you.' Gerald rested his gloved hand on her arm. 'Fire away, my dear, fire away.'

A few minutes later Gerald's face was thunderous, but Daisy had to admire how well he was keeping his cool.

'Just so I'm clear,' said Gerald through gritted teeth and narrowed eyes, 'you'd like to take my wife and my son on an all-expenses-paid skiing holiday. On Friday.'

Daisy smiled winningly. 'I would. I know it's short notice, but the opportunity only just came up and it would make my daughter very happy. And your son, I should think.'

'And why exactly does my wife need to go?' The sharpness of Gerald's tone could slice holes in the frigid air.

'Because I think it would be more appropriate. For Will. He's only seventeen, and it seems only right and proper that his mother should be there.' Gerald continued to look mutinous, so she continued. 'And if I'm being entirely selfish, it would be lovely company for me, too. Usually, Ruby and I spend our holiday time together, but I suspect she's going to want to be with Will – you know how teenagers are?' Daisy giggled, although she found it hard to be believe that Gerald had ever been a teenager. He gave the impression of being born in a tweed shooting jacket and raised by wolves.

'Melanie and I have become friends and I'm sure we'll be good company for each other.' Daisy had vague hopes on this point, but it was by no means guaranteed. The whole thing felt like a huge minefield, frankly, and she inwardly cursed Ruby for the fiftieth time since breakfast.

Gerald's eyes narrowed. 'Well, it's most unusual. And I have to say I feel rather cornered. Perhaps you'd give me some time to think about it.'

'Is your concern the cost?' asked Daisy. 'You really needn't worry: it's all taken care of.'

Gerald shook his head hurriedly. 'No, it's not the cost, of course. I'd be happy—'

Daisy spotted the advantage and seized it. 'Because obviously I've already spoken to Melanie and she would love to come. Will doesn't know anything about it yet. Clearly we didn't want to get his hopes up if there was an issue. So I came to see you and I wanted to set your mind at ease about the cost. I know you're an honourable man.'

Gerald's chest instinctively puffed with pride. 'Well, of course, but it's not just—'

'Surely Melanie doesn't need your permission to accept my offer?' asked Daisy, her eyes full of concern and confusion.

Gerald shuffled awkwardly, shifting his weight as he tried to find a foothold on the conversation. 'Well, no . . . of course not.'

'Well, that's wonderful,' smiled Daisy. 'I'm so glad it's all settled. Your hesitation does you credit, Gerald – most people would bite my arm off for a free holiday without giving it a second thought. I truly appreciate it.'

Gerald looked confused, as if he couldn't work out how the conversation had got away from him. 'Well, obviously, when you put it like that.' He paused for a moment. 'Of course, I'll need to track down their passports. I have no idea if they're still in date so that might be a small problem.'

'No need,' Daisy smiled. 'Melanie has already given them to me. There's so little time to organise everything. I must thank you, Gerald, my daughter will be so thrilled. You're a good man.' Daisy gave him her most dazzling, magazine cover-grade smile and hurried away through the churchyard before he could say anything else. She really should consider a new career in trade negotiations or peacekeeping. Maybe the United Nations would have her when the TV gods finally threw her on the scrapheap.

Daisy plugged her debit card details into the Swissair website and held her breath as the payment portal stuck for a few seconds, then finally flashed up a confirmation message. She let the air out slowly, then picked up a pen and ticked 'flights' off the list in front of her. There were a few other things to do, but that was the most important. The seats for Will and Melanie had cost twice what she'd paid for her and Ruby, but if Ruby was happy, especially when everything else was still so messy, it was worth it.

Her phone began to ring. Katie. Daisy swiped the screen to answer it, putting Katie on speakerphone.

'I spoke to Benny and confirmed everything,' Katie mumbled, her mouth full of something, reminding Daisy it was lunchtime. She ambled across to the kitchen and opened the fridge.

'How was it?' she asked, perusing its meagre contents.

'I feel like I need a shower. He's gross.'

'You've met him before, though.'

'Yeah,' said Katie. 'He's great at what he does, but he'd sell his children if it meant bagging one of his clients a slot on *Dancing on Ice*.'

'Does he even have any children?'

'No idea. Hard to imagine anyone in their right mind agreeing to have sex with him. Hang on.'

Daisy heard a drawer being opened, then closed. 'What are you doing?'

'Hand sanitizer. Talking about Benny gives me the ick.'

Daisy burst out laughing. 'So what did he say?' She put the phone on the counter as she fished a tub of yoghurt out of the fridge and grabbed a spoon from the drawer. There was only an inch left in the bottom – she sniffed it, then dug in. It tasted fine.

'—He was surprised, obviously. Don't think he expected

135

us to agree not to announce you and Christian had split up—'

'I bet.'

'—agreed on a statement, basically saying that you're both busy working on separate projects right now but are still very much a couple, blah-blah-blah.'

'Great. Thank you.' Daisy could feel the tension easing from her shoulders.

'I also made it very clear that you haven't changed your mind about Christian, but you didn't want or need the press attention right now. Then I reminded him that you wouldn't hesitate to drop Christian in the shit, if he messed up again and brought the press on you.'

'You are fierce, and I love you. Anything else?'

'Benny asked if we could change the wording to "Christian and Daisy", and I told him to go fuck himself.' Daisy could hear the glee in Katie's voice.

'Ha.' She rinsed the yoghurt pot under the tap and dropped it in the recycling bin. 'Anything in the press today?'

'Only one thing I wanted to flag up. Hang on,' said Katie. Daisy could hear her tapping around on her laptop.

'Here it is. It's from the showbiz page of the *Sun*, with the headline "*Daisy's dodgy country chums – TV star gets cosy with tax cheat chef and sex scandal MP*".'

'Christ, they *are* desperate.'

'It's nothing, just raking over the Gerald Forbes-Glover sex scandal and Justin Drummond's tax avoidance. Basically, it implies you have sex pests and criminals for neighbours.'

Daisy shrugged. 'Doesn't everyone?'

'Quite. I wouldn't have bothered mentioning it, but it got me thinking. No tabloid hack is wasting time doing a deep-dive into the C-list residents of whatever rural shithole you're living in. It wouldn't be worth the effort. It's much more likely that the tip-offs are coming from inside the village, presumably so somebody can make a few quid.'

'You think?' said Daisy doubtfully.

'Yeah, I do. First the headmaster, now these two. Right now, it's all fairly innocuous stuff, but these things can snowball. Have a think about who it might be. Would be good to nip it in the bud by the time you get back from skiing, if it carries on.'

'OK,' said Daisy. 'Although you should probably know that Gerald Forbes-Glover's wife and son are coming with us.'

'What the fuck?' Katie gasped. Daisy could just imagine her smacking her forehead in disbelief.

She chuckled. 'Buckle up, my friend. *This* is a really good story.'

CHAPTER EIGHTEEN

Daisy and Melanie were waiting by the gate to the rectory when Will loped out of the front door, huge headphones clamped to his head, backpack falling off one shoulder and his eyes firmly on his school shoes. It was the last day of term, and they'd decided now was the best time to tell him about the trip, away from Gerald so he didn't have to worry about any negative reaction.

Will didn't notice them until he looked up to open the gate and discovered a Two Mum Ambush.

'What is it?' he asked fearfully, yanking off the headphones. It sounded like Stormzy to Daisy, and she briefly wondered how impressed Will would be if she told him he was a good friend of Christian's, or that she'd recently watched him perform from the side of the stage at a gig in London, then partied half the night with him and his crew. Probably not very impressed at all, if Ruby was anything to go by.

'Nothing bad has happened, I promise,' said Melanie calmly, making Daisy wonder how many times she'd had to be the bearer of bad news. 'We've got something to tell you.'

Will looked from his mother to Daisy and back again. 'Is Ruby OK?' he asked suspiciously.

Daisy laughed. 'Ruby's fine! She'll be here this afternoon. Oh, and Justin is having a pig roast tonight at the headmaster's house, and you're both invited. And your dad, obviously.'

'Prue or Nigella?' asked Will.

'Prue,' said Daisy. 'Nigella's been liberated.'

Melanie looked confused, then slightly overwhelmed. 'Goodness! I don't really know Justin at all. We've really only met in passing. Why am I invited?'

'Because I asked him to,' said Daisy. 'So we can make plans.' She looked at Will. 'Do you want to tell him, or shall I?'

Melanie clapped her hands happily. 'You tell him.'

Daisy turned to Will. 'Skiing. You. Ruby. Me. Your mum. Austria. We're going tomorrow. For a week.'

Will's mouth opened then closed a few times, like a goldfish. He dropped his rucksack on the path. 'Are you fucking serious?' He turned to his mum with a blush. 'Sorry, Mum, my bad . . . What do you mean? Why? How?'

Daisy shrugged. 'Tomorrow is Ruby's sixteenth birthday, and that's what she wants for her present.'

Will said nothing as this information slowly sank in. Then his face broke into the biggest smile Daisy had ever seen.

In the afternoon Daisy drove over to Milton Park to pick up Ruby, piling her bags into the car as her friends waved them off and took sneaky photos of Daisy with their phones. On the way home, Daisy filled her daughter in on the itinerary for skiing and felt gratified by Ruby's childlike excitement. It had been a headache of a week, but already it was feeling like it had been totally worth it. Everything was organised – the flight tickets and insurance details were printed off with the help of Tom's secretary, Angela, and she'd upgraded the airport transfer taxi to a people carrier. She'd also emailed the housekeeper in the resort, asking her to make up four of the six bedrooms and attaching a list of groceries that would see them through the first day or two.

Vergallen was small, friendly and quintessentially Austrian, and they'd been going there for years, but any suggestion Daisy made about going somewhere new was always brushed off by Ruby, who liked the nostalgia and familiarity, as well as the luxury, of somewhere known and loved. Perhaps, Daisy realised now, because there was so much chaos in their lives otherwise. She tried not to feel guilty, but hopefully with Christian out of their lives that would change. Ruby would definitely be turning cartwheels when she heard.

'What are we doing this evening?' Ruby asked as Daisy turned the car onto the narrow road to Shipton Combe.

'Well, I hadn't planned anything really, since we're going away tomorrow. But if you fancy it, we've been invited to a gathering.'

Ruby looked dubious. 'What kind of gathering?'

'It's called a Pig in a Blanket – it's in the garden of the headmaster's house.' Daisy grinned at Ruby's confused expression. 'Justin next door is roasting half a pig. We've been invited to help him eat it, and drink some of his home-made cider.'

Ruby scrunched up her nose. 'Hmm, doesn't really sound like my kind of thing. Also didn't you say the headmaster was an absolute knob?'

Daisy laughed. 'He's grown on me considerably – and Justin's good fun. Also your granny will be there, and I'm sure she'd love to see you before we go away.' Ruby nodded, although she still didn't look keen. Daisy added casually, 'Oh, Will is coming. Don't know if that makes any difference.'

Ruby's face lit up, then blushed a deep red. 'Oh. Well. OK.'

Daisy huddled on one side of Tom's patio with Stella, clutching a glass of cider in her mittened hands. It was lethal stuff, and much as she was enjoying its warming qualities, she had to drive to the airport at 5 a.m., so one glass was definitely enough. Stella, on the other hand, was probably three glasses in.

'I'm just saying that it would have been nice to be invited,' griped Stella.

Daisy focused on her yogic breathing. 'Are you saying you want to come skiing? Because there's still time.' There wasn't time at all, but she was banking on Stella not remembering this conversation in the morning.

Stella shook her head vehemently, the pompoms on her rainbow-striped hat flapping madly. 'Good lord, no! Can't think of anything worse. I'd just like to know that I was welcome if I DID want to come.'

'Honestly, Mum, if I thought it was your thing, I'd invite you in a heartbeat.' Daisy smiled brightly, safe in the knowledge that any lies told at this point would not come back to haunt her. 'Ruby would *love* to have you there. But you hate flying, don't ski and can't stand being cold. So, I just assumed it wasn't your bag.'

Stella squeezed Daisy's arm, her scarlet nails poking out of fingerless gloves knitted in an alarming shade of yellow. 'Thank you, Daisy. It's absolutely *not* my bag, but it's lovely to know I have the option.' Stella beamed. 'I'll stay here and drink tea with the vicar,' she took another slurp of cider, 'and keep an eye on Justin. I helped him butcher Prue yesterday. It was actually rather fascinating.'

Daisy contemplated the horror of Stella in charge of a bone saw, then gasped as she had a flash of inspiration. 'Why don't you move into Willow Cottage while I'm away? It's nicer than the pub and you'll be next door to Justin. You can look after each other.' *Drink each other to death, more like.*

Stella's face lit up, her cheeks rosy with cold, or more likely cider. 'Oh! That would be lovely. Thank you. You're a good girl.'

Daisy smiled, making a mental note to hide her vibrator somewhere less obvious than her underwear drawer. She glanced up and saw Tom watching her from the other side of the patio. He glanced away immediately, but not before she'd clocked the heat in his stare. She filed that away for later.

As Stella drifted off to talk to the vicar, who had found out from Stella about the Pig in a Blanket and somehow invited herself in a way that only vicars could, Justin circumnavigated Prue crackling away over a half-barrel of coals and sidled over to Daisy.

'I hear you're helping Bitter Lemony break out of the village,' he smirked. 'Good for you. God knows that poor woman needs a holiday from Dreadful Gerald.'

Daisy glanced up to check Melanie and Dreadful Gerald couldn't hear them. They were by the hedge chatting to Marcus, who was demonstrating a slow-motion forehand with a pair of barbecue tongs.

'She's actually a lovely woman,' Daisy objected, 'and not nearly as bitter as others might be in her shoes.'

Justin looked suitably chastened. 'Well, you've certainly stirred things up in Shipton Combe. I think it's brilliant.'

'What you do mean?' asked Daisy.

'You've just given people something to talk about,' replied Justin gleefully. 'The gossip about you and Tom, your mother helicoptering in like the SAS, you hanging out with Melanie. People are even yakking about me for the first time in yonks. I'm actually kind of enjoying it.' He gave a barking laugh and took another swig of cider.

Daisy sighed. 'That wasn't my intention. I just wanted somewhere peaceful to hide out and write a book.'

'No sign of Mr Love Match, then.'

Daisy glared at Justin. 'Is that pig ready yet? I'm starving.'

Justin took the hint and wandered off to check, leaving Daisy looking thoughtfully at the group huddled around the fire, their vapour clouds of breath mingling with the smoke. This village was the kind of place where everyone knew everyone else's business, and it was reasonable to assume she was one of the main topics of local conversation. But would someone here really sell gossip about her to the tabloids?

There was Stella, of course. She was inevitably a prime suspect, because she'd done it so many times before. But she seemed more mellow here, almost as if she were trying to mend fences – and she spent most of her time these days hanging around with Justin and the vicar. But then again Stella was an inveterate gossip so nothing about Daisy's life was probably secret, on which basis none of the villagers could be entirely discounted. She ran through them in her head, her thoughts and eyes drawn back to Tom. Could it be him? She immediately dismissed the idea. With everything that was going on with Christian right now, Daisy needed to believe that Tom was the real deal, and that there was at least one hot man left in the world who was decent and kind.

'Did you look Vergallen up?' Ruby asked Will as Daisy drifted over. The teenagers were huddled together in a dark corner by the house, sharing a mug of hot cider and distancing themselves from the boring adults and the smoke from the barbecue.

'Yeah,' said Will, glancing shyly at Daisy. 'It looks really nice.'

Ruby jiggled up and down excitedly. 'It's gorgeous, and the chalet is amazing. It's not ours; it belongs to my godfather, Des Parker.' She glanced at Will to see if he was impressed by the clanging name drop, but he kept his cool. 'It's got a big open fire and a hot tub outside,' she continued. 'You can sit out there in the snow.'

Daisy spotted a flicker of anxiety in Will's eyes and realised how glad she was that Melanie was coming. Partly so she didn't have to take on the pressure of supporting two teenagers who were navigating the choppy waters of a first relationship, but also so she'd have some company.

'I don't think my dad is very happy about Mum coming,' Will commented.

'She seems pretty happy about it though,' said Ruby with a smirk, glancing over at Melanie. Daisy looked too – Melanie and Gerald were still chatting with Marcus, Gerald's leather-gloved hand resting on his wife's back.

'Hmm,' said Will, his brow furrowed. 'He's being really nice to her at the moment – maybe he thinks she's going to run off with a ski instructor or something.' He laughed at the ridiculousness of the idea, but Daisy didn't think he was that far off the mark. Gerald wouldn't be the first man to be a bit nicer to his wife when he realised she was about to spread her wings.

'Did you ask your mum about snowboarding?' said Will.

'Oh yeah,' said Ruby. 'Mum, can I have snowboarding lessons this year?'

Daisy looked baffled. 'Why would you want to learn to snowboard?' she asked. 'You're a brilliant skier.'

'Because Will wants to snowboard, and I've never done it,' Ruby replied. 'We can do the beginners' class together. Otherwise, I won't see him all day.'

Daisy shrugged in agreement. 'Sure, if you like.' Ruby mumbled her thanks through a mouthful of pork, then dragged Will off to a wooden bench by the garden wall.

'Young love,' muttered Justin, passing a plate to Daisy. 'I hope it's worth it.' His eyes narrowed shrewdly. 'Must be costing a pretty penny.'

'Don't ask,' Daisy said glumly, mentally adding snowboarding lessons and equipment for Ruby to an ever-growing shopping list. 'Let's just say writing the book has gone from a distraction to a necessity.'

'Tell me about it,' muttered Justin, sinking his teeth into a pork roll.

CHAPTER NINETEEN

On the other side of the patio, Tom caught snatches of Daisy's conversation about skiing and felt a familiar jolt of pain. He remembered the excitement of a winter holiday – he and Tessa had gone skiing for the first time the year after they got married, and once Tom started working at Shipton House they'd joined the Year 9 and 10 ski trip at Easter every year. But he hadn't been since Tessa died, and the idea of skiing without her made him want to hurl himself off the side of a mountain.

He caught Daisy's eye and she smiled, so he smiled back because it felt like the right thing to do, since smiling was what normal people did. As she weaved around the increasingly charred pig and picked her way towards him, he was forced to admit to something he'd been in denial about since they'd shared a flask of coffee in the car park of Mark's slaughterhouse. He was falling for Daisy. Not because she looked like Tessa or anything weird like that, but because she was kind and beautiful and funny and she made him feel like he was seventeen again.

In some respects this felt quite cheering, because it confirmed that he wasn't entirely dead inside and could one day hope to be stirred by a woman again. But it was also distinctly inconvenient, because women like Daisy didn't fall for men like Tom. As she stopped in front of him, he resisted the urge to tuck away the curls escaping from her red bobble hat, instead burying his hands in the pockets of his jacket.

'Hey.' Daisy bent down to pat Henry on the head. The dog looked at her dolefully, clearly torn between a warm bed indoors and the prospect of meaty snacks outside. 'Any plans for Christmas?'

Tom tried to hold her gaze, and wondered what she'd say about the dream he'd had last night, involving spectacular sex amid the piles of school reports on his office desk, Daisy's breasts jiggling in Tom's face as she rode him to a sweaty, vocal climax. *Probably best not to mention it.*

'Probably just a quiet one,' he forced out, wondering if he'd bother putting up any decorations this year. It was only ten days off, probably not worth it. 'Er . . . I've had some more thoughts about the recipe testing, if you'd still like to do it.'

'Absolutely,' Daisy nodded happily. 'When can we start?'

Tom thought for a second. 'I'll need to get permission from the parents over the holiday, so realistically it would be the first couple of weeks back in January. Are you still going to be here then?'

'Yes, I think so. I've got nothing to rush back to London for, and here is a good place to finish the book. And it's so close to Ruby.'

Tom noted the *nothing to rush back for* with a brief frisson of joy. Perhaps Christian was history after all? Although the gossip sites his secretary had been avidly pretending not to read at work suggested they were still very much a couple.

'Are you looking forward to skiing?' Tom wished he sounded less like a dreary teacher.

'Sure,' said Daisy. 'It'll be a bit different this year, with

Melanie and Will coming. But I'm sure we'll have a good time.'

'Is your fiancé going?' Tom asked casually.

'No,' said Daisy quickly. 'He's not.' *That's good news*, thought Tom, although he noted that she didn't correct him on Christian being her fiancé. *She gives, and then she takes away.*

The party broke up around 10.30 p.m., when the snow turned to sleet, then rain. Gerald and Melanie had left half an hour earlier, and Tom noticed Will and Ruby make a swift exit, presumably so they could say their snog-based goodbyes outside Willow Cottage before Daisy got back. Stella and Miriam gathered up all the remaining food and helped Justin and Marcus carry it to Beech Cottage for Justin to turn into increasingly depressing meals over the coming days. Which just left Daisy helping Tom clear up all the plates and glasses and cutlery, then shuttling it into the kitchen so Tom could load the dishwasher.

As he slammed the door shut and pressed start, he turned to face Daisy, realising she was much closer than he'd realised. The only light came from the spotlight above the cooker and the patio bulb shining in through the French doors, which cast dramatic shadows over her face, making her look more beautiful than ever. In that moment, he wondered how he had ever thought she looked like Tessa, when she was so uniquely, gloriously Daisy. He had an overpowering urge to kiss her, and there was something in her eyes that suggested she might not mind.

'Is that everything?' he forced himself to ask, his voice sounding too loud in the muffled silence of the kitchen.

Daisy looked confused. 'I'm sorry?'

'Clearing up,' he nodded outside. 'Is there anything else we need to do?'

'Just this.' Daisy leaned in to kiss him, her lips gentle on his. He resisted for the barest second as his brain tried to process whether the thing he'd just been imagining in his head was really happening. But the warmth of Daisy's lips on his was undeniably real, so he gathered her into his body and let his tongue tentatively touch hers. She tasted of cider and crackling and woodsmoke, and he allowed himself to surrender to chaotic desire for a few heady seconds before she pulled back.

'Oh Christ, I'm so sorry!' she said, holding her hand over her mouth.

Tom gave a short laugh, his eyes wide and his heart thumping. 'Why are you sorry? I'm not.'

'That seemed like such a good idea in the moment, but it wasn't.' Daisy stepped away, grabbing her coat from the hook by the door. 'My life is a shitshow, you really don't want to be anywhere near it.'

'Hey,' said Tom gently, walking over to her, his hands stilling hers as she fumbled to wrestle her arms in. 'You think my life isn't a shitshow? And forgive me, but you don't seem like the kind of person who just randomly kisses people.'

Daisy blushed. 'No, I'm really not. You just looked very . . . kissable. But things are a bit complicated right now, and I need to sort some stuff out before I decide whether I should be kissing anyone. I'm so sorry.'

Tom nodded thoughtfully. 'Hmm. Do you think we should do it one more time, just so you can make a more evidence-based decision?' He stared deep into Daisy's eyes and stroked the back of her hand with his thumb. It felt like a once-in-a-lifetime moment.

'Oh God. This is *SUCH* a bad idea,' breathed Daisy. 'But fuck it.' She grabbed handfuls of his jumper and pressed herself into his body, letting him relish the softness of her lips and the smell of her perfume.

She felt safe and warm and heavenly, but Tom resisted the urge to roam his hands all over her body, instead burying one hand in her hair and trailing the other down the curve of her neck. They kissed like teenagers for a long minute, Daisy's hips pressed so hard against his that he wondered if his erection might ever subside. Finally, she pulled away, then rested her head on his shoulder as he wrapped his arms around her, wishing he could freeze this moment forever.

'I need to go,' she whispered. 'Ruby will be wondering where I am.'

'OK. Can I walk you home?'

Daisy straightened up and gave him a playful look. 'Yes. But only if you promise not to make me kiss you again.'

Tom slowly zipped up her coat, which felt oddly sexy even if the zip was going in the wrong direction. 'You drive a very hard bargain . . . but OK.'

PART THREE

PART THREE

CHAPTER TWENTY

'How are you feeling?' Daisy smiled at Melanie, who was sitting next to her in the back of the people carrier. In the second row, Ruby chattered away excitedly as tiny clusters of festive alpine cottages flew by against a backdrop of rolling foothills.

'I'm a bit overwhelmed, if I'm honest,' Melanie admitted shyly. 'Your life is mad.'

Daisy laughed. 'Which bit?'

'All of it. The way people were asking for photos at the airport and on the plane, it must feel so weird.'

'For me that's pretty normal,' Daisy shrugged. 'It's been like that since I was a teenager. You definitely get used to it. Well, mostly.' She thought about the Vultures who'd driven her out of London. 'Most people are lovely, so I don't really mind.'

'I still can't believe I'm here,' said Melanie. Daisy could hear the excitement in her voice, and felt her confidence growing that this was the right decision.

'What's Gerald planning to do while you're away?'

'Keep himself busy,' said Melanie with a smile. 'He got up at four this morning just to make me and Will a coffee.' She glanced behind to check Will wasn't listening, but he and Ruby were now wearing an AirPod each, listening to all the birthday messages her friends had sent her. 'He's been lovely for the past few days.'

Of course he has. Gerald had clearly realised what he might lose. Christian had been like that whenever she'd been annoyed with him, instantly turning on the charm like it was all just a game. An image of Tom came to mind, and how sweet he'd been when they'd finally said goodbye last night. Perhaps not all men were like that.

'He gave me some money.' Melanie reached into her handbag for an envelope. 'To cover our food and drinks for the week. It's five hundred Euros. I hope you'll take it.'

Daisy hesitated for a second, meeting Melanie's gaze. She could see how important this gesture was to her, and how disrespectful it would be to refuse. Melanie was asking to be treated like an equal, not a charity case.

'Thank you,' said Daisy, taking the envelope and sliding it into her bag. 'It's not necessary, but very much appreciated.'

Melanie nodded. 'Talking of your fans in the airport, well done on not giving that guy a kick.'

'Which one?' asked Daisy.

'The one who said he didn't recognise you with your legs closed. I thought his wife was going to kill him.'

Daisy snorted with laughter. 'They'll dine out on that story all holiday. One of the things I love about Vergallen is that nobody has a clue who I am. We'll just be two mums taking our teenagers on a Christmas holiday. I can't wait.'

Melanie looked pleased, and Daisy felt gratified that she'd been able to say it and not feel disingenuous – after her initial reservations about going away with a woman she barely knew, she was now looking forward to it. There was something about Melanie that intrigued Daisy – every so often there was a glimmer of a twinkle in her eye that suggested hidden depths. Like she'd locked away all her joy years ago, and just needed a chance to let it all out.

It was pouring with rain by the time the taxi turned onto the narrow mountain road to Vergallen. Daisy could see Melanie taking deep breaths to stop feeling car sick, wiping her clammy hands on her too big, unfashionable jeans as the car swung round the hairpin bends at high speed. Fifteen minutes later their ears had popped and they were driving through a thick whirlwind of flakes in a snow-covered pine forest, like something from a Christmas card. As a cluster of fairy-lit chalets and the onion dome of Vergallen church came into view, they all craned their necks to watch the cable car disappearing through the trees and up the mountain like a chain of glass bubbles. Finally, they had arrived.

Daisy gasped as she climbed out of the taxi; she always forgot how cold ten degrees below zero felt, particularly in the thin air of the mountains. They were all still in their travelling clothes of jeans and trainers, and she couldn't wait to get everyone kitted out with thermals and fur-lined boots.

'Everyone grab a bag!' she cried happily. 'Let's get inside in the warm.'

The chalet was just as she remembered it – a stone-tiled boot room that led into a huge open plan space with pine panelled walls, soft rugs, heavy red curtains and an enormous open fireplace that was already laid with logs and pinecones, waiting for someone to strike a match and fall into the horseshoe of squashy cream sofas, scattered with colourful blankets and cushions. On the far side of the room was a sleek modern kitchen with an oak dining table that seated twelve and a breakfast bar lined with wooden stools. Daisy walked over to peek in the fridge – it was already filled with the groceries she had ordered, and the wine was perfectly chilled. Des's housekeeper had draped festive garlands on the banisters and over the fireplace, and a Christmas tree festooned with delicate glass ornaments and warm white lights twinkled in the corner of the room. It was perfect.

On the first floor were two en-suite bedrooms which she and Melanie were taking, and two further double bedrooms for Will and Ruby with a shared bathroom. All the beds were made up with fluffy duvets, huge pillows and soft white bedlinen, and after such an early start Daisy was tempted to keel sideways into the feathery nest and take a nap.

'It's so beautiful.' Melanie's eyes were on stalks as she looked at the dramatic vista of snow-capped mountains from her bedroom window. 'It's like something out of a movie. Does this place really belong to Des Parker?'

'Yes,' Daisy nodded. 'He took me under his wing when I started out in TV as a teenager; I was about the same age as Ruby. He's the closest thing to a father I've ever had and he's Ruby's godfather. We've had this week booked since she was a toddler.' She grabbed Melanie's arm, steering her back towards the stars. 'Come on, let's go and have some tea. And I'll find us all some warm stuff to wear, then we can go outside.'

Will carried all the bags to their bedrooms while Melanie lit the fire and made tea for everyone, using the box of Yorkshire teabags Daisy had brought with her. Austria was good at many things, but a decent cup of tea wasn't one of them. Ruby and Daisy headed back upstairs to raid the racks of ski clothes, which were stored in a wardrobe in the master bedroom. There were two decades' worth of ski jackets, trousers, thermal layers and ski accessories. A sign stuck to the inside of the door read:

> **Three rules for the ski gear store:**
> *1) Wash, dry and put away whatever you use before you go home OR leave it in a pile for the housekeeper and she'll wash it for you. Please leave cash – two Euros per item.*
> *2) Add your outgrown/unwanted stuff to the collection – all decent quality ski wear welcome.*
> *3) Feel free to recycle anything that is damaged or worn beyond repair, or so embarrassingly unfashionable that the locals will openly laugh in your face.*

They grabbed armfuls of hangers and carried them downstairs, draping everything over the back of the sofa. It all smelled a bit fusty, but nobody would notice once they were outside in the fresh air.

'What size are you, Melanie?' Daisy was rooting through a pile of women's ski jackets and trousers.

'I'm not sure,' Melanie frowned. 'An eight, I suppose, maybe a ten? Long in the leg, though.'

This quietly confirmed Daisy's suspicion that Melanie had a killer body under all that shapeless frumpwear. She pulled out some turquoise and white trousers with a fitted matching jacket. 'Here, try these.'

Will chose some black trousers and a red jacket, until Ruby told him that the instructors wore red jackets and he swapped it for a burnt orange one instead. Ruby picked out the same hot pink outfit she'd worn last year, and Daisy went for black with a red trim.

157

'What do you think?' asked Melanie, padding down the wooden stairs in a ski suit that hugged her body and showed off a figure that hadn't been seen in public since Tony Blair was Prime Minister.

'Wow, Mum.' Will walked forward slowly, his eyes wide at the sight of a version of his mother he'd never seen before. 'You look great.' Melanie beamed, as Daisy nodded in agreement.

'That really suits you. Have a rummage in the big cupboard in the boot room, you'll find loads of snow boots and socks and hats. Gloves and goggles too. Ruby, go and help.'

By five, everyone was kitted out for the week and the sun had started to sink behind the mountains. Ruby and Will decided to go and sort out their snowboarding gear and sign themselves up for classes, offering to book Melanie into the beginners' ski class while they were there. Melanie looked at Daisy, her face anxious. 'Are you sure it's OK? This hasn't cost you a lot of money?'

'It really hasn't,' lied Daisy. 'Our friends had already booked classes, you're just using up the space they had already paid for.' Daisy glanced at Ruby, who surreptitiously raised her eyebrows. No doubt she was wondering who the imaginary friends were, but she didn't say anything.

'OK then,' Melanie smiled, looking visibly relieved. 'Well, yes please to beginners' lessons. It seems a shame to come all this way and not learn to ski.' She looked relaxed and startlingly pretty, like swapping the rectory for the mountains and her usual clothes for ones that fit had ironed out the tension in her face.

Ruby slid Daisy's debit card out of her purse with practised ease. 'We'll get lift passes for everyone too. See you later.' She grabbed Will's hand, dragging him out of the door.

'Be back by seven for dinner,' called Daisy. She and Melanie smiled fondly at their happy children, then looked at each other and grinned.

'Glass of wine before we unpack?' said Daisy, and Melanie nodded.

'So you turned forty last month?' Daisy tossed the empty bottle of Grüner Veltliner into the recycling, unscrewing the cap on another.

'Mmm,' said Melanie, draining her glass and holding it out for a refill. 'I confess to having sneaked a look online, so I know yours is next month.'

'So we'd have been in the same school year.'

'I guess we would. You went to stage school though, right?'

Daisy nodded, flumping down in the corner of the sofa and dropping the bottle into the ice bucket. 'Yes, in London. What about you?'

'A Catholic girls' school in Suffolk,' said Melanie. 'It's where I grew up. I was a last-chance baby, the final one of four. I've got three brothers but I never see them. They're all a lot older than me.'

'And your parents?'

'Both gone. Dad in 2010 after a stroke, Mum two years later, ovarian cancer.'

'I'm sorry,' said Daisy. Even though Stella often drove her to despair, she was glad she and Ruby had her.

'Thanks. They were both quick, so I guess that's a blessing.' She smiled a tad bitterly, raised her glass, took a swig. 'There was a bit of money, but they left it all to my brothers.'

'Ouch,' said Daisy. There was a story there – perhaps they hadn't approved of Gerald, or perhaps they were just the kind of people who didn't think girls were worth very much.

'What about you?' asked Melanie. 'Is your dad still alive?'

Daisy hesitated. The story of her father wasn't in the public domain – she and Stella never talked about him to the press, mostly because they didn't know much, but also because neither of them wanted him to be tracked down. He'd been a whirlwind romance who wandered into the *Waste Not, Want Not* café where Stella lived and worked in the spring of 1978, then wandered out again a few days later and was never seen again. All Stella knew was that his name was Karl and he was a German Erasmus student. By the time she realised she was pregnant, it was too late to do anything about it. So Stella went it alone with the help of friends and extended family, and Daisy learnt early on never to mention him. Three glasses of wine down was definitely not the time to start.

'I have no idea,' she said vaguely. 'We're not in touch. But what about you? What made you leave Suffolk?'

Melanie took the hint and moved on. 'I moved out as soon as I finished my A levels, couldn't wait to escape. I lived in a shared house in Battersea with four other girls while I trained as a secretary.'

'That sounds kind of fun.'

'It was, actually,' said Melanie wistfully. 'Five penniless girls sharing a house full of wet laundry, empty vodka bottles and a trail of worthless boyfriends.'

'I'm actually jealous.'

Melanie laughed. 'It was fun. I moved out after a year and lived with my boyfriend for a while.'

'Then what?' Daisy topped up Melanie's glass.

'Then I met Gerald.'

Daisy's phone buzzed on the kitchen counter. 'You can tell me about that later,' she said, standing up to fetch it only to realise she wasn't entirely stable on her feet.

'We really should think about some food.'

CHAPTER TWENTY-ONE

In the headmaster's house in Shipton Combe, Tom sat in front of the wood burner and gently scratched between Henry's ears. He'd been unable to get Daisy out of his head all day, wondering how she felt about what had happened in his kitchen last night. Did she regret the kissing and plan to head straight back to London after her holiday in a flurry of embarrassment, or was she also imagining a time in the future when they might do it again, but naked? Tom was definitely focusing on the naked stuff, even though he was well aware that any relationship between them was a no-no. Daisy was TV Presenter of the Year and queen of London's red carpet, despite the wardrobe debacle at the NTAs. She was also engaged to an extremely handsome sporting hero, whereas Tom was a messed-up headmaster of a struggling independent school in the arse end of nowhere. Very much not a match made in heaven. But those kisses had definitely meant something. He knew they did.

My God, thought Tom grinning. *I kissed Daisy Crawford.* No, not Daisy Crawford. He'd kissed *Daisy*. She wasn't the glamorous TV personality; she was the funny, gorgeous woman who was happy being in his kitchen in no makeup and a red bobble hat and mittens. They felt like two very different people, somehow.

He picked up his phone and tapped out a WhatsApp.

Hope you had a good trip. Been thinking about you today.

He stared at it for a while, then deleted it, then typed it again.

Hope your trip was good. Kitchen feels empty today.

The second version felt less needy, more like a secret joke between them that nobody else would understand. He took a deep breath and pressed send, then stared at the two grey ticks for a full minute until they turned blue. Dots appeared, indicating that Daisy was replying.

Here safely. Melanie and I have accidentally got
drunk. Kitchen here entirely open plan, no good at all

Tom smiled and felt a liquid warmth in the pit of his stomach. It was enough to keep him going for now, and he didn't want to be the kind of person who messaged incessantly and made her feel under pressure to reply. He typed another message.

Have a good week, see you when you get back

Will do. Can you maybe check in on Gerald at some point?
Reassure him that his wife and son are in safe hands?

I'm having dinner with Justin and Marcus later,
I'll pop over first

You are lovely, thanks x

'Hot', 'irresistible', 'my idea of a perfect man' – all of those would have been preferable. But in the absence of those, 'lovely' would definitely do.

Tom found Gerald in the freezing cold rectory, halfway through a shepherd's pie that Melanie had left in the fridge. She'd left cooking instructions sellotaped to the door, along with details for all the other meals she'd made that were currently in the freezer. How long to defrost, which oven of the AGA to put it in, how long to leave it for. He offered Tom a glass of wine, then waved at him to sit down at the kitchen table.

'Melanie's made sure I won't starve,' he said with a grim laugh.

'Cooking not your thing?' Tom looked about him, wondering, not for the first time, how anybody could ever relax in a house that was so cold you could see your breath. No wonder Will did his homework in the pub.

'I genuinely don't think I've ever cooked a meal in my life,' replied Gerald, like this was some kind of stellar achievement. 'I went from Winchester to Cambridge then back to my mother's house in Surrey, and they all kept me fed and watered until I met and married my first wife. Melanie is a much better cook than Felicity ever was.'

'Well, I just wanted to check in,' said Tom. 'Let you know I'm always happy to keep you company while Melanie and Will are away.'

Gerald looked at Tom thoughtfully, like he was seeing him for the first time. 'It does feel a little lonely, I suppose. Not what one is used to, I keep expecting them to wander in.' He glanced at Tom, his cheeks reddening. 'I'm sorry. I suppose being alone is something you'd know about.'

Tom gave a sad smile. 'It's definitely one of my fields of expertise.'

'Except in my case, they're coming back.' He poked the shepherd's pie dolefully. 'Well, at least I hope so.'

'Was that ever in any doubt?'

'My dear Tom,' said Gerald, his face bleak. 'Currently British television's most shining star is showing my wife and son the high life. I don't think that's ever going to be good news for me, do you?'

Tom leaned forward and looked at Gerald intently, wishing he could shake him by the shoulders and make him realise how lucky he was. 'They're your family, Gerald,' he said. 'Melanie has stood by you through . . . everything.' All he knew about Gerald's transgressions was what he'd read in the papers, but he suspected that wasn't the half of it.

'I suppose that's true.' Gerald stood up and put the half-eaten food container into the fridge.

'They'll be home in a week, and you have a choice. You can spend this week feeling miserable and bitter about them being away, or you can decide how to welcome them home.' Tom felt his voice catch, thinking about all the things he'd have said to Tessa if she'd come home for just one more hour.

Gerald rubbed his hand across his jaw, then reached out to shake Tom's hand. 'You're a good man, Tom. I know it was our wives who were friends, really, but I've always respected you. And Will does, too.'

Tom patted him on the shoulder in what he hoped was a

show of manly solidarity. 'Come and have dinner with me next week.'

'I'd love to,' said Gerald. 'Shall I bring two of Melanie's meals?'

Tom laughed. 'Sounds like a plan.'

'I forgot to bring salt,' said Marcus, poking his fork glumly into Justin's pork and vegetable stew. 'Tom, did you bring any?'

Tom shook his head and sipped his glass of mead, his head still full of his messages from Daisy, his conversation with Gerald and thoughts of Tessa. It felt all jumbled together somehow, like a tangle of sheets in a tumble dryer.

'Schoolboy error,' Justin grinned at them both. 'Sorry it tastes like shit.'

'It's fine.' Marcus stabbed a carrot. 'I'm trying to imagine the flavour.' He chewed, his eyes squeezed tightly shut.

'You're a twat,' said Justin genially, 'and you're welcome to fuck off and eat elsewhere.'

Marcus snorted with laughter. 'You'd miss my company and my sparkling conversation,' he said. 'Or have I been replaced by Stella Crawford?'

'Hardly,' said Justin. 'My relationship with Stella is purely professional, but I still hold out hope that one of you two might fall for my many charms.' Justin winked at them both playfully.

Tom shook his head and rolled his eyes. 'I love you, man, but I'm afraid you're not my type. Also you're a bloody terrible cook.'

'You wait,' said Justin. 'When I'm back in London I'm going to cook you an epic dinner. The full works. You'll both be in my bed before dessert, begging for my dick as an *amuse bouche*.'

Marcus put down his fork, apparently no longer hungry. 'It's never going to happen, my friend. I'm a woman's man through and through.'

Justin huffed, looking dubious. 'Hmm, if you say so. What's so great about women?'

'Women are magnificent.' Marcus's eyes glazed over as he revisited the parade of women he'd bedded over the years. 'Take Daisy, for example. She's rich. She's famous. She's got a body to die for. You'd take her home to meet your parents, then fuck her on the sofa as soon as they left for church.'

Tom clenched his fists and took deep breaths, reminding himself that Marcus was nothing but hot air and testosterone. The easiest way to kill this conversation dead would be to tell them what had happened in his kitchen last night, but that definitely wasn't happening.

Justin raised his eyebrows at Marcus. 'I don't know much about women, but I'm pretty sure she doesn't fancy you, mate.'

Marcus sighed and folded his arms, looking first at Tom, then at Justin. 'She's definitely a challenge. I've been trying to get her back on the tennis court but haven't had much luck so far. I even got my mum to leave a note when she cleaned Willow Cottage, just to give her a nudge.'

'I think she likes her tennis players a little more professional,' said Tom, knowing it was a cheap dig but not being able to help himself. He wished he had half of Marcus's confidence and all of his six pack.

'I know it's hard for you to get your head around the idea that a woman might not want to shag you,' said Justin, his voice laced with fake concern.

'I honestly don't think it's ever happened before,' replied Marcus, his brow furrowed in confusion. 'Even the faithful ones soak up the attention.'

Tom laughed into his murky bowl of pork. 'Yeah, I'm sure attention is something Daisy's really desperate for right now.'

'Still, maybe I'm losing my touch.' Marcus's eyes darted in all directions as he processed this worrying possibility.

'Have you never thought about settling down?' asked Tom. 'What are you, thirty-four?'

Marcus looked mildly affronted. 'Not until March. And, yes, I have, actually. I'm thinking about it right now. The Glorious Gloria.'

'Is she the one from the tennis club?' asked Justin.

'Yeah,' Marcus grinned. 'Captain of the ladies' team. Used to be married to Phil, the Club Treasurer.'

'Isn't that all a bit awkward?' asked Tom, marvelling at the ease with which Marcus navigated the relationship trenches.

'He's left for another club.' Marcus smirked. 'Gloria sent a message to a friend on Facebook saying Phil should change his name because he couldn't fill a tickbox, let alone a woman. But she accidentally posted it on the main club page instead.'

Justin honked with laughter. 'And you think she's the woman for you.'

'Maybe,' said Marcus with a shrug. 'She's dynamite in bed, is financially independent and thinks I have boyfriend potential.'

'So, what's stopping you?' asked Tom, trying not to let his mind drift to Daisy and Tessa, who somehow didn't cohabit well in his brain.

'Not sure,' said Marcus blankly. 'I guess part of me was holding out for Daisy.'

Justin shook his head. 'Yeah, I'm not so sure.'

Marcus grinned. 'Do I look like a man who gives in that easily?'

'Sadly not,' said Justin, glumly chewing another forkful of pork.

CHAPTER TWENTY-TWO

'Mum!' Ruby was standing in the doorway with her hands on her hips, looking very much like her father. 'We're *starving*. Can we get some dinner?'

Daisy glanced at her watch, then at the half-empty wine bottle, then at Melanie, who had tears rolling down her face at a story Daisy had just been telling about Dermot O'Leary and a static caravan.

'Oh crap, I'm sorry.' She just about suppressed a hiccup as Ruby's eyes narrowed. 'We lost track of time. Let's go up to Eva's. We can show Melanie the town.'

'That will take about six minutes,' said Ruby, rolling her eyes at Will. 'It's just one road. No nightclubs, no bars that are open late. How are we supposed to have fun?'

'You're both too young for nightclubs and bars,' Daisy commented. 'But when you're eighteen you can pay for your own skiing holidays and go to places with as many nightclubs as you like.'

Ruby looked alarmed and started back-pedalling. 'It's fine, I like it here. Can I have a cocktail with dinner? As a birthday treat?'

Daisy pursed her lips, 'Hmm. We'll see.'

Melanie wobbled off to the bathroom as Will and Ruby pulled their winter gear back on and bundled out into the snow. Daisy glanced at her phone, but there were no more messages from Tom. She kicked herself for wanting to hear from him, but the thought of his body pressed against hers gave her a fizzy feeling in the pit of her stomach that had nothing to do with wine.

'I just need to grab my bag,' said Melanie. 'I'll be two minutes.' Daisy quickly opened WhatsApp and tapped out a message before she changed her mind.

Just off for dinner and a play in the snow.

The grey ticks went blue within seconds, and Daisy realised she was holding her breath.

Wrap up warm. Sorry I'm not there to zip your coat up.

Daisy grinned and quickly put her phone away, just as Melanie jogged back down the stairs.

'What are you smiling at?' asked Melanie, pulling on her snow boots.

'Nothing,' replied Daisy quickly. 'Here, you two, grab a sledge.'

'What do we need those for?' asked Will, taking the rope of one sledge and passing the other to Ruby.

Ruby smiled and started to drag her sledge down the path towards the road. 'They're how we get home.'

The village was quiet and beautiful as they walked up the hill to Eva's Pizzeria, past the cable car station and rows of wooden chalets twinkling with Christmas lights. The snow crunched and creaked under their boots as they puffed vapour clouds with every step; but even though the air was freezing, it wasn't long before Daisy felt hot in her ski suit.

She glanced at Melanie, who was taking deep breaths as she tried to focus through the wine. Daisy stayed quiet, instead letting her mind wander to Tom. In the context of her plan to keep him safe from press scrutiny, kissing him last night had not been a good idea. But the memory of it induced a feeling of delicious warmth that she could feel in her toes. For Christian, kissing was always a precursor to sex; he had no concept of snogging for the sheer thrill of it. But Tom had felt entirely different – tender and romantic, a little hesitant. He was an entirely different type of man altogether, and Daisy was struggling to put her finger on why she found him so attractive. It was something she'd love to talk to Melanie about, but also the one thing she absolutely couldn't mention.

'Just out of interest,' asked Melanie breathlessly, 'how long is this hill?'

Daisy laughed. 'It's about another half a mile, sorry. It takes half an hour to walk there and about two minutes to get back.'

'Maybe it would be easier if I wasn't so pissed,' said Melanie, using Daisy's footprints as a guide. Ruby and Will were dragging the sledges fifty metres ahead, occasionally stopping to push each other into a snowbank or throw a snowball. Their laughter echoed in the frigid air and made Daisy smile. It was lovely to see them both so relaxed and happy, away from the pressures of school and exams. Regardless of what happened in future, Daisy felt sure that neither of them would ever forget this trip.

The path widened as they neared the top of the hill, so

Daisy fell back alongside Melanie and laughed at their huffing and puffing.

'God, I'm so unfit,' said Daisy. 'My personal trainer is going to be furious.'

'What's that like?' asked Melanie. 'Having a personal trainer?'

'Oh,' said Daisy, kicking herself for chatting to Melanie like she was one of her London friends. She must sound so vacuous. 'It's . . . helpful. I don't have to motivate myself, Scott does it for me. I just do whatever he says until he tells me to stop.'

Melanie gave Daisy a sideways look. 'That sounds awful.'

'Yeah, it's grim,' laughed Daisy. 'But the alternative is having gossip magazines speculate on why my bum has got bigger.'

'OK, that sounds more awful,' said Melanie, her brow furrowing. 'Do they really do that?'

'Sure,' said Daisy. ' "*Daisy flaunts her new curves on a family beach holiday.*" Haven't you ever read that in a magazine?'

Melanie blushed. 'Oh. Well, yes.'

'It's code for "*Daisy's put on a few pounds.*" It's fine,' said Daisy, sensing Melanie's discomfort. 'You get used to it. And then you get a personal trainer.'

They trudged in companionable silence for a few minutes as the hill flattened out and the lights of Eva's appeared in the distance. Daisy's thighs were burning from the climb, and she dreaded to think how they were going to feel tomorrow after a day's skiing.

'It feels strange to be here with you.' Melanie's voice was quiet and a little shy, but she was emboldened by all the alcohol. 'I've been watching you on TV for so many years.'

173

Daisy looked at her. 'Really? I didn't realise you were a fan of *Spotlight*. You never said.'

Melanie shrugged. 'Not just *Spotlight*. I used to watch you on *Pop Party!* in the nineties, and then on the house make-over show, what was it called?'

Daisy laughed, '*First Time Fixer-Uppers*.'

'That's the one,' Melanie nodded. 'I was living in London then, in my boyfriend's flat. He worked in the City and had a little place in Farringdon. We loved that show, copied loads of your ideas.'

Daisy remembered how they'd never finished their conversation earlier. 'What happened to him? The boyfriend.'

Melanie let out a slow breath. 'I went to work for Gerald after he won his seat in the 2001 election. I was only twenty-two and bit naive, I suppose. Didn't see him coming.'

'Until he was coming,' said Daisy, then let out a horrified snort of laughter. 'Oops, did I say that out loud?'

'You did!' Melanie dissolved into giggles again.

'What are you two laughing at?' Ruby called. She was waiting with Will at the top of the hill, both of them equally knackered from the climb.

'How awful our children are,' Daisy stated with a grin. 'So awful that we both stopped after just one in case we got another that was just as bad.'

'It's true,' agreed Melanie. 'One was enough.'

'Ha!' said Will, rolling his eyes at Ruby, although his mouth twitched as if he wanted to laugh.

'So how are things going?' Daisy nudged Ruby's shoulder with hers. They were waiting at the bar to order their food, watching the waiters run in and out of the kitchen with huge trays of pizza and drinks.

'Really good,' replied Ruby, tucking her hair behind her ears. 'I'm really glad that Will could come.'

'Me too,' said Daisy. 'You seem to be getting on well.' Daisy felt like she was treading on eggshells, not wanting to ask the wrong question or force Ruby to retreat. Teenage relationships were such a minefield, and all she needed to know was that Ruby was OK.

'Yeah,' Ruby nodded. 'I like him.' She glanced round to check Will and Melanie weren't listening, but they were both deep in conversation, Will showing his mum something on his phone. 'He's nice to hang out with. Not pushy or anything.'

Daisy smiled, having got the answer she wanted. Ruby was fine, and no damage had been done by making enquiries.

'Seems like you and Will's mum are getting on well too,' Ruby teased.

'We are,' said Daisy. 'I really like her. I wasn't sure we'd have much in common, but she's a breath of fresh air.'

'I bet,' said Ruby, who'd grown up around Daisy's circle of celebrity friends and called them 'The Gloss Queens' because they always looked so immaculate, including the men. She peered at the menu again, her brow furrowed with uncertainty. 'Should I avoid onions, do you think?'

Daisy registered the unspoken second half of the question – *if I'm going to snog Will later* – and resisted the urge to laugh. Ruby was asking her a woman-to-woman question, and it deserved a serious woman-to-woman answer. 'Best avoided, I think,' she said. 'Along with anything spicy.'

'Ham and cheese, then,' said Ruby thoughtfully.

'Good idea,' replied Daisy, as the owner finished taking a customer's order and turned to them with a huge smile. She was a woman in her seventies who'd run this pizzeria on the mountain for forty years, now helped by her two strapping sons.

'Hello, Eva,' said Daisy. 'Lovely to see you again.'

'You are always welcome, Daisy,' said Eva, giving Ruby a huge smile. 'And Ruby gets more beautiful every year.'

'We're celebrating a special occasion,' said Daisy. 'Ruby's sixteenth birthday.'

'Congratulations,' said Eva, giving Ruby a maternal smile. 'So grown up, I remember when you were just a little girl. Perhaps some champagne cocktails? Just small ones, at least for a couple more years.'

Ruby nodded excitedly and asked for four, then placed their pizza order. Daisy watched her happily, feeling the strings of tension she'd been carrying over The Incident and Christian and the recent press coverage slowly loosening. It was all hundreds of miles away, and for the next week all she had to do was relax and enjoy being a mum, a friend and an ordinary woman having a holiday.

At 10.30, Eva finally kicked them out, which meant Daisy was now sitting on the sledge with Melanie tucked behind her, their legs out straight and lifted clear of the snow. She glanced over at Will, who was climbing onto the other sledge behind Ruby, looking entirely terrified.

'It's only a blue run,' said Ruby reassuringly.

'It looks like a death slide,' Will muttered darkly. 'How do you see where you're going?'

'The moonlight reflects on the snow,' said Ruby, like this was the most obvious thing in the world. Daisy laughed, never having really considered how insane this must look to people like Will and Melanie who weren't used to travelling this way.

'You ready?' asked Daisy, twisting round to look at Melanie.

Melanie smiled gamely. 'I've never been less ready for anything in my life.'

'Oh, thank God it's not just me,' mumbled Will.

'Hold on tight and keep your feet up or you'll snap an ankle,' Ruby instructed. 'There's a sharp right-hand bend at the bottom by the river so just lean right when I tell you, OK?'

Will nodded, looking mildly nauseous as Ruby turned to Daisy. 'You go first.'

Daisy tipped the sledge over the ledge with her feet; it eased forward slowly at first, then picked up pace as the metal rails found their groove in the freshly groomed snow. A few seconds later they were rocketing down a long, wide piste at what felt like a hundred miles an hour and Melanie's nervous laugh had turned into a full-blown whoop of excitement and terror. Daisy glanced back and checked Ruby was just behind them, then enjoyed the thrill of the ride until she saw the dark strip of river approaching and yelled, 'Lean right!' Melanie shifted her weight sideways as the sledge turned seamlessly into the bend. They slowed a little as the gradient of the piste became less steep, and Daisy felt Melanie relax her vice-like grip around her waist. Snow-laden pine trees flew by as the sledge sailed along the edge of the burbling river for a minute or so, until it finally came to a gentle stop right outside the entrance to the cable car, next to a bar where a party was in full swing. The windows were vibrating in time to the music – some kind of techno-yodel – and a group of men in ski-instructor jackets were smoking furiously outside.

Daisy's heart was pounding with exhilaration as Ruby and Will's sledge slid to a stop beside them, all of them breathless and crying with laughter as they scrambled to their feet. Then Will froze, putting his hand on Ruby's shoulder as something moved in the doorway to the cable car station.

'What's that?' he whispered, as Daisy, Melanie and Ruby turned their heads to look.

It took a few seconds to realise what they were all seeing – the naked, bobbing backside of a man in a black jacket with the bare legs of a woman wrapped around his waist, both of them wedged into a shadowy corner by the glass door. The woman screamed, 'YES, NOW!' as the man picked up pace, her fur-lined snow boots flapping in time to his pounding rhythm and his lust-fuelled grunts.

'Oh God,' gasped Daisy in horror, as she and Melanie hustled Ruby and Will across the road towards their chalet. They howled with mortified laughter all the way home, even though Daisy couldn't shift the notion that, even in the shadows, the man's backside had looked startlingly like Christian's.

CHAPTER TWENTY-THREE

Guten morgen! Dx

Hey! Good morning to you too. Did you have fun last night?

Yes. Too much champagne and pizza, skiing is going
to hurt today.

I had a foul pork stew with J & M, then walked Henry in
the pouring rain. Our evenings were identical, really.

Sounds fun. Have a lovely day.

I will now. Tx

Daisy put her phone on the counter and made breakfast for
everyone, a warm, purring feeling in her chest. When the
dishes were cleared away, everyone gathered their ski gear
from the boot room and did final checks for lift passes, Euros
and sun cream, before trudging off to the cable car in the
shadow of the mountains, which were backed by promisingly
clear skies. They stopped at the hire shop for Melanie to be
fitted for some boots and skis, while Ruby and Will retrieved
their snowboarding gear from the locker room. The four of
them met up again in the queue for a cable car, their equipment and boots clattering as they slowly trudged forward.
Each little bubble held six people, so they put their kit into

the racks on the outside and squeezed in with an older couple who were immediately and openly mesmerised by Daisy.

'You are Daisy Crawford, yes?' gasped the woman before they had even made it out of the bottom station. She had a North European accent – Dutch, Daisy guessed. Or maybe German.

Daisy nodded and flashed her media smile. This happened all the time, although much less often in Vergallen. Silently, she prayed they weren't going to be awful because there was absolutely no escape for the next ten minutes. She noticed Ruby and Will were looking out of the window, but Melanie seemed fascinated.

'We are from the Netherlands, we watch BBC on cable,' continued the woman. 'We are big fans of *Spotlight*.' Her husband nodded, grinning excitedly.

'Thank you.' Daisy gave them a warm smile, relieved she didn't have to listen to an extended lecture on how she could be better at her job. 'Just having a little holiday right now.' This was very polite code for 'please leave me alone', and the woman took the hint.

Daisy pointed out the weaving paths of black runs and the smoking chimneys of mountain huts to Melanie and Will, as Ruby sent pouting selfies to her friends. As the top station came into view the Dutch woman's self-control imploded and she asked for a photograph, so Daisy leaned in and smiled so the husband could take a few pictures on his phone. Daisy noticed Ruby rolling her eyes at Will: this was old news as far as she was concerned.

At the top, they all trudged out of the station into the bright sunshine and a breathtaking view across the mountains. This prompted a sigh of happiness from Melanie and a barrage of photos and videos from Will before he and Ruby headed off to the flag marked for the adult beginners' snowboarding class. Melanie looked around for the beginners' ski class flag, then took a deep breath.

'Wish me luck.' Her voice was wobbly with nerves and excitement.

'You'll be fine,' Daisy assured her gaily. 'See you later!'

Daisy finished her coffee, relishing the simple pleasure of twenty minutes alone with the morning sun on her face. Streams of skiers poured out of the cable car station, but nobody gave Daisy a second glance. She was entirely anonymous in her fleece headband and huge sunglasses. Anyway, the stunning vista of mountains and huge skies was all anybody wanted to look at.

She pulled out her phone and re-read the messages from Tom last night, not for the first time this morning. She liked how tentative his flirting was; nothing like the absolute filth Christian used to send her. Although she'd enjoyed that too, sometimes. If anyone ever stole her phone they'd find some eyebrow-raising videos of Christian raising his man-flag. She took a picture of the view and sent it to Tom.

It's a beautiful day in the mountains.

Wow, that looks amazing. Who are you skiing with today?

Just on my own. I'll meet the others later.

Stay safe. Don't make me come over there.

Daisy smiled, wondering whether to reply. She wanted to say *Don't think I haven't thought about it* but that seemed like taking their gentle flirting to the next level. And she really wasn't supposed to be encouraging him, tempting and fun as it was.

She zipped her phone into her jacket and made her way over to the ski rack, strapping her helmet under her chin and pulling on her gloves, then lifting her skis out of the rack and letting them fall onto the snow so she could snap her boots into the bindings. As she looped the straps of her ski poles over her wrists, she sensed the shift in air of someone standing beside her. With some trepidation, she turned. Christian stood looking at her, his hands wedged firmly into the pockets of his black jacket.

'Hey,' he said quietly.

Daisy stared at him for a long second, her brain slowly processing what her eyes were seeing. He looked different. Nervous. Daisy realised she'd only ever seen him poised and confident. She tried to keep her voice even, though she was internally raging.

'What are you doing here, Christian?'

'I need to talk to you.' He looked down at his boots like he wished the mountain would swallow him up.

'I've told you, we're finished,' said Daisy through gritted teeth. 'What else is there to say?' *You lying, cheating—*

'Just half an hour,' pleaded Christian. 'I know you're angry with me.' He stared at her, his eyes beseeching.

'I'm on holiday, Christian. Partly to get away from you. And Ruby is here. Why on earth would you think this is OK?'

'I didn't know what else to do,' Christian said. 'I knew you wouldn't see me if I asked, and I thought this was better than turning up in the village where you're staying.'

'I don't want you turning up anywhere,' snapped Daisy, struggling to keep her voice down as people turned to look. 'I don't want to see you, full stop.'

'I know, but I'm desperate. Please.' That wasn't a word Christian often used.

Daisy narrowed her eyes and pursed her lips, taking deep calming breaths. It was clear that the only way she was going to get rid of him was to give him some time, much as she'd rather toss him into the path of an avalanche. 'Fine, but not now. I'll meet you at Helga's Bar later. One thirty.'

'Thank you,' Christian looked relieved. 'Where's Helga's Bar?'

'Halfway down red run number three,' Daisy murmured, her face grim and unreadable. 'You'll have to ski there.'

It was hard to hide her glee at the fear in Christian's eyes. 'Isn't there any other way? Or somewhere else?'

'No!' Daisy said firmly, pushing away with her ski poles.

The last thing she heard before disappearing down the mountain was Christian yelling, *'Fucking hell, Daisy!'*

She grinned as she whisked off towards her favourite warm-up blue run, feeling a tiny bit evil and frankly all the better for it.

Daisy sat outside Helga's with a tall glass of cold beer, watching Christian tentatively snowplough the final few metres and come to a juddering stop, looking very much like a man who'd had an urgent appointment with his own mortality. He was led by an unfeasibly handsome male instructor, who looked even more relieved to have reached their destination than Christian. Daisy wondered how much falling and getting up and gentle coaxing it must have taken to get him here, and how painful Christian's thighs must be if he'd snowploughed the whole way. She almost felt bad, until the image of him shagging a woman in a doorway last night popped into her head. There was no doubt in her mind that Christian was the owner of the Bobbing Buttocks – which Ruby and Will had also seen – so frankly there wasn't enough thigh pain in the world for him.

She sipped her beer, watching Christian as he tried to release his boots from the bindings, getting increasingly frustrated and tangled. The instructor walked over and clicked the release levers with his ski pole, leaving Christian to tumble out of his skis and flounder in the snow on wobbly legs, like a newborn giraffe. The Daisy of a few months ago would have gone to help him. Instead, she drank some more beer and helped herself to a handful of French fries from the bowl in front of her.

Christian scrambled upright and clumped over to Daisy, leaving the instructor to deal with his skis. 'I made it,' he whispered, his face etched with trauma.

Daisy scanned his bloodshot eyes. 'You look like you need a drink.'

'Definitely.' Christian hefted himself onto the stool opposite.

The instructor walked over and smiled bleakly down at him. 'Christian, we are finished with your lesson now.' He said in careful English, 'If you like I can come back in an hour and we can do more this afternoon.' He looked like he'd rather roll naked down the mountain.

'Thanks, Lukas,' mumbled Christian. 'I . . . oh, God. No—Yes. I don't know. What are my options?'

'It's fine, thanks, Lukas.' Daisy put her hand on Christian's

184

arm. 'I'll get him back down the mountain. We'll give you a call if we want to book for tomorrow.' Even though Daisy was determined that Christian would be back in the UK by then.

Lukas grinned, his relief obvious. 'OK, no problem.' Then he looked at her properly. 'You are the woman from the singing television show, no? I did summer in Manchester last year, working in BBC canteen. I watch your show. You are very famous.'

'Just having a little holiday right now,' smiled Daisy.

Lukas gave them both a conspiratorial nod and waved as he swished expertly off down the mountain, spraying a wave of snow behind him as he took the corner at high speed. Christian watched him go, his face now ashen. Daisy waved her beer glass at the waiter and held up two fingers.

'So, remind me again why you're here?' Daisy crossed her arms over her chest in a gesture that she hoped communicated *I am not to be messed with, you bastard*. She'd calmed down since seeing Christian this morning and decided that yelling at him further was only going to prolong the meeting and attract unwanted attention. She'd hear him out and then get rid of him.

Christian took a deep breath. 'I wanted to apologise in person,' he muttered. 'For being such a dick.'

Yeah, right. Your regret is so deep you shagged a woman last night. In public.

'You could have emailed, like a normal person. How did you find me?'

Christian relaxed a little, clearly relieved that Daisy wasn't going to scream at him. 'You asked me if I wanted to come ages ago. Sent me a link.'

185

'How very foolish of me,' she said coolly. *One of the many things.*

'I was hoping to find you last night. The guy who owns my B&B told me to go to the Berge restaurant, because that's the most popular place in town. Apart from a pizza place that's apparently a hike up the mountain.'

'We hiked up the mountain.'

'Of course you did. Anyway, I hung out at the Berge for ages, but you didn't show. So I came up in the cable car this morning this morning to find you, and saw you on the terrace.'

She waited for him to continue but he stayed silent, sipping his beer. Unable to help herself, she blurted out, 'I thought we were doing OK, Christian. So why all the cheating the minute my back was turned?' She eyed him carefully. 'Or was it before that?'

Christian's head snapped upright. He looked offended. 'No. Not before,' he insisted, although he didn't quite meet her eye. 'I was completely faithful the whole time up until you left London. I promise.'

Daisy was inclined to believe him, unable to imagine how Christian could have crammed in more sex on top of their daily encounters. 'So what happened?'

He shrugged helplessly. 'I was stressed, I guess. About the contract, the whole NTAs thing, the engagement, all the press stuff, you know. You called and said you were going away, and then my personal trainer came over and . . . I don't know. It just happened.'

Daisy's eyes widened. 'Wait, hang on. You had sex with your personal trainer *the day* I told you I was going away?'

'Yeah,' said Christian, dropping his gaze to the table.

'But that was the same day you announced our engagement on Twitter.'

Christian's gaze dropped to his shoes. 'Yeah.'

'Jesus, Christian,' snapped Daisy. 'Why would you tell the world we're getting married, then screw your personal trainer a few hours later? *What's wrong with you?*'

'I didn't want to,' mumbled Christian. 'Benny told me I should.'

Daisy shook her head like she was fighting off a cloud of wasps. 'Benny told you to fuck your personal trainer?!'

'NO!' shouted Christian, then lowered his head as people turned to look at them. 'No. Benny told me to announce the engagement. He said it would make me look like a hero.' He turned his palms to face upwards in a gesture of apparent openness. 'I didn't want to. I knew you'd be upset. The whole thing just messed with my head.' *Messed with his head?* But Daisy believed him, and for the first time she saw him for what he was: a handsome, spoiled, weak man.

'You really need to deal with the whole "using sex to deal with stress" thing. Maybe try yoga instead. Or mindfulness. Download an app.'

Christian nodded. 'I know, but it's the only thing that keeps me together since I retired from the tour.'

'What?' Daisy frowned.

'Sex. I need it all the time. And if I'm not doing it, I'm thinking about it. It's been like that ever since I stopped playing.'

'Wait, what?' Although that did explain his insane libido. And Daisy had just thought she was entirely irresistible. 'Jesus, Christian. You need to see someone.'

'I was seeing you, but then you dumped me.'

'No, not like that. A medical professional.'

'What, like a therapist?' Christian said scornfully.

'Well, that might be better for your career than having sex with strange women in doorways.'

Christian choked on his beer. 'Shit. Are you having me followed?'

Daisy looked deadpan. 'No.' *Not any more.* 'Ruby and I happened to be passing last night and saw the show. We probably weren't the only ones.'

Christian rubbed his hand across his jaw. 'Oh, fuck. I'm so sorry.'

'Who was she? Do you even know her name? Or was she just another convenient vagina?'

Christian had the grace to look ashamed. 'Sophie. Her name's Sophie. She's twenty-four, a ski instructor from Vienn—'

'As I said, seek help.' Daisy's voice wavered a little. 'If it's some kind of sex addiction, I'm pretty sure it's something that can be treated. But I'm hardly an expert, am I?'

Christian shrugged, then looked at her consideringly. 'So, now that you know I'm an addict rather than a complete arsehole, is there any chance you might take me back?'

Daisy gave a hollow laugh, wondering what life must be like in Christian's head. Such a simple place. What had she ever seen in him? An image of Tom flashed into her head – the way he'd looked after he'd kissed her, like she was the only woman on the planet. Christian had never looked at her like that.

'No,' she said firmly. 'There is no chance. Aside from you

probably having every STD going, we're not right for each other. I think we both know that.'

Christian pouted. 'Why?'

'OK,' said Daisy, moving her face closer to his. God, he was beautiful. 'Look me in the eye and tell me you love me.'

Christian's dark eyes tried to hold her gaze, then darted away.

'You never have, you know,' she said quietly. 'You've never said it.'

'I–I can't,' he admitted. 'I've never said it to anyone. I don't know – if . . . I'm even *able* to feel like that.'

Daisy swallowed. If there was ever evidence she had truly crap taste in men, this was it.

'Benny says we need to get back together.'

Daisy rolled her eyes. 'Benny is a dick. It isn't going to happen, but if it helps, tell him I said I'd think about it, pending you getting professional help. That should get him off your case for a while.' She stared at him intently. 'Just don't make a fool out of me, Christian. Or at least, any more than you have already.'

Christian nodded solemnly. 'I won't, I promise.' He looked at her sadly. 'I'm really sorry, Dais.' And for a moment she believed that he really was.

She shrugged, fighting the temptation to cry. She took a deep breath and gestured to the waiter for the bill. 'I think we should go. The piste can get icy and dangerous in the afternoons.' It was a bit mean, but there was a grim satisfaction in seeing how much Christian looked like he wanted to throw up. Especially as he watched a couple of skiers take the corner at high speed.

189

'Any chance you could piggy-back me down?' he asked faintly.

Daisy snorted. 'Nope. But the rest of the way is a blue run. Piece of cake.'

Christian looked unconvinced.

She didn't notice the photographer until Christian was wrestling himself back into his skis; a man in a white jacket snapping furiously from behind a tree opposite the bar. He'd made very little effort to hide, and his camera had a huge telephoto lens. God knows how long he'd been there and what pictures he'd taken, or what spin the tabloids would put on them. She sighed as she gripped Christian's elbow to hold him steady, and decided not to say anything about it right now. She couldn't discount the possibility that Christian or his manager had arranged for the photographer to be there – it was all too convenient, but it was too late to worry about that now. Daisy's phone buzzed in her pocket, and she quickly pulled it out in case it was Ruby. But instead it was from Tom.

Hey! How's your day going? Found your ski legs yet?

Daisy sighed, feeling suddenly exhausted. Tom and Christian felt like two different worlds, and juggling them both in one day felt knotty and complicated. She put her phone back in her pocket, deciding she'd unravel it all later in the peace and tranquillity of the hot tub.

CHAPTER TWENTY-FOUR

'So, who's got the best bruises?' asked Ruby, as they all relaxed on the chalet terrace. The air felt brittle and fat snowflakes fell from the inky sky, but Daisy had cranked up the water temperature to the equivalent of a hot bath and made mugs of hot chocolate. After a challenging afternoon dealing with Christian, it was just about as blissful as it got.

Will was a clear winner in the bruise department – his knees and elbows were a patchwork of purple blotches. Melanie had a corker on her hip where she'd got her skis crossed during a shambolic exit from a chair lift and landed heavily on one of her classmates, and Ruby had several on her backside which she refused to show to the assembled group. Daisy just had a sore arm from when Christian had lost his balance and grabbed her in a panic, but she didn't mention that.

'Snowboarding is HARD,' Ruby announced. 'I thought it would be easy to switch from skiing, but it's completely different. Will is way better than me.' She gave him a playful splash and he grinned.

'We both spent a lot of time sitting down,' he corrected. 'Or with our heads buried in the snow.' He smiled at Ruby. 'Apparently that's normal for the first day and we'll be better tomorrow.'

'You have four more days of lessons,' said Daisy. 'By the end of the week you'll be brilliant.'

'I'm being moved to a different class tomorrow,' Melanie murmured. 'The instructor said I got the basics really quickly, so he's moving me up a level.' She blushed and smiled as everyone applauded and whooped.

'Did you enjoy it?' asked Daisy.

'I loved it.' Melanie's eyes were sparkling in a way that Daisy had never seen before. She'd borrowed a navy swimsuit from a box in the clothing store, revealing a body that women fifteen years her junior would kill for. Daisy couldn't help but wonder why she'd kept it hidden for so long.

'I wasn't sure I would, but it was amazing,' she continued. 'And I thought I'd be rubbish at it, but I did OK. I can't wait to go again.'

They sat in contented silence for a minute, watching the snow fall into the hot water as the moon rose behind the mountains. The hot tub could fit eight, so there was plenty of room for them to stretch their aching limbs and sink down so only their heads were above the water line. It made Daisy think of those Japanese monkeys in hot springs that she'd seen on an Attenborough documentary. Ruby closed her eyes and floated on her back, her long hair spreading out into the water. *Like Millais' painting of Ophelia*, thought Daisy, although thankfully a little less morbid.

'Rubes, I have bad news,' Daisy announced.

Ruby sat up with a splash, her tranquillity broken. 'What?'

'I'm afraid you and Will have to get out and make dinner. It's your turn tonight; Melanie and me tomorrow.'

As Will and Ruby clattered around in the kitchen, Daisy and Melanie stayed where they were, wallowing silently in the hot tub. After a few minutes Will brought them both a glass of wine – *well trained*, thought Daisy – so they sat in the steaming water, each lost in their own thoughts as the snow settled on the deck around them.

'We'll get out soon,' Melanie yawned.

'Definitely,' mumbled Daisy. She caught her friend's eye and they both snorted with laughter.

'This place is amazing,' said Melanie. 'I still can't quite believe I'm here. It's a shame Gerald . . .'

Daisy was silent for a few seconds, then placed her wine glass on the side of the hot tub. 'What are you going to do, Melanie?'

Melanie turned to look at her. 'About Gerald?'

Daisy nodded. 'You seem like a different person here. More relaxed, happy.'

Melanie gave a tight smile. 'I know.' She turned her head towards the house and the sound of Will and Ruby laughing. 'I think things will have to be very different when we get home. I just haven't worked out how.'

After dinner Melanie and Will both headed for bed, exhausted after their first day on the slopes. Daisy and Ruby cleaned up the kitchen, then took a couple of mugs of peppermint tea back out to the hot tub. The snow had stopped and the stars were out, and the air felt crisp and icy.

Daisy had been thinking about whether she should tell Ruby about Christian. On the one hand she didn't want him to intrude on their holiday any more than he had already; but on the other, it didn't seem fair or respectful to keep Ruby in the dark. And Daisy couldn't discount the possibility that those photos might appear in the press. Tom drifted into her thoughts and induced a flicker of anxiety, but she pushed it aside.

'I saw Christian today,' Daisy said in what she hoped was a casual tone.

'What?!' demanded Ruby, her head snapping upright from recumbent stargazing. 'What's HE doing here?'

'It's fine,' said Daisy, 'he's going home tomorrow. He came to see me, to talk about our relationship.'

'What about it?' asked Ruby, her eyes narrowing.

Daisy took a deep breath. 'We've split up. It wasn't working out.'

Ruby's eyes widened. 'Really? Like, properly broken up? You won't get back together?'

'No,' Daisy shook her head. *Not in this lifetime.*

'Wow,' said Ruby. 'Just when I thought today couldn't possibly get any better, you throw in a final glitter bomb. I could sing!'

Daisy shook her head, hiding a smile. There was no pretence with Ruby. 'Actually, please don't. You're tone deaf like me.' She gave Ruby her serious face. 'But listen, Rubes, nobody knows yet. We haven't made a statement to the press or anything, so you need to keep it to yourself.'

'Why?' asked Ruby, looking confused.

Daisy sighed. 'Because I'm trying to keep out of the news for a while. And I don't want it to spoil our time here.' She dismissed the photographer for now. It might never happen, and if it did, Katie would deal with it.

Ruby nodded, then looked at her mother shrewdly. 'Are you going to tell me what he did?'

'No,' said Daisy, sipping her peppermint tea. 'But I'm

fine. Although I suspect Christian would have won today's bruise competition.'

Ruby sat up, her eyes glittering. 'Oh my God, did you deck him?'

'No!' laughed Daisy in horror, then recounted the saga of getting a petrified Christian down the mountain at approximately two miles an hour, plus breaks for tantrums and crying. Ruby howled with laughter.

'What are your plans when we get back?' asked Ruby finally, when she'd calmed down. 'Are you going back to London, or to the village?'

'The village,' Daisy said decisively, her thoughts drifting to Tom as anxiety bloomed again. 'I want to finish the book, and the school is going to run a cooking club straight after Christmas so I can test all the recipes.'

'By "the school" you mean the headmaster, right?' Ruby grinned knowingly.

Daisy ignored her and threw in a deflection. 'I'm thinking of asking your granny if she wants to help.'

Until that second Daisy hadn't been thinking anything of the sort, but now it seemed perfectly obvious – Stella had spent years testing recipes with schoolchildren, she had far more classroom experience than Daisy did. Why hadn't she thought of it before? Stella could do the teaching, and it would free Daisy up to observe, ask questions and take photos for her Instagram. Plus her mother would love the attention, so she'd get Brownie points. A win–win.

'So, you'll be around for a few more weeks,' said Ruby.

Daisy nodded. 'Yes, I should think so. Why?'

Ruby shrugged. 'Just means I can come home on weekends

when I don't have play rehearsals, even if it's just for a few hours.'

Daisy smiled. 'You really like him, don't you?'

Ruby blushed and fidgeted. 'Yeah. He's fun to hang out with, and he's nice to me.' She glanced at Daisy from under her lashes. 'Christian was never that nice to you,' she whispered.

'Oh, Rubes.' Daisy's heart hurt. She pulled her daughter to her. 'Never ever underestimate that quality in a man. Niceness, *kindness*, is seriously underrated.' *Tom is kind*, she thought, thinking about his hands on the zip of her coat again. She needed to reply to his message. Maybe she'd do it in the morning, when her head felt clearer.

Ruby rested her head against Daisy's shoulder, splashing her feet in the water, her face turned to the sky. They both contemplated the stars in companiable silence.

'Mu–um . . . I wanted to ask you something.'

Daisy looked down at Ruby, her face patient but questioning. 'What is it?'

'Nothing bad,' Ruby said quickly, 'I just wondered how you'd feel if I wanted to hang out here with Will.' She blushed awkwardly. 'In the hot tub. Just the two of us. Would that be weird?'

Daisy was silent for a moment, before giving her daughter a soft smile. 'Well, it wouldn't be weird for me. The big question is, would it be weird for you?'

Ruby chewed her lip. 'No. At least, I don't think so.'

Daisy rubbed Ruby's arm. 'Rubes, you don't have to ask my permission to be alone with your boyfriend. But it's lovely that you want to talk about it.'

'I don't know,' said Ruby with a shrug. 'Things feel confusing sometimes.'

Daisy smiled. 'Will seems lovely, but you haven't been seeing each other very long. This trip is a great opportunity for you to get to know each other better, but it shouldn't feel like pressure.'

'It doesn't,' said Ruby. 'He isn't like that. I was just thinking how nice it would be just to hang out here with him and talk about stuff. Kind of romantic, you know?'

'I do know,' smiled Daisy. 'The first time we came here, your dad and I did exactly that. After you'd gone to bed, we'd get a bottle of wine and sit out here. It was a different hot tub then. This one is much nicer.'

'Do you miss him?' asked Ruby.

Daisy thought about it for a moment. 'Yes. But I also always knew that something wasn't quite right. Your dad is much happier now, and I'm happy for him.'

'But what about you?' asked Ruby. 'When do you get to be happy?'

Daisy smiled, blinking away tears. 'I'm happy whenever you're happy. Talking of which, do you want me to go to bed so you can summon Will for some stargazing?'

Ruby looked at her wrinkled fingers. 'Nah. I'm getting a bit pruny now. Not a great look. Maybe tomorrow.'

Daisy nodded solemnly. 'Nobody ever fancied a prune.'

'Prunes start out as plums though,' said Ruby. 'Much more tempting.'

Daisy laughed and lifted her arm, pinching a flap of skin under her armpit that definitely hadn't been there a few years ago. 'I used to be a plum,' she said glumly, 'but I think it's all prune from now on.'

'You won an award though,' said Ruby happily. 'For best prune on TV. I know we haven't talked about it because of everything else that happened that night, but I'm really proud of you.'

Daisy put her arm around Ruby and pulled her head onto her shoulder again, so her daughter couldn't see her cry. She hadn't realised how much she'd needed to hear somebody say that. 'Thanks, Rubes. That means a lot.'

They sat in silence for another minute, the steam from the water rising around their heads. Daisy felt her eyes closing; they should get off to bed soon.

'Do you think I'll ever be able to think about that night without cringing?' Daisy asked.

Ruby considered the question seriously. 'Honestly, Mum? I doubt it.'

Daisy laughed, realising for the first time that she didn't care any more.

CHAPTER TWENTY-FIVE

Tom sat on the sofa in front of the fire, Henry asleep next to him with his jaw hanging open and his pink tongue lolling out of one side. He sipped his coffee, which tasted as bitter as his cold, widowed, miserable heart. He'd been stalking Daisy online all weekend, wanting reassurance that she was fine and happy and not lying at the bottom of some crevasse. Served him right for being nosy, because instead he found photos of her and Christian sharing an intimate beer in the mountains, then laughing together as Christian fell over in the snow.

He scrolled back to the top and read the story again. The headline alone made him feel nauseous:

SNOW In Love – Daisy and Christian Snuggle Up on the Slopes.

Why had she lied to him? He'd asked her outright at Justin's Pig in a Blanket – *'Is your fiancé going?' 'No, he's not.'* That was just three days ago, and nothing in her WhatsApps since had mentioned *anything* about Christian being there. In fact, she'd explicitly said she was skiing alone yesterday.

He kept reading, every line feeling like a gut punch.

Smashing all those rumours that their surprise engagement was about to double fault after THAT tumble at the NTAs, 39-year-old TV treasure Daisy Crawford and her 33-year-old tennis toyboy

Christian Walker were smitten in mittens as they enjoyed a pre-Christmas cosy ski trip for two in an exclusive Austrian mountain resort. But it was tennis ace Christian falling head over heels this time, as queen of the slopes Daisy provided hands-on support for the snowsports novice.

Underneath were half a dozen pictures, each with a caption explaining exactly what was happening in case you were so extraordinarily stupid you needed someone to spell it out – *Here's Daisy laughing with Christian . . . Here's Daisy helping Christian up from the snow, because he has fallen over . . . Look at them laughing, ha ha!* Honestly, what was the readership age for this shit?

He paused again at a further sub-heading halfway down and rubbed his hands across his tired face. '*Home Alone for the Heartbreak Headmaster*'.

Meanwhile back in the UK, Daisy's hunky headmaster is rumoured to be nursing a broken heart after developing a close relationship with the TV star. According to a source close to the couple, they've shared a kiss or two in his cosy Cotswold kitchen at £14,000-a-year Shipton House School, but now he's home alone while Daisy frolics in the snow with fit fiancé Christian.

The paragraph was accompanied by a picture of him from the school website. It had been taken four years ago, after Tessa had suggested shunning boring, formal portraits in favour of more casual shots of the staff in their classrooms, perching on desks or leaning against colourful bookshelves. She thought it made the school look more like a family and less like an institution. So the picture was of Tom in an open-necked plaid shirt, his hair a little ruffled and untidy, crouching down in front of the fireplace in his office with his arms around Henry. It was supposed to look candid and homely, but Tessa had said he'd looked like a model on the cover of *Country Life*.

The comment about kissing in his kitchen made him uneasy – how would anyone know? Obviously, he hadn't told anyone, which suggested that Daisy had. But who? And why?

Tom scrolled down a bit further and briefly dived into the readers' comments. The first three were *'I've never heard of her, I don't even have a TV'* – why bother commenting then? – *'She's only famous for getting her minge out in public, what a talentless whore'* – charming – and *'If my headmaster had been that shaggable I'd have stayed on for sixth form'*. Tom closed his laptop, feeling grubby and confused. Whichever way he looked at it, Daisy was trouble – the school governors were hardly going to be happy with this kind of attention, and she definitely hadn't been honest with him. She was obviously very much still with Christian. There was no head-or-heart argument to grapple with here – right now they were both in agreement, telling him to stay well away from Daisy Crawford.

The last thing Tom wanted was to be around people, but his day was full. Stella had offered him brunch at Willow Cottage yesterday, when he'd bumped into her while he was walking Henry. Tom had accepted happily, because the run-up to Christmas always made him feel lonely. He'd also arranged to meet Gerald later; Tom had got the impression he wanted his help with something.

'Tom,' said Stella, pulling him into the cottage by way of a crushing hug. 'I'm so glad you came.' Her tone was breathless and grave, like war had just been declared on the wireless. She pressed her hand to her chest, as if clutching imaginary pearls.

'All right, mate.' Justin wandered out of the kitchen. Miriam was also there, warming her socks in front of the wood burner, giving him her best concerned tilted-head vicar face. Henry immediately bagged his favourite spot on the sofa, then looked outraged when he realised that Miriam wasn't Daisy.

'You've seen the news, then,' said Justin, never one to hold back.

'Just call me the Heartbreak Headmaster,' replied Tom with a forced smile. 'Although I regret to inform you that none of it is true.'

'See, I told you he'd think it was funny,' said Stella, clearly relieved. 'Such nonsense. Did YOU know Christian was going skiing, Tom?'

'No,' he shook his head. 'I asked Daisy in passing on Friday and she definitely said he wasn't.' He shrugged casually, avoiding Justin's beady-eyed stare.

'See?' said Stella. 'I asked her the same, so it wasn't just me. I can't think why she would lie about it.'

'Maybe he just turned up, like an early Christmas present,' said Justin. Tom rallied briefly at this thought, but what kind of man gatecrashed a holiday? You'd have to be a special kind of arsehole.

'I wonder if reporters will come to Shipton Combe,' said Miriam, breathless with excitement.

Tom shot Justin a glance that he hoped communicated a

full morse code distress signal; Justin caught it and shook himself into action. 'Right, let's get you some coffee,' he said, leading the way into the kitchen. 'Eggs and bacon on the way. Stella's made some bread which I'm not allowed to eat, so I'm banking on you letting me watch you enjoy every mouthful. With moans.'

Tom smiled and leaned against the kitchen worktop, rubbing his face with his hands.

'You all right?' said Justin quietly, glancing over Tom's shoulder to check Stella and Miriam weren't earwigging. They were chatting away on the sofa; Tom heard the words 'church fete' and relaxed a little.

'Yeah,' Tom shrugged then at Justin's narrow-eyed look. 'Actually, no.'

'Wanna talk about it?'

'Not really.'

Justin sighed as he picked up a spatula, gave the eggs a poke. 'It's just tabloid gossip, mate. It's your own fault for being so fucking handsome.'

'Tom, come and hear our plans for the fete,' shouted Miriam from the lounge.

'Uh-oh.' Justin winked. He slathered a quarter of an inch of butter on a slice of bread the size of a Russian novel, then gasped with longing as Tom picked it up and chewed off half of it.

'Stop watching me eat, you weirdo,' Tom muttered as Justin practically drooled. 'How many weeks left?'

Justin groaned. '*Ten.*'

Gerald and Tom sat in Gerald's car outside the sweeping crescent of Regency townhouses in Cheltenham, waiting for the estate agent to arrive. Tom still wasn't entirely clear why he was here, but Gerald had seemed stressed and anxious enough for Tom to simply agree to go with him, then wait patiently for Gerald to offload.

'My cleaner showed me the news story about Daisy Crawford this morning,' Gerald drawled. 'I'm so sorry you've got dragged into it all.'

'Thanks,' Tom said. 'It's all a bit bewildering.'

'I must say Melanie never mentioned that Daisy's fiancé was joining them on holiday.'

'No,' Tom said, catching the edge in Gerald's voice. Clearly Gerald had been imagining his wife partying with Daisy and Christian and a whole host of other unknown celebrity friends, and didn't like it one bit.

'Gerald,' Tom asked gently. 'I still don't know why we're here.'

'Of course, I'm so sorry.' Gerald looked out of the car window at the elegant terrace, then took a deep breath. 'My mother left me this house along with the rectory, and since her passing I've been renting it out to students.'

'Right,' said Tom, none the wiser.

'The monthly income has kept the rectory standing and covered Will's school fees.'

'We're very glad to have him. He's an exceptional student.'

Gerald nodded in acknowledgement of the compliment. 'I also inherited some land, a dozen or so acres near Burford. My sisters have already sold their share to a property developer who has reached out to my solicitor with a very encouraging first offer.'

'That's all good. Melanie must be pleased.' He'd got the

impression that money was tight. Then he saw Gerald's face. 'Wait. Does Melanie actually know about any of this?'

Gerald shook his head, looking a bit sick. 'I confess I've hidden it from her, just in case I decided to move on to pastures new. I'm not proud of myself,' he added.

'No,' said Tom. 'I should think not.'

'I've spent the weekend doing some thinking, much of which has been rather painful.' He turned to look at Tom, his face bleak. 'I think I may have been a bit of a bastard.'

Tom stayed silent. It was something of an understatement, but he was a bit at a loss as to why Gerald had chosen him as a confidante and therapist. Didn't he have enough to deal with?

'Things were very difficult after I retired from office,' continued Gerald.

Got fired for screwing an intern, you mean.

'I'm ashamed to say I rather took that out on Melanie. I'd lost my career, my professional identity, my hairline.' He gave a hollow laugh. 'If she doesn't come home from Austria, I shall only have myself to blame.'

Tom cleared his throat, worried this conversation was about to plunge into wailing melodrama. 'Have you spoken to her? To Will?'

'I see this as a time of reckoning.' Gerald sat upright, straightening his tie. 'So I'm going to sell this house and the land, and put it all on the table. See if we can build something out of the mess I've made.' He looked at Tom uncertainly. 'And, er, I was rather banking on your support.'

Tom frowned. 'I'm not sure what I can do—'

'There's a poem by Philip Larkin—Ah, there he is.' The estate agent pulled into the parking space behind them, so

Gerald stuck his hand out of the window in greeting. 'Er . . . I forget the name of it, the Larkin. It includes the line "*We should be kind, while there is still time*".'

Tom knew the poem; it was about killing a hedgehog with a lawnmower, but now probably wasn't the time to mention it. He wondered if there was still time for him and Daisy. Then he thought of Tessa, who'd run out of time all too soon. Gerald and Melanie and Will were lucky; they had everything to play for.

'There's still time, Gerald.'

CHAPTER TWENTY-SIX

Daisy waved Melanie, Ruby and Will off to another day of ski classes, pulling her scarf up over her nose. The weather felt as dark as her mood, with battle-grey skies and heavy snow. She ordered a coffee in the bar by the top cable car station and sat down in the window, her legs pressed against the radiator.

Deep cleansing breaths, Daisy.

Katie had sent her a link to the news story first thing, with a WhatsApp that just said *??? WTF call me???* She'd meant to tell Katie about Christian and the photographer yesterday, but part of her had hoped it was just an opportunist pap and would all come to nothing. But that was wishful thinking, because the *Daily Mail* had featured them as the top story on their website as an exclusive, and it was clear whoever had taken those pictures was a pro, which suggested it had all been organised in advance. By Christian, probably, or more likely that manipulative little shit Benny. Now she wondered if Christian's nerves were less to do with facing Daisy and more to do with looking like a dick on skis in the tabloids; he never liked doing anything badly.

Daisy had explained Christian's appearance to Melanie and Will over breakfast, giving them the same version of the story she'd shared with Ruby. They'd all read the online coverage and dismissed it as the usual tabloid rubbish, although

Will had been massively weirded out to see his headmaster implicated in some kind of celebrity love triangle. But nausea and anxiety were still wriggling in Daisy's belly, worrying that right now some hack in London had got their hands on a picture of Tessa and was writing a gleeful follow-up.

'*Dead Ringer! Hunky Head's Tragic Wife was TV Star Daisy's Double.*'

And it would all be her fault for dragging Tom into her mess of a life. He hadn't signed up for this, and she absolutely shouldn't have kissed him. That was perfectly clear now. So should she set him straight on Christian turning up? Or would it actually be better for everyone if he thought she was a liar and a cheat? The thought made her feel sick.

Christian first, then. She needed to know he'd definitely left Vergallen and wasn't going to stir up more trouble. She pulled out her phone and tapped out a message.

> There are some pap shots of us from yesterday in the Mail.
> Did you organise them?

The blue ticks appeared almost immediately, then a reply.

> No, I promise. Why would I do that? It could have been
> pics of you slapping my face

This was a fair point.

> OK. I had to ask. Where are you now?

> In taxi to Zurich. I thought about what you said, decided to
> check into a clinic. Four weeks.

Daisy briefly tried to imagine how much that was costing, then dismissed it as not her problem. She wondered if it was their conversation that prompted this decision, or whatever had happened afterwards. A question wormed its way into her head, and she'd asked it before she could stop herself.

Did you see Sophie again last night?

No, I deleted her number. Farmer couple who own B&B cooked me foul dinner

Daisy smiled.

Did they have a daughter?

Yeah but she was 17 with hands like snow shovels. I'd have died on those mountains.

Daisy snorted with laughter, despite the headache that had set in several hours ago. Christian could be funny when he was on form. Probably a good time to wrap this conversation up, while things between them were on a high.

Take care, Christian

I will, thanks. Sorry about everything x

'So you definitely didn't know he was coming?' clarified Katie, having listened to the entire saga in silence. Daisy had moved outside to avoid being overheard, taking shelter under an overhanging roof that was dangerously heavy with snow. It would be just her luck to get dumped on from a great height on top of everything else.

'No, he just turned up,' Daisy repeated. 'He asked me to take him back, I said no, and now he's on his way to a sex addiction clinic in Switzerland.'

'Yeah, I heard that bit the first time,' Katie commented wryly. 'Do I need to know the details?'

'You definitely don't,' said Daisy quickly. 'Those places are super discreet, so hopefully things will go quiet for a bit.'

'How discreet? We could really do with keeping Christian's bonkathons out of the press.'

'I don't know. The Swiss are pretty tight about stuff like this. Christian used to tell me stuff about Swiss tennis players that would make your eyes boggle, but none of it ever ended up in the papers.'

Katie sighed. 'OK. So, what about the headmaster? Have you actually been banging him over the kitchen table?'

Daisy hesitated for a second, reminding herself that nothing good ever came from keeping important information from her manager. 'We kissed,' she said talking over Katie as she started to interrupt. 'It was nothing, but it was in the kitchen of his house, which makes me think he must have told someone, because everyone else had left the party. Or maybe someone was looking through the window, I don't know.'

'Honestly, your life.' Daisy could practically hear Katie rolling her eyes. 'OK, none of this is a big story, but little ones can snowball. Clara called earlier, wondering if you have any plans to stay out of the news for a while, like we all agreed.'

Now it was Daisy's turn to roll her eyes. 'I'm doing my best here. It's not my fault if someone is talking to the tabloids every time I change my knickers.'

'Or don't wear any,' added Katie wryly. 'I think we should release the statement that you and Christian have split up. Get that out of the way so it's one less thing hanging about.'

'No,' said Daisy decisively. 'As long as I'm still living in Shipton Combe they'll name Tom as a third party and turn his life inside out. That would be disastrous for him. Christian being in a clinic is good news; now we've been seen together the press will assume he's here with me all week. I'll stay off Instagram so nobody asks questions and get Ruby and Will to leave me off theirs. So let's stick with the original plan and wait until I'm back in London in a few weeks.'

'And what about you and Tom?' asked Katie gently.

'There is no me and Tom,' Daisy said firmly. 'I shouldn't have kissed him. It was a stupid thing to do. And if he thinks I'm messing him around, he'll stay away.'

'Hmm,' said Katie doubtfully. 'If you say so.'

Daisy's phone buzzed as she shuffled forward in the queue for a ski lift. She waited until she was safely in her seat and soaring up the mountain before she gingerly pulled off her gloves and extracted her phone from her pocket. If it slipped out of her hands it would fall twenty metres into the untouched powder snow below and not be seen again until spring, so this was a delicate operation.

The message was from Simon. She felt a flurry of panic that he needed the cottage back, then briefly considered the possibility that Stella had burned it down and panicked a bit more.

Darling, I need a massive favour. On Saturday
Archie's off to do a garden project in New Hampshire—

Archie was an award-winning garden designer who special-ised in creating beautiful outdoor entertaining spaces, at least according to his website. His clients were usually rich Americans who wanted him to create a classic English coun-try garden for their McMansions, but with a swimming pool and a barbecue the size of a small car.

—It's three weeks over Xmas/NY, the owners are in Aspen so he can live in their house. But I'm taking Ruby to Des's and then first week Jan I'm going on a spa break with Fern Britton. Could you have Hank until Archie gets back? I can drop him off and pick up Ruby at the same time, he LOVES Shipton Combe.

Oh God. Hank was Archie's Jack Russell terrier and Daisy wasn't really a dog person. But she couldn't possibly say no; Simon had lent her his house. At least Hank seemed fairly low maintenance and well behaved.

No problem, messaged Daisy, adding a paw emoji to make her message sound more enthusiastic.

Hank was only a small dog, and it was only three weeks. How hard could it be?

212

CHAPTER TWENTY-SEVEN

'So which run shall we do next?'

Daisy turned her face to the sun in the cable car. Melanie, Ruby and Will had all finished their five-day course of lessons yesterday, and today was everyone's final day of skiing before they all travelled home tomorrow. Last night they'd all agreed that they wanted to spend today together, although Daisy would bet good money on Ruby and Will getting bored of their mothers and going off to do their own thing before lunch.

'Number three!' cried Ruby. 'It's my favourite.' She turned to Will and Melanie, explaining, 'It goes through the forest all the way back to the village, and there's a bar on the way down called Helga's that does amazing hot chocolate. We didn't do it during our lessons. Did you?'

Ruby looked at Melanie, who shook her head. 'We did a few reds but only short ones. Isn't number three a red all the way down?'

Daisy smiled reassuringly. 'The final third is blue,' she said. 'And it's really gorgeous. You should definitely see it, and we can take it steady. There's no hurry.'

Melanie nodded happily, and Daisy thought how different she looked from a few weeks ago. Her face had caught a touch of sun, adding some colour to her ghostly pale cheeks. But it was more than that. She was less jittery and anxious,

213

like her frayed edges had been smoothed off by laughter and mountain air and good company.

Melanie wasn't the kind of person Daisy would normally be friends with, simply because Daisy's friendships had all been formed within the bubble of stage school and the TV industry. But lack of glitter aside, Melanie had the qualities that Daisy really valued in a friend – she was smart, funny and kind and clearly adored her son. Wasn't that what really mattered, at the end of the day? She realised she wanted to keep the friendship going after she went back to London – not just for Ruby and Will, who she suspected might be in each other's lives for quite some time – but for herself too. With the exception of Des, hardly any of her showbiz pals had checked in on her beyond the first couple of weeks after The Incident. Life moved fast in those circles, and there were always a thousand other things to think about.

They headed out of the cable car station into the sunshine, then clipped on all their gear and pushed off down the mountain. Ruby and Will went on ahead, leaning back on the edges of their boards as they expertly weaved in wide loops across the piste. Daisy stayed close behind Melanie, watching her soften her knees and push her shins into the front of her boots as she shifted her weight into the turns. She'd clearly paid attention in her lessons, and her skiing had a nice fluidity and rhythm to it. Already she'd got the hang of parallel turns, albeit Daisy could see the concentration etched on her face as she worked through the mantras she'd been taught. With more practise, it was easy to see that Melanie was going to be a lovely skier.

At the end of the first section the piste narrowed and flattened out a bit, so Melanie kept her skis parallel and let herself speed up, tilting her face to the sun and letting her arms drop by her sides. Daisy pulled alongside her, feeling the wind in her face and the exhilaration of being somewhere so quiet, pristine and beautiful. She hoped this wouldn't be the last time she and Melanie ever went skiing together, but if it was, she realised she'd stored up enough joy and friendship from this week to keep her going for a very long time.

Will and Ruby were already waiting inside when Daisy and Melanie arrived at Helga's, having bagged a table for lunch and ordered themselves hot chocolates. Daisy turned and waved at the waiter, who nodded and came over with a handful of menus. If he recognised her from the other afternoon with Christian, he didn't acknowledge it.

'How was that?' Will looked expectantly at his mother, although it was obvious how she felt from the huge grin that almost split her face.

'It was brilliant. I didn't fall over once.'

'She was amazing,' confirmed Daisy. 'Really impressive. Took that final corner like a pro.'

Will smiled proudly, then dropped a kiss on his mother's cheek. Melanie looked shocked, then delighted. 'What are we eating?' he asked.

Daisy perused the menu. 'Well, as long as it's not your leftover salad, I'll eat pretty much anything.'

Will and Ruby gasped and pretended to be offended. The previous night they'd made dinner from all the bits and bobs left in the fridge, and it had ended up being an eclectic salad featuring dried-up heels of cheese, scraps of cooked meat, cold pasta and shredded bits of stale garlic bread, garnished

215

with black olives and served on a bed of moist Doritos. They'd all ended up laughing so hard that nobody was hungry any more, which was just as well because it had tasted foul. In the end Daisy had sent Will and Ruby to the village shop for crisps, popcorn and Haribos, which they ate while watching *Paddington 2* on DVD. They'd all agreed it was one of their favourite meals of the holiday.

Daisy's phone buzzed on the table, so she took a quick peek. It was Tom. She hadn't heard from him since just before Christian appeared, and a swooping, sick feeling landed in her stomach. Whatever the message was, she couldn't read it here.

She smiled at Will and stood up. 'Can you order me a schnitzel and a beer? I just need to pop outside and deal with a few messages.'

Will nodded and smiled, a look of mild concern on his face, the one he usually saved for his mother. It was nice to be worried about, Daisy thought as she hurried outside, but right now, she'd give a great deal for her life to be less of a shitshow.

Daisy sat on the wooden bench under the eaves of the mountain hut and read Tom's message, looking for any sign of humour or mild flirting.

Hey it's Tom. I've got a plan for the classes if you want to discuss when you get back?

OK, zero flirting. Not so much as a winking smiley.

She watched the steady snowfall for a minute, a dull ache in her chest. He'd obviously seen the photos – they were everywhere – so it was hardly surprising. Daisy wished she could explain and apologise, but if her plan to keep him out of the press was going to work, Frosty Daisy was how it had to be. It was painful but necessary.

Daisy took a deep breath and composed a reply.

> Hey thanks, can we catch up on Sunday? I know
> it's close to Christmas so no probs if you're busy/away.

She waited a few seconds, watching the dots that told her he was writing.

> Sure – I can email parents on the 27th, then give it a push
> on the school Facebook page. We'll need to apply for a
> DBS check for you – usually takes 48 hours. Is that OK?

Daisy had done talks and events in schools before and was pretty sure she had an up-to-date certificate stating she wasn't a criminal or a sex offender, but it didn't hurt for Tom to look.

> Sure, message my manager if you need any details.

She added Katie's email address. More dots.

> OK. Enjoy the rest of your trip.

Ouch. Tom was clearly upset with her. But honestly, who could blame him?

Daisy sat next to Ruby and watched her scrolling through the photos on Will's phone, deleting the ones of her that didn't make the grade. Ski wear and sunny mountains were actually pretty forgiving so most of them were allowed to stay, but there were a few where Ruby's eyes were half-closed or she'd decided her hair looked sweaty and weird. Will had taken some amazing film of her snowboarding too: he had a real talent for video.

'This is a great picture.' Ruby tilted the phone to show Daisy a selfie of the four of them in the cable car. 'Can I put it on Instagram?'

Daisy considered the request for a moment. 'Actually do you mind if I say no? I don't mind pictures of you and me, but I'd prefer no group photos if that's OK?'

Ruby was quiet for a moment, scrolling through more pictures. 'I want a normal job,' she muttered. 'Like a teacher or a lawyer or something.'

'I'm not going to argue with that,' Daisy replied.

'Like, why shouldn't you be allowed to mess up occasionally?' Ruby said, clearly referencing The Incident. 'Why do your mistakes have to follow you around for the rest of time?'

'I wish I knew,' Daisy smiled gamely. Although the fact she was a woman probably had something to do with it.

'Yeah, well, it sucks.' Ruby's mouth was set in a determined line. 'Fame can absolutely do one!'

'Amen to that.' Daisy wondered if Ruby would still feel the same if she reminded her that fame had scored them this holiday.

CHAPTER TWENTY-EIGHT

Tom lay on the floor of his office, feeling cold and hollowed out. He'd been hoping to hear from Daisy all week, just a *hello* or a *how are you?*, maybe something that implied 'I'm sorry I wasn't honest about Christian', but he'd heard nothing. In the end he'd taken the initiative and messaged Daisy himself, and the conversation hadn't made him feel any better at all.

He stood up and walked over to the window of his office, Henry loping along behind him. It was raining hard, the trees in the school grounds bent over against the howling wind. Being cooped up in this place wasn't good for him, especially at this time of year. He should have gone away instead of staying here with nobody but ghosts for company. But where would he go? The mountains reminded him of Tessa, his brother and sister were both abroad and his mother was on a cruise ship somewhere. He briefly considered spending the afternoon drinking red wine in the bath, but the knock at the door saved him.

Angela poked her white-haired head into the office. She was wearing an orange cardigan and a green scarf that made her look like a Halloween pumpkin. She'd been the Shipton School secretary for decades and was generally thought to be older than the building itself, which was early eighteenth century. She was a widow and should have retired years ago to put her feet up and potter around her garden, but her children and grandchildren had all moved away and she was clearly lonely. So, each day, she slowly made her way from her house in the village to her desk outside Tom's office.

Her continued presence raised a few eyebrows among the teachers, mostly because she was breathtakingly rude in a way that only elderly people can get away with, and categorically refused to acknowledge the existence of the school IT system. But Tom defended her till the end. She'd pretty much saved him when Tessa had died, moving into his house for weeks to make sure he ate and washed and didn't kill himself. She liaised with Tessa's parents on funeral arrangements, managed visits and calls from Tom's family, dealt with the wave of cards and frozen meals from teachers, parents and local ghouls, and forced him outside to walk Henry every day. She'd arranged with the governors for the deputy head to take over the running of the school for the rest of the autumn term, while she spent each day with Tom, gently nursing him through a living nightmare, until he could face the world again.

So, the best way he knew how to thank Angela was to keep her in a job for as long as she liked, while quietly doing eighty per cent of the school admin himself. He'd also bought her a mobility scooter when the walk from her cottage to the office started to take longer than the first lesson of the day, not realising this thoughtful gesture would unleash a menace on four wheels. Barely a day went by when a parent wasn't forced to do an emergency stop on the school drive, and the kitchen cat rarely ventured outside these days.

'That bloody vicar is here again,' she whispered, rolling her rheumy eyes. This was the third visit from Reverend Miriam since the story about Daisy and Christian had appeared in the press, and Tom couldn't work out whether she was worried for his tortured soul or just wanted to be in the thick of the gossip. Either way he couldn't face another facile chat about the winter fete: he'd rather cut off an arm with school scissors.

'Can you let her know I'm busy with prep for mocks?' said Tom, gesturing towards the untouched pile of folders gathering dust on his desk. 'It's really not a great time. I'll stop for a chat after the carol service on Friday.'

Angela winked conspiratorially and quietly closed the door. Tom sat on the floor again, his back against the scalding radiator, and waited for Henry to haul himself over to join him. The dog draped himself across Tom's legs, imparting a furry warmth that felt lovely now, but would at some point cut off the circulation to Tom's lower limbs so he couldn't stand up. He stroked Henry's head until he huffed contentedly, then pulled out his phone to call Tessa's parents. It was a call he made three or four times a year that was guaranteed to make everyone involved feel like utter shit, but since he felt terrible anyway, he might as well go for gold.

CHAPTER TWENTY-NINE

Daisy's first stop in Shipton Combe was the rectory, where she and Ruby helped Melanie and Will unload their luggage. The drive back from Heathrow had been a ninety-mile battle against driving rain and side winds, and Daisy needed a cup of tea and an hour in front of the fire with her eyes closed.

Gerald came out to meet them, giving Melanie an awkward hug and shaking Will's hand like he was about to help him open his first bank account. Daisy braced herself for some over-familiar kissing and was slightly taken aback when Gerald opted for just a polite arm pat, then shook Ruby's hand warmly. Daisy spotted Will surreptitiously raise his eyebrows at his mother, who gave him a stern look in return.

Melanie invited them in for tea but Daisy made their excuses, so they hugged goodbye. It was strange how close they had all become in just a week.

'How are you feeling?' Daisy asked her daughter as they pulled out of the rectory and turned into the school drive. Will and Ruby kept their goodbyes brief, subtle and chaste, but Daisy knew they were planning to see each other again in the morning before Simon picked her up.

'Pretty good,' smiled Ruby. 'Thanks for an amazing trip.'

Daisy beamed. 'You're really welcome.' She reached over to briefly squeeze her daughter's hand.

'I'm knackered now though,' Ruby yawned. 'Do we have to do anything else today?'

'Nope,' Daisy smiled. 'I'm thinking a cup of tea and a movie in our pyjamas. Let's see what we can find in the freezer for dinner. Hopefully your granny's been cooking while we've been away.' Even the prospect of seeing Stella couldn't ruin her post-holiday joy.

Ruby sighed happily. 'That sounds perfect.'

'SURPRISE!' shouted Simon, bursting out of Willow Cottage with his arms in the air like he'd been picked from the audience on *Wheel of Fortune*. Stella and Archie followed closely behind, both beaming and waving. Archie was holding a small brown and white dog who wriggled with excitement at all the noise.

'Oh God,' mumbled Daisy, closing the car door as their cosy evening in front of the fire slipped away before her eyes.

'We thought we'd surprise you!' Simon gave Ruby a huge hug. 'I'm sorry I missed your birthday, sweetheart, but we can celebrate this evening instead.'

'That's OK,' said Ruby, rallying from her tiredness at the sight of her dad. Daisy's mother stood in the doorway behind them, arms folded, watching.

'Are you staying tonight?' asked Daisy, hoping very much they weren't.

'No, Archie's flying to New Hampshire tomorrow morning, so we thought we might give you a crash course on caring for Hank over dinner, then take Ruby back tonight.'

Daisy pasted on a happy smile. 'Well, that sounds lovely.' She caught Stella's eye and tried not to look too pained.

223

'We can go to the pub,' suggested Stella. 'Save anyone having to cook.' Daisy could have hugged her.

'Do you want Will to come?' Daisy asked Ruby. 'So he can meet your dad?'

'Ooh, YES', Simon exclaimed. 'I can do my fatherly stern face, ask him about his intentions for my little girl.'

'Actually, that's a no,' said Ruby quickly. 'He's going to want to spend some time with his dad after a week away, but I'll pop round before dinner to say goodbye if we're going tonight.'

Daisy nodded sagely. 'Very wise decision.'

Simon quickly rallied. 'And since we're talking about inviting boyfriends,' he said casually, turning to Daisy, 'how about the hunky headmaster?'

Daisy rolled her eyes and unloaded the bags from the boot of the car. 'I've only been back five minutes, Si,' she mumbled. 'Just put the kettle on, will you?'

Despite not really having the space or the availability four days before Christmas, Lesley the landlady was more than happy to squeeze a table for five into a quiet nook of the Shipton Arms, particularly when Daisy put the call in. By the time they arrived it felt the whole village was in situ, craning their necks to get a look at Daisy and Simon as they walked through the bar. Daisy waved at Justin, who was sipping water at the bar with Marcus, while Miriam was sat in the far corner with various people from the church committee, nursing what looked like an orange juice. She was too busy gesticulating to acknowledge the new arrivals, although everyone else in the group was rubbernecking. Daisy scanned the pub for Tom, torn between wanting to see his face and desperately hoping he wasn't there. But there was no sign of him, so she breathed a little more easily.

Ruby sat at the head of the table with Simon on her left and Daisy on her right, so Stella sat next to Simon and Archie took up the final chair opposite her. He'd brought Hank, who sat on his lap with his tongue hanging out, happily observing the goings-on around him. Archie was older than Simon by a good decade and was, without question, the most stylish man Daisy had ever met. This evening he wore an exquisitely tailored tweed waistcoat with a fitted cream shirt and designer dark green cords, and had a red handkerchief tucked into his breast pocket. He'd been in the Cotswolds for barely a few hours and had already assumed the look of the perfectly groomed, country gentleman à la GQ. Not many men could pull that off with such panache, but Archie absolutely nailed it. Daisy had to admire him, even if he had stolen her husband.

It takes two to tango, thought Daisy. And by all accounts they'd been dancing for some months before Simon came clean and told her the truth. Over time she'd trained herself to think about it without pain; the fact that Simon was so happy and Archie so charming made it considerably easier.

'He's not food-motivated like other dogs.' Archie looked lovingly at the dog, who in turn looked at Daisy and panted happily. 'He wants love and attention. So you need to show him that good behaviour will mean you'll give him lots of fuss.' Daisy raised her eyebrows. Archie rarely seemed to put Hank down, so he was in for a bleak and lonely few weeks with Daisy.

She smiled and patted Hank's head reassuringly, half-listening to Ruby telling her dad all about their trip. Ruby had Daisy's fair skin and hair, but her cheekbones and brown eyes were all Simon's. They'd been quite the celebrity family back in the day – Simon was still remembered fondly from his time on Breakfast TV, but now he wrote erotic thrillers for a living and was more than happy to tap away in the attic room at home and leave the spotlight to Daisy. For a while though, they'd been TV's dream couple, so it was no wonder half the pub was tying themselves in knots to get a look at them.

When the wine arrived Daisy noticed Stella covering her glass and shaking her head, which made her wonder if she'd spent last night getting hammered with Justin. It wasn't like her mother to refuse a drink. Daisy surreptitiously watched her for a minute or two, observing that she didn't look hungover. In fact, even in the dim light of the pub, Stella looked remarkably well – clear-eyed and healthy, without the veiny cheeks and saggy skin that were signs that she was well into the drink. She'd brought all her belongings back to the pub with her, checking back into the room with the horrible wisteria wallpaper without any fuss. Daisy hadn't spent much time in Willow Cottage before they'd left for dinner, but she did notice that it had been cleaned and the sheets changed. So maybe she wasn't giving her mum enough credit.

'I have a question for you,' Daisy said nervously. She'd been battling with the logic of this idea ever since she'd thought of it in the hot tub in Austria, and still wasn't completely convinced it was the way to go. She and Stella had a turbulent relationship, and there was a risk this would dial up the drama.

'Go on,' Stella encouraged, taking a sip of water.

'It's about my cookbook—'

'OUR cookbook,' interrupted Ruby with an exaggerated glare.

Daisy rolled her eyes. 'You haven't even looked at the recipes. But you'll still get your picture on the cover and take half the royalties without doing a single minute of work.'

Ruby shrugged and grinned. 'You need me. I'm your angle. You can't write a cookbook for teenagers without a teenager.'

'Hmm.' Daisy turned back to Stella. 'Anyway, I need to test all the recipes and the headmaster—' she glared at Simon and Archie, whose ears had pricked up, 'the headmaster has offered to organise some after-school sessions.'

'I bet he has,' smirked Simon, making Archie snort.

'*With the kids*,' Daisy hissed, 'like a cooking club. So, I wondered if you might help.'

'Me?' Stella's eyes widened in surprise. 'What kind of help?'

Daisy took a deep breath, wondering if she might live to regret this. 'Well, actually I was hoping you might run the classes. That's your speciality, after all.'

Stella's face softened into a beaming smile. 'Well, that's very kind of you to say so. I'm sure I can help.'

'Lovely.' Daisy watched as Stella placed her hand over her glass, refusing Simon's offer of wine again. Maybe it would all be OK.

'How many are you going to have in a class, Mum?' asked Ruby.

'Quite a few, I think. Maybe twenty or so, and four or five classes. It's going to be brilliant research for the book.'

Stella frowned and pondered for a minute or two while everyone perused the menu. 'Twenty is quite a lot of pupils for one teacher. Could Justin help too?'

Daisy hadn't thought about Justin, but it made a lot of sense. He was an experienced chef and the kids already knew and liked him. 'That's an interesting idea,' she said slowly. 'Do you think he'd want to get involved?'

Stella gave a booming laugh. 'Darling, he's bored out of his mind and *you're* Daisy Crawford. Of course he'll want to get involved.'

'What are you doing for your birthday, Mum?' Ruby asked as Archie settled the bill and everyone else was putting their coats on. Daisy wondered why Stella was bothering when she was only going upstairs, but the rooms in this place were probably freezing.

Daisy shrugged. 'I haven't really thought about it.' She was due to turn forty in three weeks, and she and Christian had talked before about a trip to the Caribbean. A little house on stilts, swaying palm trees, lots of hammock sex. *Not happening.*

'Remind me when it is again?' Simon looked a little mortified at failing to remember the birthday of a woman he'd been married to for six years and with whom he had a child.

'Twelfth of January.' Daisy rolled her eyes at him. 'It's a Saturday.'

'What's happening on the twelfth of January?' asked Archie, returning from the bar.

'Daisy's turning forty,' said Stella, 'but she hasn't made any plans.'

'Well, that won't do at all,' said Archie. 'Simon's dropping Ruby back at school that week, but we were planning to come back together to fetch Hank that weekend, so perhaps we can stay overnight for a little celebration.'

Ruby clapped her hands. 'That's a brilliant idea. Granny and I will organise something.'

'Fine.' Daisy looked dubious. 'But just a family thing. I'm heading back to London straight after that so don't drag any of my friends down here.'

'Not until after the twenty-sixth of January, though,' said Stella, her brow furrowing.

'Why?' said Daisy. 'What's happening on the twenty-sixth of January?'

'The church winter fete,' said Stella. 'You need to be here to help me with the judging.'

Daisy looked confused. 'Judging for what? That's the first I've heard.'

'Really?' said Stella innocently. 'I was *sure* I'd told you. I must have agreed on your behalf. You're declaring the fete open, then judging the cake competition. Nothing you can't do with your eyes closed.' She paused for effect then put her hand on Daisy's arm. 'It's a small ask. Miriam is counting on you.'

Daisy took a few deep yogic breaths. She looked at Simon, who raised his eyebrows in amusement, his fingers pressed to his lips. Archie turned away to face Ruby, both of them shaking with silent laughter as they waited for Daisy to let rip.

'For God's sake, Mum,' said Daisy through gritted teeth, conscious that everyone in the pub was eavesdropping. *'We'll talk about this another time.'*

CHAPTER THIRTY

Melanie and Will sat at the kitchen table with Gerald and Tom, eating a beef stew that Gerald had paid the chef at the Shipton Arms to make, soon to be followed by an apple crumble that was currently warming in the AGA. Gerald had wanted his wife and son to have something nice to eat when they got back, and Tom had suggested he outsource the job to avoid burning the house down.

The kitchen felt warm and cosy with the heating on, even though the wind was whistling through one of the windows and the cat was sitting in the hole in the floorboards again. According to Gerald it wasn't even their cat; she just wandered in every now and then and slept in the hole for a while, then disappeared again, sometimes for months. Nobody knew her name, so everyone in the house just called her Cat. She was currently eyeing the baubles beadily on the tree that Gerald had hastily put up, again at Tom's urging. Melanie usually handled that kind of thing.

'Have you had a good week, Tom?' Melanie asked, then blushed furiously. Tom smiled awkwardly, assuming she'd read the story in the *Mail* and wondering how much Daisy had told her.

'It's been fine,' said Tom. 'Gerald and I have kept each other company.' He'd pushed back hard against coming along to dinner this evening, feeling strongly that Gerald should have an evening alone with his family, but Gerald had insisted. He had things to discuss with Melanie and Will, and he wanted Tom there for moral support. Tom had agreed to come but it was more for Will than Gerald, whom he thought had behaved questionably.

'Tom has been helping me with a project I've been working on,' Gerald stated, prompting Melanie and Will to both freeze mid-mouthful and stare at him. 'We've . . . well, I've been doing some work on our finances while you two have been gallivanting in the mountains, and I thought we should talk about it. As a family.' He tried to keep his voice upbeat and friendly, which just made him sound like a bullshitting politician.

Melanie and Will looked at each other, then at Tom, then at Gerald.

'I didn't realise we had any finances.' Will's face was deadpan.

Tom cleared his throat. 'I'll just clear these plates and check on the apple crumble.' He quickly crossed the room before anyone could say anything, busying himself at the sink, listening in to the conversation while making sure he was far enough away not to intrude.

'Well,' he heard Gerald say. 'As you know things have been quite difficult for a number of years since I . . . lost my job.'

Tom could see Melanie's eyes had narrowed into tiny slits. Gerald looked away, then quickly rallied. 'But the remainder of my mother's estate has finally been resolved, so we have an opportunity to improve things.'

He waited but Melanie and Will said nothing, so Gerald ploughed on. 'The legalities around it are complicated, but

Tom has kindly helped me work through the details and I've now come to an agreement with my sisters.' Tom knew that Gerald hadn't spoken a word to his sisters that wasn't via lawyers since his mother's funeral, but throwing them into the mix gave his story credibility. Even Melanie apparently thought they were grasping witches.

'OK,' Will said finally. 'But what does that mean?'

'It means we have some money.' Gerald rested his palms on the kitchen table like he was about to make a speech in the Commons. 'Enough to do some work on this house, if that's what we want to do. Or we could sell this place and buy something different.' As if on cue, a window slammed shut in a distant corner of the house. 'Perhaps a little less draughty.'

Melanie remained silent, her eyes boring into the depths of Gerald's soul. It was clear to Tom that the timing of this revelation wasn't fooling her, but was it too little, too late?

Will glanced between his parents, clearly unsettled by his mother's long silence. 'What do you think, Mum?'

Tom silently scrubbed down the sink, thinking of second chances, and how important they were. He and Tessa had loved each other deeply, but they'd also taken each other for granted, become complacent in their marriage. Why make every moment count when you have years of moments laid out ahead of you? And then their very last moment together involved Tom shouting from the kitchen to ask Tessa to pick up some screenwash. Tessa had died a few hours later, and the last thing he'd said to her was 'Get one of the five-litre ones', not 'I love you' or 'You mean the world to me' or 'I can't wait for our baby to arrive', but a request for fucking screenwash.

Gerald had a second chance here; an opportunity to make sure Melanie knew she was loved and valued every single day. And Tom wanted that second chance too, so maybe if he did a good thing for Gerald, karma would reward him with the woman he now knew he had fallen hopelessly in love with. How pathetic was that?

'I think we should sell this place,' said Melanie, the clatter of her fork on the plate pulling Tom back into the room. 'It's far too big and expensive to run. I'd love somewhere cosy and light that we can look after properly. Maybe three bedrooms and a nice garden.'

Don't blink, Gerald, thought Tom. *Let her lay her cards on the table.*

'I'm also thinking of going back to college,' continued Melanie, the slight wobble in her voice betraying her nerves. 'Getting my skills up to date so I can get an admin job. So that would help with our finances too, particularly once Will finishes school.'

Tom started filling the dishwasher and resisted the urge to give Melanie a cheer: she was offering to negotiate on the terms of a future partnership, rather than seeking punishment and reparations like many people in her situation would. She was a better person than all of them, but Gerald already knew that. His thoughts drifted to Daisy again, wondering what she was doing this evening. Maybe Christian had returned to Shipton Combe with her and was currently making Daisy's dinner. It hurt to think about.

'I've been considering that too,' said Gerald. 'Getting back to work, making myself useful. Property was always my thing and I've still got some contacts in the industry.'

'Can I learn to drive?' Will interjected. Tom turned and

233

briefly caught his eye, feeling a small burst of pride. Will may have inherited his mother's mild manner, but he'd learnt the importance of choosing your moment from his father.

'Of course,' Gerald replied jovially. 'Your mother will need a little car if she's at college or working, so perhaps you and she can share it until we see what the future holds for you.'

Will beamed at him. 'This is going to be brilliant. I'm sorry you couldn't come skiing, Dad. You'd have loved it.'

Gerald's voice wobbled with emotion as he patted his son on the shoulder. 'Well,' he said quietly. 'Perhaps next time.'

My work here is done, thought Tom, taking the apple crumble out of the AGA and putting it on the table with a jug of cream. 'Thanks for dinner,' he said with a warm smile as he grabbed his coat. 'I'll see myself out.'

CHAPTER THIRTY-ONE

Daisy decided to take Hank to her meeting with Tom on Sunday morning, primarily so she could give him a walk on the school fields and introduce him to Henry as a potential playmate, but also so she and Tom would have something to talk about that might make things a little less frosty. She was banking on Tom being less upset with her if she had a cute dog in tow, particularly two days before Christmas.

Hank's first night at Willow Cottage had been surprisingly successful – he hadn't seemed remotely bothered about Simon and Archie's departure and had settled down on Daisy's lap for an hour or so of head scratches and belly rubs while she drank a peppermint tea and watched *Love Actually* before bed. Daisy had made a feeble attempt to get him to settle on his blanket in front of the wood burner but had given up after a few minutes of whining to let him sleep on her bed. Archie had warned her that he often slept with him and Simon, so Daisy hadn't really expected to win that battle. Hank had curled up behind her knees and slept soundly, then licked her face urgently at 7 a.m. until Daisy carried him downstairs, put her coat and wellies over her pyjamas and let him outside. Daisy had to admit she'd found his furry warmth rather comforting, and at least he didn't snore.

She packed Hank's lead, snacks and a couple of chew toys in her shoulder bag along with her laptop and recipe notes, then tucked him under her arm as she opened the front door to the cottage. Yesterday's wind and rain had given way to a sunny, mild day, a world away from the cold of the mountains. Daisy buttoned up her jacket and dug her sunglasses out of her bag; her hair was still damp from the shower but she left it to dry in the breeze. In the absence of her favourite blow-dry bar in Camden, nature would do nicely.

Minutes later, Daisy climbed the stairs to Tom's office, noting with a tinge of regret that she hadn't been invited to his house this time. She passed Reverend Miriam on the stairs, looking stressed and flustered and very much like she was running late for an impending birth in Bethlehem. Miriam mumbled a harried 'Good morning' and scuttled off, her yellow scarf flapping in her wake.

Tom was standing by the window when Daisy poked her head around his office's open door. Henry was sitting nobly by his side.

'Hey,' she said, and he turned to give her a weak smile, before brightening up considerably at the sight of Hank in her arms.

'Hey. Who's this?' Tom crossed the room, reaching out to relieve Daisy of either her bag or the dog. She passed him a wriggling Hank, who licked his face appreciatively.

'His name's Hank,' Daisy said. 'He belongs to my ex-husband and his husband.' Tom's brow furrowed briefly as he worked that concept through. 'I'm dog-sitting for a few weeks.' Daisy put her bag down and smiled at Tom fussing Hank's ears. 'Will Henry be OK with him?' she asked.

'He'll be fine,' Tom grinned. 'Henry loves other dogs, don't you?' Henry gave a vague sniff in the direction of the new arrival, but otherwise looked unimpressed. 'Do they hunt with him?' he asked, putting Hank down next to Henry. 'Jack Russells are amazing at flushing out rabbits.'

'They live in north London,' Daisy said with a wry smile. 'The only thing Hank flushes out is bins and picnics.'

Daisy and Tom watched as Hank investigated every inch of Henry with his nose before doing a few laps of the office and finally cheekily settling into Henry's bed. Henry huffed and settled down by the radiator, eyeing the intruder moodily.

'Working this close to Christmas?' said Daisy airily.

'Writing school reports.' Tom gestured towards the pile of cardboard folders on his desk. 'The teachers have done their bit, now I'm supposed to read them all and write some personal remarks on each one before parents' evenings in January. I've nearly finished.' Daisy noticed the dark circles under his eyes. His hair needed a cut and there was another hole in the elbow of his navy jumper.

'How was Reverend Miriam?' Daisy wondered if there was any chance she might be offered a coffee, then decided it was unlikely.

'Concerned for my spiritual welfare,' said Tom. 'She came over to ask if I'd accompany her to church. I said no thank you. Tessa was the churchgoer, not me.'

'I imagine rejection must be part and parcel of being a vicar,' she said, then immediately wished she could take the words back. She blushed and looked at her hands.

'Not just vicars,' mumbled Tom.

Ouch.

'—How was your holiday?'

'Great,' Daisy smiled. 'The kids had a fabulous time. Melanie too.'

'And you?' asked Tom pointedly.

Daisy took a deep breath, unable to meet his eyes. 'I had a fabulous time too. Christian coming was very last minute, but it was good to see him.'

A brief wince of pain crossed Tom's face. 'I'm glad.'

I'm doing this for you, Tom. I can't explain it because you'll never understand. But it's the right thing to do.

Tom opened the door to the domestic science classroom and stood aside to let Daisy pass. 'We had some people in last week to sort this place out,' he told her. 'Electrician, plumber, decorator. The ovens are a bit old but they still work.'

Daisy looked around, breathing in the smell of fresh paint and kitchen cleaner. 'It looks great,' she said, giving him a genuinely grateful smile.

'A couple of the teachers went to IKEA on your behalf.' Tom opened a drawer in one of the five workstations, each with an oven and hob and space for four pupils. 'They got some stuff for each group – bowls, knives, peelers, that sort of thing. Funnily enough I found one of your mum's old textbooks and used the equipment list from that.'

Daisy looked in the drawer, then opened a cupboard, impressed to see new mixing bowls and saucepans.

'Wow, this is amazing,' she muttered. 'Can you give me the bill?'

Tom shook his head, leaning against one of the counters with his arms folded. His expression was hard to read but she could see what he was – a decent, kind man. In many ways it would be so much easier if he was less nice; more smug and arrogant like Christian, or self-obsessed like Marcus.

Instead he was just incredibly attractive on multiple levels, which made this whole situation so much harder to bear.

'No need,' said Tom. 'The governors have agreed to free up some funds. To be honest this is great publicity for the school – the parents are already talking and it will be a big story locally.' He gave a small laugh. 'Not much happens around here. We might pick up a few new pupils, at which point a few hundred quid for saucepans and tin openers is kind of irrelevant.'

Daisy nodded, her face lined with uncertainty. 'OK, but my reputation isn't exactly pristine right now, were all the governors OK with it?'

Tom shrugged, picking up a fork and turning it over in his hands. 'The thing at the NTAs was obviously unfortunate—' Daisy looked away, feeling the familiar cringe of embarrassment, '—but it's old news now. Nobody died, and you're still a big name. You also have to remember that most of the parents are our age,' added Tom. 'They've grown up with you. We can't cancel now, if that's what you're thinking – everyone's buzzing about it. I'd have a riot on my hands.'

Appeased, Daisy boosted herself up to sit on one of the worktops and rummaged in her bag, drawing out her lists. 'OK,' she said briskly. 'Shall I talk you through my plan?'

Twenty minutes later, Daisy had outlined her ideas for what each year group would cook and agreed to do five classes in total – Years 8 and 9 the first week back after Christmas, and Years 10, 11 and 12 the week after. Year 13 were up to their necks in prep for mock A levels and were a bit old for the book anyway.

'I've been thinking about some extra pairs of hands,' Daisy said. 'Twenty kids is quite a lot for me to handle.'

'Who did you have in mind?' Tom asked, his voice softer and friendlier than when she'd turned up in his office. Maybe he was thawing, thought Daisy, and they could find a neutral space where they could at least be friends.

'My mother and Justin,' said Daisy. 'Mum is an expert on teaching schoolkids to cook, and I figure they already know Justin.'

Tom nodded slowly. 'That's a really good idea. Do we need to get them over now?'

Daisy shook her head. 'No. I think we should probably focus on the email to parents today. I'll speak to Justin later on.'

'OK. Let's go back to my office, see if the dogs have trashed it.'

Daisy laughed, thinking how different Tom was to the first time she'd met him. In less than three months she'd gone from hating his guts to snogging his face off to putting him in the friend zone for his own safety. It occurred to her that some people were married for decades and went through fewer ups and downs.

The walk back to Tom's office seemed to take forever, both of them walking side by side in silence, the air between them electric with unanswered questions and unrequited yearnings. At one point they both reached for the same door handle and their hands touched, and Tom leapt back like he'd trapped his fingers in a sandwich toaster.

'I'm sorry,' said Daisy, feeling like any apology she made wasn't even going to touch the sides.

'It was entirely my fault,' said Tom, and Daisy suspected he wasn't talking about the door handle either.

Henry and Hank were both in Henry's bed when they got back to Tom's office, looking very cute, although the pile of reports on Tom's desk looked suspiciously like they'd been snuffled about by a small animal. There didn't seem to be any damage, however, so when Tom popped out to make coffee Daisy hastily straightened up the pile and did a quick frisk of the office for any smelly gifts Hank may have left behind. Hank watched her with a frantically wagging tail, and Daisy had to admit he was kind of adorable. She squatted down and stroked his pure white back, where a brown patch down each side met under his barrel of a belly. His head and ears were entirely brown apart from an inch of white that ran down his nose to his whiskery chin.

Archie had acquired Hank from a client whose husband had spent two years training the dog as a devoted companion, then dropped dead of a heart attack in Waitrose. The woman couldn't bear to keep her dead husband's pining dog and didn't want to give him to a rescue centre, so she spent the time it took for Archie to design her a memorial garden persuading him to give Mr Tumnus a home. Simon had agreed on the condition they changed the dog's name, since he categorically refused to shout 'Mr Tumnus' in any public space. Daisy remembered Simon's call a year earlier, informing her that Archie was 'on his way home from Narnia with a fucking dog.' Since Archie's surname was Williams, Hank was both suitably manly and secured his place as a fully fledged member of the family.

Tom came back with two mugs of instant coffee, so they sat on opposite sides of his desk and drafted the email to parents, detailing the dates and inviting children from each year group to sign up on a first-come, first-served basis. Classes were free, and they'd be welcome to take home whatever they cooked. Daisy insisted on covering the cost of ingredients but agreed that the school could order everything for her through their wholesalers. After a few minutes Hank abandoned Henry's bed for Daisy's lap, nudging her hand until she gently stroked between his ears while she and Tom worked through the details.

'How do you feel about them bringing their phones?' asked Tom. 'I'm guessing some of them will want a photo.'

'Definitely no phones,' said Daisy emphatically, 'apart from mine. I need to take pictures for Instagram.' After what happened at the NTAs Daisy would happily ban smartphones entirely. 'We should include that,' she added, gesturing at the draft on Tom's laptop. 'Permission to use the pictures or video on social or in the book or whatever. I can't be doing with having to remember which kids I can and can't take pictures of. So if that's a problem, parents shouldn't sign them up.'

'Fair enough,' said Tom, tapping another paragraph into the email. 'Anything else?'

Daisy thought for a moment. 'No food allergies,' she said. 'Vegans are fine, but after the few months I've had, I'd probably kill someone with a walnut.'

'Agreed,' said Tom. 'That's everything, I think. I'll get Angela to send it out to parents next week.'

'Right,' said Daisy, feeling like she was being dismissed. 'Is there anything else?'

'I don't think so,' said Tom, eyeing her carefully. 'Do you?'

Daisy took a deep breath and gathered up her belongings,

wishing she could just tell him everything, then reminding herself that it was better in the long run if he thought she was a shitty human being.

'No,' said Daisy. 'I think we're all done.'

Daisy walked Hank back across the school field, letting the fresh air blow away her sadness and pain over Tom, and hoping it would all be worth it. Justin was unloading his wheelbarrow when Daisy walked round the corner from the stables, so she stopped to introduce Hank and ask him about the classes. Stella had already mentioned it and he was more than happy to help.

'Right now I'll do anything that isn't milking a goat or peeling vegetables,' said Justin gloomily. 'You could ask me to clean out your septic tank and I'd bite your arm off.'

'How many weeks left now?' asked Daisy with a smile.

'Six,' replied Justin, looking a little brighter. 'Or forty days, to be exact. The book is pretty much finished, thanks to your mum. Just got to write the final chapter about what I've learnt from the experience.'

'And what have you learnt, Justin?' asked Daisy, grinning playfully.

'Never to sign up for anything this fucking stupid again,' Justin muttered. 'I want a quiet life from now on.'

'Sure you do,' said Daisy. 'I've just been to see Tom,' she added, ignoring Justin's suggestive eyebrow raising. 'He suggested we all get together to talk about the classes after Christmas. You, me, Stella and Tom. I might invite Will too, see if I can rope him in to doing some videoing for my Instagram. He took loads of great videos while we were skiing, he's got a real talent for it.'

'He's coming to mine for Christmas lunch.'

'Who, Will?' asked Daisy, thoroughly confused.

'No, Tom,' said Justin. 'I didn't want him to spend it alone.'

Daisy ignored the implication that it was somehow her fault that Tom was alone; she had no idea what he'd told Justin, but suspected not very much. 'I'm spending it with Mum. She's cooking.'

'I know,' said Justin. 'She told me. But it seems mad to me that you and Stella are in one house, and Tom and me are next door. Why don't we all eat together?'

Daisy hesitated. The reason was Tom, of course, but she couldn't tell Justin that. 'I can't eat what you're eating,' she said with a playful smile. 'No disrespect, Justin, but even Mary and Joseph's donkey wouldn't eat your shitty diet.'

'I thought I might take a day off,' said Justin. 'As long as nobody tells. It's what the baby Jesus would have wanted.'

Daisy laughed, trying to buy herself some time to think of another excuse. 'Have you mentioned this idea to Tom?'

'Yeah,' said Justin. 'Yesterday. He was all right with it as long as you were.' He raised his eyebrows questioningly, but Daisy looked away so he didn't see her blush. This all felt horribly awkward, but she couldn't see any way out if Tom was OK with it. And at least it meant not spending Christmas Day alone with her mum, which was a bleak prospect indeed.

'We'll come to yours, shall we?' said Justin, not willing to let this go until he had a firm agreement. Daisy nodded reluctantly, then pulled out her phone to call Stella. The number of people at their Christmas table had just doubled, which meant an emergency trip to Waitrose tomorrow.

CHAPTER THIRTY-TWO

In the end it was Daisy who ended up doing most of the festive cooking and preparation, because Stella decided to go to church at 9.30 on Christmas morning to show support for Miriam. As far as Daisy knew, Stella had never been to church for anything other than a wedding or a funeral, but it gave Daisy a peaceful couple of hours in the kitchen to make a trifle and peel vegetables while listening to 'Carols from Kings' on the radio, watched beadily by Hank. She reached down to scratch between his ears every few minutes, remembering that he needed lots of love and attention. At least one of them was getting some. Her thoughts drifted to Tom, then she berated herself for thinking about him. But even as she put on a dress and proper makeup for the first time since she'd arrived in Shipton Combe, she found herself wondering if he'd like this slightly more polished look, or was actually quite taken with the everyday version.

Ruby called mid-morning – she and Simon were joining Des Parker and his family for Christmas lunch. Daisy felt a pang of longing to be immersed in festive spirit with her friends and family, but also knew there would be too many questions, too many concerned looks. She'd finish the project she'd set herself when she arrived in Shipton Combe, then go back to London with renewed focus and energy. If she left now, she'd probably never come back.

'Merry Christmas!' shouted Stella as she opened the front door, telling someone else to hang their coat on the hook. Daisy took a deep breath and headed through to the lounge, wondering if Stella had somehow persuaded Justin to go to church with her. But it wasn't Justin, or even Tom. For reasons best known to herself, Stella had brought the Reverend Miriam Mayhew back with her.

'I hope you don't mind,' Miriam said sheepishly. 'Your mother absolutely insisted I join you for lunch.'

'She was going to eat alone,' said Stella in an undertone. 'I thought we could easily find an extra place at our humble festive table.' She delivered this with the gravitas of Kenneth Branagh at the RSC, like suddenly they were a refuge for the single and lonely of Shipton Combe.

'Of course.' Daisy reminded herself of how helpful Miriam had been in keeping her mother occupied and forced herself to think charitable thoughts. There was plenty of food, and at least it provided another buffer against Tom.

'I brought you a present,' said Tom a couple of hours later, as he and Justin bustled through the door and Henry immediately bagged a space on the sofa next to Hank. Tom was holding a tiny Christmas tree in a pot, tied with a red ribbon and decorated with miniscule baubles and lights. 'I thought you might not have one, since you only got back a few days ago.'

Daisy took the tree and blinked away tears, recognising it as a peace offering. Tom had worked through his issues over the news story about her and Christian and decided to surrender gracefully. She adored him for it, but also felt immeasurably sad that this was the way it had to be between them.

'Thank you,' she said quietly. 'By the time I went to Waitrose yesterday there was nothing nice left, so I don't have a single decoration.' She leaned over and kissed him gently on the cheek, giving his arm a squeeze for good measure. He smelled of lemony soap and shampoo, without a hint of designer aftershave or skincare and hair products. Most of the men in Daisy's life smelled expensive; Christian's skin and haircare regime took twenty minutes every day, and she'd never really appreciated the appeal of someone who just smelled . . . clean. Her mind briefly wondered what Tom might look like naked, and she had a sudden urge to kick everyone else out and bundle him up the stairs.

'Should I open some fizz?' asked Justin, grinning gleefully. Daisy blushed as she noticed the group in the kitchen doorway, transfixed by them both; Miriam looking slightly embarrassed and Stella all misty-eyed, like she was witnessing their wedding vows. She and Tom quickly moved apart and made themselves busy with coats and dogs as Justin popped a cork with great enthusiasm. He'd freed himself from the shackles of a highly restrictive diet for one day only, and clearly didn't plan to waste it.

'This looks wonderful, Daisy,' said Miriam, raising an elderflower cordial in her direction as they all took their seats an hour later. 'Merry Christmas to you.'

'Merry Christmas,' added the others, although Justin was already half-cut and louder than everyone else combined. Daisy glanced at Tom, who gave her a half-smile that turned her loins to mush, then raised his glass in a gesture that felt like it was just for her. Her breath caught in her chest and her cheeks flushed, and it dawned on her exactly how difficult it was going to be to stay away from Tom Clark.

They were on opposite sides of the small dining table, which in some ways was better because she could see his face and catch his glances. But she also wanted to be next to him, breathing in his scent and feeling the heat of his body, holding his hand in hers as Miriam said Grace. She tried to focus on her food, but every time she looked up he was *there*, passing over a dish or looking at her in a way that made her neck feel hot. How was she supposed to focus on *anything*?

By the time the meal was finished, Daisy had decided that she really didn't object to this eclectic collection of people at all. Miriam was quiet and appreciative and didn't drink, and that seemed to have had a knock-on influence on Stella, who only put away one glass of champagne and half a glass of wine over the whole of lunch, which was practically unheard of. Justin was plastered but also a natural storyteller with a brilliant ability to involve everyone in the conversation, and Tom was his literal and figurative straight man, taking his gentle ribbing with good grace.

'Come on, Tom,' slurred Justin, waving his empty glass in Daisy's direction, apparently hoping for a refill. 'Are you seriously telling us you've never responded to the advances of any of the school single mothers?'

'Never,' said Tom, giving Daisy an apologetic glance. 'It would be unprofessional and far too complicated.'

'Not even a quick snog behind the bike sheds?—'

'That was a wonderful lunch, Daisy,' said Miriam loudly. 'An absolute treat to be with friends on this holy day.'

'—We don't have any bike sheds,' smiled Tom. 'They all

248

turn up in four-wheel drives. And anyway, does anyone *snog* any more?'

'Let's make some coffee,' said Stella, patting Daisy's hand as she stood up. Daisy gathered up all the trifle bowls and followed her into the kitchen. Justin was going to have a terrible hangover tomorrow, but he was too drunk to rein in now.

'You need to talk to him,' whispered Stella, closing the kitchen door behind them.

'Who, Justin?' asked Daisy.

'No,' Stella rolled her eyes, looking just like Ruby. 'Tom. You need to talk to Tom.'

'About what?'

'About you and him.'

Daisy busied herself loading the dishwasher. 'There is no me and him.'

'Daisy, I'm your mother, and I'm not blind. I don't know what's happened between you, but there's definitely *something*. You both keep looking at each other, then looking away. It's like a bad film.'

'Nothing's happened,' blushed Daisy, wishing her mother wasn't quite so eagle-eyed. 'Christian and I are working through some issues, and Tom has absolutely nothing to do with any of them. It's very important that nobody thinks he does.' She gave Stella a pointed stare.

'Who do you think I'm going to tell?' hissed Stella. 'I came to this village for you, remember. I've discovered I rather like it here, but I'd stay either way. I'm on your side, Daisy.'

Daisy took a deep breath and forced a smile. 'If you really want to help me, you'll keep the gossip about me and Tom at bay. As far as the world is concerned Christian and I are still getting married and I'm here to write a cookbook and be near Ruby. I'll be back in London after your bloody fete, and everything is absolutely fine and normal.'

'Of course it is.' Stella eyed Daisy sceptically. 'But you should still talk to Tom. He's worth twenty of that tennis playboy.'

'I'm just going to take Henry out,' said Tom, sticking his head into the kitchen. 'But I'll be back for coffee. Do you want me to take Hank?'

'Oh,' said Daisy. 'Actually, yes, that would be great.'

'Why don't you go with Tom?' said Stella pointedly. 'Get some fresh air after all that cooking?'

Daisy rolled her eyes at her mother for being so obvious, but rationalised that five minutes alone with Tom might not be the worst bit of her day. She grabbed her coat and wellies and Hank's lead, then followed Tom around the stables and onto the school field.

'That was a lovely lunch,' said Tom as she fell into step beside him. 'Thank you.'

'You're welcome,' said Daisy, not wanting to waste the few minutes they had together. 'I'm sorry that this week has been a . . . rollercoaster. I didn't intend for it to—'

'—No,' interrupted Tom. 'It definitely didn't pan out quite how I'd hoped. But I suppose that's life, sometimes. We all move on.'

'Yes,' said Daisy bleakly. 'I hope we can still be friends, at least while I'm still here.'

Tom gave her a look of such steadiness and kindness that she thought she might cry. 'I'm sure I can manage that,' he said quietly. 'It is Christmas, after all.'

★

Miriam started to make moves to head back to Church House once coffee was cleared away, so Tom offered to walk her and Stella back to the village. He gave Daisy a chaste kiss on the cheek with a flurry of thank yous, then buried his hands in his coat pockets and hurried out into the yard after Stella and Miriam without looking back. Justin closed the door behind him, then hummed 'Last Christmas' as he danced back into the kitchen to help Daisy do the final clearing-up.

'God, I'm stuffed.'

'Then why are you still eating?' laughed Daisy as Justin popped a cold pig in a blanket into his mouth then dropped another on the floor for Hank, who sniffed it suspiciously.

'Because after today I'll be back to sawdust and vegetables,' Justin mused. 'If you're going to cheat, you might as well do it properly.'

'You'll be sick if you're not careful,' replied Daisy, rinsing glasses in the sink.

'Not as sick as Tom,' smirked Justin. 'That man is lovesick, and it's terminal. In the immortal words of Mariah Carey, *all he wants for Christmas is you.*'

Daisy gave him a stern look. 'Don't you start. I've already had all this from my mother.'

Justin looked serious for a moment. 'Are you going to tell me what's going on?'

'Absolutely not,' said Daisy emphatically, yanking off her rubber gloves. 'There's nothing to tell.'

'Ooh, stern face,' laughed Justin. 'It's quite sexy, even on a woman. I like it.'

'Fuck off, Justin.'

Justin put his hands up. 'Fine, I can definitely fuck off.

But I'm also available to spend the rest of the day eating cheese and watching bad Christmas movies on your sofa, should you so desire.'

Daisy thought about the Christmas movie version of this situation where Tom would return, make a breathless speech on her doorstep and they'd end up a tangle of sweaty limbs on a fur rug in front of the fire as flakes of snow began to fall outside. But real life was considerably more complicated, and they both knew that Tom wasn't coming back.

'Fine,' said Daisy. 'But only if you stop drinking.'

'I promise.' Justin scooped up Hank and fell into the sofa. 'I won't drink, or mention your elusive fiancé, who by the way you haven't talked about once today. Nor will I mention our handsome headmaster and how much you very obviously want to bang him into New Year.'

Daisy gave him a stern look, prompting Justin to press his fingers to his lips.

'I still need to organise a get-together to talk about the student cooking sessions,' she said, seizing the opportunity to change the subject. 'I thought I could do it later in the week before Will goes back to school.'

'Why don't you all come to dinner at mine on the twenty-ninth?' said Justin. 'Give us something to look forward to in the festive perineum. Stella and I can cook, you can all see what our vibe is.'

'Your vibe?' Daisy raised her eyebrows in amusement.

'Our double act, our chemistry, our blend of personalities. Whatever you want to call it.'

'Sounds good to me.' Daisy crammed another plate of leftovers into the fridge. Her mother would do something magical with them tomorrow. 'I'll message everyone.'

'About seven thirty,' Justin decided. 'I'm sure Stella mentioned a fete meeting in the church until seven.'

Daisy rolled her eyes. 'Honestly, she's obsessed with that bloody church fete.'

Justin laughed. 'I think she's found Jesus. Or Miriam. Which is kind of the same thing.'

CHAPTER THIRTY-THREE

On the twenty-eighth, Daisy got up early to let Hank out, doing a lap of the stables in the frigid morning air so the dog could sniff around and do his business. It occurred to her that any camera-wielding paparazzi lurking in the shadows would have a hell of a job convincing the tabloids that the crinkly-faced woman in wellies, pink pyjamas, a huge puffy coat and bed hair was the same dolled-up Daisy Crawford who'd gone commando and flashed her bits to the world at the NTAs. Daisy felt a million miles from the glitz and glamour of her normal life. She was surprised to discover how much she was enjoying it.

Once they were back in the cottage, Daisy hauled in a barrow of logs from one of the old stables, then built a little tepee with firelighters and kindling in the wood burner. She relished these morning rituals. There was something quite satisfying about getting her hands dirty in the wood-pile at 7 a.m. You weren't allowed to burn firewood in London, only that smokeless fuel stuff that didn't have the same crackle or woodsmokey smell. While the fire kindled, Daisy went back outside and filled up Justin's wheelbarrow too. It had never been formally discussed, but whichever one of them got up first filled up both barrows. It was a small thing, but rather lovely to open the front door and find a pile of dry logs waiting to be carried inside.

Once the wood burner was blazing and she'd fed Hank and made a cup of tea, Daisy huddled under a blanket with the dog beside her and called Katie. It was a Monday-morning ritual to check in with her manager and see what rubbish had appeared in the press over the weekend, and it saved Daisy googling her own name, which was never good for anyone's self-esteem. But since it was Christmas week and Katie had gone home to her girlfriend's family in Belfast, they'd delayed their call to Friday instead.

'There's nothing much,' said Katie, as Hank wriggled onto his back so Daisy could scratch his belly. 'Just a snippet in the *Sun Showbiz* about a rumour you're not loving village life.'

'Really?' asked Daisy, intrigued. 'What have I done now?'

'You've been spotted hanging out with Simon and his husband, not getting involved with the community, blah-blah-blah,' Katie dismissed. 'The implication is you hate the locals so much that you're shipping in friends and family from London.'

'Jesus,' said Daisy. 'It's Simon's cottage!' She sighed. 'I'm guessing someone heard me having words with my mum in the pub. She's trying to get me involved in the village fete.'

'What's wrong with the village fete?' Daisy could hear the smile in Katie's voice.

'It's not until the end of January,' replied Daisy. 'And I'd kind of hoped to be out of here by then.'

'Well, I'll leave that one up to you,' said Katie, 'but in the meantime try to embrace rural life. Plant a tree or something. Go on a ramble.'

'Thanks for the advice,' Daisy replied drolly. 'I've got a dog, does that count?'

'Wait, what?' said Katie. 'When did you get a dog?'

'It's Simon and Archie's.' Daisy stroked Hank's fat little belly. 'I'm looking after him for a few weeks.'

'Can you keep him for longer? Everybody loves a dog.'

'No,' Daisy laughed, 'although he is kind of adorable.' Hank's upside-down face made it look like he was smiling, so Daisy took a quick photo with her phone. She'd send it to Archie later.

'Any news from Christian?' asked Katie.

'Not a peep. He's locked up in the sex clinic for a month then I'm guessing he's heading back to London. I'll let you know if he gets in touch.'

'OK, thanks. What are you doing this week?' Daisy could hear Katie flicking through the pages of her notebook.

'Writing the intro for the book,' Daisy replied, 'and I need to start getting fit again. I've put on a few pounds without my trainer yelling at me. So some long dog walks, maybe a bit of tennis. All good, wholesome stuff.'

'Excellent!' Katie sounded satisfied. 'Roger's been in touch with some work offers, you know he doesn't believe in Christmas. There's an email in your inbox.' Roger had been Daisy's agent since before she'd landed the job on *Spotlight*, and he and Katie had a solid working relationship. It wasn't always the case with agents and managers, but since they each took ten per cent of Daisy's earnings it was in both their interests to collaborate.

'Give me the highlights,' said Daisy, taking a swig of her tea.

'My favourite is the luxury knicker brand that wants you to be their ambassador,' Katie smirked.

Daisy spluttered tea over the blanket and Hank. 'You're kidding,' she gasped.

'I'm not,' said Katie. 'Apparently they're willing to pay a

hundred grand for two seasonal photo shoots and a couple of social posts a month, plus a shitload of free knickers. Roger says to call him if you want more info.'

'Fine, I'll call and tell him absolutely *not*.'

Katie burst out laughing. 'I told him you'd say no.'

'Anything else?' asked Daisy breezily, still trying to get her head around why any company would think she'd want to capitalise on The Incident by promoting their pants. Who would do that? Although Daisy could name a lot of celebs who would do pretty much anything for a hundred grand, but she'd already surrendered her dignity once this year.

'A couple of charity things in the spring that you'll be fine with, Roger's sent the details over. Also *OK!* – apparently, since there's no sign of an engagement interview, they've asked to do a shoot to celebrate your fortieth birthday instead. An "at home with Daisy" type thing. They're offering megabucks; even more if Christian's there.'

Daisy barked out a laugh that made Hank jump off the sofa. 'Sorry, Hank!' she squealed.

'Who's Hank?' asked Katie suspiciously.

'The dog . . . And that's absolutely *no* to letting *OK!* into my home.'

'I told Roger you'd say that as well. He said . . . hang on.' Daisy could hear Katie riffling through the pages of her notebook. 'He said can you please say yes to something because he needs a new car.'

'I've said yes to dog-sitting Hank,' Daisy muttered darkly, 'and it's looking very likely I'll say yes to judging homemade cakes at the Shipton Combe village fete. There's no fee, but tell Roger I might be able to get him a half-price lemon drizzle.'

'I'll let him know,' said Katie dryly. It was one of the

many things that Daisy loved about her – she never tried to persuade Daisy to do anything she didn't want to. She and Roger both worked incredibly hard on her behalf, so she should probably throw them a bone.

'I'll tell you what,' said Daisy. 'Tell Roger I'll do a "Forty, newly single and happier than ever" interview with *OK!* in a month or two, once all the Christian stuff is out in the open. But not in London. Maybe in Portugal at half-term.' Her London house would have been empty for over four months by then and she really couldn't be bothered to give it a glossy magazine overhaul.

'He'll be so excited!' They both had a chuckle. Roger was well-known for being a bit dry and rarely getting excited about anything. 'Talking of your fortieth, what's the plan?'

Daisy drained her tea and shuffled her legs so Hank could snuggle into the crook of her knees. 'Just a quiet family thing here, I think. Simon and Archie are back down to pick up Hank, so it'll be them and Ruby and my mum, no big celebration. I might get together with some friends when I get back to London, but to be honest I'm happy to let it pass without making a big fuss. It's been a rubbish year.'

'Fair enough,' said Katie. 'Roger and I have got you a present, I'll send it down.'

Daisy felt a rush of warmth for Katie and Roger; they'd had her back for so many years. 'You didn't need to do that.'

'I know – turns out I'm a sentimental bitch.'

'Well,' said Daisy. 'I appreciate it.'

She heard Katie close her notebook decisively. 'I need to go. Have a good week, stay out of trouble, don't snog any randoms.'

'I'll do my best,' Daisy responded with a smile. She hung

up the phone and planted a kiss on Hank's head. 'You don't count.'

Daisy messaged Melanie after breakfast to see if she fancied a walk or lunch out somewhere, but by midday she could see from the absence of blue ticks that Melanie hadn't even read her message, let alone replied. She felt a flurry of concern, wondering what Melanie could be doing that meant she hadn't glanced at her phone all morning. They hadn't seen or spoken to each other since she'd dropped her and Will home last Friday, and she had no idea what Gerald's behaviour had been like over Christmas. After drumming her fingers on the kitchen counter thoughtfully for a few minutes, Daisy grabbed her coat and handbag and clipped Hank onto his lead.

It took a few minutes of persistently ringing the bell to the rectory before Melanie appeared with her hair in a nest, her cardigan on inside out and dark shadows under her eyes, crusted with yesterday's mascara.

'My God,' gasped Daisy. 'Are you OK? You look terrible.' She glanced around for Gerald, but there was no sign of him.

'I'm fine,' Melanie smiled weakly, squatting down to stroke Hank. 'Sorry, I'm a bit all over the shop.'

'Who is it?' bellowed Gerald's voice from upstairs.

'It's Daisy,' replied Melanie with an apologetic glance.

'Tell her to bugger off!' came the voice from above.

Daisy raised her eyebrows in horror. What on earth had happened?

Melanie laughed awkwardly, then grabbed her raincoat from the peg and dragged on a pair of trainers. 'I'm popping out for ten minutes,' she called up the stairs. Gerald didn't reply, so Melanie hurried outside and closed the door behind her. Daisy caught a whiff of cheese and fish and wondered if anyone in this house had emptied the festive bins.

'What on earth is going on?' Daisy hustled Melanie over to the gate to the churchyard. 'I messaged you earlier to ask you out for lunch, but you didn't reply.'

'Oh God, sorry,' said Melanie. 'I haven't looked at my phone all morning.'

'Is everything OK?' Daisy put her hand on Melanie's arm, stopping her so she could look closely at her puffy face and wildly dishevelled hair. She really did look dreadful, as if she hadn't slept in days.

Melanie started to laugh and this time Daisy could see the genuine joy in her expression. 'We were having sex, Daisy,' she announced happily. 'Gerald pretty much chased me up the stairs the second Will left to visit his cousins in Bath yesterday.'

Daisy's mouth fell open, her eyes boggling. Melanie laughed even harder.

'Will's back later this afternoon. When you rang the doorbell I was over Gerald's desk in heels and some skimpy knickers that haven't seen the light of day in a decade. We ignored you for a while, but you kept ringing!'

Melanie's shoulders shook as Daisy clamped her hand over her mouth, in turn delighted at this revelation, and relieved that Melanie wasn't being kept hostage in the attic.

'Oh God, I'm so sorry!' said Daisy. 'What the hell happened to Gerald while we were away?'

Melanie smiled. 'Tom. Tom happened.'

CHAPTER THIRTY-FOUR

Justin wasn't much of a morning person, so he and Tom had agreed early on in the sustainable year project that Tom would let the chickens out and collect the eggs. He often combined it with Henry's first walk of the day, but Tom usually brought Henry down to the allotment at lunchtime too, just to get some fresh air before classes began for the afternoon. He kept up the routine even in the school holidays, because right now routine was the only thing that got him out of bed in the morning.

He watched the chickens first, counting the sixteen laying hens and nine cocks that Justin kept for meat, although their numbers had rapidly dwindled due to Justin's largely chicken-based diet. He knew he should be in his office preparing for parents' evening, but instead he headed over to Nancy's goat enclosure and offloaded his woes. Despite not having much to say beyond the odd bleat, she was a good listener.

'—Anyway I've given up,' Tom murmured, in summary, leaning on the fence as Nancy observed him intently, her head tilted to one side. 'I'm done with women. They either die unexpectedly or lie to you.'

'About fucking time,' yelled Justin, bringing his bike to a skidding halt and making Tom jump. 'I've been trying to

261

convince you to turn your back on women for months. A man like you is entirely wasted on them.'

Tom shook his head and lifted the flaps to collect this morning's eggs. 'Fourteen today. How many do you want?' Justin took whatever eggs he needed each day and Tom took the rest.

'I'll have them all today,' Justin announced. 'I'm making goat's milk custard for dinner this evening, and I'll hard boil the rest for scotch eggs.'

'Anything else I can do while I'm here?' Tom asked, stacking the boxed eggs in Justin's wicker bicycle basket.

'You can either kill two chickens or pull some veg,' Justin replied, always keen for free labour. 'Enough to roast for five.'

'I'll do the veg,' said Tom hurriedly. There were still some leafy greens and root veg left in the soil, covered with a bed of straw to protect them from frost, and some onions and potatoes keeping dry in the shed.

'Fine by me,' said Justin glumly. 'These days it's the only chance I get to yank on a cock that isn't my own.'

'It's fine, I'm getting enough for both of you,' said Marcus jogging up behind them from the direction of the lake. Tom and Justin rolled their eyes at each other as he bounced around on the spot, wearing black running leggings and a hoodie that said *new balls please* in neon yellow lettering.

'Going well with Gloria then?' Tom asked mildly.

'Very much so,' Marcus preened. 'If she's not riding my dick, she's sending me dirty pictures.'

'Make sure she doesn't accidentally put them on the tennis club Facebook page,' Justin chortled. 'What are you doing over here anyway?'

'Just out for a run, so I thought I'd swing by for a gloat.' Both men groaned. Marcus looked too smug for words. 'I've had a message from Daisy; she's requested my services on the tennis court.'

'Has she specifically requested you show her your winning smash – or is it just tennis for now?' asked Justin wryly. Tom said nothing, noting his throat felt dry and his hands were clammy.

Marcus rolled his eyes. 'Tennis, obviously. But it's one-on-one time, so an opportunity for me to have another go at working my special Marcus Elliot magic.' He kept bouncing, a bundle of hormones and nervous energy, until his phone buzzed and he fished it out of his pocket.

'She cancelled on you already?' Justin sneered as Marcus tapped the screen, his brow furrowed.

'Oh, fucking bollocks,' muttered Marcus. 'It's worse than that. She wants to play mixed doubles with you, me and Melanie.'

Tom grinned and disappeared into the shed as Justin dissolved into howls of laughter.

CHAPTER THIRTY-FIVE

Squeezing five people and two dogs into Beech Cottage was definitely a challenge, but they managed it somehow. Daisy and Tom stayed in the lounge, sitting either side of the wood burner with a dog each. Justin and Stella were in the kitchen, clattering pots and dishes and cackling at each other, while Will hovered in the doorway between the two rooms shooting videos on his phone.

The atmosphere in the lounge was amicable, if not exactly relaxed. Daisy sat on the sofa with Hank tucked behind her knees, reading the introduction to one of Justin's cookbooks. He'd been a proponent of instinctive cooking – chuck in a bit of this, sprinkle in a handful of that – before it was the defining feature of geezer chefs on the internet. For Justin a recipe was simply a direction of travel, but how you got there was very much open to artistic interpretation. Experimentation was encouraged, with a lot of tasting along the way: as far as Justin was concerned that was how every classic recipe had started out. It was a method that definitely wasn't to everyone's tastes, but Daisy rather liked it.

Every now and then she glanced up at Tom, who was stroking Henry and staring intently into the wood burner, periodically kneeling forward to feed in another log. He'd switched his Christmas Day red jumper for soft grey cashmere over a blue check shirt, paired with dark grey cords and tan brogues. The whole outfit was pure rural headmaster; all he needed was a tweed jacket with suede elbow patches.

'How's your day been?' asked Daisy as another burst of laughter rang out from the kitchen. Tom looked up at her, and for a second Daisy had a glimpse of what normal life must be like – just two people getting home from work and chatting about their ordinary days. She had no concept of this – every man she'd ever dated had been in the public eye to some degree or other. There'd been the odd date with TV presenter colleagues after her split with Simon, then a brief relationship with a pop star that was doomed from the minute they realised their hectic schedules rarely aligned. He married a minor royal in the end; Daisy had even gone to their wedding. Normality was a foreign concept.

'Fine,' said Tom with a hint of amusement. Daisy assumed he was also thinking about the little tableau of domestication they had created. A fire, two dogs, inane conversation. 'I've had loads of positive responses to your classes; pretty much all the slots have gone already.'

'That's good news. I'm looking forward to it.' Another barrage of clattering emanated from the kitchen, along with a whoop of joy. 'Are you sure you want to let those two loose on your pupils?'

'I'd sort of assumed your mum would keep Justin under control,' Tom smiled.

'I think it might be the other way round, actually,' said Daisy, suddenly feeling a little nervous.

Will came back into the lounge and sat on the arm of the sofa, looking from Daisy to Tom like he was trying to work out a particularly tricky equation. The kitchen noise continued behind him.

'Is everything OK?' Daisy finally asked.

'Have you ever seen those two cooking?' Will shook his head, as if dazed. 'Like, together?'

Daisy sat up. 'No. Why?' She felt another flurry of concern and wondered if all her carefully laid plans were about to come crashing down.

'They're . . . AM-AZ-ING! Here.' He held out his phone and tapped play. Daisy scooped Hank onto her lap and scooted along the sofa so Tom could watch too. His arm pressed against hers as he leaned over to see the screen, and the warmth and closeness of him made her feel a little giddy.

It was clear from the off that Stella and Justin had something unique going – the kind of natural rapport that couldn't be forced or manufactured. They chopped and fried and told stories about their careers as chefs, writers and presenters, stopping every now and then to fall about laughing. Occasionally one of them would remember to explain a technique, but mostly it was about two people cooking and chatting and bouncing off each other, like they'd been doing this routine all their lives. Daisy had seen a lot of TV partnerships over the years, and there was no question this was something special.

'Wow!' She looked at Will. 'I had no idea.'

'I'm not sure they did either,' Tom smiled. 'You can't fake that.'

'No,' Daisy shook her head. 'You really can't. What are you thinking, Will?' He was sitting on the arm of the sofa, staring at the screen with a furrowed brow.

'I'm thinking we should get these two on YouTube as soon as possible. They could be massive.'

Daisy didn't argue with him; she knew Will was right. 'Do I need to call some people? I have a few contacts in the TV industry.'

Will and Tom both laughed, as Tom leaned back to make room for Hank, who clambered over from Daisy's lap onto his, turning a couple of circles before sitting down with a yawn. Feeling left out, Henry loped over and jumped into the tiny space between Tom and the arm of the sofa, forcing Tom to move even closer to Daisy. He mouthed a 'sorry' and blushed, as Daisy clicked to the next video and watched intently, hyper-aware of the heat of his strong thigh against hers. She'd seen enough, but it gave Tom a reason to stay there.

'No, I think we should put them on YouTube. Nothing feels too . . . I don't know, what's the word—'

'Polished?' suggested Tom.

'Exactly,' Will nodded vigorously. 'Then if it does numbers, it'll be because of their thing. Nothing that's been messed about with.' He looked from Daisy to Tom. 'Does that make sense?'

'It does,' Daisy said; Tom nodded in agreement. She was all too aware of how a barrage of TV executives could pull the arms and legs off a perfectly good idea.

Will stood up. 'I'm going to film some more.' He looked at Daisy. 'Can we talk to them about it?'

Daisy smiled. 'We probably should, before we make them internet famous. Let them cook for now, get a bit more video. Then we'll talk about it over dinner.'

Will nodded and took his phone back to the kitchen,

leaving Daisy and Tom floundering on the sofa under a pile of dogs.

'Well, I wasn't expecting that. Er, do you want me to move?' Tom waved his arms helplessly; Henry and Hank were both sprawled across his lap.

'It's fine.' Daisy shuffled to the edge of the sofa so she could stand up. 'You stay there.'

'No.' Tom placed his hand on Daisy's back. Her shirt had ridden up as she leaned forward, and the feeling of his warm skin on hers felt like electricity. She gasped and he immediately whipped his hand away. '*Sorry*.'

'It's OK.' Daisy twisted round to look at him, still buried under the unrepentant dogs and looking entirely delicious. She paused for a second, then made an impulsive decision. 'Don't go home.' The words were out of her mouth before she could take them back.

'What?'

'After dinner. Don't go home,' said Daisy, twiddling her hair awkwardly. 'Come next door. We should talk.'

Tom nodded, giving Daisy a smile of such tenderness that she had to force herself not to kiss him right there and then. Now wasn't the time. Maybe at some point, but not now. She just needed to help him understand.

'So, let me get this straight,' Justin repeated to Will. 'You want to put videos of me and Stella cooking on the internet.'

'Yep,' Will nodded. 'On YouTube.'

'And why would we do that?' asked Stella politely.

'Because I think lots of people will watch it.' Daisy had to admire Will's patience; it was like he was trying to explain the functioning of NATO to a class of six-year-olds. 'And if you make lots of videos and lots of people watch them, you could start making money out of it.'

'How much money?' asked Justin, perking up.

'It's hard to say. You need to build up a following, which could take a bit of time. But Daisy could help, probably.' He looked at Daisy, who nodded. 'Some people who do You-Tube videos make a LOT of money.'

'And how much does it cost?' asked Stella. 'The Tube thing?'

'It doesn't cost anything,' Will explained. 'I can edit the first video and upload it tomorrow. Then Daisy can give it a nudge on social media and we'll see what happens.'

Stella and Justin looked at each other, then at Daisy and Tom. 'Do you really think it's good?' Stella asked, seeming uncharacteristically unsure.

'You're both amazing,' Daisy reassured. 'I think people are going to love you.'

Tom nodded in agreement. 'You'll probably have your own TV show by Easter.'

'Really?' Justin's face lit up.

'You might not want a TV show though,' said Will. 'A lot of YouTubers make more money online.'

Stella looked even more confused, so Daisy stepped in. 'OK, let's focus on one thing at a time. I think Will should put this first video on YouTube and we'll see if people like it. I can give it a push too, as he said. Then later we can add more stuff from the classes. It might work; it might not. But if you're both up for it, Will is offering to help. So am I.'

'Well, I don't really know how any of this works but it sounds fun,' Stella grinned. 'So count me in.'

'Me too,' Justin agreed, looking at Stella with a smile. 'Looks like you might be stuck with me for a while.'

'I want ten per cent,' blurted out Will, prompting everyone to stop and look at him. 'I'll do all your video editing, manage your YouTube channel, look after your social.' He swallowed and ploughed on. 'If you don't make any money, you don't have to pay me anything. But if you do, I want ten per cent. As your manager.'

Everyone was silent for a moment, then Daisy spoke. 'That seems fair. You can't do this without Will – and it was all his idea.'

Justin shrugged. 'Fine by me.' And Stella nodded.

'Cool,' said Will, his face breaking into a big smile.

Good for you, thought Daisy proudly. *You've just landed yourself one hell of a gig.*

'Come in,' whispered Daisy as she opened the door for Tom and Henry. He'd hung around at Justin's for a little while after Will offered to walk Stella back to the pub and Daisy had returned to Willow Cottage. No doubt he'd done a lap of the stables in case Justin was watching out of the window.

Daisy poured Tom a glass of wine, a welcome relief from the gut-stripping qualities of Justin's homemade cider. He sat on the sofa with Henry at his feet and looked up at her, clearly anxious at what she was about to say. She sat on the sofa opposite, making room for Hank.

Daisy straightened her shoulders. This was long overdue. 'Look, I need to explain something. It might not make sense at first, so I'm asking you to trust me.'

'OK,' Tom said. 'I trust you.' He smiled nervously, and

Daisy realised in that moment that she was a little bit in love with Tom Clark. She pushed the thought aside, focusing on not messing this up.

'Two things,' Daisy murmured. 'First, I really like you—' she blushed and took a deep breath, '—a lot, actually. And,' she held up her hand when Tom looked like he might speak, 'Christian and I have split up. A while back.'

Tom's eyes widened as he processed this information. 'Well, that's a good thing. A great thing. I really like you a lot too, so—'

'Wait,' she interrupted. 'I know this seems like good news, but it's not that simple. Just bear with me for a minute.'

Tom nodded, even though he looked confused. He sat back on the sofa. Hank hopped off Daisy's lap and went to join him, so she stood up and started to pace the room.

'I didn't know Christian was coming to Austria,' she told Tom. 'He turned up, apparently to try to persuade me to take him back.' Daisy reached the front door and turned around to pace back the other way. 'I said no and he left, but there was a pap hiding in the trees. Christian's got some issues. It's complicated, so that's why there's been no announcement.'

Tom stayed silent so Daisy kept talking and pacing. 'If things were different, I'd ask you out on a date, like normal people do. But I'm not a normal person.'

'But—'

Daisy held up a hand again. 'No, please. Let me finish.' She took a deep breath. 'I'm not saying we can't ever go on a date, but the timing is really important here.' Daisy stopped pacing and finally turned to face Tom, wishing she had a flipchart so she could make notes and draw circles and arrows to connect all the important things.

'If I go back to London, and then I announce that Christian and I have split up, that's one small bit of news, right? Later, you and I go on a date, which is another small bit of news. No big deal. OK?'

'OK.'

'BUT,' Daisy continued, 'if I were to announce that Christian and I have split while I'm still living in this village, and then you and I start dating, you will become the REASON we split. That's much bigger news and the tabloids will rake over every inch of your past.'

Tom looked away, clearly torn. 'But what if I don't care?' he said finally.

Daisy sat back on the chair and leaned towards him, her hands pressed together like she was praying. 'No, listen. They'll write about Tessa. They'll find old pictures and make a big thing about how alike we look. They'll paint you as a homewrecking headmaster and me as a love cheat. They'll interview your friends and family, then move on to school staff and parents and governors. It will be horrible in every possible way. You don't want that.'

Tom took a deep breath. 'No. I can't imagine anybody would want that.'

'So, I'm asking you to wait until after February half-term. Eight weeks from now.' Daisy's look was beseeching. It was all or nothing now. 'I'll go back to London at the end of January, then Christian and I will announce we split amicably over Christmas. Ruby will go on the school ski trip at half-term and I usually go to my villa in Portugal, so maybe we can go on a date after I get back.

'We'll stay under the radar for a while, see how things go. When the press gets wind, there'll be a brief flurry of interest, but nothing compared to what would happen if I announced it now.'

Tom nodded slowly. 'I understand.'

Daisy exhaled, letting go of all the breath she'd been holding in. She felt a little dizzy. 'So for the time being we can't be anything more than friends working on a project together. Nothing can happen that might implicate you when Christian and I officially split.'

Daisy turned her palms upwards, feeling like she'd emptied her soul onto the rug in front of him. 'I'm sorry it has to be this way, but I'm just trying to protect you. It will be better in the long run.'

'OK. I believe you.'

Daisy sighed heavily. 'You should probably go.'

Tom looked torn, but finally he nodded and stood up, then walked to the front door with Henry shuffling reluctantly along behind him. He turned back to look at Daisy with those intense, beautiful eyes. 'Eight weeks, right?'

Daisy nodded. 'Eight weeks.'

'OK.' Tom took a deep breath, then giving her a soft smile, he murmured, 'But before I go, is there any chance I could kiss you? Just once, to keep me going?'

Daisy hesitated for a moment, then took two huge strides across the room and pressed her lips against his before she changed her mind. She let herself go for a long moment, emptying her mind of everything but the feel and smell and taste of him. After ten seconds that felt like several blissful years, she pulled away and stepped back, holding his gaze until he smiled softly and slipped through the door, closing it quietly behind him.

PART FOUR

PART FOUR

CHAPTER THIRTY-SIX

Daisy sat on the edge of the bed applying her makeup using a plastic-framed mirror propped up on the windowsill. She could feel cold air creeping around the edges of the glass, condensation pooling in the flaking paintwork. These old cottages had bags of charm, but there was also a lot to be said for double glazing.

It wasn't lost on Daisy that the last time she'd been getting ready for a big night out was the NTAs nearly four months ago. Today was her fortieth birthday and there was no red carpet, no towering heels, no Victor the stylist with his dress bag and diamonds. Today it was just her and a small dog curled up like a croissant on her pillow.

Ruby was home from school for the weekend, but she'd gone over to the Shipton Arms to see Stella. Presumably they were organising some kind of birthday surprise, although hopefully nothing too ridiculous. Daisy just wanted a small family dinner, a few glasses of half-decent wine and an early night. Maybe being forty meant you swapped falling out of a nightclub at 4 a.m. for stretchy joggers, fluffy socks and a mug of tea. She tried not to think what Tom might be doing.

The past two weeks since school had restarted had been hectic – she'd completed all five classes and finished edits to the recipes, on top of managing Justin and Stella's new status as YouTube sensations. She'd called Roger and asked if he

277

knew any agents who dealt with social media influencers, and it turned out one of his colleagues was a specialist. So at least now they had some support to deal with all the press and publicity and were no longer turning to Daisy for advice every hour of the day. She was thrilled for them, but had more than enough on her own plate without being an unpaid agent to her needy mother and the sweary but endearing chef next door.

She'd kept up her regular calls with Katie, and thankfully there'd been a lull in the gossip, possibly because she'd done very little apart from work. A daft story about her getting a dog, an article that essentially printed the contents of some Tweets from parents about her classes, as if this was hard news, a report that Christian was also currently working at a tennis academy in Latvia or Lithuania – Daisy couldn't remember which, nor cared. Presumably it was Benny Bull-shit and Christian was still in Switzerland, although it was always possible that he'd checked out of the clinic and was now shagging his way around the Baltics. Either way there was no further mention of Tom, which was a relief.

To his credit he'd upheld their agreement and kept a respectful distance since their chat, even though their paths had regularly crossed during the cooking classes. Christian would have texted her all manner of filth by now, and she had to remind herself that he and Tom were very different people; that was *definitely* a good thing.

Daisy finished putting on her makeup and sat back on the bed to stroke Hank. She was sorry he was going home tomorrow; he'd been such unexpectedly lovely company. Looking after a dog gave her structure to her day and a reason to get out of bed on chilly mornings. Last weekend they'd had a dump of heavy snow and walking through the grounds had entirely blown Hank's mind. In places, it was deep enough to cover his furry head, so Daisy had taken him into the fenced-off area where the netball courts were so he could zoom about in circles and roll in the snow until he looked like a tiny polar bear. She'd been so tempted to message Tom so he could bring Henry down to play, but in the end decided that it wasn't worth the risk of them being seen together. If he could wait, so could she. Every so often she worried he'd given up on her, but then she'd catch him looking and feel the heat in his stare from the other side of the room.

She glanced at her new watch, a fortieth-birthday present from Stella. It was a delicate platinum and diamond bracelet with a rectangular watch face that felt too expensive to wear to the Shipton Arms, but was also beautiful to leave behind. Ruby had given her a photo of the two of them from their skiing trip, a selfie of them smiling in the hot tub, clutching their mugs of peppermint tea, which made her grin every time she looked at it. Justin had made the frame for it out of wood from the school estate, and it now stood in pride of place on the mantlepiece above the fireplace.

Katie and Roger had made her a book, which had arrived earlier in the week, wrapped in tissue paper. It was a beautifully bound photographic journey of her twenty-five years in television, including messages of love and birthday wishes from her friends and the co-presenters she'd worked with over the course of her career. Flicking through the pages had brought a full bag of mixed emotions – a small part of her missed all the parties and dinners and awards shows, but a much bigger part of her felt relieved to be away from it. Like she'd unzipped a dress that was too tight and could finally breathe, but also knew that at some point she was going to have to zip the bastard thing up again, and it was going to feel tighter than ever before.

CHAPTER THIRTY-SEVEN

'Will says we've had over a million views. Whatever that means,' said Stella, handing a silver balloon to Ruby, who tied the neck and attached it to a string with several others. She then passed the whole bunch to Tom. 'He says we've gone viral, which is apparently a good thing.'

Tom laughed at her expression and climbed onto a chair to tie the balloons to a wooden beam in the function room of the Shipton Arms, which was more like a fancy conservatory clamped onto the side of the pub.

'It's only three weeks since I was last here,' huffed Ruby moodily. 'Loads has happened since then. I've got the school play in a couple of weeks so I can hardly ever get home.'

'It's definitely all been going on,' said Tom, thinking about all the things that definitely hadn't been going on, mostly involving Ruby's mother. 'Is that a million views per video, or all together?' he asked.

'All together, I think,' Stella shrugged helplessly as if to say 'what do I know?' 'You'd have to ask Will. He's the master.'

'How did the cooking classes go?' asked Ruby, starting on the next bunch of balloons. There were four bunches in total, one in each corner of the room. Stella had brought some fortieth-birthday bunting to string between them and Ruby wasn't sure how Daisy would react. She'd said she didn't want a fuss.

'They were SUCH fun.' Stella all but bounced. 'Your

mother has written a *wonderful* book and the students had a great time. Daisy got lots of feedback and the videos Will took were smashing.'

'It's my book too,' grumbled Ruby. 'I hate being stuck at school when all the exciting stuff is happening here.'

Tom gave her a sympathetic look, having already listened to Ruby tell him about her weekend and evening commitments in the school play. From what Tom had gathered, it was a modern version of Shakespeare set in space, called *A Moonsummer Night's Dream*. Tom was no expert on Shakespeare but it sounded terrible.

'I know, sweetheart,' said Stella. 'When the royalties start rolling in, it will feel a lot more like your book.'

'But I'm missing out on all the fun,' sulked Ruby. 'The book's not even out until October. You and Justin will be megastars by then.'

'Well, I don't know about that,' Stella preened. 'Will says it's early days, and we have to keep doing more videos. I expect we'll run out of things to talk about eventually.'

'I'm sure you'll find something, Granny,' replied Ruby affectionately. 'Shall we do the bunting?'

'Can you and Tom do that?' Stella scanned the room. 'I need to do the place settings.' She fished a sheet of paper out of her giant handbag.

'Why do we need place settings?' Ruby frowned. 'There are only five of us.'

'Ah,' said Stella, shuffling awkwardly. 'Well, that didn't feel much like a party, so I've invited a few of your mother's friends from the village.'

Uh oh. Tom watched as Ruby marched up to her grandmother, hands on her hips. Her eyes narrowed in a very

Daisy-like way as Stella tried to avoid her piercing gaze. 'Granny, *what have you done?*'

Tom busied himself unravelling fortieth-birthday bunting as Ruby expressed relief that there were only twelve guests rather than the entire village. Ruby could understand why she might invite Tom, Will, Justin and Melanie, but she was less clear on Gerald, Marcus and Miriam.

'We couldn't invite Melanie and Will and not invite Gerald. It would be rude,' scolded Stella.

'Fine, whatever,' Ruby waved her hand dismissively. 'But why Marcus?'

'Your mother's been playing a lot of tennis with him. Doubles, you know, with Melanie and Justin. I think they've become friends. He's also a bit younger and I thought he might be a bit more fun than us old farts.'

Ouch, thought Tom. Ruby grinned at him mischievously.

'And Miriam?' she asked. 'Why the vicar?'

Stella pursed her lips and glanced in Tom's direction for help. 'Because she's a very nice woman, and to be honest I don't think she gets many party invitations.'

Ruby laughed and rolled her eyes. 'Honestly, Granny, why didn't you invite the cleaning lady while you were at it?'

'I seriously considered it,' Stella said pensively. 'But Miriam made twelve, which seemed like a nice number. Sadly five women and seven men, but for the purpose of the seating plan we can count Archie as a woman.'

'Granny!' exclaimed Ruby, glancing at Tom in horror. '*You can't say that.*'

Stella smiled sweetly at her granddaughter. 'Darling, Archie will be the best-dressed person at that table, he should take it as a compliment. And also I'm sixty-two and I can say whatever I like.'

Ruby sighed and snatched the seating plan from Stella's hand. 'Who have you sat me next to?'

Stella leaned over her shoulder and pointed to where Ruby was sitting. 'You've got Will on one side and Justin on the other.'

'OK, that's fine, but why have you put Mum between Marcus and Gerald?'

'I had a bit of a crisis,' Stella said, her hands flapping. 'It felt wrong to seat her next to your dad or Archie, and poor Will shouldn't be sandwiched between his girlfriend's mother and her grandmother.'

Ruby nodded in agreement, running her finger over the hastily drawn plan. 'Will would prefer being next to me, even if that does mean Miriam on his other side. Although Will quite likes the vicar; he reckons she has hidden depths. Why can't we sit Mum next to Tom?'

'Oh.' Stella looked at Tom, her hands flapping awkwardly. 'I'm so sorry, Tom, I wasn't sure if that was a good idea. What with all that silly gossip about you two a few weeks back. I didn't want to add fuel to the fire.'

'Don't be daft, Granny.' Ruby rolled her eyes. 'It's Mum's birthday, put her next to the people she'll actually have fun with.' She grabbed Stella's pencil and did some crossing out. 'Look, I'll move Gerald to the other side of Miriam so Tom can sit on Mum's left. There. That's much better.'

Ruby gave Tom a beaming smile, and he tried not to blush. If there was one thing he'd learnt about teenagers over the years, it was that they didn't miss much.

*

284

At 5 p.m. Tom sat at his desk, his pen hovering over the birthday card he'd bought for Daisy. The picture on the front was a brown dog that looked a bit like Henry, with a bunch of daisies dangling from its mouth in a dopey but charming fashion. He'd spent ages this afternoon scouring the local gift shops for a card that didn't look like the kind of thing you'd buy an elderly aunt, but also didn't communicate: 'I've been thinking about little else but getting naked with you for several weeks.' Most fortieth-birthday cards for women seemed to imply they subsisted on a diet of gin and Prosecco, and he had no idea if Daisy liked either. There was a lot he didn't know about Daisy. He was looking forward to that changing.

He'd written several drafts of his message, including a jokey poem that was so bad he'd set fire to it then flushed the ashes down the staff toilet to eliminate the risk of anyone ever reading it. He reminded himself that there was a reason he'd started his career teaching Geography rather than English, and now was probably not the time to decide he could be the next Lord Byron.

There was a gentle knock at the door, which could only be Angela. She sometimes came in on a Saturday and pretended to work, presumably so she didn't have to put the central heating on at home. She poked her head around the door, followed swiftly by a bowl of white hyacinths. Tessa had always hated the smell of them, which was unfortunate as she always got loads as Christmas gifts from parents trying to butter up the headmaster's wife.

'I thought these would look nice on your desk,' Angela said gaily. 'They're rather cheery.'

Tom smiled and stood up, wafting an arm to indicate she

should find a space among the stacks of files that littered his desk like cardboard cairns. 'Thank you, that's kind of you.'

Angela put the bowl on the corner of the desk and looked at Tom, wringing her hands. 'I also wondered if you could spare me a moment.'

'Of course.' Tom redirected his wafting arm to the visitor's chair. It was worn and ancient and had lost a few of its springs, rather like Angela. She fell into it awkwardly and fidgeted for a while, which made Tom wonder if she was sick, or had done something terrible with the school computer system. Again. 'Is everything OK?'

'Yes, I'm fine,' Angela said in hushed tones. 'But I'm afraid I have some difficult news which you may find upsetting.'

Tom raised his eyebrows. 'Go on.'

'I've decided it's time for me to retire.' Angela spoke in the same grave voice the police officers had used to tell Tom Tessa was dead.

'Goodness!'

'I know.' Angela's eyes filled with tears. 'It's been a difficult decision. I know how much you depend on me.'

Tom arranged his face into an expression of brave acceptance. 'You'll be very much missed, Angela, but I'm sure this is the right decision.'

'I think so.' Angela gave a weak smile. 'I'm thinking of selling Holly Tree Cottage and moving to a retirement community. There's a new one in Cheltenham. It has a swimming pool and a snooker table.'

'It sounds wonderful,' Tom smiled, already thinking ahead to a time when he could hire a new secretary and not spend his life drowning in admin. 'When were you thinking of leaving us?'

'At half-term, if you don't mind. Although obviously I'm happy to stay until Easter if that's helpful.'

'No, I won't hear of it.' *I really won't.* 'Let's sort out all the details on Monday, shall we?'

He walked round to the front of the desk and offered her an arm so she could winch herself out of the chair. She patted his arm affectionately and smiled. 'You're a good man, Tom. I hope she looks after you.'

Tom stared at her, momentarily confused. 'Who?'

Angela shrugged and smiled conspiratorially. 'The reason you're sweating over that birthday card.' She gave him a wink and closed the office door behind her.

Tom stood in silence for a moment, then returned to his chair. He took a deep breath and wrote 'To Daisy, with best wishes on your 40th birthday.' He signed it 'Tom' without a kiss, in case anyone at the party read it. He had a thousand kisses stored up for her, but they could all wait just a few more weeks.

CHAPTER THIRTY-EIGHT

Once Daisy had got past the initial surprise of unexpected guests at her birthday dinner, she decided she was rather enjoying herself. The function room at the Shipton Arms was hardly the VIP area at Mahiki, but honestly, what did it matter? So much about the past few months had been new and unconventional. The heavy damask curtains that covered the patio doors at the front of the room had been drawn, making the space feel cosy and ensuring people outside the pub couldn't gawp in. Her family was here. Her daughter and her mother. Simon and Archie. And then there was the man who gave her butterflies in her stomach like a teenager with a crush, and that definitely wasn't her ex-husband. Whichever way Daisy looked at it, she'd had worse birthdays.

Seeing Tom's name next to hers on the table placement had given her a guilty frisson of anticipation. She should have moved him really, put him down the other end of the table where she wouldn't be able to feel the heat of him, but she had to admit she was kind of looking forward to spending a legitimate couple of hours in his company. His birthday card had made her smile, and she wondered how long he'd laboured over the message to make it that bland and innocuous.

Stella tapped her champagne glass with a dinner knife to

invite everyone to take their seats, which Daisy thought was a rather grandiose gesture for such a low-key assembly. But she took her place anyway, in the middle of the table on the side nearest the wall. Tom slid in next to her and smiled, trying to avoid eye contact as his cheeks flushed pink. Daisy wondered if it was the warmth of the room or the champagne, or maybe he felt the same way she did about being so close to each other for the first time in weeks.

He looked adorable in his charcoal grey cashmere sweater over one of his many check shirts; it looked kitten-soft and cosy. She resisted the urge to stroke him and looked over at Gerald, who was sipping red wine and inspecting the label on the bottle with an expression of appreciation, then periodically glancing across the table at his wife. She and Melanie had played a lot of tennis and had several lunches together over recent weeks, so Daisy was fully up to speed on the restructure and renegotiation of their marriage. Gerald had finally realised Melanie's worth and so far everything was going well between them.

Things were better between Gerald and Will too, particularly after Will had shown enough business acumen to ask for a ten per cent share of Stella and Justin's YouTube earnings. Apparently, Gerald's solicitor had drafted up a simple contract which Stella and Justin had been happy to sign, so Will's interests were protected for now. Gerald and Melanie had discussed buying him a second-hand car for his eighteenth birthday next month, but right now there was a good chance Will would be buying his own, and an even better chance it would be considerably more glamorous than Gerald's Mondeo.

Melanie was on Daisy's side of the table, happily sandwiched between Simon and Tom. At fifty, Simon was the older of the two men, with an enviable head of salt-and-pepper hair that made him look rather distinguished and dashing. Tom wasn't as groomed or well-dressed, but he was definitely more effortlessly good-looking. It was hard for Daisy not to think about where things might lead for her and Tom, once the dust had settled around Christian and the Vultures had moved on to pastures new. In two weeks, she would head back to London and the quiet announcement about her and Christian's relationship would be made. Then later next month she and Tom would be free to spend time together. It felt closer this side of the new year, and the flutter of anticipation in her stomach seemed almost permanent these days.

Melanie looked ten years younger, her hair cut in a shorter, more elegant style and wearing a green wrap dress that flattered her figure and complemented her pale colouring. She and Daisy had gone shopping in Oxford, booking a personal shopper at John Lewis so they could try on outfits without Daisy having to stop for endless selfies. Then Daisy had taken her to Soho Farmhouse for a surprise fortieth-birthday treat for them both, booking them in for a facial and a manicure, then a cut and colour in the hair salon. It had been a lovely day, with Melanie bringing Daisy up to speed on the online IT training she'd already started, and the extra courses she was planning to do at the local college after Easter. The rectory was now on the market and they'd already looked at a lovely house in a village a few miles away, but Melanie had thought that the garden was a little small, particularly if they were planning to entertain in the summer or maybe get a dog. Melanie's life now seemed like it was full of possibility, and Daisy couldn't be happier for her.

Archie was on Gerald's right, regaling him with tales of the landscaping commission in New Hampshire over Christmas. Apparently the owner was a distant Kennedy cousin, with a husband who worked in timber and spent most of his time deforesting Brazil. Daisy caught Simon's eye and smiled, glad to see her ex-husband so settled and happy. Now perhaps fate might deal her the same; God knows she'd waited long enough.

Miriam was on Gerald's left, currently listening to Will explain how YouTube worked and doing a sterling job of looking fascinated. Presumably they gave classes in attentiveness at theological college; it felt like an important quality for a vicar.

'—they've got well over a million views now,' Will enthused, 'and over a hundred thousand subscribers on their YouTube channel.'

'Goodness,' exclaimed Miriam, clearly having no idea of what that meant. 'Who are all these people watching cooking shows on the internet?'

'There are loads of students,' replied Will. 'You can tell from the comments. They think Justella's really funny. Apparently they explain things really well. One comment said it was like being shown how to cook by your grandparents.'

'We had an email from *This Morning* yesterday,' added Stella. 'They want us to go on and cook something.'

'Are you going to do it?' asked Ruby, looking from her grandmother to Justin.

Justin shrugged. 'Not sure. Our agent is looking into it.

She looks after lots of influencers. That annoying woman who bangs on about cleaning – what's her name?—'

'That's what we are now,' interrupted Stella. '*Influencers*—'

'Who thought of Justella?' asked Ruby. 'It's genius.'

'Will did,' Daisy smiled. 'Your granny still isn't sure about it.'

'It's distinctive,' Will proclaimed with the confidence of a seventeen-year-old boy who'd been in the social media game for two solid weeks. 'Justin and Stella sounds boring, but Justella sounds cool. It's a . . . what's the word?'

'A portmanteau?' suggested Tom.

'Exactly. One of those. Like Kimye.'

'Or Jedward,' added Melanie from the other end of the table.

'I have no idea what any of you are talking about,' said Stella, folding her arms and looking sulky when everyone burst out laughing.

'How's your starter?' Daisy asked Justin.

He moodily poked a lump of potato with his spoon, visibly salivating over Daisy's dish of pan-fried scallops with pancetta.

'Fucking awful,' he said. 'Leek and potato soup needs blending and seasoning, and this miserable bowl of fucking sadness has neither. I tried beating it with a whisk to break up the vegetables, but in the end I didn't have the energy to push it all through a sieve as well.'

Daisy gave him her best sympathy face while trying not to laugh. 'What else did you bring?'

'There are two tubs in the kitchen,' he grumbled. 'Beige chicken with beige vegetables, followed by the last of my stewed plums.'

'Yummy.'

Justin cast her a baleful look. 'I swear to God I will never touch another fucking plum unless it's dangling between the legs of a comely gentleman.' Archie arched an eyebrow from across the table.

Daisy snorted into her wine. She'd miss Justin when she left Shipton Combe, but his sustainable year finished in February so hopefully they could hang out together when he was back in London.

'Talking of comely gentlemen,' whispered Justin. 'Your ex and his bloke are both gorgeous. I'm hoping you're going to move us all around before dessert so I can flirt shamelessly and wheedle my way into their celebrity gay circle.'

'Is that even a thing?' asked Daisy, not keen on moving away from Tom, whose thigh was now pressed firmly against hers and burning a hole through her dress.

'No idea, but it will give me something to think about later.' He turned to Miriam and raised his voice a notch. 'So Vicar, how's the plan for the fete coming on?'

'Oh,' stuttered Miriam, dabbing the corners of her mouth with her napkin. 'Very well, I think. Especially now you and Stella have offered to do some cooking demonstrations. It's created a lot of excitement on the Facebook page, and the local paper has confirmed they're sending a reporter.'

'That's great news,' Daisy said, genuinely delighted that the celebrity spotlight wasn't all going to be on her. 'Hopefully you'll raise the funds you need to get the vestry repairs done.' She turned to Marcus before Miriam launched into a monologue about the specific jobs that needed doing in the vestry. 'More wine?'

Marcus nodded and smiled, clearly happy to be seated

next to Daisy and the focus of her attention, however briefly. They'd played tennis four times in the past couple of weeks, always mixed doubles where she partnered with Justin and Marcus played with Melanie. Now Marcus had finally realised that Daisy categorically didn't fancy him and had stopped strutting like a peacock, she'd decided she rather liked him. He was a good coach with a dry sense of humour, and always had an encouraging word for Melanie. Daisy had heard from Justin that he was thinking of moving in with his girlfriend; a woman called Gloria who played at his tennis club. Hopefully things would work out for him. Much like Christian, once you stripped away all the bullshit and bravado, Marcus just needed the love of a good woman. Or in Christian's case, several women at once.

CHAPTER THIRTY-NINE

Tom had lost his appetite somewhere around the time Daisy's left hand slid onto his right knee, beginning its painfully slow navigation north. Occasionally she'd change course and head south again or withdraw her hand briefly to innocently tuck her hair behind her ear or top up her wine glass. Then the hand would return to where it started, beginning again on its excruciating but delicious journey.

His face felt hot and he couldn't imagine a time in the future when his erection might have subsided enough for him to leave the table. He might have to live in the function room of the Shipton Arms forever. He silently cursed her for playing games with him this way, then cursed himself for wearing jeans that didn't include room for a raging hard-on. He willed her to stop, then prayed she wouldn't.

When the main course of beef wellington and gratin dauphinoise arrived, Daisy removed her left hand so she could hold a fork, giving him enough of a break for things to calm down. He made small talk with Melanie until everyone had finished eating, then excused himself to go to the bathroom, instead heading outside. The night air was cold and clean and frosty, so he sat on the stone wall outside the pub, taking deep, calming breaths and smiling to himself. He'd forgotten what it was like to feel this level of desire for a woman;

the kind that writhed like a basket of snakes in the pit of your stomach and made your balls ache.

He didn't register the man getting out of the taxi at first, other than he was tall and lean with dark hair, an expensive-looking coat and a leather holdall. Only when the man turned and paused in the glow of the streetlight, did Tom realise it was Christian Walker. He smiled at Tom briefly, whisking past him with an 'All right, mate?' before disappearing into the pub.

After the briefest pause, Tom followed him inside, his heart pounding, trying to work out why Christian Walker would turn up in Shipton Combe on the night of Daisy's birthday party, barely a few minutes after she'd had her hand on Tom's crotch. None of it made sense, but he had a very bad feeling about it.

Christian was leaning on the bar, giving his most dazzling smile to Steph the barmaid, who was in her mid-twenties. She had copper hair and huge boobs that habitually spilled out of a top that was at least two sizes too small. She held a glass cloth in one hand and a giant gin glass in the other and seemed momentarily unsure what to do with either. Tom sidled up to the bar, stopping a few metres away and straining his ears to listen to their conversation.

'Hi,' said Christian with his best showbiz smile. 'I know this is a strange question, but can you tell me where Daisy Crawford lives? I'm her fiancé.'

Steph smiled and nodded, leaning over the bar and lowering her voice. 'She's actually in there,' she nodded towards the door that connected the pub to the function room. 'Having a birthday dinner.'

Tom drummed his fingers on the bar nervously, realising

that Christian was just about to gatecrash Daisy's party and he had absolutely no idea what, if anything, he was supposed to do about it.

'Well, that's ideal.' Christian glanced appreciatively at Steph's impressive breasts, which were now squashed together between her elbows, creating a shelf she could have rested the gin glass on. 'I'll just go in.' He moved towards the door, but stopped when Steph waved him back. Tom exhaled.

'Wait,' she whispered. 'Does she know you're coming?'

Christian walked back to the bar and leaned over so Steph's face was only a few inches from his. 'What's your name?'

She gave him her most dazzling smile. 'Steph.'

'Well, Steph,' said Christian, glancing from her face to her freckly cleavage. 'Let's just say I'm her birthday surprise.' Tom felt like gagging.

Steph giggled and blushed. 'I've got an idea,' she said, her eyes glittering with excitement. 'We've just cleared away their mains, so we'll be doing the cake in a minute. Justella made it, it's going to be on YouTube. Why don't you take it through?'

Tom could see Christian pondering this suggestion, weighing up the pros and cons of such a grand public gesture. He watched the cogs turn slowly in Christian's brain, hoping he would naturally come to the conclusion that doing the equivalent of bursting out of a birthday cake and yelling '*Surprise!*' was a very bad idea indeed. Tom took a step towards him, wondering if he should introduce himself and offer to fetch Daisy for him, but he hesitated too long and Christian had scurried off after Steph into the kitchen.

'*Oh bloody, fucking hell!*' muttered Tom, striding back into the function room, his heart pounding in his chest, his head feeling like it was underwater. Daisy wasn't in the seat where he'd left her – she'd moved further down the table and was deep in conversation with Simon and Ruby. He spotted Justin and hurried over to ask for his urgent help, but before he could get the words out a switch was flicked and the room was plunged into darkness.

CHAPTER FORTY

Daisy clapped her hands as the lights in the function room went out, joining in with the obligatory nervous giggles and ghostly 'woo' noises. A chorus of 'Happy Birthday' started up as a dazzling halo of candles and sparklers appeared through the door, then bobbed across the dark room as if it was levitating. Somebody placed the huge cake in front of Daisy, and she watched the sparklers burn out one by one as the song finished.

'Don't forget to make a wish,' called Stella.

Daisy's head felt woozy as she breathed in a new scent in the room, something that felt strangely familiar but also made her inexplicably anxious. Her face felt warm and her head was spinning, she'd almost certainly had too much to drink. She took a deep breath and blew out the candles, then pressed her palms together in front of her lips, the faint smell of Tom's jeans on her left hand mingling with the unsettlingly overpowering fragrance in the air and making her heart pound. She closed her eyes and made a wish.

'Don't tell us what you wished for,' she heard Ruby say.

Yeah, that's definitely not happening.

Everyone clapped and cheered as the lights came on again and the waitress stepped forward with a huge cake knife. It took a few seconds for Daisy's eyes to adjust and focus, and even longer for her brain to process the inarguable fact that

Christian was standing next to her, grinning like a naughty schoolboy.

'*Surprise!*' he announced, doing half-hearted jazz hands. He was wearing a fawn wool coat over a black turtleneck and looked like a Columbian drug baron. '*Happy birthday!*' Then when Daisy continued to stare at him, added a feeble '*Yay!*' for good measure.

The table had fallen silent, staring at them in a mix of shock, horror and confusion at the new arrival. Daisy saw a few pennies drop as Melanie and Justin realised finally who Christian was, and Tom had his hand clamped across his mouth, looking like he might throw up. Marcus was staring at Christian with a steely glare, like he wanted to strangle him, but that was nothing compared to the killer death stare on Ruby's face. Gerald cleared his throat and brandished two bottles of wine. 'Anyone for a top-up?' Multiple glasses were thrust in his direction and everyone started chuntering awkwardly.

Daisy glanced at the waitress, who silently withdrew the cake knife. 'Outside!' she spat at Christian, standing up and dropping her linen napkin on the table. 'Now.' The table fell silent again as they left.

'What the fuck are you playing at?!' Daisy stage-whispered.

They were standing in the road outside the pub, far enough away from the cluster of smokers to avoid being overheard, although it was clear from the fevered whispering that everyone was trying their hardest. She searched the crowd for Ruby and Tom and saw two people who could be them, but everything was in shadow and she couldn't be sure.

'I wanted to surprise you on your birthday,' Christian said feebly. 'I've got stuff I need to say.' His icy breath formed tiny clouds above his head, like speech bubbles. God, he was infuriating.

'How did you find me?' she demanded, unable to believe she was having this conversation for the second time in a month.

'I knew you weren't in London. I got a friend to do a drive-by and your house was all locked up and dark. And there were no photos on Instagram of you sipping a pina colada in a hammock under a palm tree.' He tried a brief smile but it withered under Daisy's glare.

'How did you find me HERE?' She gestured to the pub, wondering not for the first time who in the village was sharing her whereabouts.

'Oh,' Christian muttered, avoiding her eyes. 'I got lucky. I thought I'd ask at the pub where you lived, but it turned out you were actually here.' He looked about him. 'Bit slummy for you, isn't it?—'

'You can't keep doing this,' Daisy shrieked. 'Just turn up, demanding to speak to me. This isn't OK, Christian. We had a deal.' Daisy felt like she was on stage, spotlit by the sodium glow from the street lights. She saw someone push back the curtains in the function room and open the glass doors, flooding more light out onto the street. She should really take Christian back to the cottage, away from all the phone cameras, but what she wanted was for him to leave so she could get back to her friends and pretend this had never happened.

'I got a taxi here from Heathrow. I needed to see you,' he said quickly before she could interrupt. 'I've changed, Daisy. I've spent four weeks in therapy, peeling back the layers of my life like a mouldy onion. All my fears, failures, instincts, compulsions.'

Daisy said nothing, in no doubt that he'd been practising this little speech for ninety miles. Her head throbbed, unwilling to accept that Christian had done this to her again. But just like Vergallen, the quickest way to get rid of him was to let him make his little speech and get whatever alleged burden he was carrying off his chest.

'I've learnt about my issues with intimacy, my attitude to women, the way I use sex to boost my self-esteem. I've written you so many letters, but I didn't send them. I wanted to tell you in person.'

'Tell me what?' Daisy suddenly felt jittery and nervous. *Please, no!*

'I love you, Daisy,' Christian declared, his face pleading and desperate. 'You asked me once to say it and I couldn't. But now I can. I want to spend the rest of my life with you. So I got this in Switzerland.' He fumbled in his pocket and brought out a tiny blue box.

Oh Jesus fucking Christ, thought Daisy, wondering how this evening had spiralled out of control so quickly. Ten minutes ago she'd been happily drunk and feeling Tom up under the table, now her ex-fiancé was about to drop to one knee.

Christian opened the box, revealing a ring with a diamond the size of an almond. It was hideous, not her kind of thing at all. Her stomach churned with panic and booze. 'Christian, don't. It's absolutely a no. I don't want—'

'Daisy, is everything OK?' Marcus appeared in the road, his arms folded like a nightclub bouncer. His eyes darted to the ring glittering in the streetlights and he visibly faltered, backing away with his palms up. 'Oh. Fuck. I'm so sorry.'

'Marcus, it's fine,' said Daisy, not wanting him to misread the situation. She saw Tom framed in the doorway behind him and her heart sank.

Daisy turned back to Christian, but he'd closed the ring box and was edging across the street towards Marcus, his eyes narrowed. 'Who the fuck are you?' he asked, puffing out his chest.

Marcus gave a hollow laugh. 'Like you don't already know.' Daisy wondered if she'd misheard and tried to make sense of it, but it all felt other-worldly, like she was watching a crappy film full of terrible actors. Their voices were too loud and now everyone from the pub was either outside or leaning out of windows to get a good view. Most of her guests were now on the street. She could see the pinprick lights from phones, either taking photographs or videos, probably both. It was just like the night of The Incident, and she could feel the panic rising in her chest.

'You've got to be kidding me.' Christian had squared up, his face a few inches from Marcus's. Daisy noticed that the ring had gone, presumably back into his pocket. Christian looked back at Daisy with a bitter, taunting smile. 'Is Marcus Elliot the best you could do, Dais? Really?'

The punch came from nowhere, on the side of Christian's face while his head was still half-turned towards Daisy. She heard a scream as he landed like a sack of potatoes at her feet, then realised the noise was coming from her. Christian moaned in pain, curling up into a ball to shield his major organs.

Marcus moved towards them, his breathing heavy and his face white as a sheet as he tried to throw in a few extra kicks before Justin charged in from nowhere, pinning his arms down and wrestling him away. Tom weighed in and crouched down to restrain Christian, who was now hurling abuse at Marcus's retreating back, but not actually attempting to follow him. Daisy was aware of a lot of noise and bustle, but her head was spinning. She stood there for a few seconds, taking in the scene, unable to make sense of what had just happened.

Ruby appeared at Daisy's side, gently taking her elbow. 'Come on, Mum, let's go home,' she said softly, holding up Daisy's coat so she could slide her arms in. Stella and Miriam both loomed out of the darkness, their arms outstretched like zombies.

'No.' Ruby put her hand up to keep them away. 'We'll be fine. Dad, can you walk us home? Archie, can you settle up? The rest of you, deal with Christian and all these people.'

Daisy was only vaguely aware of her daughter's voice, sounding decades older than her sixteen years. Her head still felt woozy, but the fog of shock was lifting. Christian had done it again, she thought bitterly. Where had he gone? And what was the whole thing with Marcus?

Daisy hung up on Katie and flopped back onto the sofa, taking the mug of peppermint tea that Ruby was holding out for her. 'Thanks, Rubes. Katie's on the case. She'll call me in the morning.'

Ruby sat down on the sofa next to her, pulling a blanket over both their legs. Hank jumped up to settle in the space between them – Simon and Archie were staying in the pub tonight and were due to pick him up in the morning. Daisy was glad of his solid, warm little body, his obliviousness to the chaos going on around him.

'So, what happened?' Ruby whispered. 'All I saw was you and Christian talking, then Marcus throwing punches.'

Daisy ran her hand through her hair, feeling like maybe a shower would be nice before bed. 'I'm not really sure. Christian had a massive Tiffany diamond that looked like something off *Real Housewives*.' Ruby's eyes widened in horror, so Daisy gave her arm a reassuring pat. 'It's fine, I said no. Then Marcus came out and things started getting even weirder, it was like they knew each other or something. Then Christian said something snarky, like he thought me and Marcus were an item. So Marcus decked him. And the rest, as they say, is history.'

'Wow! I'm living for all this drama.' Ruby sipped her tea, then giggled. 'Just so I'm clear, were you actually having a thing with Marcus?'

Daisy started to laugh, all the nervous energy from earlier bubbling to the surface. 'God, no.'

'Poor Christian,' said Ruby, joining in with the laughter. 'He came all that way to propose and ended up getting smacked in the face.'

'But he spoiled my birthday party, the bastard,' wailed Daisy. 'Why did he have to turn up unannounced? Why couldn't he just phone or email or something?'

Ruby was quiet for a moment, then reached out to take Daisy's hand. 'Are you OK?' she asked quietly.

Daisy smiled reassuringly and squeezed Ruby's hand. 'I'm fine,' she lied. 'Katie's going to put out a statement tomorrow confirming our split. She's emailing Christian's manager tonight. Oh God, this is going to be all over the press! Loads of people were taking videos.'

Ruby shrugged and sipped her tea. 'At least you had some pants on.'

Daisy snorted and started laughing again, and Ruby joined in; soon they were both clutching their sides with tears streaming down their faces. But at the back of Daisy's mind was one big question – where was Tom?

CHAPTER FORTY-ONE

'Hold still.' Tom pressed a bag of frozen peas wrapped in a tea towel to the side of Christian's face, resisting the urge to batter the stupid twat around the head with it.

'That fucking hurts.' Christian's eyes were watering from the pain.

'If we can get the swelling down you might have less of a black eye tomorrow.'

'I'll fucking kill him,' mumbled Christian. 'I swear to God.'

Tom laughed. 'With the greatest respect, I'm not sure either of you are the fighting type. Unless you're planning to battle it out on the tennis court. Here, hold this.' He twisted the corners of the tea towel so Christian could keep the ice pack in place, then stood up and walked into the kitchen. 'Do you want a cup of tea, or a beer?'

'Tea,' said Christian. 'Thanks. I'd beat that fucker on court too. Not for the first time.'

Tom stood in the doorway while the kettle boiled. 'So, an old rivalry, then?' Suddenly the memory came back to him. He'd entirely forgotten Marcus telling him about their tennis history.

Christian nodded, then winced again. 'I thrashed him in the Wimbledon Boys' tournament when we were fourteen.

Twenty years later he fucks my fiancée and punches me in the face. Doesn't seem quite fair, does it?'

Tom swallowed, putting his hands in his pockets so Christian didn't see them shaking. 'What makes you think he and Daisy were a thing?'

Christian was quiet for a moment, staring at his shoes. 'I just assumed because he came trotting out after her like a fucking puppy. But I suppose he could have been looking for me.'

Tom breathed out slowly and walked back into the kitchen, trying to calm himself. He poured hot water onto a tea bag and added milk, then squished the bag with a spoon before dumping it in the sink and carrying the mug back through to the lounge. Christian had his head in his hands, still clutching the ice pack to this left eye.

'Here,' said Tom, putting the mug down on the table. He sat in the other chair, trying to feel like he was comforting a sixth former who'd just ballsed up his A levels and not the arrogant prick who'd spoiled Daisy's birthday party.

'Thanks.' Christian picked up the mug and took a sip. 'I didn't catch your name.'

'Tom. I'm the school headmaster.' He figured he might as well get that out in the open sooner rather than later.

Christian gave a short laugh, followed by another wince of pain. 'The famous headmaster. I should have guessed.'

'What's your plan?' asked Tom, steering the conversation back to Christian.

Christian shrugged. 'Well, I fucked up Plan A, and currently don't have a Plan B.' He gave Tom a weak smile. 'This is going to be all over the press, isn't it?'

Tom nodded. 'I think there's a good chance. People were

definitely videoing and taking photos. You should speak to . . . whoever you speak to when stuff like this happens.'

'Benny,' winced Christian. 'My manager. He's going to lose his shit. When can I get a train back to London?'

Tom looked at his watch, surprised to see it was gone eleven. Earlier he'd had visions of continuing the pub fondling with some WhatsApp sexting, or at least some quality time with his own thoughts. Fat chance of that now.

'On a Sunday?' he said. 'Not until after nine.'

'Can I get an Uber?'

Tom gave Christian a withering look. 'You can crash in my spare room if you like. I'll drive you to the station in the morning.'

Christian gave him a penetrating stare, only able to narrow one eye because the other one was already swollen and rapidly turning purple. Tom hoped he had some sunglasses in that holdall.

'Why would you do that?' asked Christian. 'What do you care?'

Tom leaned forward and gently repositioned the bag of peas. 'I don't care about you at all,' he said lightly. 'But if I watch you leave, I can reassure Daisy that you've definitely gone.'

By the time Tom messaged Daisy it was after midnight, so he didn't really expect to get a reply. But he wanted her to have something positive to read when she woke up.

Just wanted to let you know that Christian's at my house. He's fine, I'm putting him on a train to London tomorrow at 9. Don't leave your house before then.

Tom's breath quickened as he saw that Daisy had read the message, then the three dots that showed she was writing a reply. It seemed to take forever.

Thank you. You are amazing. Will message you tomorrow once Ruby's gone back to school. Simon's going to take her.

Tom stared at the message for a few seconds, the words spreading through his limbs like a hot bath on a frosty day. He smiled at his phone, wishing Daisy was here so he could say what he felt in person. Sometimes it paid to play it cool, but other times you just had to open your heart.

Happy birthday. I like you very much x

It's been a memorable one, for lots of reasons. I like you very much too x

CHAPTER FORTY-TWO

Daisy kept her usual scheduled call with Katie on Monday morning, despite having spoken to her at least five times since Saturday night. She sipped her tea under her usual blanket on the sofa as her manager gave her the rundown of what was currently happening.

'My phone is still ringing off the hook,' Katie complained, 'mostly hacks trying to piece all the rumours together. I'll be amazed if they've left your village yet, so stay indoors.'

'They're still here. Fortunately, they're not allowed on school grounds. Tom's secretary is chasing them off on her mobility scooter.'

'What about the tennis coach?' asked Katie. 'Where's he?'

'No idea. His girlfriend lives in Cirencester so I guess he's hiding out at her house.'

'Lucky girlfriend,' Katie chuckled. 'I've done some digging and it seems like he and Christian did know each other from playing tennis when they were kids, I'll see if I can find out the details. But in the meantime, the press consensus seems to be that you've dumped Christian for the local tennis pro and they had a street brawl over you. Like Hugh Grant and Colin Firth in *Bridget Jones*.'

Daisy sighed. 'It's a non-story. I've played tennis with Marcus half a dozen times, mostly with other people. That fight had nothing to do with me.'

'I believe you, though thousands won't. Any news from Christian?'

'Nothing after his message yesterday.' Christian had sent Daisy a WhatsApp apologising for gatecrashing her party, presumably while he was on the train back to London. Daisy had replied curtly, informing him that Katie was putting a statement out saying they had split amicably and hoped to remain friends. Christian's response was, 'OK, I'll let Benny know,' and she hadn't heard from him since.

'So that's that,' Katie concluded. 'Congratulations! You're officially a single woman.'

'Apparently so.' Daisy thought about Tom, who'd been waiting so patiently in the wings, and had come through for her again on Saturday night with Christian. She shivered at the memory of the hard urgency of him under the table on Saturday, then tried to focus. 'Have you heard from *Spotlight*?'

'Yeah. Clara's left several messages. I'm pretty sure she'll do some squawking, but it's nothing I can't handle.'

'Thanks.' Daisy felt exhausted. 'And *thank you* for the birthday present. I didn't get a chance to say how much I loved it. I'll call Roger later.'

'You're welcome.' Daisy could hear the smile in Katie's voice. 'So, what are you going to do today?'

'Stay indoors with the curtains closed,' Daisy parroted. 'Edit the book and enjoy the peace. Ruby's safely back at school and Hank has gone back to London with Simon and Archie.' She looked at the space on the sofa where Hank would normally be, curled up in a tight ball behind her knees. 'I really miss Hank, but at least I don't have to walk him.'

'No walks. The village will be crawling with press, so sit tight,' Katie murmured.

'Melanie lives next door to the pub. She can see them from her husband's office window. She's promised to let me know when they leave. It can't be more than a day or two, surely?'

'Depends on how welcome the village makes them and how willing people are to talk to them.' Daisy could hear Katie moving around, shuffling papers, opening drawers. 'Did you ever find out who the leak was?'

'No.'

'Who's your best guess?'

'Honestly? I have no idea.' Tom, Stella, Justin, Melanie . . . she didn't want to think any of them were capable of it.

Anybody walking past Willow Cottage on Monday would have assumed from the drawn curtains and the cold chimney that nobody was home – only Daisy's friends in the village knew she was hunkered down in the kitchen, warmed by the AGA. As Radio 2 played softly in the background, Daisy propped her laptop on the kitchen counter and tapped out the Acknowledgements – her heartfelt thanks to Stella, Justin, Will, Tom and the staff, parents and students of Shipton House School. It was strange to think how important they'd all been to the book even though she'd only known them for less than four months. So much had happened in that time.

She took a break to watch Justella's latest YouTube video, filmed by Will in the pub kitchen on Saturday morning, while they'd iced and decorated her beautiful birthday cake. She'd never had a chance to taste it, although apparently the chef at the Shipton Arms had put a chunk of it in the pub freezer for her. The video made her laugh: they were so naturally funny and charming, especially when Stella tried to teach Justin, with his giant sausage fingers, how to make delicate sugar paste daisies.

The video already had nearly a million views, no doubt helped along by the press coverage of what happened later, but it was also clear from the comments that Justella were starting to get some traction in the States. There was a lot of love for Justin and Stella's accents and their British humour. Perhaps they were going to be the next biggest British invasion since *Downton Abbey*. Her mother would love that.

After lunch Daisy did some chores, cleaning the cottage and doing some laundry, and by late afternoon Melanie had confirmed that the remaining Vultures had gone. Daisy breathed a sigh of relief, feeling like she could relax for the first time in an age. She stood in the garden for a few minutes, enjoying the frosty winter air. Sometimes you just had to absent yourself from all the noise and let it burn itself out.

Her phone buzzed while she watched the sun disappear behind the trees in a haze of pink sky; her stomach flipped when she saw it was Tom. They hadn't spoken since their late-night WhatsApps on Saturday, and he'd sensibly stayed well away from Willow Cottage yesterday, although she probably wouldn't have said no if he'd knocked on her door.

Are you OK? Tx

Daisy smiled, happy that he was thinking about her. She quickly tapped out a reply.

I'm fine, holed up in the cottage working hard. Thank you
for asking.

I was just thinking about you. Just thought you'd like
to know.

What were you thinking about?

Lots of things. Most of them not suitable for work, so I'll
save them for another day.

Daisy grinned, feeling suddenly very warm despite the
frigid air. She thought for a moment about her reply, then
her phone rang.

'Hey,' said Daisy breathlessly.

'I thought I'd call,' Tom laughed nervously. 'Call me
old-fashioned.'

'You're old-fashioned. But I find it rather charming.'

'Thank God,' Tom muttered fervently. 'I just walked
Henry through the village and the reporters have gone.'

'That's good news. I might be able to leave the house
soon.'

There was a moment of hesitation. 'Can I come over? Just
for ten minutes? I'd like to see you.'

Daisy thought about it for about three milliseconds. 'That
would be nice, actually. When's a good time?'

Tom laughed. 'Well, I'm currently standing outside your
front door trying to pluck up the courage to knock, so I
guess now?'

Daisy poured Tom a glass of wine – it was definitely 5 o'clock
somewhere, and somehow it felt like there was something to

celebrate. Also going into the kitchen gave her a chance to run a brush through her hair and pinch her pallid cheeks.

Tom took a sip and perched on the arm of the chair. He was back in his headmaster uniform – dark grey cords, a pale blue shirt and a black coat that could at best be described as an anorak. The whole look was incredibly *Rural Dad at M&S* and yet somehow oddly sexy.

'So, you and Christian are officially finished?' asked Tom, not even attempting to hide his smile. They watched as a confused Henry did a final lap of the cottage, before giving up looking for Hank and flumping onto the sofa next to Daisy.

'We are. Katie put out a statement yesterday. All very amicable, still friends, blah-blah-blah. The usual stuff. Is everything OK at school though? Not too much outrage from the governors?'

Tom shrugged. 'Not really. Today has been a bit of a fuss, but what happened on Saturday was nothing to do with me. And apparently I'm no longer being named as the other man in your life.' Tom raised his eyebrows playfully.

Daisy smiled. 'It seems I'm now part of some love triangle with Christian and Marcus.'

'So I'm not the Homewrecking Headmaster any more.' Tom put his glass down on the table and moved over to the sofa, hoofing Henry off so he could take his place next to Daisy.

'No, it would seem not.' Daisy's heart was racing at how close Tom was. 'But listen, before you ravish me on this sofa – and I do very much hope that's your intention – you need to know that this isn't the end of it. If we're seen together, they'll rake over your life. You have to be prepared for that.'

316

Tom reached over and tucked a loose strand of hair behind Daisy's ear. 'Listen to me, Daisy. I want this. I've been through more pain in the last three years than most people go through in a lifetime, so there's nothing the papers can do or say that will make a difference. I'm ready to start living again.'

Daisy nodded vehemently. 'So. Where would you like to start?'

'Much as I'd very much like to ravish you on this sofa, sixth form parents' evening starts in about twenty minutes. So, let's do what normal people do, and go on a date. What are you doing next Saturday?'

Daisy thought for a second. 'Nothing. Ruby isn't home, she's got play rehearsals.'

'Then let's go somewhere. Take a picnic, get in the car, spend the day together.'

'That sounds lovely.' Daisy took in every detail of his features, wondering if she'd ever get tired of looking at him.

'Just so you know – I might ask to kiss you at the end of it.'

Daisy laughed and pulled a face. 'I know it's not traditional, but how do you feel about kissing me now?'

Ten minutes later Tom pulled away reluctantly. 'I need to go,' he whispered, adding the lightest of kisses to Daisy's lips.

'It's fine,' Daisy grinned. 'That will keep me going until next weekend.'

'Really?'

'No.'

Tom looked at her, his face tender. 'I meant what I said on Saturday night. I like you a lot.'

'I like you a lot too. Is that too forward, considering we haven't even had our first date?'

Tom laughed and stood up, pulling Daisy with him. 'Ours has been an unconventional courtship. I'm sorry if I'm not very communicative for the rest of the week. I'm drowning in admin. Luckily my antique secretary is retiring at half-term so I can advertise for someone who knows how to turn on a computer.'

Daisy reached down her jumper and shuffled her boob back into her bra. 'Or you could just hire Melanie now and save yourself the bother.'

Tom paused for a second, then turned his palms upwards like he'd had a revelation. 'Oh my God, you're a genius! Why didn't I think of that? I'll call her as soon as I get back to the office.'

Daisy leaned over and straightened the collar of his shirt, then patted his shoulder before stepping back. 'Go charm some parents and I'll see you on Saturday. I'll bring a picnic, but I don't have a rucksack or anything practical like that.'

'I'm a Duke of Edinburgh expedition leader,' Tom assured her. 'Leave that to me. I'll pick you up at ten.' He put his coat on and grabbed Henry's lead, giving Daisy a final kiss on the lips before checking the coast was clear and sliding out of the door into the darkness.

Daisy breathed out slowly and fell back onto the sofa, a huge grin on her face as she tried to calm the butterflies in her stomach and the hot, throbbing ache between her legs.

CHAPTER FORTY-THREE

'What did you decide in the end?' asked Stella. 'For the picnic?'

'I made Cornish pasties,' replied Daisy, pulling a paper bag out of the fridge. 'Easy to eat standing up, not too fancy, no plastic packaging.'

Stella raised an eyebrow. 'I hadn't realised Tom was an environmentalist. Are you sure he wouldn't prefer some hot soup? There's six inches of snow out there.'

'We'll never know. Because he's getting a pasty.'

Stella pursed her lips disapprovingly, watching Daisy pack lunch into a Selfridges tote bag. 'Is that it? *Just* a pasty?'

Daisy rolled her eyes, wondering whether it had been wise to tell Stella about spending the day with Tom. They'd been getting on so well lately, and it had been a long time since Daisy had taken her mother into her confidence. 'I've also got bananas and chocolate. Honestly, Mum, if we're that hungry or cold, we'll just go to a pub.'

Stella sniffed. 'I'm just saying that you could have made more effort.'

'It's just Tom.' Daisy sighed. 'We're going for a walk. It's not that big a deal.'

'So not a date, then?' Stella's stare was penetrating.

Daisy's neck started to itch, so she stopped packing her bag. 'Jesus, this is like being fourteen again. Fine, it's a date!

I like him. He likes me. So we're going to spend the day together to see if we still like each other at the end of it. Happy?'

Stella clapped her hands together with delight. 'Can I tell Justin?'

'Is there any point me asking you not to?'

'No. Not really.' Her grin was unrepentant, and Daisy felt a flow of warmth for her mother that she hadn't experienced in years.

'What are you doing today?'

'Making a new Justella video,' Stella announced proudly. 'Will's meeting us at Justin's allotment in a bit. We're going to milk his goat, then come back to the cottage to make goat's cheese.'

Daisy grinned excitedly as a car horn sounded outside. There was no point pretending to be cool about it. She'd been jittery all week. 'I'm off.'

Stella winked. 'Behave yourself.'

Daisy paused in the doorway. 'Do I have to?'

'I'd be very disappointed if you did.'

'Don't kiss me, my mother is watching.' Daisy handed Tom her bag and climbed into his car.

'Sorry about the state of my car.' The ancient Toyota Land Cruiser showed signs of being dark blue, although there was more mud than paintwork. Inside was considerably cleaner, like it had been given a hasty vacuum. 'I cleaned the dog hair from the seats but didn't dare wash the outside in case the mud is actually holding it together.'

Daisy didn't care; the idea of spending a whole day with Tom made her giddy. 'Where's Henry?'

320

'I left him with Angela. He's getting a bit old for long walks and he doesn't like being cold. She'll take him out for a spin on her scooter and feed him treats.'

Daisy gave a happy sigh, then turned to study Tom in the steamy warmth of the car. He looked like one of the dads who eyed her up at Ruby's school, all rumpled but yummy with those gorgeous blue eyes, tidy stubble and the tiniest smattering of grey about his ears. He was wearing black canvas trousers and a moss green jumper that hugged his arms and chest, neither of which were particularly toned or exceptional. He wasn't that tall – maybe 5'8 or 5'9 – so in heels Daisy would tower over him. He was about as far from Christian, who looked like a male model and had the attitude to match, as he could be. Tom looked like he might wear John Lewis pyjamas to bed, and right now Daisy couldn't imagine anything sexier.

'Hello.' Daisy realised she was smiling at him.

'Hi.' Tom gently pressed his lips on hers. He leaned back and looked into her eyes. 'Do you think your mother saw?'

'I don't care.' She pointed at the road ahead. 'Get me out of here.'

As Tom headed north through the snow-covered hills of the Cotswolds, Daisy tried to calm her nerves. She'd been so on edge at the prospect of spending the day with him, she'd purposely paid little attention to her appearance, so as not to look desperate: black leggings, walking boots, a shapeless grey sweatshirt under a padded coat, and her hair carelessly tucked into a bobble hat, her makeup-free face hidden behind huge sunglasses. The white knuckles gripping the steering wheel suggested Tom was nervous too, so they made small talk about Justin and Stella's videos, the increased enquiries on the school website after Daisy's classes and what Daisy was planning to do next.

'I've got the fete next weekend, then I'm heading back to London.'

'Can I come and visit?' Tom immediately blushed and fixed his eyes on the road.

'I rather hoped you would,' replied Daisy, imagining what it might be like to wake up next to this beautiful man. 'It's so gorgeous here though, I don't know how I'll be able to leave.' She wound down the window, breathing in the icy air. 'Did you grow up here?'

'No, East Sussex. My first teaching job after qualifying was in Cheltenham, then I moved to Shipton Combe about eight years ago.'

'What did you teach?' asked Daisy.

'Geography. This is a nice bit of the country for teaching kids about weather and land use, topography, that kind of stuff.' He glanced sideways at Daisy, like he was checking she hadn't fallen asleep. 'I even know where there's an oxbow lake.'

Daisy sat up, her eyes wide with fake shock. '*No way!*'

Tom laughed. 'Yup. It's on the River Severn, but I can't tell you where. It's a secret only geography teachers know.'

'I'll force it out of you. Get you drunk and make you tell,' she teased, pleased when Tom grinned. 'What about your family? You never mention them.'

Tom shrugged. 'Not much to tell. My dad died when I was fifteen, then six months later my mother married an old family friend. He had a truckload of money so as soon I went to university they retired and started travelling the world. They've now been on holiday for nearly twenty-five years.'

'You're kidding.' Daisy's eyes were wide at the idea.

'Nope. They spend half the year in the UK for tax and residency reasons, although they're always off touring the lakes or Cornwall or wherever. They're currently on a six-week cruise of the Pacific. I had a postcard from Tahiti last week.'

'Wow! No brothers or sisters?'

'One of each. Both older than me; both abroad. My sister Ellie is married to a former Swedish popstar; they run a record label in Stockholm. My brother Jonathan owns a beach bar in Honduras.'

'Stop it. You're making that up!'

'I'm not,' Tom grinned. 'I spent last October half-term with Jonny. We drank beer on his boat and caught fish like real men.' He puffed out his chest.

'OK, you're definitely making it up.'

Tom shrugged. 'I don't know what to say. We're less than an hour into our first date and you're already calling me a liar.'

Daisy leaned back into her seat, feeling that warm feeling again. 'So, how's this first date going for you so far?'

Tom was silent for a moment. 'Well, you're in my car, we've got a whole day together and there's a good chance I might get to kiss you again . . . I'd say it was going pretty well.'

By the time they finished their hike almost five hours later, Daisy had seen enough snowy fields and winter hedgerows to last a lifetime, although she obviously wouldn't tell Tom that. The boutique hotel and gastropub where they parked was a very welcome finish point, with honey-stone build-ings clustered around a gravel courtyard scattered with snow-capped ornamental trees. They dumped the rucksack in the car and headed to one of the picnic benches outside the pub, laughing at how Daisy had fallen in a patch of brambles, got a splinter in her hand from an ancient farm gate and ended up with leggings that were cold and damp from the snow. But she'd also laughed until her sides hurt and climbed a couple of thigh-burner hills at a pace that made her feel more alive than she had in weeks. Even her pasties hadn't been bad – or maybe it was the fact she'd eaten them with a man who kept looking at her like she was a goddess.

At one point Tom had taken her hand to help her over a wooden stile and not let go, stroking his thumb along her palm in a way that made her insides dissolve. She wondered if he might kiss her at some point, maybe press her up against the trunk of a snow-laden tree like one of those crappy Netflix films she and Ruby liked to watch at Christmas, but he was clearly determined to spend their first date courting her like some Jane Austen hero. It was delightful and arousing in equal measure, particularly after six months dating a man like Christian who'd had his fingers inside her before she'd finished saying good morn-ing. Tom's chivalry made a rather refreshing change, but it also made Daisy all the more determined to get him naked as soon as possible.

'Here you go, half a cider.' Daisy put the drinks down on the table. She held hers up until Tom chinked her glass. 'Cheers. Thank you for a lovely walk.' Daisy sat down opposite him, straddling the wooden bench.

Tom smiled and took a sip. 'You're very welcome.' He gestured to her glass. 'You don't strike me as the cider type.'

'I'm not usually,' she admitted, 'but we're in the West Country so it feels like the done thing. I'm not much of a drinker at all, really.' Daisy thought of the occasions Tom had seen her knocking back wine and added hurriedly, 'My birthday party was an exception to a strict three-drink rule. But I usually drink white wine. *Never* red.'

'What happens if you drink red?'

'Pray you never find out.' Daisy crossed her eyes and stuck her tongue out. Tom laughed. She looked up at the beautiful old buildings around them, the stone glowing almost orange in the afternoon sun. 'What's this hotel like?'

Tom shrugged. 'No idea, never stayed here. But I've heard it's pretty swish.'

Daisy closed her eyes, took a deep breath. Sometimes it paid to seize the moment. 'Good. Because I booked us a room when I went to the bar.'

Tom's eyes widened with surprise.

'I'm feeling impulsive, among other things. Do you think Angela would keep Henry for the night?'

Tom put down his glass and swallowed. 'I'm sure she would.'

Daisy drained her glass then stood up, fishing a key attached to a huge oak tag out of her coat pocket. 'It's called the Stable Loft. I'll go and check it out. Finish your drink, call Angela then come and join me when you're ready.' She hesitated for a second. 'Unless . . . this is a bad idea?'

Tom was already reaching for his phone. 'Daisy, this is the best idea you've had since you kissed me in my kitchen.'

*

325

The Stable Loft suite was exactly as Daisy had hoped – a beautiful room with a steeply pitched roof and exposed beams, decorated with deep carpets, a vast bed and a rolltop bath positioned in front of huge windows overlooking miles of snow-covered fields. The colour scheme was neutral and stylish, all mushroom-coloured curtains, duck egg cushions and soft white bedlinen.

Daisy switched on table lamps feeling jittery and nervous, conscious that this had been a spur-of-the-moment decision that might backfire horribly. She hadn't been naked with a man for nearly four months, and the fallout from The Incident had prompted her to reject all forms of body hair grooming on the basis that it was winter and nobody was going to see her without her clothes on for a very long time. Tom was probably expecting the smooth, hairless Daisy he'd almost certainly seen on social media, and instead he was going to get a petting zoo.

And what if someone in the hotel called reporters and told them she was shacked up in a Cotswold hotel suite with the famous headmaster? Was this a mistake? She paced up and down, willing Tom to arrive before she made a run for it; then cast around for something to do other than downing neat whisky from the minibar.

She turned off her phone, then walked into the enormous bathroom and splashed water on her face, looking at her reflection in the mirror. Her hair was flat on top and frizzy at the ends from her bobble hat, and a bit of mascara wouldn't have killed her. Being sexy and spontaneous had felt empowering in the moment, but now she just felt inadequate and stupid and some three hundred pounds poorer than when she'd arrived. Tom probably thought she was a slag and was sitting outside the pub trying to come up with excuses not to stay.

The room didn't look lovely any more, it looked like a magazine interior for idiots with more money than sense. Who actually needed two sinks and a shower head the size of a dinner plate? What was the point of six scatter cushions on the bed?

A gentle knock at the door made Daisy's heart pound out of her chest. She took a few deep breaths to stop herself being sick, tucked her frazzled hair behind her ears and wiped her sweaty palms on her leggings as she opened the door, praying that she wouldn't regret this in the morning.

'Hi,' said Tom, his voice catching as he gave her a look that was pure, unadulterated lust. *We've both been thinking about this for so long*, thought Daisy. *And now it's finally going to happen.*

'Hi,' whispered Daisy, backing into the room as Tom bore down on her with a level of fierce intensity she'd never seen from him before. He kicked the door closed and gathered her into his arms, pressing her against the wall with his whole body and kissing her like she was the only thing in the world that mattered.

'I haven't done this in a while,' breathed Daisy, pulling back and searching his face for reassurance. 'And I haven't waxed or anything.'

Tom laughed softly. 'I haven't done this in over three years,' he said, curling a tendril of her hair around his fingers. 'And I haven't waxed either.'

They both started to laugh and Daisy felt herself relax into him, knowing that nothing – *nothing* – she had experienced with Christian or Simon or any other man was going to come close to this night with Tom.

CHAPTER FORTY-FOUR

Tom watched the finer details of the hotel room emerge from the darkness, listening to the dawn chorus as Daisy slept beside him, her breathing deep and steady. The bed was warm and soft and comfortable and there was absolutely nowhere else he needed to be, so he burrowed his head further into the mountain of pillows and enjoyed the unfamiliar feeling of serenity and contentment.

The previous evening played like a movie in his head – the passionate kissing, then the brief period of awkwardness where they both admitted they felt like inexperienced, fumbling teenagers. Daisy had also been shy and hesitant, clearly used to a man taking the lead and not nearly as comfortable in her body as he might have expected for someone so entirely, utterly glorious. But there wasn't an inch of Daisy that Tom didn't find alluring, from the chipped red nail polish on her toes to the downy fluff under her arms.

They'd taken things slowly, luxuriating in the knowledge that the whole night stretched out ahead of them and there was no need to bang each other like they had a bus to catch. Daisy had taken a shower to wash off the sweat and grime of their hike while Tom ran a bath in the enormous tub in the bedroom. Then Daisy had wallowed in the bubbles until Tom had finished his shower and padded across the soft carpet to join her.

Daisy had lain with her back against Tom's chest, in a bath so deep that the water had been barely more than an inch from the top. Any sudden movements would have flooded the floor, so instead they just relaxed and familiarised themselves with the strange and novel sensation of each other's nakedness, with nothing more than lingering, featherlight touches. Tom was pretty sure it was the single most erotic experience of his life. And strangely he felt no guilt about that. He'd worried that he might compare Daisy to Tessa, but Daisy was so different in every respect, and the intimacy he'd shared with this late wife was firmly in the past. His future, he hoped, was the woman lying next to him.

Once the water had started to go cold they'd moved to the bed, burrowing under the duvet to lose themselves in a tangle of damp limbs. That bit hadn't been quiet and lingering at all – instead, it had felt like the weeks of simmering tension finally had the chance to boil over. At one point Daisy had accidentally elbowed him in the jaw, but mostly it had been incredible.

Afterwards Daisy had nestled her body into Tom's shoulder so they could both catch their breath and languish in the post-coital glow, lying in comfortable silence for a few minutes until Daisy asked if he was hungry. Tom had been a little bit in love with Daisy since the day he'd watched her feeding the ducks from the window of his office, but hearing her ask 'Shall we order pizza?' had pretty much sealed the deal.

In the throes of passion neither Tom nor Daisy had remembered to put the little hanging card on the door to order room service breakfast, and he could completely understand why Daisy didn't want to do a walk of shame to the hotel dining room in yesterday's hiking clothes. So instead he offered to go down and pick up a tray of food and coffee, and try to procure a couple of toothbrushes from reception. The bathroom was full of tiny bottles of expensive toiletries, but apparently if you wanted a toothbrush you had to ask.

The Receptionist was the same woman who had checked Daisy in yesterday, and was more than happy to discreetly help with whatever Tom needed. So when he casually passed back through reception with a tray of toast, juice and coffee from the restaurant, she slid toothbrushes and toothpaste onto the tray along with a folded copy of the *Mail on Sunday*.

'You might want to read that,' she said gravely. 'Page four.'

Tom hurried back upstairs with a sinking feeling that this blissful time with Daisy was about to come to an abrupt end.

Daisy turned the paper to face him. In bold black letters, the headline read: *Daisy's doubles! TV star's love-all triangle is a game, set and match rivalry that goes back TWENTY YEARS.'* Under it were two photos – one of Christian and Daisy looking like Hollywood royalty on the fateful night of the NTAs, next to another of Marcus looking tired and hostile, clearly being papped outside the tennis club where he worked.

'Shit!' said Tom. 'Read it out.' He handed Daisy a slice of toast, then started buttering another.

The story started out with a recap of the Wimbledon Boys' final in 1999 and Marcus's bike accident shortly afterwards. Then there was a load of irrelevant stuff about Daisy which she skipped over, before the article ended with:

A source close to Marcus Elliot said, 'Christian wasn't expected that night, he turned up as a surprise for Daisy's fortieth birthday with a Tiffany engagement ring. I think seeing him there opened old wounds for Marcus, as Daisy had told him she'd split up with her famous tennis beau.' Neither Christian Walker or Marcus Elliot were available for comment.

'Well. I guess you have to admire how these idiots can pull together a handful of random facts, fill in the cracks with made-up sources and quotes and call it an "exclusive". Poor Marcus.' Daisy put the paper down and took a forceful bite of her toast.

'How do you feel about it?' asked Tom curiously.

'It's something and nothing,' Daisy shrugged. 'I'll talk to Katie about it,' – she'd bet there were missed calls and messages from her manager when she turned her phone back on – 'see if it's worth actively denying Marcus and I had a thing going on. She'll probably say no; they don't have any photos or videos to dump later because it never happened, so chances are it will go away on its own.'

Tom sat down next to her, his face full of concern. He hated the fact Daisy looked so grim, that her reality had intruded on theirs. 'Is this your life? Stuff like this, week after week?'

Daisy gave him a tired smile. 'Sometimes. The split from Simon was awful, and whenever I've dated someone the press Vultures have started circling, which is why I haven't dated much.' She put her coffee cup on the table and swung her feet onto Tom's lap. 'This last year has been particularly bad.'

'Do you know why?' asked Tom.

'The thing at the NTAs, obviously,' Daisy continued,

closing her eyes as he started to gently rub her feet. 'But afterwards there were other stories, about me being a drunk, taking medication, having a temper. There was even a story about me throwing a shoe at my dog. I don't even have a dog.' Tom snorted. 'And now all of this. Somebody is definitely making up stories about me. And somebody in Shipton Combe is helping.'

'What makes you think that?'

'It's here.' Daisy tapped the newspaper and read aloud.

'According to a source close to the TV star, top of the chat agenda at Daisy's fortieth birthday party was the new YouTube venture of Daisy's mother Stella Crawford and her cooking partner, Justin Drummond, who announced that Cook with Justella *will soon be featured on ITV's* This Morning.'

She raised her eyebrows at Tom. 'See? Only people in that room heard Justin mention that, so one of them must have told the press.'

'Shit, Shipton Combe has a mole.' Tom looked suddenly alarmed. 'You know it's not me, right?'

Daisy laughed. 'I'd assumed it wasn't you. It would put quite the dampener on this first date if it were.'

Tom shook his head. 'But who can it be?'

'I have my suspicions,' she waved Tom off, 'but I can't think about that today. Right now I need to call Katie, then turn my phone off again so I can take you back to bed. We need to make the most of this room for at least a couple more hours.'

She shot Tom her most seductive smile, then laughed when he almost choked gulping down the rest of his breakfast.

CHAPTER FORTY-FIVE

Since Daisy had spent a decent chunk of Sunday on the phone to Katie, they'd decided to skip their normal Monday morning phone call unless something urgent came up. So when her phone started ringing when she was in the shower at Willow Cottage, she immediately thought it was her manager and felt a frisson of worry. She played out all manner of doom scenarios in her head while she finished washing her hair, wrapped it in a towel and put her bathrobe on before she padded back into the bedroom to return Katie's call. Daisy sat on the bed and looked at the screen, surprised to see the missed call was from Christian, not Katie. The worry was replaced by a weary heaviness, but on the upside at least he wasn't hammering on her front door.

Daisy had just made the decision to call him back later when the phone rang again, Christian's name lighting up the screen in the gloom of the bedroom. It was lashing down with rain outside and the room felt damp and cold. She decided she might as well answer it – she'd been on the receiving end of Christian's persistence before. Her mind briefly flickered to Tom's relentless tongue and fingers yesterday morning, but she pushed those thoughts aside. *Not* a good time.

'Hey,' Daisy said, trying not to sigh.

'Don't hang up,' said Christian hurriedly. 'I need to talk to you.'

Daisy rolled her eyes. 'First, I'm not a hanging-up kind of person, and second, if I didn't want to talk to you I wouldn't have answered the phone in the first place.'

'Sorry,' mumbled Christian. 'I just need to tell you something. About the story in the *Mail on Sunday* yesterday.'

'Go on.' Daisy closed her eyes, lying back on the pillow.

'All the stories about you since the NTAs, they've come from Benny.'

'Why am I not surprised,' she sighed. 'How did you know it was him?'

'The bit about the Tiffany ring and opening old wounds, I said that to Benny when I told him what had happened. Nobody else could have known that but him.'

'Right.' Daisy sat up, her weariness turning to anger. 'Did he say WHY he's been making up bullshit stories about me for the last four months?'

'He and Damien cooked it all up. I think at first it was about trying to protect my career, make me look good with the engagement stuff, but also making you look bad in case things went south with *Spotlight*. So I didn't get burned by association, I guess.'

This was just a game to people like Benny – a series of chess moves where sacrifices had to be made in order to claim the win. And Damien, Christian's agent, was just as bad, if not worse. And Daisy was just meant to sit back and be collateral damage? *Not*.

'Then when it was clear *Spotlight* weren't going to sack you off, Benny persuaded me to go to Austria to win you back, then sent the photographer to make us look all loved up. He thought it might help get the Wimbledon deal over the line. He's been hedging his bets the whole time. And now we've officially split up, he's trying to get you fired so he can put one of his other clients in your job.'

'Of course he is.' *Well, isn't that just great?* 'I think we can all agree that you picked a brilliant manager, Christian. Well done.'

'I'm really sorry, Dais,' Christian said bleakly. 'Obviously I've fired both of them. The Wimbledon job is off the table anyway, the BBC got cold feet after all the rumours.'

Daisy said nothing, her mind still buzzing with fury at Benny and Damien for trying to derail her career. She was even a little sorry that things hadn't panned out the way Christian had hoped, but this interlude wouldn't do him any harm in the long run. He was young, handsome and charismatic, and the rules were simply different for men.

'I'm really sorry about last Saturday,' he mumbled. 'I really did come to ask you to marry me. I didn't mean to cause trouble.'

'I know.' That Daisy believed. Christian really wasn't that smart. 'Did you manage to get a refund on the ring?'

'Yeah. Tiffany were cool about it. I guess they've seen it all before.'

'It was beautiful,' lied Daisy, 'but I'm not the right person to wear it.'

'No,' Christian agreed. 'I get that now.' He was so silent Daisy wondered if he'd hung up, then he said, 'Look, I won't bother you again, I promise. I've been thinking about taking some time out anyway, maybe going to coach a tennis season in Spain. I know loads of people who can hook me up with a job. I'll take my parents, rent a villa or something. Carry on with my therapy.'

'How have your mum and dad taken everything?' She'd

met them a couple of times and had rather liked them. Nice, ordinary people who were hugely proud of their son.

'Oh, OK. I'm actually living with them at the moment. Best not to be alone until my head's less fucked up.'

'Do they know about your . . . issues?'

'Yeah.' He gave a wry laugh. 'I don't ever want to have to say the words "sex party" in front of my mum and dad again.'

Daisy laughed, trying to imagine how mortifying that conversation would be. Christian's mother was on first name terms with Jesus, for a start.

'They've done some reading and spoken to my therapist in Switzerland,' Christian continued. 'Mum seems to think that food can replace women in my life, and Dad and I watch classic Wimbledon men's finals together, so we don't have to talk.'

'Sounds delightful.'

'Hey, don't knock it! Yesterday we watched Bjorg v. McEnroe 1980, today we've lined up Agassi v. Ivanisevic 1992.'

'What's tomorrow?' This was the Christian she enjoyed. She unwrapped the towel from her head, raking her fingers through her damp hair as she listened.

'Federer v. Nadal 2007.'

'I'm glad you're OK.' She was surprised to find she meant it. 'And I think you coaching in Spain is a great idea. Give me a call when you get back.'

'I will.'

'Christian – wait!' she shouted before he could hang up. 'Did Benny say how he was getting the information on me?'

'Yeah. He said he had a source in your village.'

'Did he say who it was?' asked Daisy, sitting upright on the bed.

'No, sorry.'

Daisy nodded, disappointed but not surprised. That would have been too easy. 'OK. Take care of yourself, Christian.'

'I will . . . You know where I am if you ever want a chat.' He paused, before adding, 'Or, you know, phone sex . . . Too soon?'

'Waaay too soon, Christian.'

CHAPTER FORTY-SIX

Daisy was eating her breakfast when her mother knocked on the window, then immediately stuck her head in the back door without being invited. Evidently Stella was easing into the norms of village life quicker than Daisy was.

'How was your walk on Saturday?' asked Stella, not bothering with any pleasantries.

'Hello, Mum, I'm fine, thanks for asking.'

Stella waved her away. 'I popped over yesterday morning and there didn't seem to be anyone here, and then there was all that nonsense in the paper, so I wanted to check that you were OK.'

As there was a ring of truth to it, Daisy relaxed, folding her arms and leaning back against the counter. 'We had a lovely walk, and the reason I wasn't around yesterday morning was because we booked ourselves into a very expensive hotel and had lots of great sex.'

Stella clapped her hands and hooted, 'Oh, I AM glad! *That's my girl.*'

Daisy held her hands up. 'Don't get too excited, it's early days.'

'I know, I know. I promise not to buy a hat.'

'Very funny.' Daisy felt herself wobble a little, her bravado suddenly replaced by a wave of self-doubt. 'Tom wants to come and stay when I'm back in London. What if he doesn't like that Daisy Crawford nearly as much as the country version?'

Stella looked at her for a moment, her brow furrowed. 'Well,' she reached out and took her daughter's hand between both of hers. 'I think first you need to ask yourself which version YOU like more.'

Daisy couldn't deal with the ramifications of that thought right now. 'How are you, anyway?' she asked.

'I'm fine,' Stella smiled. 'Actually, I came over because I have something to tell you.'

Daisy looked up at her mother, wondering what on earth she had done now. 'OK,' she said, immediately reaching for the kettle.

'It's about Miriam. Well, me and Miriam really,' Stella corrected, sounding nervous.

'What about you and Miriam?'

Stella cleared her throat. 'We've acknowledged that our friendship has . . . feelings.' She glared at her daughter defiantly.

Daisy turned on the tap, trying not to hide the huge smile on her face. 'Mum, are you saying that you've fallen for the local vicar?'

'I'm not a teenager,' Stella stated. 'But I like her very much and we seem to have some kind of connection.'

'And forgive me for asking,' asked Daisy, grabbing a mug from the shelf, 'but have you had a connection with women before?'

Stella blushed. 'Well, not in the relationship sense, no. I wouldn't call myself a . . . lesbian, or . . . what's the other one? Bilingual—'

'Bisexual,' Daisy corrected, wondering how on earth

she'd ended up discussing her mother's sexuality before ten on a Monday morning.

'This feels like something different, more of a personality thing. I suppose it's more about love than sex, although I'm not saying I don't find her attractive. It's just that the fact that she's a woman seems rather . . . incidental, I suppose.'

'What's the deal with Miriam's job?' Daisy asked.

Stella wafted a bejewelled hand dismissively. 'It's too early days to worry about that. But we can spend time together, and there's no need to make a big fuss about us being a "*couple*".' She made quote signs with her fingers.

'Fair enough. Does that mean you're planning to stay in Shipton Combe indefinitely?'

Stella nodded. 'I think so, or at least nearby. I'm hoping to persuade Justin to do the same. That way we can carry on with *Cook with Justella* and keep Will involved too. I thought I might ask Archie if I can rent this cottage after you leave, then see if Tom will let us hire the old domestic science classroom as a studio for our videos. We'll do it up a bit, and Will wants to add some proper lighting. I thought we could run an after-school club for the students too.'

Daisy nodded along, impressed with how much thought Stella had given this. 'Do you think Justin will stay?'

Stella shrugged. 'I think he might, especially once he can eat whatever he wants and the book is finished. The situation has changed for both of us in the last few weeks. Our agent seems to think we could make a great deal of money. But we have to keep up the, er, momentum.'

'And this way you can see how things go with Miriam. I'm really happy for you, Mum.'

Stella beamed. 'Thank you, my dear. I've pretty much given up drinking too. Miriam doesn't touch it, so I've got out of the habit. Thought I might see if I can live a bit longer.'

Daisy stared at her mother, her eyes wide. 'That's amazing.'

'It's funny really,' laughed Stella. 'I came to Shipton Combe to help save you, and it turns out I've saved myself instead. All rather unexpected.'

Daisy pulled her into a hug. Today felt like it was full of new beginnings.

Another surprise arrived just after school finished, in the shape of Melanie. She looked fabulous in a grey pencil skirt, cream blouse and sensible heels after her first day as Tom's new school secretary. She was standing taller and had a new glow of confidence about her.

'I just thought I'd pop in and say hello. Is it a bad time?'

'Absolutely not.' Daisy boiled the kettle for what felt like the seventeenth time today. 'Do you want tea? Or wine? Is it too early for wine?'

'It's 4 p.m., Daisy,' Melanie smiled. 'Anyway, I'm off wine at the moment.'

'You as well?' Daisy exclaimed in mock horror. 'It must be this village! My mother's given up the booze, now you too. Who am I going to drink with in my last week?'

'Oh, well, I have a good reason.' Melanie looked at Daisy awkwardly. 'Actually, I'm, um, well. I'm *pregnant*.'

'Oh my God!' Daisy yelled, crossing the tiny kitchen to hug Melanie. 'That's amazing news! You're pleased, right?'

Melanie nodded, clearly still unused to saying it out

loud. 'I'm thrilled. Gerald's a little shocked – and Will looked like he might be sick.' She giggled. 'I think the idea of his parents having sex was a bit much for him.' Melanie tucked her hair behind her ears. 'But yes, I'm pleased. We tried for years after Will and couldn't quite get there, so I never imagined . . . anyway, it's still very early days. I've had miscarriages before, and I'm not exactly in my first youth. So please don't tell anyone.'

'Of course.' Daisy laid her hand on Melanie's arm, squeezing gently. 'I won't say a word.'

'But look,' Melanie took the mug of tea from Daisy, leaning her hip against the worktop, 'since I've told you, can I ask your advice about something?'

'Sure.'

'I haven't told Tom. I just want to see what happens first, get past the first scan. Is that bad?'

'Of course not,' replied Daisy. 'Tell him when you're ready. He'll be delighted for you, even if it means you're only there for a couple of terms.'

'I'm rather hoping I can go back afterwards. At least part time. I thought Gerald might share the parenting load this time round, be more of a modern father.'

Daisy raised her eyebrows. 'Is that likely?' Gerald didn't seem like the kind of man to put the baby in a sling while he pegged reusable nappies on the washing line.

Melanie laughed. 'A couple of months ago I'd have said absolutely not. But an awful lot has changed since then.'

'Tell me about it . . .' laughed Daisy.

'Well, actually, that's why I'm here,' said Melanie with a grin. 'You and Tom. Tell me ALL about it.'

★

The final surprise of the day came about three minutes after Melanie left, when another knock at the door heralded the arrival of Will. He hurried into the cottage, dropping his school bag by the door.

'Sorry,' he mumbled, as Daisy stared at him in surprise. 'I've been hiding behind the stables waiting for my mum to leave.'

'Is everything OK?' Daisy took his wet coat, hanging it over the back of a chair. 'It's not Ruby?'

'She's fine,' Will said reassuringly. 'Bit nervous about her play on Friday, I think.'

'Well, that's normal. So what's the urgency?'

Will took a deep breath. 'It's about the thing in the paper yesterday. The story in the *Mail*. I think somebody from the village has been talking.'

Daisy tried not to smile; Will looked so intense and grown-up and she didn't want to burst his bubble. 'What makes you think that?'

'Because there was something in the story about Justella going on *This Morning*. Nobody could have known that unless they were at your birthday party.'

Daisy beamed. 'You, Will, are a very smart young man. I'd actually already worked out the same thing but hadn't got much further than that.'

'I wanted to tell you it wasn't me,' Will blurted, his feet shuffling with nerves.

Daisy gave a soft smile, wishing she could give him a hug without it seeming weird. 'It never crossed my mind.'

'Really?' he looked surprised.

'I'd already discounted you as a suspect, because you seem like a person with integrity and Ruby is a very good judge of character. She can sniff out a bad egg from a mile off.' Daisy thought of Christian: Ruby's reservations about him had turned out to be bang on. 'Also I don't think you're a very good liar.'

Will gave a short laugh. 'No, I'm rubbish.'

'That's a good thing,' Daisy told him. 'And I just couldn't see you coming on that skiing holiday with us if you were selling stories behind my back. That takes a special kind of . . . what's the word?'

'Duplicity?' suggested Will.

'Ooh, that's a good one. I was going to say treachery, but yours is better.'

'I'm doing *Julius Caesar* for English Lit, so I know all about that. "*And some that smile, have in their hearts, I fear, millions of mischiefs.*"' He blushed at his impromptu performance and picked at a loose thread on his sleeve.

'Mmm, that sounds about right.'

'So do you want to find out who it is?' asked Will.

'I've thought about that a lot, actually. I'm leaving Shipton Combe on Monday, so does it matter? The stories have been nothing more than idle gossip – bruising, but there's been no real damage. I could just let it go.'

'Aren't you even a bit curious? Don't you want to find out which one of the people around that table betrayed you?'

Daisy laughed. 'You make it sound like Judas at The Last Supper.'

'I'd want to know, that's all,' Will shrugged. 'And if you were interested, I thought I could help you.'

Daisy sighed and stood up. 'Would you like a cup of tea?'

Will beamed at Daisy, reaching over to take a notebook out of his schoolbag. 'Thought you'd never ask.'

CHAPTER FORTY-SEVEN

On Friday morning, Daisy woke up in Tom's bed with a large brown dog flumped across her legs. She barely had time to stretch before Tom came in with a tray of coffee and toast, balancing it on the edge of the bed while Daisy sat up and tucked the duvet around her. He was fully dressed in his usual headmaster gear of cords, white shirt and a dark green jumper. To Daisy he looked solid and dependable and sexy as hell.

Daisy brushed the hair out of her face as Tom leaned over to kiss her. 'Been a while since I've had breakfast in bed.'

'I'd stay but I have to go to work, I'm afraid. Got a load of kids heading off on their Duke of Edinburgh Gold Expedition in about twenty minutes. I should go and wave them off. Are you off to Milton Park later?'

'Yep,' Daisy nodded happily. She picked up a piece of toast, biting into it, talking between chews. 'Ruby's play starts at four . . . then I'll bring her home after . . . Will's coming with me . . . Simon and Stella are meeting us there . . . Back about seven.'

'Are Simon and Archie staying the weekend?' asked Tom.

Daisy nodded, her mouth full of toast. 'Mmm. They're booked into the pub for the weekend. The plan is to hang around for the fete tomorrow, then fumigate the cottage when I leave on Monday.'

Tom hung his head, looking a little deflated. 'Selfishly, I hate the idea of you leaving. We're just getting started.'

Daisy felt the same way but tried to sound upbeat. 'It'll be fine. You can come and visit me in London, and I can come back when I've got a free weekend. Ruby's going to want to come here to see Will anyway.'

Tom nodded thoughtfully. 'Exam season is coming up, so I'm going to be pretty busy anyway. It's probably just as well you won't be around to distract me.' He slid a hand under the duvet and up Daisy's thigh, smiling playfully.

'Oi, stop that.' Daisy swatted away his hand. 'You'll spill my coffee.'

Tom laughed, then asked more seriously, 'Does Ruby know about us yet?'

'No, not yet. I'll talk to her later, but I'm sure she'll be fine about it. My guess is she'll see you as a considerable upgrade from Christian.'

'Kind of boring though, in comparison.'

'There is no comparison,' replied Daisy firmly. 'You are from entirely different worlds. And I can't begin to tell you what a good thing that is.'

Tom looked cheered by the thought. 'So I'll see you tomorrow then. At the fete?'

'Actually, I wondered if you could come over tonight,' replied Daisy. 'About seven thirty? There's something I need your help with. Will and Ruby will be there too.'

'How very cryptic.'

Daisy gave him a broad smile. 'I'm working on projecting an air of mystery.'

'Right. Because that's absolutely what I look for in a woman.'

★

Daisy didn't bother to wash or put on any makeup, planning instead to slip quietly across the fresh snowfall on the school grounds back to Willow Cottage and have a long shower. She wanted to make a bit of effort before going to Ruby's school play later. People always asked her and Simon for photos at these things, and it felt rude to say no. So she put on her coat and fished her bobble hat out of the pocket to cover up her bed hair, then added a pair of sunglasses for good measure. She'd heard the bell go twenty minutes ago, so all the students would be in their first lesson right now.

As she gently closed the back gate, two teenage boys walking backwards with a large table almost reversed into her, forcing Daisy to back into the snowy hedge to avoid being mown down. The boys at the other end of the table appeared around the corner, along with several more students carrying chairs and what looked like the poles and canvas for a small marquee. They all stopped and stared at her as Justin brought up the rear, looking stressed and harried.

'Why have you all fucking stopped?' he bellowed, then spied Daisy wedged into the yew hedge. He took in the hat and the glasses with a knowing eye.

Daisy cleared her throat and gave one of the boys holding the table a smile. He had bright pink cheeks from the exertion and shifted his weight from foot to foot in that restless way teenage boys do when they want to look cool, although he actually just looked like he needed the toilet. 'Hi. Is this all for the fete?'

The boy nodded, temporarily mute in the face of a bona fide celebrity who also happened to be a really hot older woman.

'This is Year 9,' Justin explained. 'The school trailer has a flat tyre, so I've rescued them from PE to help me lug some stuff down to the lake. Miriam's planning a last-minute snowman-building contest, and that apparently needs a gazebo so the spectators can buy hot drinks.' The group glared at him. Clearly lugging furniture in lieu of hockey or rugby wasn't considered a good trade. Justin rolled his eyes and sighed heavily. 'Honestly, give me a fucking break. You think this is what I want to be doing on a Friday? Is it fuck. If we get it done without you lot whining like fucking babies, we might get ten minutes for a snowball fight.'

Daisy idly wondered if the governors knew that Justin talked to fourteen-year-olds like they were skivvies in one of his restaurant kitchens, then decided that the students probably quite liked it. Daisy noticed a couple of the girls nudging each other with their elbows. One of them flicked her long hair and eyed Daisy beadily.

'What are you doing at Mr Clark's house, miss? I thought you lived over by the stables?' Everyone stared at Daisy again, a few trying to hide their gleeful smiles.

Justin came to her rescue, waving the students on. 'Come on, leave Miss Crawford alone. We need to get moving.'

Justin gave her a surreptitious wink as the group trudged off towards the lake. The girl turned back to give Daisy a snarky look, then muttered something to her friend, who snorted with laughter. Daisy definitely heard something about 'giving head'. Apparently the cat was now out of the bag regarding her and Tom: it surprised Daisy to realise how little she cared.

★

The trip to Milton Park for Ruby's play was an unexpectedly lovely evening, even though *A Moonsummer Night's Dream* had an entirely impenetrable plot that veered cosmically from the original. The cast of aliens and astronauts prompted Daisy to wonder if the whistling blizzard outside was actually Shakespeare spinning in his grave. But Ruby made the part of Titania, Queen of the Space Fairies, her own, and even Simon managed to turn up on time, having left Archie and Hank at The Shipton Arms. He played the part of doting father who clapped a bit too loud and charmed all the teachers, as well as spending some quality time with his former mother-in-law on the drive over. Will managed to withstand the appraising stares of Ruby's schoolmates with a seemingly cool, brooding silence that only Daisy knew was crippling shyness. By the time they left, Daisy wasn't sure which of them had the biggest Milton Park fan club.

On the way home, Daisy decided to capitalise on the positive mood by telling Ruby about Tom.

'So I have some news,' said Daisy, glancing at Ruby in the rear view mirror. Her daughter had insisted on sitting in the back with Will, which made Daisy feel like a taxi driver.

'Is it about you getting it on with Tom?' asked Ruby with a smirk. 'Will told me.'

Daisy raised her eyebrows at Will in the mirror; he managed to look both sheepish and embarrassed.

'I didn't say it was definite,' mumbled Will to Ruby. 'I just said I thought it was possible.'

'Based on what?' asked Daisy, feeling somewhat put out despite having spent four nights out of the past six naked with Tom in one of three different beds.

'He's just been in a really good mood.' Will gave an embarrassed shrug. 'Like he's won the lottery or something. Usually he's kind of grumpy.'

'Well,' said Daisy, torn between annoyance that her news wasn't news, and delight that Tom was clearly as happy about it as she was, 'it's true. We're "getting it on" as you so eloquently put it.'

'It's fine,' Ruby told her mother. 'I like him. You have my permission.'

Daisy snorted. 'I wasn't asking your permission, thank you very much.'

Ruby shrugged and smiled. 'Well, you have it anyway. Look, I'm starving, can we get a KFC?'

They arrived back at Willow Cottage just before 7.30 p.m., having taken a harrowing twelve-mile detour in driving snow for a ten-piece family megabucket. Daisy refused to let them eat it in the car, so by the time they got back to Shipton Combe everyone reeked of fried chicken and was visibly salivating. The three of them ate standing up in the kitchen, reducing the meal to a graveyard of bones and cardboard packaging in a matter of minutes. Daisy hastily cleared everything away before Tom arrived, wiping the grease off her face and adding a slick of lipstick and a spritz of Dior that would hopefully obscure the whiff of the Colonel's blend of eleven herbs and spices.

Tom arrived on time, looking as handsome as ever in faded jeans and a chunky turtleneck jumper, his hair still wet from the shower. He stood to one side in the doorway so Henry could slip through and bag his favourite corner of Daisy's sofa, then raised his eyebrows questioningly. Daisy nodded and smiled, squeezing his hand as she gave him a quick kiss. Ruby and Will wandered out of the kitchen to say hello, Will very obviously not comfortable with hanging out with his girlfriend's mother and her boyfriend, who was also his school headmaster. *Better get used to it.*

Daisy organised drinks – tea for Ruby and Will, and white wine for her and Tom. Then she perched on the arm of the sofa and stroked Henry's head as everyone looked at her expectantly.

'So, it's the church winter fete tomorrow,' Daisy began.

Ruby rolled her eyes. 'Highlight of my social calendar.'

'You don't HAVE to come, you know.'

'I want to see Granny and Justin do their thing live, in front of real people. I'm hoping for a real-time disaster.'

'Fine, be quiet then.' Daisy glared. 'The reason I've got you all together is because I want to find out who the village mole is, the person who's been sharing stories about me with Christian's manager. Or, former manager.'

Tom furrowed his brow. 'What does it matter if you're leaving on Monday?'

Daisy gave Tom a significant look. 'Because there may be times when I want to come back. But let's just say I'm curious.'

'Fair enough,' Tom said easily. 'But didn't we decide it could be any one of the twelve people at your birthday party? Or eleven, not including you?'

'We did,' Daisy glanced at Will, 'but Will and I have narrowed it down to a possible four.'

Tom and Ruby looked at Will, who blushed and gave a shrug. 'It's a quiet village. I've got time on my hands.' He looked at Daisy, who nodded for him to continue. 'OK, so we started with twelve, right? At Daisy's party. But the mole must also have been at Justin's Pig in a Blanket. Before Christmas.'

'How come?' Ruby frowned. Will looked a little awkward, so Daisy picked up the thread.

'Because there was a story a few days after about Tom and I kissing in the kitchen. So somebody at that party must have seen us.'

'Seen you doing what?' Ruby was clearly scandalised.

Daisy smiled, her cheeks flushing at the memory. 'Kissing. In Tom's kitchen.'

'When?' demanded Ruby, her eyes wide.

'After the Pig in a Blanket. You'd already gone home. Look, it doesn't matter. The point is, somebody who left the party must have snuck back and seen us through the kitchen window. It's too much of a coincidence otherwise. Which means the mole must have been at both parties.'

'But that's pretty much everyone.' Ruby frowned. 'Other than Dad and Archie, the same people were at both parties.'

'Yes, but we can also exclude my parents,' Will interjected. 'They went home from the pig thing early, remember?'

'Any chance one of them could have been hanging around in the dark?' asked Ruby. 'Sorry, I don't mean to pin this on your mum and dad. I'm just considering all the possibilities.'

'No.' Will shook his head. 'Mum was in the bath when I got back, and Dad was already in bed. I'd have known if one of them had just been out.'

Ruby nodded and looked at Daisy. 'OK, so how do you know it wasn't me? Or Will? Or Tom?'

Daisy smiled sadly. 'Because I trust all of you, and I don't think any of you would sell me out to the press. Am I right?'

Everyone nodded solemnly. 'Good. So that narrows it down to four – Mum, Miriam, Marcus and Justin.'

'Do you really think it could be Granny?' Ruby looked distraught.

'I really want to say no, Rubes, but I can't discount the possibility. She hasn't always been as together as she is now, and she's done this kind of thing before.'

'I suppose.'

'But look,' Daisy couldn't bear the sadness on Ruby's face, 'this isn't about punishing anyone. I'd just like to know who it was, and why. Nobody will know apart from me.'

'Fair enough.' Tom rolled his sleeves up. 'So, what's the plan?'

Ten minutes later, Will and Daisy had outlined their idea and invited Tom and Ruby to add their thoughts.

'Just so I'm clear,' Ruby looked sceptical, 'because to be honest this sounds like the plot of a really crap film, we're going to make up four random bits of gossip about you, then you're going to pass one on to each of our suspects, so you can see which bit of gossip gets leaked to the press via Christian's evil manager, who's not his manager any more.'

'*Exactly!*' Daisy shouted. 'And because I'll decide who gets told what, I'll be the only one who knows who the mole is. It was Will's idea. It's worth a try.'

'What kind of gossip?' Tom looked a little uneasy. 'Like you're going to be the new presenter of *Bake Off*?'

'No.' Daisy drummed her fingers on the arm of the sofa. 'It needs to be something a bit rubbish, that feels like a come-down from *Spotlight*. Benny won't share something that looks like I'm doing well.'

'So you could be a contestant on a gameshow?' asked

Ruby. 'Or reality TV? Like *I'm a Celebrity . . . Get Me Out of Here!*'

'Yes, that kind of thing,' Daisy beamed. 'But not so ridiculous that Benny would dismiss it as nonsense or look for confirmation. *I'm A Celeb* is ITV, that would be a contractual nightmare. Benny would check.'

'And you really think he'll tell the press?' asked Will.

'If it's stupid gossip and makes it look like my career is on the wane or might embarrass me, he won't be able to resist,' Daisy mused. 'It will be online by Sunday morning, at which point I can get Katie to officially deny it.'

'Does it have to be a TV thing?' asked Tom, standing up to pace the room in a headmasterly way. He looked like a man who needed a whiteboard and a selection of coloured pens.

'No, not necessarily. It could be, like, I don't know, theatre. Or politics. Or a public appearance.'

'So . . . for example, you could have agreed to turn on next year's Christmas lights in, I don't know, somewhere random. Evesham, or Stow-on-the-Wold.'

'YES,' exclaimed Daisy, clapping her hands. 'That's exactly the kind of mediocre nonsense I'm looking for.'

'What about another BBC TV show?' asked Will.

'Ooh,' said Ruby, sitting up. 'You could do *Celebrity Mastermind*.'

'I like that,' said Daisy, nodding thoughtfully. 'But what would my specialist subject be? That's the bit that makes it interesting.'

'It needs to be really nerdy,' suggested Will. 'Norse mythology, or *Dungeons & Dragons*.'

'Vampire fiction,' suggested Tom.

'Hmm,' said Daisy. 'They're all good, but I'll take vampire

books, I think. I definitely read *Twilight*.' The smile Tom gave her was so sweet it made her stomach turn cartwheels.

'OK, we've got two.' Ruby looked at Will. 'What else?'

'What about a survival show?' he suggested. 'The kind where you live in the wilderness with whatshisname. *Bear Grylls*. And then you learn to kill animals with your bare hands.'

'Or you could be the new presenter of *Crufts*?' suggested Ruby.

Daisy shook her head. 'Clare Balding would never let that go. And anyway, I allegedly threw a shoe at a dog, remember?'

Ruby's face fell. 'Oh yeah. Nobody's booking you for Crufts.'

'OK.' Tom clearly felt the need to keep this class in order. 'Let's go with a new Bear Grylls show. And we've got Christmas lights and *Mastermind*. We need one more.'

'I've got it.' Ruby's eyes glittered at Daisy. 'Now you're officially single, you could be in discussion to do *Celebrity Love Island*. For charity, obviously.' She glanced at Tom awkwardly. 'Sorry, Tom.'

Tom held up his hands. 'It's absolutely fine. If your mum wants to hang out on an exotic island with lots of hot celebrity men, I won't stand in her way.'

'Thanks,' said Daisy with a sarcastic smile, '*Love Island* it is, although honestly I can't think of anything worse.'

Yeah, right, Ruby's expression said.

CHAPTER FORTY-EIGHT

Daisy met Miriam, Stella and Justin outside the school hall half an hour before the fete was due to open, conscious that she'd had precisely zero involvement in the organisation of this event and had no idea what she was supposed to be doing. The blizzard had cleared to reveal a beautiful winter's day of blue skies, sunshine and a fresh carpet of snow, and vehicles were already carving a path in the school field that had been turned into a makeshift car park, directed by members of the local Scouts in hi-vis jackets.

'It's very easy.' Miriam bustled around the stalls, waving to her fellow helpers as Daisy followed her more slowly, sipping coffee from a thermos cup, Justin and Stella trailing in their wake. 'Just a few words at 11 a.m. to announce the fete open, thank the school and all the volunteers, that sort of thing. You'll be fine.'

'I'm sure I will,' said Daisy, rolling her eyes behind her sunglasses. She'd presented live TV for twenty-five years, so this wasn't her first rodeo.

'Then I'll show you round all the stalls,' said Miriam, either missing or ignoring Daisy's sarcasm. 'Introduce you to the volunteers, take some photos. Maybe you could have a go on the tombola, wang a welly on the school field, help build a snowman, that sort of thing.'

'I'd be delighted.' Daisy caught Justin's eye and tried not to laugh.

'Then at 1 p.m. Stella and Justin will judge the chocolate brownies while you judge the best Victoria sponge cake.'

'Wait, all the cakes are Victoria sponges?'

'Yes,' Miriam nodded. 'It's a village tradition.'

'Don't all Victoria sponges taste the same?'

Miriam huffed impatiently. 'Of course not, that's ridiculous.' Justin snorted with laughter again. 'Then it's prizegiving at two, and everything wraps up at two thirty. Do you need to know anything else?'

'No,' Daisy shook her head. 'I think I'm fully briefed.'

'Good,' Miriam beamed. 'I need to go and speak to the Bishop. He's brought all kinds of important people from the diocese.' She smoothed down her black clergy blouse and straightened her dog collar before hurrying off, entirely ignorant of Daisy's raised eyebrows.

Stella put her hand on Daisy's arm. 'She's in a tizz about the Bishop,' she explained. 'He doesn't normally come to this kind of thing, but everybody expects this fete to be something a bit special. I think Miriam's feeling the pressure.'

'She'll have a seizure if she's not careful,' Daisy muttered.

'A dioceizure,' Justin whispered, making Daisy snort her coffee.

Daisy asked Stella to accompany her to the staff loos after Justin had gone off to start setting up *Cook With Justella* in the old domestic science classroom, taking her mother's arm as they strolled down the school corridors. They were getting a lot of stares.

'You look lovely. I like your dress, darling.'

Ruby had persuaded Daisy to wear a mustard yellow dress

with elbow-length sleeves and tiny embroidered daisies, cinched in at the waist with a fabric belt. There'd been a minor crisis over what footwear was appropriate for a winter fete, but in the end they'd gone with a pair of black fur-lined ankle boots and purple opaque tights that matched her padded coat.

'Thanks, Mum.' Daisy gave Stella's arm a squeeze.

'But it's not just the dress that's making you look lovely. You're glowing with happiness.'

Daisy gave her a shy smile. 'I am happy, Mum. It's early days, but things are good.'

'It feels like we've both turned a corner.' Stella put her arm around Daisy's shoulders. 'We should be very proud of ourselves.'

Daisy swallowed and plunged into her prepared story, feeling terrible about lying to her mother but also wanting to out the mole. 'I like it around here. I might spend more time here in future. In fact I've been asked to turn on the Christmas lights in Stow-on-the-Wold in November, and I've said yes.'

'Really?' Stella gave a hoot of laughter. 'Not very fancy for you, but lovely for Stow-on-the-Wold.'

'Well, maybe I'm tired of fancy.' Feeling ridiculous, Daisy felt she should defend herself for something that absolutely wasn't happening. 'I think I'd quite like to be a bit less fancy sometimes. But it's a long way off. Don't tell anyone. It won't be announced for ages.'

Stella nodded slowly. 'Of course. Good for you. Are you *sure* it was Stow-on-the-Wold? Not Bath or Cheltenham or somewhere more impressive?'

Daisy laughed, wondering whether she should now offer to turn on Stow's Christmas lights just to spite her mother.

★

After wanging several wellies and guessing the weight of a jar of mint humbugs, Daisy found Reverend Miriam milling about in the hall where the cake competition was being held, making sure all the entries for the chocolate brownie and Victoria sponge competition were properly labelled and aligned in a tidy fashion. She looked stressed and sweaty, her neck glowing pink above her dog collar.

'Can I help?' Daisy gave her best celebrity smile.

Miriam beamed back at her. 'I think we're fine, Daisy, but thank you. Everything seems to be going well.'

'Big crowd in the Justella classroom. Heard lots of laughing as I went by. I think they're a hit.'

Miriam nodded enthusiastically as she secured the clingfilm under a three-tiered sponge. 'It's extraordinary, really. I'd imagined that you would be the big draw for the crowds, but actually it's Stella and Justin. I hope you aren't disappointed.'

Daisy laughed. 'God, no! I've had my fair share of attention in the past six months. I'm more than happy for someone else to lighten the load.'

'Well, yes.' Miriam's cheeks flushed as she remembered the reason for Daisy coming here. 'I have to say your stay in Shipton Combe has been such a blessing, though.'

'Well, off back to London on Monday. Lots of exciting new projects in the works.' Daisy crossed her fingers behind her back and prayed she wouldn't mess this up. She tried to convince herself that this was acting rather than lying, but it still didn't feel right to fib to a vicar.

'Oh yes?' Miriam leaned forwards slightly. 'What kind of thing?'

'I've just been booked for *Celebrity Mastermind*,' Daisy

whispered. 'You'll laugh at my specialist subject: it's not commonly known how much I know about vampire fiction.'

'Goodness.' Miriam's eyes were wide with surprise. 'I wouldn't have guessed anyone knew very much about that. And you're going on *Mastermind*? How fascinating.'

'I'm very excited about it,' Daisy lied shamelessly, 'but it's not public knowledge yet.'

'Of course,' said Miriam. 'Oh look, it's almost time to judge the cakes. Do you know where Justin is?'

'Don't worry, I'll find him for you.' Daisy gave Miriam a friendly pat on the shoulder. As she left the gloom of the classroom and headed out into the school quad, she glanced up at the dazzling blue sky and politely requested forgiveness for her lies.

Daisy hovered with Justin at the edge of the cake display, waiting for the judging to begin. 'Couldn't they have picked something a bit more interesting than a Victoria sponge?' Daisy lamented. 'How do you choose?'

'Half of those will be the same Mary Berry recipe,' laughed Justin. 'If I were you, I'd just pick one at random and then head for a hot cider down by the lake.'

'Only a few days left before you can eat cake,' observed Daisy.

'Can't wait,' replied Justin. 'I don't want anything fancy, just a tray of supermarket jam doughnuts. I'm going to push them into my face one by one until I puke.'

Daisy giggled, then spotted her window of opportunity. 'I'll have to stock up on cake too. I'm going to be eating grubs and roots soon.'

Justin turned to look at her, his brow furrowed with interest. 'How come?'

'I've signed up for a new celebrity survival show,' whispered Daisy. 'One with Bear Grylls where you live on an island and kill your own food.'

'Fucking hell!' Justin took in Daisy's flowery dress and the bouncy curls escaping from the pins in her hair. 'No offence, but you don't seem like the survival type.'

'I think you inspired me,' Daisy smiled. 'I'm not sure I was supposed to say anything, though, so don't tell anyone.'

'No problem,' said Justin, looking pleased. 'It's been a while since anyone gave two fucks about anything I know.'

By 2.30, Daisy had eaten her bodyweight in cake and was reasonably confident she'd never touch another Victoria sponge for as long as she lived. She'd eaten dry ones, moist ones, ones with homemade jam, ones that were four layers deep, ones bigger than her mother's handbag. In the end she'd stuck the rosette on one that was particularly light and buttery, which turned out to be the creation of Lesley the landlady from the Shipton Arms.

Once her fete duties were done, and the crowds of visitors had stopped asking her for selfies and started to drift off towards the car park, Daisy spotted Simon, Archie, Stella, Will and Ruby admiring the snowmen by the lake and wandered down to join them.

'Here she is,' announced Archie, letting go of Hank so he could bound over to Daisy. 'The guest of honour.'

'Hardly.' She pointed at her mother. 'Justella were the big draw today. I'm just making up the numbers.'

Stella smiled indulgently and shuffled over so there was a space on the bench for her to perch.

'Do you want a hot cider?' asked Simon. Daisy briefly considered it, then thought of her mother and asked for a tea instead.

Daisy sipped her tea and watched Hank shuttle up and down the edge of the lake, clearly excited by the novelty of mallards and swans swimming in circles in the steaming water, but frustrated at being unable to reach them. She turned to look back towards the school and spotted Marcus walking along the footpath with his mother, heading in the direction of the gate leading to the village. Daisy had been keeping an eye out for him all day.

'Give me a minute.' Daisy scrambled to her feet and jogged after Marcus, calling his name when she was twenty metres away. He turned, then said something to his mother, who glanced at Daisy, then carried on without him.

Daisy was a little out of breath when she reached him. 'Sorry to hold you up.'

'It's fine.' Marcus fiddled with the cords on the neck of his hoodie, unable to meet Daisy's eye. They hadn't seen or spoken to each other since the ill-fated birthday party.

'I wanted to say sorry,' Daisy told him, 'about all the press stuff after the party. It wasn't fair that you got caught up in all that.'

Marcus shrugged. 'It was my own fault. I shouldn't have punched him. It was out of order and he probably didn't deserve it.'

'No,' replied Daisy, 'he probably didn't. But it's done now. How are things with you?'

'Good, actually.' Marcus looked a little more cheerful.

'I've moved in with my girlfriend and got loads of new coaching clients off the back of the publicity, so life could be worse. Happy to be out of this village, if I'm honest.'

Daisy smiled. 'I'm sure you're right. And there's a fresh start for me too. I'm heading back to London on Monday. Got some fun new projects.'

'Like what?' Daisy could hear Hank barking frantically by the lake but kept her focus on Marcus, who was clearly enjoying finally having Daisy's undivided attention after months of attempting to catch her eye.

'Oh, I shouldn't say, really.' She tried to look enigmatic. 'I've been asked to do a charity show. *Celebrity Love Island*, actually, but I haven't decided yet.'

'Wow.' Marcus looked genuinely surprised. 'I'm not sure if . . .' His head turned to the lake. 'Is that dog OK?'

Hank, it turned out, was very much not OK. The barking had prompted a number of mallards to take flight, which was the catalyst for Hank to take a plunge into the lake and start paddling frantically towards the swans on the island. He was already several metres out before Simon and Archie made it to the edge of the water, by which time he had his eyes on the prize and no amount of calling was going to bring him back.

Archie grabbed Daisy's arm as she appeared at his side, his face distraught. 'Oh God, I don't know if he's going to make it.'

Daisy chewed her thumbnail, her heart thumping as she worked her way through various scenarios. If Hank got near the swans they might attack him, and there were also a lot of overhanging branches that could get hooked on his collar. One way or another, he was going to need help.

Archie called Hank's name again but Daisy grabbed his wrist. 'No, don't make him swim back. If he panics, he could drown. I'll get him.'

Daisy pulled off her boots and coat decisively and waded into the water, which was so cold it felt like knives were being poked into her ankles. The mud and silt sucked at her feet, but she kept moving, oblivious to the shouts on the bank behind her. Once the water was chest deep, she plunged forward and started to swim, trying to breathe through the searing cold and keep her head above the water. The fabric of the dress felt heavy and clingy around her legs, but she kicked it away and kept going.

Hank reached the island about ten metres ahead of Daisy, veering away from the frantic hissing of the swans and hunkering under a bush, no doubt surprised to discover how big and angry they were at close quarters. Daisy could see him shivering, although it was hard to tell if that was from cold or fear or both. She pushed through the mud and branches and dragged her wet skirt up the bank, mud smeared in long streaks up her arms. The swans took to the water as she reached out for Hank, who leapt into her arms and buried his head in the crook of her elbow.

Daisy squatted for a minute on the edge of the bank, stroking Hank's head and whispering, 'It's OK, you silly thing,' as she tried to impart any remaining warmth into his body and stop her teeth chattering. She waved at the group on the lakeside and gave them a thumbs up, seeing Archie's body visibly relax as he realised his dog wasn't in any immediate danger. Hank slowly started to calm down, lifting his head to Daisy's face and giving her cheek a lick as his tail began to wag.

'Now listen,' Daisy told him sternly. 'We're going to have to swim back. Which means you're going to have to be a brave boy, but I promise not to let you go. What do you think?' Hank wagged his tail and scraped his claws down Daisy's cold arm, which she took as encouragement even though her eyes were watering with the pain.

Holding Hank tightly against her body as they both shivered, Daisy untied the belt from her dress and looped it through his collar, setting him down on the bank so she could secure it with a knot and tie the other end around her wrist. Taking a deep breath, she tucked Hank under her left arm and waded back into the freezing water, observing that it hadn't got any bloody warmer in the past three minutes.

She swam on her right side, paddling with one arm only, until Hank's little legs started to kick and Daisy tentatively let him go so he could power himself along. They swam the last ten metres side by side, applauded and cheered on by the group of spectators on the lakeside, which appeared to have got considerably larger since Hank and Daisy had taken the plunge.

As soon as Hank found his footing, he raced into Archie's waiting arms, leaving Daisy to scramble through the mud just behind him. She was wading through the last couple of feet of soft silt when Archie stood up, causing the belt on Daisy's wrist to pull tight. It yanked her body forward and gave her feet nowhere to go but backwards. She heard Archie shout, 'Oh shit!' then moments later she lay with her face pressed into the cold, slippery bank, a throbbing pain in her right ankle and the familiar horror of being sprawled out and helpless in front of a crowd of strangers. She raised her head slowly and Tom's face appeared in her line of vision, his fingers working deftly to untie the belt from her wrist before he hooked his arm under her armpit and helped her to sit up. His eyes never left hers as he dipped a handkerchief into the lake and gently wiped the mud off her face. 'Are you OK?'

'I think I've twisted my ankle,' whispered Daisy, her face burning. 'And my dress . . .'

'It's all fine.' Tom pushed Daisy's hair out of her eyes. 'It's just wet, and you've got black tights on. Nobody can see anything.' He took her hand and squeezed it gently. 'I'll help you up, just smile and wave.'

Daisy scrambled to her feet and smiled at the crowd, acknowledging the ripple of applause as she let Tom help her hobble over to Archie so she could check Hank was OK. The ankle felt sore, but it could bear her weight.

She let Tom lead her away towards Willow Cottage, his arm tight around her shoulder as he helped her undress and get into a hot shower and dry, clean clothes. Nobody followed them or chased them down with cameras. No one cared. And it occurred to Daisy that most people here wished her nothing but happiness.

CHAPTER FORTY-NINE

Benny's latest gossip website news leak on Sunday was much as Daisy expected; he'd clearly heard about the dramatic dog rescue and tried to play it down, making up a quote from a villager that read: '*It all seemed like a fuss about nothing, really; the dog was fine and there was no need for Daisy to swim across the lake in front of everyone. Everyone thought it was a bit attention-seeking.*' Daisy rolled her eyes and rubbed her sore ankle, thinking of how terrified and shivery Hank had been when he'd jumped into her arms.

She scanned the rest of the copy, glossing over the paragraphs about how she had been seen talking to Marcus Elliot just before the incident, but had left the scene with Tom Clark, which left the journalist unsure what conclusion to draw about Daisy's complex love life. Further down she found what she was looking for — an irresistible rumour about something that Daisy was lined up to do in the future, of no real consequence to anyone apart from Daisy, who now knew who the mole was.

She reminded herself that the true villain here was Benny, who had clearly decided that causing death to Daisy's career by a thousand tiny cuts was a fun game. Today the best he could do was snipe about a dog at a village fete and a booking that must have seemed unlikely, even to him. Such a pathetic little man. She'd go and see him when she was back in London, tell him what she knew and give him a choice – learn to play nicely or have his transgressions laid bare and never work in this industry again.

Daisy wasn't entirely surprised to find her mother having breakfast in Miriam's kitchen, although it was unclear whether she'd just popped over for coffee and toast before the Sunday church service or if she'd stayed the night. Either way Stella looked a good deal more relaxed about it than Miriam did. She spotted a mustard yellow scarf and matching gloves on the hat rack inside the door and remembered seeing Stella in the gloves at Justin's pig roast, then Miriam in the scarf a week or two later. The signs were always there, she just hadn't noticed. She took a deep breath and sat down at the kitchen table, knowing this wasn't going to be an easy conversation.

'You're lucky to find me here,' said Stella, 'I've only just arrived.'

If you say so. 'Actually, it wasn't you I was looking for. I came to speak to Miriam.'

'Oh,' Stella sounded put out. 'Is it a private chat, or can I stay?'

Daisy looked at Miriam and raised her eyebrows questioningly. The vicar's face was pale and tired, and she looked like she might be sick.

'No, it's fine,' whispered Miriam, her voice wavering. 'I think I know why Daisy is here, and you'll find out soon enough.' She put the kettle down and tucked her hands under her armpits to stop them shaking.

'Goodness.' Stella's eyes swivelled between Daisy and Miriam. 'What on earth has happened?'

Daisy waited until Miriam had sat down, not wanting to intimidate the vicar in her own kitchen. 'I think Miriam may have been sharing stories about me that might have ended up in the press.'

Miriam dropped her head, her shoulders shaking as she started to cry.

'Good lord.' Stella stared at the older woman. 'That can't be true. Miriam?'

The vicar nodded, now sobbing heartily.

'Miriam, it's OK.' Daisy reached over to put a hand over hers. 'I'm not here to yell at you, just to understand what happened.'

Miriam took a few shuddering breaths and sat upright, wiping the tears away with a loaves and fishes tea towel. She looked from Daisy to Stella, trying to compose herself.

'The money wasn't for me; it was for the vestry.' She gave Daisy a beseeching look, then tore off a sheet of kitchen roll and blew her nose noisily. 'A man contacted me through the church Facebook page. I never knew his name. He said he'd pay five thousand pounds, which meant I wouldn't have to beg people for money any more. The fundraising has been so stressful for years and I couldn't see an end to it.'

'I can understand that,' Daisy murmured. Her mother's expression was hard to read.

'At the time you were a stranger and it seemed so easy,' Miriam said, her eyes welling up again. 'Then I got to know you and Stella and felt terrible, but I couldn't back out. He said he'd tell the Bishop what I'd done.' Her face was bleak and exhausted. 'I'm so sorry.' She dissolved into tears again.

'Has the man paid you yet?' asked Daisy.

'No,' sobbed Miriam. 'He said what I've given him wasn't

good enough. I have photos of Tom leaving your house and you walking a dog in your pyjamas, but I never sent them. I couldn't.'

Daisy smiled gently. 'Miriam, it's fine. Please don't cry. Block the man's number, delete any messages and leave him to me.'

'Do you know who he is?' Miriam's eyes widened.

'Yes, and he won't be bothering you again. How much money do you need for the church?'

'That's the worst thing about it,' Miriam wailed. 'You and Stella and Justin meant we got hundreds more visitors to the fete and raised five times what we usually make. So I don't even need the money. I feel awful. I'm so sorry.'

Daisy patted her hand again, nodding fervently at her mother to do the same. 'Miriam, there's no real harm done, so please don't be upset. I'm not angry with you, and neither is Stella.' Daisy intensified her glare until finally Stella put her arm round Miriam.

'I'm sure everything will be fine,' Stella said grudgingly, prompting another round of crying.

'How did you know?' sobbed Miriam. 'Was it *Celebrity Mastermind*?'

'I'm afraid I made that story up.' She didn't mention Tom and Ruby and Will, there was no need for Miriam and Stella to know they were involved.

'What story?' asked Stella.

'I told Miriam that I was going to be on *Celebrity Mastermind*.'

'With what specialist subject?' demanded Stella, her mouth hanging open.

'For God's sake, Mum, what does it matter?' replied Daisy with an eyeroll. 'Fine. Vampire fiction.'

'Goodness,' Stella snorted. 'I had no idea you read that kind of thing. Some of it's quite racy, isn't it?'

Daisy ignored her mother, who seemed to have entirely missed the point. Instead she looked at Miriam, who threw her a bleak smile. Daisy squeezed her hand, then rose and headed towards the door, taking Stella by the arm as she passed.

'Don't be angry with her,' whispered Daisy in the doorway. 'She made a stupid mistake, but she's a good person. She wouldn't be the first to sell stories to the press then regret it later.' Daisy gave her mother a significant look.

'No. No,' Stella had the grace to blush, 'she wouldn't.' She pulled Daisy into a hug and sighed heavily. 'You're too good for this industry, Daisy. Don't ever lose that.'

CHAPTER FIFTY

'I brought you a cup of tea.' Melanie appeared behind Tom in the churchyard, carrying a blue-and-white-striped mug in each hand. He turned to face her from his kneeling position in front of Tessa's gravestone, using his hand to shield his eyes against the glare of the sun on the snowy ground. Henry was lying on a waterproof picnic blanket nearby, his head on his paws as his eyelids flickered in a dream.

'Thanks.' Tom stood up and took the mug gratefully. 'Just so we're clear on your job description, you're not obliged to make me tea during office hours, let alone on a Sunday.'

Melanie smiled. 'I saw you from the window and thought you looked like a man in need of a hot drink. I've got some gardening tools if you want them.'

'No, it's fine. Tessa never liked things too tidy.' He sipped his tea and looked across the churchyard to the road as a tractor rumbled by.

'When's Daisy leaving?' asked Melanie.

'Tomorrow.' Tom kicked a few stray pieces of gravel off the grass and back onto the path. 'Which one of us is going to miss her more, do you think?'

Melanie laughed. 'It sounds silly to say it out loud, but she's changed my life. You both have.'

'Stop it,' Tom teased. 'You'll make me blush.'

'I mean it, Tom. Tessa was my friend, and you and I have

never really connected in the same way since she died. But you've done such a lot for me and Gerald. I really can't thank you enough.'

'Tessa was very fond of you, and I've always had time for Gerald. And Will, of course. I'm just glad things have worked out for you. For all your family, current and future.' He gave Melanie a significant look.

'Oh.' Melanie's eyes widened. 'Did Daisy tell you?'

Tom shook his head. 'She didn't have to. You have the same glow that Tessa had. Like you're carrying around the most wonderful secret.'

'I'm sorry I didn't say anything. I was going to tell you soon. I just wanted to be sure—'

'Don't be silly.' He held up a hand to silence her. 'I want you to know that I'm delighted, and we'll do whatever we can at the school to make things easy for you. Whatever you need.'

Melanie glanced at Tessa's gravestone. 'Thank you. I can't tell you what a relief that is. What names did you and Tessa choose, for your baby? If you don't mind me asking.'

Tears pinpricked the corner of Tom's eyes, but he blinked them away. 'Daniel for a boy. Elizabeth for a girl. Why do you ask?'

'No reason.' Melanie smiled gently. 'Gerald and I were just wondering.'

Will walked past a few minutes after Melanie headed back to the house, his hands deep in his pockets. Tom gave him a wave, then wandered over to the wall by the road to say hello.

'Hey, Mr Clark.'

'Can we agree on Tom at weekends?' Tom smiled. 'Nobody needs to know.'

'Bit weird, but sure.' Will shrugged. 'I'm just off to the pub to meet Justin and Stella. They want to have a brainstorm.' He rolled his eyes, like brainstorming with adults was a colossal drag.

'Got to earn your ten per cent.' Tom bumped his shoulder. 'Keep the clients happy.'

'Yeah,' Will smiled. 'It's turning out to be a pretty good gig.'

'A word of advice, if you'll take it,' Tom said, leaning on the wall. 'Lots of people are going to try to take that gig away from you. Professional video people, social media experts – the bigger and more successful *Cook with Justella* gets, the more others will try to muscle in.'

'Really?' Will's brow furrowed with worry. 'What should I do?'

'Look after them. Justin and Stella. Keep them ahead of the game. Know their audience, be the expert in everything there is to know about social media, online cooking trends, building a YouTube brand. You need to be all over the details. And if they want a brainstorm, give them a brainstorm.'

Will's eyes glazed over thoughtfully. Tom could see the cogs whirring in his brain.

'Don't just be on their team, Will. *Lead* their team. You're the perfect man for the job, but it's a cutthroat business and you're going to have to keep your wits about you. I'm always available if you need help or advice. As is Daisy.'

Will nodded, his eyes blazing, his mouth set into a determined line. Tom felt a pang of paternal pride for this clever, shy, awkward boy. So much had changed for him in the past couple of months, and now the future was his for the taking.

What a remarkable thing it was to be excited about what was around the corner – it had been so long for Tom, he'd almost forgotten what that felt like. But Daisy . . . she was a world of possibility.

'Thanks, Tom . . . OK, that feels weird.'

'We'll get used to it.'

Tom waved and headed back to Tessa's grave. He was wiping off the snow with a cloth when he saw Daisy coming out of Church House. He hesitated for a second before raising his hand in greeting. If she was going back to London tomorrow, he'd rather one of their final conversations in Shipton Combe didn't take place in such close proximity to his late wife, but it couldn't really be helped.

Daisy hobbled over, bits of hair from her bun breaking free in the breeze. A dusting of snow dislodged from an overhanging tree and rained down on her like confetti, and for a second Tom imagined her walking the same path towards him in a wedding dress. The thought gave him a feeling in his chest that was somewhere between joy and pain, and he mentally apologised to Tessa. Daisy stopped in front of him and tipped forward on her toes like she was going in for a kiss, then spotted the gravestone and rocked back, brushing his arm instead.

'You OK?' asked Tom searching her face.

'I'm fine.' Daisy's eyes darted to Tessa's grave then back again. 'It turns out that Miriam's the mole.'

'Christ! Or one of his messengers, at least.'

Daisy smiled. 'I'm not angry about it. It was done out of desperation.'

Tom nodded and thought for a moment. 'I suppose I should thank her, really. Without her causing trouble you might have gone home sooner. So maybe it was divine intervention.'

'Do you believe in that kind of stuff?' Daisy started to pick snow out of her hair.

Tom leaned over and gently brushed a few flakes from her shoulders. 'I don't believe in God, but I believe in fate.'

Daisy nodded at the gravestone. 'Is that how you cope with what happened to Tessa? Fate?'

Tom nodded, looking up at the clear blue sky. 'We had a happy decade together, but we'd been talking about moving before the baby arrived – a job at a bigger school, a town where there were more young families. She loved this church but found the village rather stifling. But because she died, I stayed, and that meant I got to meet you. And because of what Miriam did, you stayed long enough for me to fall in love with you.' He smiled shyly, wondering if he'd said too much. 'Sometimes you have to read the signs, I guess.'

Daisy was quiet for a long moment, looking at him with a far away expression that he couldn't quite fathom. He wondered if using the 'L' word was a mistake.

'I have a call I need to make. Give me an hour, then I'll come to your place.'

'You look serious,' said Tom. She had a determined look in her eyes, like something important had just happened.

'I am serious, but in a good way.' She leaned over and kissed him softly on the cheek, then hurried off towards the school gates. Tom stared after her until she disappeared, then turned back to Tessa's grave.

'Sorry you had to see that,' he whispered. 'You know I'll always love you, but it's time for me to move on.'

CHAPTER FIFTY-ONE

Daisy ended the call and breathed out slowly, feeling like she'd just shed ten pounds she hadn't even noticed she was carrying. She rushed to the bathroom and ran a brush through her hair, adding a touch of lipstick and a pair of sunglasses. It was a big day, and that called for a very small effort.

Ruby had gone for a walk with Simon, Archie and Hank, so she dropped her a message and hurried out of Willow Cottage and across the field to Tom's house. The snow on the fields glittered like diamonds in the sunshine, and the row of snowmen by the lake politely watched her progress like spectators lining a red carpet. It felt like a sign, and today she was reading the signs.

Daisy could see Tom waiting by the gate with Henry and quickened her pace; he must have been watching out of the window. He looked worried and unsure, so she pulled him into a long kiss, then decided not to keep him waiting any longer.

'I've made a decision. I'm quitting *Spotlight*.'

He didn't say anything at first, then his eyes widened with shock. 'What? Are you kidding?'

Daisy rolled her eyes. 'Of course I'm not kidding.'

'I don't understand.'

'I don't want that life any more,' Daisy explained patiently.

'It's been twenty-five years. I need – *want* – something different.' Her eyes searched his.

'What did you have in mind?' Tom looked like he was holding his breath.

'I'm going to move to the countryside. I've been thinking about it for weeks, really. I want somewhere I can grow my own food and chop my own firewood. Maybe write my memoirs. I definitely want to spend more time with my mum and Ruby. And never wear high heels again.'

Tom pretended to be horrified. 'No heels? Not even for special occasions?'

'Love me, love my sensible shoes.'

'I do love you.' Tom pulled Daisy into his arms. 'Even in sensible shoes.'

Daisy looked at him, her eyes blazing. 'I love you too.' His eyes flared and a grin lit up his face. He bent to kiss her.

'Will you help me find a cottage?'

'Of course. What did you have in mind?'

'Something pretty,' Daisy responded happily, 'big kitchen, nice garden, space to write and have guests, no nosey neighbours. Not too far from you.'

Tom held her shoulders at arms' length and looked at her intently. 'Are you sure about this?'

Daisy nodded furiously. 'Absolutely. I'm not saying I'll never work in television again, but right now I need a break. I want to breathe, do normal things. I don't know exactly what, but something else.'

'And what about me?' asked Tom, looking a little nervous.

Daisy smiled. 'You're definitely *something else*.'

Tom pulled her into a hug, letting out a long and slow

breath. To Daisy it sounded like a release, the beginning of letting go of some of the burdens he'd been hauling around for the past three years. His were much bigger than Daisy's, but they could work through them together. She was convinced of it.

'So what's next?' Tom took Daisy's hand and led her out onto the field. They strolled in the direction of the lake, the morning sun in their faces.

'I'm still going back to London tomorrow. But Katie and Roger are making calls to the team at *Spotlight* now and working on a statement. They've got time to find a new presenter, I've always had the option to do this as long as I told them by the end of January.'

'That's next week,' said Tom.

'I read the signs just in time,' said Daisy. 'I'll need to have some meetings, do some interviews, wrap up some loose ends. I reckon it will take a week or two.'

'Can you come back for half-term? I've got a week off. Usually I'd have tons of admin to do but I've got a new secretary and she's fabulous.'

Daisy smiled, glad that things were working out for Melanie, and crossing her fingers that the pregnancy would go well. 'I have a lovely little villa in Portugal. We could go together if you can find someone to look after Henry.'

Tom grinned. 'Angela would be delighted. She's already asked if she can keep him as an emotional support dog when she moves into her retirement village. That's obviously a no,' he added hastily. Daisy couldn't imagine Tom without Henry.

'I figure if we can spend twenty-four hours a day together for a week, we're in with a good chance.' Her face glowed with excitement.

Tom pulled her into another hug, holding her tight like she might disappear if he let her go. 'That's a chance I'm very willing to take.' Daisy could feel his heart thumping through his shirt.

'Well,' Tom whispered into her hair. 'Today hasn't turned out quite how I imagined. I woke up feeling a bit crap about you leaving tomorrow, and now you're moving to the countryside and we get to go on holiday together.'

'We should celebrate.' Daisy waited for Tom to suggest they had sex. But he wasn't Christian. He was a million miles from Christian.

'Definitely. When's Ruby going back to school?'

Daisy looked at her watch, struggling to process how much had happened in the past couple of hours. 'I need to drop her back about five. I haven't told her my plan yet, but she'll be cool about it as long as I can still get her free tickets for stuff.'

'It's not even twelve. Go talk to Ruby, then let's meet in the pub in an hour. Ask Simon and Archie if they want to join us.' He grinned and squeezed Daisy's hand happily. 'I'll message a few people in the village, see if anyone else is at a loose end.'

Daisy laughed. 'What are the chances?'

'Very high. But that's village life, so you might as well get used to it. No red carpets, no fancy parties. You ready for that?' He lifted Daisy's hand to his lips and kissed it, his eyes meeting hers with an intensity that she felt all the way to the tips of her toes.

'Yes.'

And Daisy knew without a shadow of a doubt that she really was.

PART FIVE

JULY

The barbecue had been Melanie's idea, to celebrate Daisy finally moving into Holly Tree Cottage after three months of renovations. But then other people came up with extra reasons to celebrate – Justin and Stella hitting three million subscribers on YouTube, Will passing his driving test on the first attempt, the end of exams and the start of the school summer holidays, Gerald's new role as a non-executive director for a big property developer. In the end Daisy decided to invite Simon, Archie and Des Parker and his wife down to the Cotswolds and make a weekend party of it.

The weather was hot and dry in a way that can make England in July briefly feel like Spain, but Archie had done a wonderful job of creating little patches of dappled shade around the edges of Daisy's beautiful garden. There was a further quarter of an acre on the other side of the orchard still to be landscaped, but that was on hold for now as Daisy considered whether she actually wanted to grow vegetables, or whether that was some romantic country fantasy, particularly since the school smallholding kept her well supplied. Archie had suggested seeding the whole area with wild flowers to create a bee-friendly meadow, while Ruby was still pitching for a swimming pool.

It was Tom who'd first suggested Daisy buy Angela's cottage. On first inspection it hadn't seemed very promising, but once she'd looked beyond the eighties decor and the overgrown wilderness outside, she'd seen the potential and snapped it up before the local estate agents had even got a sniff of a rare sale opportunity in Shipton Combe. The place had been crawling with builders ever since, gutting the interior and starting again. The broken roof tiles, peeling windows and rickety fences and gates had all been replaced, and within three months the cottage had been transformed into a beautiful four-bedroomed country home.

Daisy's townhouse in London had been sold for a price that left more than enough to buy a small flat in town if she wanted to. But she was in no hurry to decide – when she needed to be in London there were plenty of old friends who were happy to loan her their guest room in exchange for dinner and a proper catch-up.

There'd been no word from Christian, other than an email letting her know that he was setting up a tennis academy in Spain with some other former players and would be living over there for a while. He and Daisy had both moved on, and blessedly the Vultures had done the same, finding new carcasses to feed off.

'Are you OK?' Tom wrapped his arms around her waist as she stood in the kitchen, looking up at the collage of pictures stuck on the fridge door. Shots of them together in Portugal back in February and skiing in Tignes with the school at Easter, Ruby at her Year 11 prom, wearing a beautiful designer gown that Daisy had once worn to a movie premiere. A cover photo from *OK!* of Daisy wearing a pink chiffon dress on her white sofa in Portugal, with the headline '*Out of the Spotlight – TV star Daisy Crawford tells OK! why she's feeling fabulous at 40*'.

'Fine.' Daisy sent him a reassuring smile. She knew why he was asking – ordinarily this would be the first weekend of *Spotlight* live shows, but this year the whole summer stretched out ahead of her, the first time in over a decade. 'Absolutely *no* regrets.'

Tom buried his face in her hair, breathing her in. 'I'm glad. You living here makes me incredibly happy.'

'Me too.' Daisy leaned back into him, enjoying the moment of quiet togetherness. 'But we should go and join the party.'

She handed Tom the tray of canapes she'd originally come inside for, then followed him out into the garden, taking a moment to appreciate how incredibly gorgeous he looked in shorts, a linen shirt and a pair of flip-flops. Justin and Stella had commandeered a corner of the garden for a barbecue and a preparation table, which was set up with two cameras on tripods, another rigged to a tree so it could take overhead shots. Will was prowling around them taking mobile footage as Stella chopped salads and Justin talked to one of the cameras about the elements of a perfect sausage.

'Do you feel like my housewarming party has been hijacked for YouTube?' Daisy smiled.

'They'll make enough money off that video to pay for this party ten times over, so you should probably send them the bill,' Tom quipped.

'I might just do that.'

Daisy took a moment to marvel at how healthy and content Stella looked as she helped Miriam arrange the salad bowls on the table. The two women moved around each other with such ease and familiarity, it was easy to forget they'd only been a couple for six months. She wasn't sure how the bedroom logistics worked, given Miriam's job – but it was unquestionably a loving partnership that seemed to make them both very happy.

With Gerald's help and advice, Justin, Stella and Will had set up Justella Productions Limited, which formalised their profit-share arrangement and made it easier for them to employ extra staff. They now had a proper accountant and a part-time video editor, a woman called Lauren who Melanie had met at ante-natal classes. That took the pressure off Will, who would be starting his gap year in September. There was talk of taking Justella on a European tour, but the details were still a little vague. But they'd all agreed to make hay while the sun shone, hence Will shamelessly using Daisy's party for a content opportunity.

'I know I said I was in favour of the bee meadow,' said Melanie, waddling across the lawn and easing her huge pregnant belly down into a camping chair next to Daisy and Ruby, 'but right now I'd kill for the swimming pool. My feet look like boiled hams. I can only see them when I sit down.' She lifted her legs and pulled a face at her pink, puffy feet.

'See?' Ruby crowed triumphantly. '*Everyone* wants the swimming pool.'

'Apart from the bees,' Daisy interjected dryly. 'Perhaps you could get Melanie a bowl of water for her feet?'

'It's fine. I'll get Gerald to do it in a minute.'

'You could plant a bee meadow NEXT to the swimming pool,' Ruby pressed on. 'Or in the orchard? How many wild flowers do bees actually need?'

'A bee meadow would cost about fifty quid for seeds, maybe a hundred at a push. A swimming pool is going to cost a bomb, and I've only just got rid of the builders,' Daisy chided. 'And I'm technically unemployed.'

'Right. And how much was your advance for the new book?' Ruby asked cheekily.

It was more than enough for a swimming pool, but Ruby definitely didn't need to know that. 'None of your business.'

'HAH, I knew it,' Ruby shouted triumphantly.

'How's the writing going?' Melanie interrupted, giving Gerald a thumbs up as he waved a jug of lemonade and an empty glass at her, his eyebrows raised in question.

'We haven't really started yet. Mum and I are both still making notes, working out how to structure the story.' Daisy had loved the idea of using her career break to write her autobiography, but she'd been intrigued by the suggestion that she write it in conjunction with Stella, telling a forty-year story of two celebrity women that started and ended with Stella cooking up a storm.

Daisy leaned back in her chair, sipping a glass of Pimm's and watching Tom standing on the patio with Des and Simon, looking relaxed and happy with a bottle of beer in his hand. Three beautiful men who had played such a huge role in her life. Des, her protector and mentor. Simon, the first man she'd truly loved, who'd also given her Ruby. And Tom? What had he given her?

'What are you thinking about, Mum?' Ruby asked. 'You look a million miles away.'

Daisy tilted her face to the sun and closed her eyes. 'Peace, Rubes,' she murmured quietly. 'I'm thinking about finding peace.'

Acknowledgements

The Only Way Is Up was the second book I wrote but my third to be published – I wrote most of it in the late summer and autumn of 2020, during the second Covid-19 lockdown. By this point, I had signed with a literary agent but not a publisher, and for good measure had been made redundant from my job. So in the midst of uncertainty and confusion, writing a second book seemed like as good an idea as any. After *Two Metres From You* I really wanted to write a book set in a pre-Covid time where people could meet and travel and snog with wild abandon, so this story is set in late 2018/early 2019. It felt liberating at the time, and hopefully now doesn't feel too other-worldly.

So to be honest I don't have many people to thank, because I didn't really tell anyone I was writing this book at the time. But now we're a little further down the line there are a few people I want to mention. As ever I'm most grateful to my partner, Pip – my biggest supporter, chief coffee maker and fellow dogwalker. I'd also like to thank my amazing family who have given me their unending love and support as I've found my feet as an author. You have always had my back and I truly appreciate it.

Two other extraordinary people helped get this book over the finish line – my agent Caroline Sheldon and my editor, Bea Grabowska, at Headline Accent. You have both been incredible and I am permanently in awe of your patience and wisdom. Thanks also to Isabelle Wilson for PR expertise, Aruna Vasudevan for being a copy-editor extraordinaire, Versha Jones for the beautiful cover and Jill Cole for being a legendary proofreader. It takes a top team to make a book, and my words are just the beginning.

A huge thanks to everyone who bought my first two novels and said such lovely things about them, you give me strength and motivation during the darker moments.

Finally, a massive thanks to the *Guardian* Strictly Liveblog Glitterati for brightening those autumn lockdown weekends when I'd spent all day trying to find the right words. I'd be lying if I said you weren't in my thoughts when I wrote bits of this story, so this one's definitely for you.

Discover more hilarious and hugely uplifting romcoms from Heidi Stephens . . .

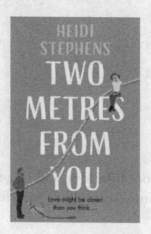

Gemma isn't sure what upsets her more. The fact she
just caught her boyfriend cheating, or that he did it on
her *brand-new* Heal's cushions.

All she knows is she needs to put as many miles between
her and Fraser as humanly possible. So, when her
best friend suggests a restorative few days in the
West Country, it seems like the perfect solution.

That is, until the country enters a national lockdown
that leaves her stranded. All she has for company is
her dog, Mabel. And the mysterious (and handsome!)
stranger living at the bottom of her garden . . .

Available to order

ACCENT

Emily Wilkinson has lost everything. Literally. In a hair-straightener fire. Oh, and her boyfriend (and boss) has announced he's going back to his wife. So, she needs a new job, a new plan, and somewhere to live that isn't her childhood bedroom.

Charles Hunter is looking for a live-in PA to help run Bowford Manor and Emily thinks she's the perfect fit. Well, she's spent ten years propping up demanding men, so she can definitely handle some tricky characters – like Charles's eldest son and heir, who's got plans for the estate that might raise a few eyebrows.

No one's mentioned Jamie though. The stable hand – and youngest Hunter. Dashing, of course, but totally unsuitable. And Emily's not about to make that mistake again.

Definitely not. No, really.

Available to order

ACCENT